I0729031

BLOOD MOONS

BLOOD & SHADOWS BOOK 1

BOOKS BY ALIANNE DONNELLY

BLOOD AND SHADOWS
Blood Moons
Blood Trails
Blood Debts
Blood Hunt
Shadow Hawk

DAWN OF RAGNAROK
The Royal Wizard
Dragonblood
Prince of Deceit

THE BEAST
Bastien
The Beast

OTHER TITLES
Wolfen
Virtual
Function: L1VE

ALIANNE DONNELLY

BLOOD MOONS

BLOOD & SHADOWS BOOK 1

THIS IS AN ALIANNE DONNELLY BOOK PUBLISHED BY ALIANNE DONNELLY
It's not bragging if it's true.

BLOOD MOONS is a work of fiction. Names, characters, places, and incidents either are the product of the author's imagination or are used fictitiously, and any resemblance to actual persons, living or dead, business establishments, events, or locales is entirely coincidental.

Copyright © 2010 by Alianne Donnelly

All rights reserved.
No part of this book may be reproduced, scanned, or distributed in any printed or electronic form without permission. Please do not participate in or encourage piracy of copyrighted materials in violation of the author's rights. Purchase only authorized editions.

aliannedonnelly.com

ISBN: 978-1-948325-00-4

Published in the United States of America

*To Ms. Lyn Isbell, whose encouragement led me here.
You believed I would be a published writer one day, and you were
right. I am honored to have had the privilege of being in your class. I
am a better writer and human being for having known you.*

Facilis descensus Averni:
noctes atque dies patet atri ianua Ditis;
sed revocare gradium superasque evadere ad auras.
Hoc opus, hic labor est.

It is easy to go down into Hell:
night and day, the gates of dark Death stand wide;
but to climb back again, to retrace one's steps to the upper air –
there's the rub, the task.

-Virgil (The Aeneid, Book VI)

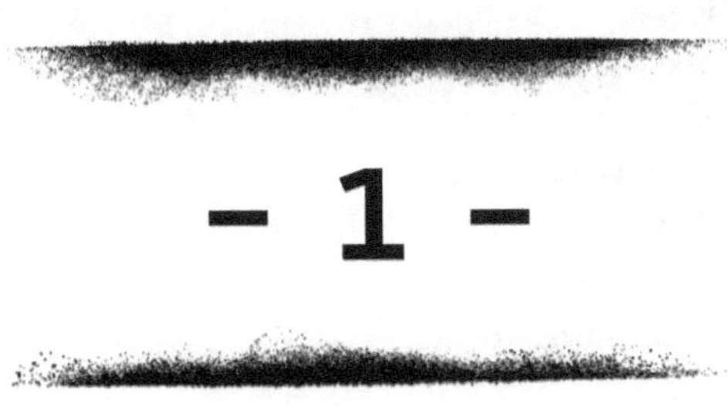

- 1 -

27th day of the 3rd Blood Moon, 3028

The man behind the desk didn't notice the two guards and their prisoner approaching. He was bobbing his head in rhythm to the music coming from his tiny music player while he filled out forms, consulting the computer screen a few times. He sang out a couple of words in a high-pitched voice that cracked. It didn't seem to bother him that he was singing offbeat—and why should it? He was there by himself.

Dara winced listening to him. He was a terrible singer, but at least his voice drowned out the other ones—those in her head.

Can't believe I pulled transport duty…

If we get out of here in time, I can make the flight to Lotus Three…

…cares about one chick, anyway…

…the beaches are snow-white…

Dara squeezed her eyes shut. *I'm not hearing you…*

…and the best thing—no sharks. Ha! A deep blue ocean, and no sharks!

She massaged her temples, humming a tune in her mind. The one the clerk was listening to. It was all she had to distract herself with.

It wasn't enough. Desperate now for a break from the constant chatter, she went over everything the guards had let slip from their minds. Facts were her saving grace. Facts gave the rest of it meaning, so she didn't have to drown in the flood of random thoughts.

The bigger guard was the one in charge. His rank was higher. His name was Michael J. Jennings; he was thirty-nine years old, married with a kid on the way, and he thought guard duty was a short stick he'd gotten in some sick universal draw. His idea of dealing with criminals was shooting them in the head.

Impatient, Jennings cleared his throat.

The clerk didn't notice.

Fucking lazy-ass bureaucrat!

Dara flinched.

Facts. The other guard was a newbie and this was his first prisoner run. He annoyed Jennings because he kept jabbering on and on about vacation spots he would go to the next time he had some time off. He was young, fresh out of the academy—or wherever it was that people went to learn how to strike terror into someone with just a look or a gesture. Charles Timmons. He still thought the world was his oyster. Still hadn't realized that none of the places he talked about were affordable for a guard of his station, and all the talking about it made Jennings even more miserable.

Jennings cleared his throat again, this time banging his ham-sized fist against the metal net that separated them from the clerk.

The clerk jumped, dropped his pen, and pushed away from the desk so abruptly that the wheeled chair carried him nearly to the end of the room. "Goddamn! Show some respect, man," he complained. The headphones came off his ears.

"Get up off your ass, and do your job," Jennings growled in return. "We have more work to do today." He was cracking his knuckles again. He'd done that the entire way here—that, and pat his gun like some sort of talisman—and Dara gritted her teeth, wishing the clerk would sing again.

...fucking shithead cop, Dara picked up from the clerk. She agreed wholeheartedly. "Awrightawright," he said. "No need to shout at the brotha." He left his chair behind as he stood up and returned to his desk to check the prisoner in. Once the surly Jennings signed the form, both he and his partner made their exit, leaving Dara alone to face the clerk.

The clerk put his headphones back on, but turned the volume

down on his music. When he faced her again, he grinned and said in a mocking TV announcer voice, "Welcome to the sunny New Alaska underground prison facility." He was holding an imaginary microphone to his mouth. "As our final contestant, you get a pick out of our five very luxurious blocks." Bobbing his head again, he passed her five brochures in a bunch and Dara was morbidly glad for his sense of humor. She hadn't enjoyed much laughter lately. Not since this had all begun.

The chief of police had stood as witness both for her and against her. Ultimately, it had been his voice that had condemned her. At first, she'd been glad. She'd wanted it all to be over. But then he had stood up again and pleaded with the court to spare her life. Once more, his voice had been heard and, instead of a death sentence, she had received life in a maximum security prison on Alpha Beta Nine, better known as New Alaska.

She really wished they'd just killed her and had done with it.

The planet was ten light years from Earth and no easy journey. The prison itself was underground.

Dara picked technical information out of the clerk's mind without giving it conscious thought. Turning her attention to the pamphlets the clerk had given her, she simply glanced at the covers, not bothering to flip through them. That she was even being given a choice was baffling. But Dara supposed that it didn't really matter in the end. Prisons didn't get more maximum security than this.

Each pamphlet had a name on it and an animal symbol. Each animal meant a different level of security. There was a hamster, a humming-bird, and cat for the lower security blocks, and a human and wolf for maximum security. But if there was any real difference between them, Dara couldn't see it. As she looked at the pictures, the clerk followed her gaze, and she could easily read their descriptions from his mind.

Hummin' bird's got all the hot chicks. Hamster's all crooks and ac-countants. Hate those fucking pricks. Kitty cat…soap opera, twenty-four seven. "Make your choice," he said cheerfully, still in character. *Wouldn't wanna be caught in Human… But Wolf…* "Time's a'tickin.'" He was still grinning as he executed a small salsa step and turned full circle on the ball of one foot with a flourish.

But he stopped and his smile faded when he noticed her pointing at one of the pamphlets. "The Wolf," he said, eyeing her doubtfully. "That is *maximum* maximum security, lady. Ain't no one there but messed-up motherfuckers." *Be kidding. Please.*

Didn't make a difference. Dara didn't reply, only kept pointing.

"You sure? I was thinking more along the lines of the Hummin' bird, or Cat. I mean, men and women are kept together, sure, but there's only three in Wolf block. And two hundred men."

Again, she didn't reply. This was where she wanted to go. Didn't know why, only knew that she had to. It was an instinct so strong, she was afraid to go against it. Accountants, hot chicks, soap operas… he hadn't thought anything about Wolf block.

"Think about this, lady," he tried again, the jovial announcer gone. He really wanted her to change her mind. "The guards only step in when the men fight. They ain't gonna risk their necks for a woman. Shit, for a sweet thing like you, they might even be worse than the inmates."

Now he was making her nervous. She couldn't tell from his mind whether he was just being dramatic, or really concerned for her safety. He wasn't thinking in words at the moment, just silently willing her to point to something else. Dara looked over the choices one more time. None of them drew her as that one did. She met his gaze again, made her own calm and steady, and nodded once.

"You'll be dead or worse within a week," he told her, enunciating each word with cruel precision. "Once you give a thumbprint, that's it. Ain't no such thing as transfers."

It would be a relief, she thought. Nodding to him, she held out her thumb. It would be an end. She would welcome it, even. Maybe she'd finally be able to sleep in the silence.

The clerk—Herbert Jones was his name—frowned at her. "You don't talk much, do you?" He scratched his head when she didn't answer and eyed the pamphlets. He was easy to read. Right now he was considering whether he should just decide for her. For a moment there, he wanted to play the hero.

Then he remembered she was a criminal. *Her funeral,* she heard him think. *If she wants to go…* He sighed capitulation, but it still didn't sit well with him. "Awright, Wolf block it is." He looked her over as he gathered the pamphlets back up. "Good luck."

And that was all, apparently. He didn't ask her name, or the time she would have to serve; didn't say anything else, in fact. He opened a small window in the net and took off her handcuffs, then pressed her thumb to a little lighted pad built into the desk and pointed at the cage door opposite the one she'd come through.

"Straight down to the end, turn left, take the items on the shelf on your right and continue on to the next desk." He went back to his work, then added, almost as an afterthought, "Oh, and don't worry about tryin' to escape. There ain't nowhere to go. Trust me."

She did.

With a nod, she went where he'd told her to, turning left at the end of the long corridor. There was only one shelf on her right and it disappeared back into the wall as soon as she took the items.

She came to the second desk where a different clerk was typing on his computer. He said without looking up, "Herb says to put you up in a safe cell." He snorted. "Yeah, right. As if there is such a thing in Wolf block." This one all but broadcast his thoughts and Dara winced at his mind-tone. *Son of a bitch's got me running errands now. And that guy is supposed to be* safe? He snorted again. *Hey, not my problem.*

The thoughts came accompanied with background noise, like grumbling, that gave Dara a headache. This man had a lot of frustration built up inside his head and he was leaking it all around. *Great,* she thought. *Another person who hates their job as much as me. How refreshing.*

"You're holding spare clothing, soap, a comb, and the pills, yes?" When she didn't answer, he looked up to check for himself. "Good. Take the largest pill now. It will take care of every female problem from now until the end of your stay. No mood swings, menstrual cycles, PMS, cramps, no babies or any of that shit. The rest are painkillers, in case you happen to get a headache. There's a cup of water over there." He pointed to where the wall opened onto a compartment no larger than her head. A plastic cup of water stood there.

She hesitated, eyeing the pills doubtfully. She'd never thought about having children, but the idea that the choice might be taken completely out of her hands was not exactly welcome.

As if reading her mind, the clerk spoke again. "Effects are temporary. Will be rendered null and void with another pill if or when you get out of here."

That was something, at least.

"Drink up; I can't let ya in until you do."

She smiled at that. What would they do with her if she refused?

When the clerk shot her a cold glare, she opted for the safer course of complying.

The clerk nodded in satisfaction then pointed farther down the hall. "Straight on till the end, then to your left. Follow the noises. There is a guard at the end that will take you the rest of the way."

Dara followed the corridor, feeling colder with each step. She could hear her heart beating out a frantic staccato against her ribs. The sound drowned out any noise her shoes might have made on a regular floor. This one had been designed to muffle it. Her palms were sweating as she turned left again and continued along the down-sloping path.

The noises the clerk had mentioned started off as nothing but a soft hum. It gave Dara pause, and her step slowed. For the first time apprehension hit her. Not for her safety, but for her sanity. So many people… so many voices. She might not be able to block them out. Her arms shook. She wanted to drop everything and cover her ears.

By the time she got to what looked like a solid wall, the hum was a roar of noise she couldn't drown out. The clothing she held nearly tumbled from her grasp, and she began to shiver.

She would probably have been more comfortable in the Hamster block—if such a thing as "comfort" was even possible in prison—but her gut told her this was where she was supposed to be. Somehow, this felt safer than all the alternatives.

The solid wall suddenly disappeared, leaving her standing in front of a heavy metal gate. The guard stood on the other side, already grim-faced. He was tall and bulky, with a wide nose that had seen straighter days. His eyes were hard as he stared at her. He might have been handsome if it wasn't for that ugly thin line that his mouth formed. There was no kindness to him; his mind was uninterestedly blank.

When he let her through, he added a pillow and a blanket to her load, and then led her along a catwalk to the other side. There was no other way to approach the one exit, except by this catwalk. On the other end, however, it connected to a walkway on either side that ran along the perimeter, connecting the cells on different levels. There were nine levels—four below her and four above her—and none of their walkways came close enough to the exit to jump.

There would be no point in attempting an escape. Even if she did somehow manage to get to the exit and out, there were no doubt many more gates and metal nets to keep her underground. And if she reached the surface? What would she do—jump into the air and fly back to Earth?

She chanced a look up at her escort. There was no point in trying to talk to this guard. Though she couldn't see inside the cells to their inhabitants, the noise they were making both inside her mind and outside was deafening and anything she might try to say would be drowned out. That was assuming he might even be interested in what she had to say.

Doubtful.

They stopped in front of an open cell. They were all open, but something had to hold the prisoners inside. With one finger, the guard touched the wall next to the cell and something like electricity sparked in the open doorway.

A force field, then, Dara thought. Swallowing hard, she resolved to stay far away from it, just to be safe.

At her stalling, the guard nudged her inside and then resealed the cell.

Someone stirred in the shadows on the top bunk. Dara could tell it was a man, but she couldn't make out anything about him. "What the fuck is this?" he demanded in a rough, rumbling voice. Dara got the impression of an angry bear.

Oh, hell, she thought, *I'm in a bear's lair.* Bear's lair in Wolf block. And Dara, the tiny little mouse. It would be funny if she wasn't about to be *dead or worse,* as Herbert Jones had put it.

"Your new cellmate," the guard mocked him. "Behave yourself, Hunt."

"You have got to be shittin' me!" Hunt slid off the top bunk and stalked toward the guard, stopping just shy of the force field.

Dara shrank back slightly. He was the largest man she'd ever seen. More than a head taller than she, with unbelievably wide shoulders and arms that bulged with muscle. His hair was brown and fell to his shoulders, but it was pulled back from his face and neatly tied in a ponytail. She would have expected someone like this in ancient Scotland, tending a forge, not here—not now. He had hands that would dwarf a twelve-pound domestic cat. At the moment, they were balled into fists at his sides.

He was not happy with her presence. *I'm not happy with it, either,* Dara thought sullenly, but bit the inside of her cheek to keep from making any noise. Safer for her *not* to draw his wrath. She waited in pensive silence to see what would happen. Or rather, how long she could expect to survive here.

"You're saddling me with a *female*?" Her new roommate said the word as if it was dirty, and Dara frowned. She couldn't read him.

The guard shrugged as if it didn't matter to him, but there was a smirk on his face he couldn't get under control and in his mind he was laughing at Hunt. "Hey, I don't make the rules. Herb said to stash her here, that's what I'm doing." *Oh, man. This is going to be fun…*

There. Proof positive that her telepathy hadn't disappeared. The guard's thoughts: clear as bells.

Hunt's, though?

Nope, nothing. Not a single one. No thought, no emotion—although he made those obvious enough. How could this be? Did she care?

"Do I look like I give a shit about what Herb wants? Get her the hell away from me!"

Okay, so it might be useful to know what this one was thinking. It would make an attack a little more predictable.

The guard grinned maliciously. "The way I see it, Herb did you a favor." He winked with a mischievous eyebrow waggle, and Hunt tensed.

Dara half thought he would lunge for the guard, and she wouldn't have been surprised if he was able to withstand the force field and tear the guard's head off with his bare hands.

Then the tension left his back. "That son of a bitch," he snarled.

With a hearty chuckle, the guard left, shouting back something Dara didn't catch.

As soon as he was gone, she missed the guard.

Hunt turned on her next.

His face was fierce, his nose the slightest bit crooked, as if it had been broken once, and he had intense eyes that flashed green fire, even in the darkened cell. His mouth was compressed into a thin line, his jaw was shadowed and, belatedly, she wondered if she had gotten a death sentence after all. The prospect didn't seem so welcome now.

He stalked up to her, crowding her against the wall. "Not one peep out of you," he warned, low and quiet. "Do you understand?"

Cowering, wide eyed, Dara nodded, hugging her things to her chest as if they could shield her from him.

Tristan stared her down for a moment longer, making sure she understood, then hopped back up onto his bunk, determined to ignore her. Fucking hell.

Of all the fucked-up pranks Herb had pulled, this was the worst. *Goddamn piece of shit.* It wasn't enough that the prick spread rumors to the others for fun, to see them rip into each other; Herb delighted in making all the nutjobs in this place hate each other—and Tristan in particular. Which Tristan wouldn't normally give a shit about, except he couldn't kill any of them. And the paper pusher hated Tristan's guts; he'd been trying to get rid of him one way or another almost since he'd gotten here. Did everything he could to provoke him.

And now, with this little package of delights, Herb had the perfect solution. Because Tristan would sure as shit end up in a brawl over the female at some point, whether he wanted to or not. A body like that did not just go unnoticed in a glorified underground cave that housed a ratio of over two hundred men to three women.

Four now, he amended darkly. *Jesus.*

The only thing keeping this place from turning into a sick, grown-up version of *Lord of the Flies* was the illusion that the guards were in charge and the cells kept the men separated. But here, there was no Jack's camp and Ralph's camp, no voice of reason among them. There was only Simon, surrounded by all the others. Only one person who had the sense to realize something the others were in denial about: all of them were monsters. It was why Tristan was still alive. He lived day after day here with the knowledge that all it took was one tiny spark for the whole operation to fall into chaos.

But Simon hadn't fared so well in the book. And now here was this tasty little thing, so completely out of place, who might just be the spark that would blow this place sky-high. Just what the hell could she have done to get in here? Tristan could read people like open books and nothing about this female said *killer.*

Don't get involved. Just keep to yourself, like always.

He closed his eyes, blocking her completely out of his mind. He didn't even want to acknowledge her presence. Didn't want to know she was really real. And he definitely did *not* want to know her name.

But he still heard her soft sigh—of relief or resignation, probably both—and the light rustle of fabric as she settled her things in a small cabinet under her bed and arranged the pillow and blanket before she sat in the center of her bunk.

Tristan punched the mattress. This was going to be a shitstorm waiting to happen.

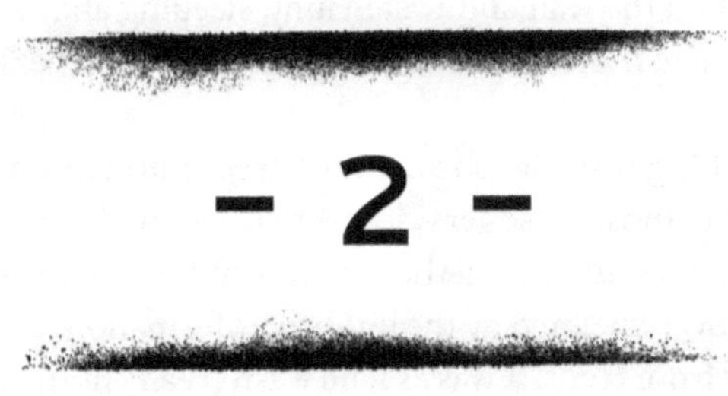

28th day of the 3rd Blood Moon, 3028

Dara tossed and turned, afraid of falling asleep again. She'd slept earlier in the night, having practically fallen unconscious. But she'd had The Dream again; the same dream that had plagued her since her incarceration.

She was before the court again, pleading with them to keep looking for the real killer, that she hadn't done it. She wasn't begging for herself. She was begging for the people she knew would die horribly if this man wasn't caught.

The jury was stone-faced. They never acknowledged that they heard her. They just stared at her as she shouted and cried and begged, then they turned their backs on her and refused to listen anymore.

And then he was there. The killer.

She felt his presence like a cold chill running up her spine, and she turned around just as he reached out and snatched her around the neck. His eyes were feverish and he had the look of a maniac. This was more than a kill for him. It was an obsession he was helpless to stop. He *needed* to kill.

Just as his cold fingers closed around her throat, Dara woke up gasping so loud it was almost a scream. She instantly remembered where she was and scrambled deeper into the shadows in case Hunt, or someone else, decided to take exception to the noise.

She shivered so much she was afraid that the involuntary spasms would travel up the wall and wake Hunt, sleeping above her. But he never even stirred. After a while, she was able to calm herself enough to lie back down.

The odd thing was that she couldn't "see" into Hunt's mind. She could see what those prisoners closest to her were dreaming, sorting through the information methodically, uninterestedly, so that she wouldn't be overwhelmed by the influx of information. But she didn't get anything from Hunt. It was as if he wasn't really human. Everyone thought, and remembered, and dreamed. If not, at the very least they perceived and had opinions about what they saw and heard.

And they most definitely dreamed. But either Hunt was some kind of very convincing AI robot, or he'd conditioned himself not to, because Dara wasn't getting a thing. He was still there, but his brain wasn't broadcasting.

Dara even tried to reach out to him, for the first time in her life taking a chance and making use of this stupid, useless ability. But when she couldn't access his thoughts, she lost interest and gave up.

It was a double-edged sword. At least if she knew what he was thinking, she could prepare herself for what was coming, instead of always dreading the unknown. On the other hand, not knowing had its advantages, in theory. Dara had read somewhere a while ago that a person's life ended on the day they found out when they were going to die. Knowledge of a possible future didn't make the wait any easier. In theory.

But in practice, here, it might be nice to know where the biggest threats were housed. One of them might be sleeping on the bunk above hers. Without being able to read him, she was as vulnerable to an attack from him as anyone else might be. With nothing else to go on, Dara was reduced to examining his actions.

He had completely ignored her last evening and hadn't done anything to her yet, she tried to reassure herself. But that *yet* was frightening to contemplate.

It doesn't mean he'll be as uninterested today.

A loud siren made her jump and scramble to get out of bed and she managed to hit her head on the top bunk in the process. She hissed and rubbed the spot.

Hunt slid off his bed and landed softly, stretching his half-naked body.

Dara stared. In his shirt yesterday he'd been impressive. Without it today… *Holy crap!* For just a second, watching those beautiful muscles stretch and bulge, she forgot where she was and who he was. The walls faded away, the other voices muted, and she was just a woman, staring at a man who'd just rolled out of bed, his pants riding low on his hips. And Dara was curious about what it would feel like to be gathered up in arms that powerful. Would he crush her without a thought? Her gut said he wasn't that kind of guy.

Right now, without that tough, menacing face he'd put on yesterday, he looked completely devastating. The type of guy for whom women fell all over themselves; and who touched his women with just enough strength to make them feel overpowered, but not threatened. Well, not *much*, anyway. A guy like that never let a woman forget she was toying with danger.

The fantasy made the region around her heart ache. Why couldn't she have met a guy like this before? Maybe if she had, her life would have turned out differently. Maybe he could have kept her thoughts and dreams occupied with more pleasant things than what those around her were thinking. Maybe she could have woken up with him, and spent her days smiling about how lucky she was, and come back home to sleep in his arms at night.

Maybe he would have kept her so busy in his bed that she wouldn't have had time to think about anything else. *Ah, sex.* Dara remembered having had it. So very long ago. Remembered not being impressed with it. She should have known better, though. Nothing was ever as good as the books made it seem. Dara had built her hopes up with a steady diet of romance novels in which the hero was… well, like this guy, and everything turned out perfect when he found his heroine.

If she let herself, Dara could pretend that this was the beginning of some steamy romance novel. Wouldn't be difficult, really. The plot had already begun with a complicated situation, and now here she was, trapped with the hero of the tale, with nowhere to turn except into his arms.

His really big, strong-looking arms…

Then Hunt spoke and quickly dispelled her fantasy.

"Wake-up call," he said and grinned, as if he'd read her thoughts and they amused him. "Six thirty."

Dara blushed, feeling as if she'd just been caught in one of those naked-in-public dreams. When he turned away, she swallowed a wistful sigh and made herself look at something besides his tight backside.

There was nothing, except a wall.

Back to reality she plunged, and it wasn't a soft landing. What was she thinking? Romance novel? Turning into his arms for help? Ha. All that strength had a completely different purpose here. Hunt probably *would* crush the life out of her, given half a chance. And he'd smile while doing it.

A spark in the doorway disabled the force field. Hunt left without a word, joining the others to go somewhere. Most likely to breakfast.

Dara felt a tingle of panic when she lost sight of him. The cell was open, and she was suddenly all alone in it. *Bad, bad.* Alone was very bad. Alone, she had no one to scream for if something happened. It was ridiculous, bordering on insane, to even think about Hunt as possibly a friend—and romance novel hero was completely out of the question. He'd have the most opportunities to hurt her in any number of ways. But she was getting a feeling—which felt a lot like the stupid, useless instinct that had gotten her into this mess to begin with—that she should stick with Hunt and take her chances.

What else could she do? Dara hadn't been born yesterday. Her experience in these situations was thankfully lacking, but her imagination wasn't. She knew she'd have to throw her lot in with someone at some point; she didn't stand a chance on her own. Plus, she would need to eat eventually, which meant exposing herself to the others in the… cafeteria?

Stay or go? Stay or go?

Making a split-second decision, Dara ran out after Hunt.

She took up the rear and followed the others, down to the bottom level, then away from the main chamber to the cafeteria. Somehow she found herself with a mangled tray in her hand, somewhere in line for food. Something was dropped onto the metal thing, and she was shoved aside as the person behind her put his tray forward.

Dara looked around uneasily. Some tables were already filled, others only had a person or two; none were completely empty. And most faces she'd rather not come close to. She got a strange image in her head of playing Russian roulette, except the gun only had one chamber empty.

The cylinder spun and spun, then settled with a chamber aligned. The hammer pulled back slowly with a loud click. No one held the gun. No one was even in the picture. And still the trigger moved back farther and farther until…

Someone cursed low behind her, and then her upper arm was gripped in the tight vise of Hunt's huge hand. How did he get behind her? He pulled her after him to the shadows under a broken lamp where a lone table stood unoccupied. She hadn't noticed it before.

Hunt pushed her down to sit in the corner. He dropped his tray across from her and sat, glowering again like he'd done yesterday.

Shaken, heart racing, Dara just stared. *What just happened?* For a second there, she'd thought that would be the end of it.

"You don't have the sense of a sparrow, do you?" Hunt demanded. No more fantasy guy. Firmly back in the scare-you-to-death-with-a-look guy mode. Obviously he didn't expect an answer. He continued, "First day and you already stand out like a sore thumb. *Get some sense, lassie!*" He hissed that last part, and she frowned at the term. Didn't know anyone still used it outside of books. "If you want to survive the week, you keep the hell out of sight."

Dara ducked her head and looked around to see if anyone had noticed her. No one was even looking in her direction. She was so relieved, she almost let herself relax. Shifting her chair farther into shadow, Dara turned her gaze to her unlikely rescuer. Hunt was angry, but her gut still said the same thing it did before. He just didn't look the type to hurt her. Not like the others did. Why else would he be hiding her now? He was right, of course. The moment those other men started to pay attention to her, she was dead.

Dara nodded once, since it seemed he was looking for some kind of response, and hunched down over her bowl.

Whatever was in that dish, it didn't smell like anything. It looked like runny oatmeal, with lumps, and she wrinkled her nose. Scooping up a small amount with her spoon, she sniffed it cautiously, and then squeezed her eyes shut and stuck the spoon into her mouth.

No taste, either. And the texture was nondescript as well.

Dara let out a tense breath and opened her eyes to find Hunt watching her with amusement. How quickly his mood changed. And damn him, he looked even better when he smiled. Looked like someone she'd want to put her trust in.

"Not used to our fine cuisine, are you? It gets better over time." He popped a spoonful into his mouth and swallowed without chewing. "We have the same in solid form for lunch and dinner. Don't ask why breakfast is different. You probably don't want to know."

The woman gave him a tentative smile, then ate some more, slowly and cautiously, as if she was afraid it was poison. He could have put her mind at ease. People didn't need poison to take someone out around here. Brute force usually worked just fine.

Tristan shook his head. What someone as timid as this creature was doing in here was beyond him. It hadn't escaped his notice when she woke with such a start close to morning. He hadn't been sleeping, but seething that Herb had done this to him. And that he couldn't retaliate.

He'd heard her tossing and turning and had been about to snap at her to keep still so that he could sleep when she'd nearly screamed. He'd even heard her huddle in a ball. But she'd never said a word. A fucking miracle—a quiet woman. Had she taken it to heart when he'd told her not to utter a peep?

Tristan looked her over again, taking advantage of her inattention while she was still eating and wouldn't notice his scrutiny. She was beautiful in a way that was rare these days. Then again, after so many years with only men for company and those three that looked more like men, he supposed anyone would look beautiful to him.

She'd braided her raven hair for the night, but it was now mussed, giving her a look of a woman who'd just rolled out of someone's bed. She had pale skin, big honey-brown eyes, a thin nose, and full, naturally red lips he wanted to feel all over him.

She held her spoon like a lady of old, in delicate fingers that were clean of all dirt, with elegant fingernails that were neat, not fancy. All woman, the way a woman should be: without artifice.

She had a figure that was just right. Not too ample, nor too flat. Breasts that would fit perfectly into his hands, a waist he could fit his arm around, hips that were shapely, and legs that would be just long enough to wrap around him.

He straightened. Where the hell had *that* come from? He shifted so that she was better concealed and concentrated on the act of eating so as not to draw attention. Christ! If anyone noticed her, she'd end up dead within a week, just as he'd said she would. There were no conjugal visits here. The men had to make do with what was available. A woman as delicate as this one was wouldn't survive a minute in the filthy games those men played.

"What the hell did you do to get in here?" he heard himself asking.

She shook her head awkwardly, but did not look up.

"Don't wanna talk about it?" He shrugged easily. "Fine by me. I like silence."

She ducked her head, but he caught the wry grin on her face.

He didn't know what she found so funny, but oddly, Tristan felt like smiling, himself.

"*Move it, ladies! Two minutes!*" a guard bellowed, and she jumped.

"He means all of us, not just the women," Tristan assured her. He leaned forward to impart the next piece of wisdom. "If you value your life, you will stay out of sight. Stay in the cell as much as possible. Don't draw attention." Then he scoffed at the absurdity of it. "Shit, it's like trying to hide a mouse in a nest of snakes."

"*All right! Single file. Pick a fight and you'll regret it!*"

"C'mon." Tristan grasped her arm again and pulled her along. They dropped off their trays, and he led her back to their cell as quickly as he could, keeping her between him and a wall at all times to limit her exposure. It was more for her peace of mind. Neither he nor the wall would offer much concealment, but there were other ways to hide her. She just wasn't aware of them. "Get your soap and whatnot." He grinned wryly. "Just don't drop it."

She picked up her things as if she was bracing herself for battle. She didn't say a word, but he could see the unspoken question on her face. "There is only one showering area, but the women's is curtained off."

He saw the instant relief on her face and just stopped himself from lashing out. Naive was one thing, but this was bordering on idiocy. And it would get her killed if she didn't learn fast enough, which meant that Tristan had just become her teacher.

There were few who would not pity her.

"You little fool!" he hissed. "Women aren't your friends any more than the men are. Talk to no one. If something happens, you haul ass back here and hide. Understand?"

She looked startled, but still those pretty eyes of hers searched his face. It was unsettling to be looked at like that. "Why are you helping me?"

Fucking figured, even her voice would be perfect. Melodic and sweet. Soft, like a caress. "You'd be dead in a day if I didn't," he said more harshly than he'd intended, then shrugged. "Consider it my one good deed." And because benevolence made him uncomfortable as hell, he decided to distance himself so she wouldn't look at him like some fucking hero anymore.

Dara had problems. That was a given. But as she weighed her options, she came to the conclusion that fear could not be one of them. Not here. If she allowed it to get a foothold, she'd spend the rest of her days in panic-stricken catatonia. Dara had to be as badass as all the other badasses here, or at least give a convincing impression of it. She wasn't completely useless.

Yes, her mind was broken, but she'd had years and decades to get used to it. She'd even picked up a trick or two along the way. Usually when she wanted a person to leave, she could make them feel so uncomfortable that they eventually excused themselves, sweat dotting their foreheads, and all but ran away. Dara would bet that if she could just concentrate a little, she could get that result faster if push came to shove. It wasn't much, and it wasn't a guarantee. Chances were that she wouldn't be able to make it work and she'd waste precious seconds in a tight spot, but it was something. She had to work with what she had.

Taking a bracing breath, Dara left the cell again and followed the others, this time to the showers. Hunt had been right—there was a small area curtained off from the rest for the women to shower in. She ducked inside and shed her clothes quickly, stepping into the stream of water before the others got there. It was a welcome comfort, the feel of lukewarm water on her body. But she didn't allow herself the luxury of enjoying it. The other women were lagging behind and she wanted to get out of there before they could confront her.

On the other side of the curtain the men talked, some of them shouting. There was laughter and curses, and more than once she heard the impact of physical blows and people falling to the wet floor. Dara worked very hard to block out the groans and shouts of pain. She hummed to herself, focusing on the melody to get through the next few minutes, praying that no one decided to pull the curtain aside and expose her.

She scrubbed herself quickly, washed her hair, and then grabbed a towel to wrap herself in.

A moment later, Dara sensed the women's approach, but by then, she was dressed and heading out of the showers. Her hair was dripping, but she toweled it dry even as she moved. The cloth was big enough to hide her head and she made good use of it on her way back to the cell.

Hunt was still gone. Good. Making a frustrated sound, she tossed the towel into a corner. So this was to be her life now. If one could call it a life.

Determined to last at least a full month, until she would get the hell out of here, she studied her surroundings. Any advantage would help, wouldn't it? The cell was actually not that small. It was only when Hunt was in residence that it seemed to shrink around her. There were cabinets other than the ones under her bed, but she didn't look into them. They probably held Hunt's things.

A toilet and sink stood to one side, and it appeared that the tooth rinse would be provided every morning and evening for both her and Hunt above the sink.

Dara wondered if everything here was touch or voice activated. She was about to try it when Hunt returned. "There is a gym on the fourth level and an entertainment area on the sixth," he said without looking at her. "It's ancient. Sixty-inch flat screen televisions and some DVDs." He was still wet from his shower, shirtless. Dara almost sighed as she covertly ogled him for a moment. The water beaded on his pecs and abs, creating an effect similar to oil on skin. But this was no model posing for his shot. Hunt made those guys look like immature little boys.

Freaking unbelievably sexy man. She did sigh a little at that thought. So unfair.

No! *Convict.* He was a convict. Who knew what he'd done to land himself in here? What the hell was she doing thinking like that?

Dara forced her wince into a smile that felt very uncomfortable, and took up her comb. She broke off a tooth almost immediately. Her hair was soft, but there was so much of it that it took a long time to comb out the knots and snarls. Making a face, she sat on her bed to finish her task.

For a moment, she was at eye level with Hunt's crotch. *So unfair!* Had he lost weight or something since the last time they issued him pants? Why did he have to wear them so low? She could almost see his...

Do not *think it. Don't even look.* Dara plied the comb through her hair again, welcoming the sting of torn-out follicles as a distraction. It was proving feeble, at best.

Hunt bent double to look at her. "Well? What's it to be, lady?"

Dara frowned. What was it he'd been asking?

"Gym or the TV? I don't have all day. There's still some things I need to explain to you before I cut you completely loose."

He was tapping his foot at her! Definitely *not* a fairy-tale hero, no matter how hot he happened to be. But he was all she had to stake her hopes on. Dara raked the comb through her hair again, wincing as a few more hairs snapped at the tension. "And what important business do you have to keep you busy today?"

His face went blank, then a slow smile spread to reveal strong white teeth. "Touché."

Dara inclined her head in a semi-bow. She was not going to be smitten by that smile. No way.

The huge hand he extended to her had calluses, hinting at hard work, or hard exercise. She didn't know which. "Tristan Hunt," he said. "We haven't been introduced yet."

Wiping the water from her hand, she slipped it into his grip. "A pleasure to meet you, Mr. Hunt." It wasn't until he released her hand again that she noticed there were no spills of unwanted knowledge. No secrets tumbling out of his head and into hers. Physical touch tended to reveal more of a person. Apparently, Hunt was still immune. All that was left over from his touch was the warmth of his hand that seemed to stay around hers like a glove. Odd, that.

"And your name?"

"I have many," she said with an impish grin, quoting a movie from the early twenty-first century. "But we're all so much more… complicated than our names." When he only stared at her, uncomprehending, she shook her head. "Never mind."

"Okay… what do I call you, then?"

"Dara. Dara Frost."

"Strange name," he noted.

"Yes it is, Mr. Tristan Hunt," she returned pointedly, and he scowled at her.

"Pick your fancy, Dara."

"Are there any books?"

As if on command, a panel slid open in the wall, revealing a small chamber with a screen inside. It listed genres and a search window.

"I should have figured you'd be a bookworm. Guess further instruction can wait until tonight." Hunt left grumbling.

Dara didn't know what his problem was; she was delighted! She browsed through a couple of genres, then stated her selection with a voice command. The screen went blank and the bottom of the shelf opened while a book was pushed up. A real book! With a broken spine and paper pages and everything! Dara hadn't held one since grade school. She picked up her book and brought it to her nose. The old book smell almost made her swoon. Dara returned to her bunk, grinning like an idiot.

At least there was something here that she would be able to enjoy. She might never even leave this cell. Except for showers and meals, of course. And at least this way, she'd be out of sight and far enough from the others that she wouldn't be bothered by their thoughts.

Determined to keep looking on the bright side of things, she opened the book and lost herself in a story for a while.

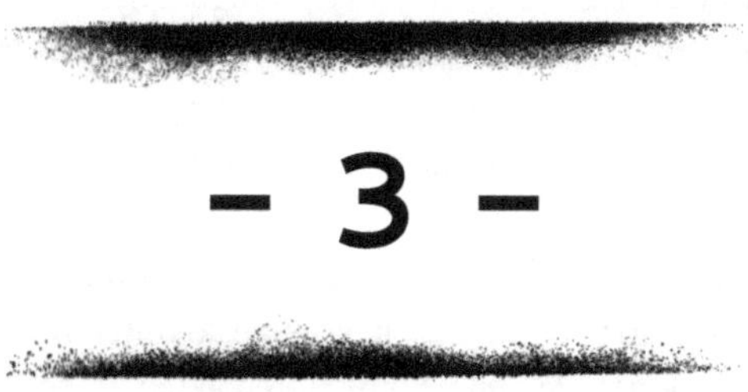

- 3 -

Later that day

The gym took up the entire second level. It was a vast expanse of equipment and fields, pools and machines. It was a haven for those who required daily physical exertion, or those who were required to get it as part of their assigned treatment.

Prisons were not just holding cells anymore. They were sophisticated laboratories in which the inmates were lab rats. Extensive studies and experiments were performed, typically without their consent, to improve the lives of all other people. If someone happened to die because of the treatment, well, it was considered a small price to pay. Most men were here for the rest of their lives anyway.

Tristan didn't give a shit one way or another. The monitoring device was a small patch that adhered to his skin and relayed information to the electronic notepads all the doctors carried. It didn't bother him while he worked out, so he didn't give it much thought.

After basic stretches and an hour-long jog on one of the machines, he dived into the first empty pool he could find. This was the only place where he still felt human. When he swam, he could pretend he was somewhere else. The pools were small, fitted to the individual, who swam against an artificial current.

Usually the swim was timed. With so many prisoners and only one gym, the limit on equipment usage prevented fights. For Tristan, exceptions were made. The doctors adored him because he never gave them any trouble. He didn't give a damn what they did to him, so they didn't hesitate to do anything and everything they wanted. In return, Tristan got to spend as much time in the water as he wished.

Today, he planned on staying as long as possible. He needed to clear his head. There was only so much meddling a man could stand and Herb had just crossed the line. It was a good thing the clerk never came to Wolf block. Tristan doubted he'd be able to restrain himself.

His new *roommate* was a monumental new headache. A female.

Not just any female, but a fucking telepath! Did they even know what she was capable of? Or was that why she was here in the first place? The thought chilled him. It was one thing to play with his chemistry, quite another to play with someone's mind. The only reason they weren't doing *that* to him was they had no idea. Oh, but one telepath always sensed another. He'd suspected Dara from the first, but when she'd tentatively reached out to his mind, he'd been certain.

She was unskilled. It took a lot of training and guidance from someone who'd mastered the art to control something like that. Dara seemed only to be able to hush the voices slightly. She couldn't even shut them out altogether. It was why he'd shielded his thoughts around her. Tristan had meant to scan her while she'd slept, but he hadn't. He'd have to do it tonight.

The alarm beeped. Tristan gritted his teeth and passed his hand in front of the sensor, turning off the flow of water. When he got to the pool's edge, the guard who'd escorted Dara to his cell crouched there, grinning. "So?" he asked, quietly so that only Tristan heard him.

"So, what?" Tristan levered himself out of the pool, forcing the guard to step back.

"How is she?"

Tristan looked him in the eye, judging his intent. Just as he'd thought. Blanc was all talk and very little game. He wanted Dara, but wasn't man enough to face off with Tristan for her. She wasn't worth that much trouble to him. "Adapting," he answered.

Blanc chuckled. "I'll just bet she is. Do you gag her, or just put a pillow over that pretty face to shut her up? Word has it Wolf block was awful quiet last night."

"You know I don't kiss and tell." Tristan took a towel and dried himself off. In a few minutes he would get to the weights.

Blanc's eyebrows shot up. "Could it be… you haven't—" He burst out laughing, drawing undue attention to them.

"Shut your mouth, Blanc," Tristan warned, keeping his voice neutral and his gaze elsewhere. "I didn't have any problem shutting it for you three months ago. I could do it again."

Blanc continued to chuckle. "I'll make a deal with you, Hunt." He stepped closer, his mouth twitching. Tristan was taller than Blanc. Stronger, too. But the weapon at Blanc's side was a great equalizer. It gave the guard far more courage than he should have had. "I'll shut up about your pretty little thing in exchange for a free ride every once in a while."

"Not a chance. I don't share."

"Better sharing with me than sharing with everyone else, don't you think?"

Tristan speared him with a sharp glare, holding the man in place with a small compulsion. He only hesitated for a moment before he projected some sense into the guard's mind. Subtle was the way. He lowered his head a little, leaned forward; added real perceptions of a threat to the projected ones and amplified all of them to suit his needs. Just enough to make him back down. Just enough to scare the fucking shit out of him for a few seconds before he eased up.

Blanc's smile fell, and he shifted nervously, unable to look away. He broadcast his fear like a scent Tristan could see. Blanc already thought Tristan was an animal. Nothing but muscle and brute force. But Tristan let him see something even more dangerous in his eyes. It was something even the guards refused to fuck with. He was not such an easy prey.

He amplified the doubt in the guard's mind. Maybe Blanc shouldn't have brought this up just yet. And a seemingly stray thought, *Maybe not ever.* It brought Blanc's shoulders back and his chin up. Tristan's control on him slipped, and the son of a bitch found his backbone again. *I am the fucking law around here!* he thought. "Think about it," Blanc said out loud, barely keeping his voice from betraying how uneasy he was. Before he walked away, he decided to give Hunt a final warning. "Word can spread mighty quick around here. I'll stop by tonight."

I knew she'd be trouble. Tristan swore and dropped the towel into the pool. It was instantly vaporized. He should have thrown the damn guard in there. No fuss, no messes.

Before he could entertain the thought a little longer, one of the doctors approached him. Adjusting her spectacles, she watched Blanc leave, her sharp gaze missing nothing. Out of all the white coats, Dr. Chase was the nicest and the sharpest. She always spoke to him as if they were equals in every respect. Unlike the others, each time she performed an experiment or procedure on him, she told him what she was doing, while she was doing it, and even went so far as to predict possible side effects. She'd used to ask if he was okay with what she was about to do. But she'd stopped after a while when he always answered the same—that he didn't give a fuck either way.

"Are you making trouble for him again?" she asked.

"Not yet," Tristan told her, and she grinned up at him.

"Try not to break any bones, will you?" she told him gamely. "I'm always the one who ends up having to set them."

Tristan schooled himself not to smile back. "What's on the menu today, Doc?"

She looked away. "I saw yesterday's population charts. Herb assigned a woman to your cell." The observation was made in a cool, neutral manner, but Tristan knew she was on the lookout for any kind of reaction.

"I don't think he wants to be friends with me anymore."

"You'd do well to be careful, Tristan. I can only help so much."

"Do you know anything about her?"

"Let's talk in my lab, shall we?" She didn't look behind her to check if he was following as she left the gym.

Tristan shook out his wet hair and went after her.

A few words to the guards and an elevator ride later, they entered the laboratory that was reserved for her exclusively. As one of the top physicians and researchers, Dr. Amelia Marguerite Chase merited it. She waved him into the exam chair that stood in the center while she reviewed his file. A computer screen took up nearly half of one wall and displayed his entire body, inside and out, in precise detail.

"You were about to tell me about my new roommate," Tristan reminded her.

Dr. Chase read through the last part of the file, then set it aside and met his gaze. "You should know that the guild is debating a new series of experiments."

"Do I want to know?"

"No, I don't think you do. But I'll tell you anyway." But she didn't. Instead, she pulled on her gloves and pushed a button to summon a hovering table. She opened a kit and neatly spread the contents on the table before sending it to Tristan's side.

"You're hedging." Tristan frowned. "That's not like you. What's going on?"

Dr. Chase looked at him for a moment, then nudged the hovering table aside to reach the keypad on the back of Tristan's chair. It beeped softly with each button she pushed, and then the surveillance cameras turned off. "Ten minutes, that's all we have. Then the system reboots and security is notified."

He nodded.

"I was recently given the results of a statistical analysis done on Earth. The sample size was big enough that I'm inclined to believe it. It shows an increasing trend of chemically… different people. They don't fit any of the original DNA profiles and are proving to be resistant to the chem treatments."

"Like me."

She nodded. "Like you."

"Are you sure they were even treated?"

Dr. Chase gave him a look. "Tristan, the treatments are mandatory. People can protest all they want, but whether they like it or not, their children will receive it with or without their knowledge. There are no loopholes. The guild and the government—since they're chief advisors to the president—think it's because these traits are being naturally selected for."

"I don't think I like where you're going with this."

It was easy to keep up with the political currents when he was being swept up in them. And Tristan had been paying close attention.

Since the last fallout, the government had taken a stronger hand in the ruling of its people. They dictated where people should live, what they should eat; they even controlled fashion trends, although why anyone would want to get involved with that was beyond him. Chem-treating people right after birth to prevent any problems was just another way to stay efficient. If that was starting to fail, people were shit out of luck. Because the next step would be engineering people according to the government's specifications.

"Believe me, I don't like it, either. But the grants have been received, supposedly with no strings attached—"

"And yet in a few months' time, officials will be knocking on your door for results on the studies *they* want done," he finished for her.

"Yes," Dr. Chase agreed unhappily, then hesitated before blurting out, "They're reproductive studies, Tristan."

It took his brain a moment to process what she'd just said.

The rest she related quickly, as if she didn't want to pollute her mind even long enough to put the thought into words. "The preliminary design is to pair inmates according to three processes—chemical traits, natural selection, and randomization."

Tristan stared at her, astonished. "Please tell me you didn't just say what I think you just said." They wouldn't dare.

"It gets worse," she said. "Interaction is necessary. They don't want to see in vitro fertilization in their results because it creates bias. As far as chemical traits and random selection go, a computer can find candidates fairly easily, but the rest of it, especially the natural selection part, is nothing more than—"

"Rape." Tristan's stomach did a nasty dive. Those bastards. "How will it be conducted? What's the scope?"

"You don't want to know."

"Yes, I do, damn it!" he growled. "How?"

Dr. Chase took a steadying breath. "Anarchy," she said succinctly. "They plan to designate an entire level to it. Men and women will be led inside in near-equal proportion, and then the guards will leave and the doors will close."

"What's the scope?"

"Total. No exceptions."

The next thing Tristan growled was not in English. Dr. Chase stared at him, her mouth agape. "Was that Greek?" she asked in amazement.

Gaelic, actually. But he spoke Greek and Latin, too. Wasn't worth it to read *The Odyssey* or *The Aeneid* in the English translation. Like paying the price of a 3-D interactive admission to watch the movie on TV. But he couldn't say that; he could barely make a sound.

Tristan was struggling to keep from lashing out. The previous studies done on him had changed him significantly, altered his mental and physical abilities. His muscles have been enhanced—a side effect of one of the serums Dr. Chase always pumped into him. They caused him to have outbursts of incredible strength that he couldn't control, because they were triggered by stress or anger—times when he didn't *want* to be in control. He was literally a primed bomb ready to go off at any moment.

Even as he gripped the armrests of the chair he was sitting in, the material indented, right down to the alloy center. There would be marks left on it.

"Tristan, listen to me. You have to breathe through this. I don't want to have to sedate you."

"Of course not," he managed to say through gritted teeth. "That would mean no more experiments today."

Dr. Chase stepped away. "You know that's not true," she said, and Tristan could hear the hurt in her voice. She wasn't one of them, he tried to remind himself. If she hadn't told him, that reproductive study would have come as a nasty surprise.

He breathed in, instinctively reaching out to the only person like him within ten light years. He *felt* Dara start and drop her book. Cursing himself, he pulled back instantly, throwing up all his shields. He told himself that the next breath came easier, and his vision settled to normal. He pretended that the details faded until he couldn't see the miniscule writing on the computer screen twelve feet away from him anymore.

Dr. Chase was next to him again, her fingers pressed to the inside of his wrist, but she wasn't looking at her watch to measure his heart rate. Tristan looked at her, and she blinked. "Your eyes have changed. The pupils contracted vertically just now, like a cat's." There was something in her voice, some kind of emotion he couldn't pinpoint in his current state.

His jaw was clenched so hard the muscles ached. "Amelia," he said, fighting to regain his senses. "I need to ask you a favor."

"What is it?"

"Keep her out of it."

She frowned. "The woman? I'm not sure if I can. I told you the scope—"

Christ, his teeth were about to start cracking. "You can try. There are ways. There are always options."

"Tristan, I can't make her disappear. She's on the list. She's coming in tomorrow for—"

"No," he told her fiercely, meeting her gaze. His hand turned up to capture hers for emphasis, though it took everything he had to control his muscles and not crush her bones. The more he fought himself, the more it enraged him, eroding his control further. Tristan focused on his breath and nothing more. In and out. He closed his eyes. In and out.

The security cameras beeped as they turned back on. A deep male voice called Amelia's name from the intercom by the door.

"Please," Tristan said and opened his eyes. If it was all he could ever do for the woman, he had to keep her away from this mess. Dara exuded innocence like an aura he could practically see around her. She'd be broken by this. Irreparably. Tristan had seen rape victims in the memories of some of the men here. Those women had lost everything that had ever defined them, leaving nothing but a shell of a human being. And if there was one thing he never wanted to see, it was Dara's eyes completely empty like that.

Dr. Chase pulled her hand free and answered the intercom. "All clear here, Sergeant. I must have punched in the wrong combination. Won't happen again."

"Need backup?"

"No, thank you. Everything's fine." She waved at the camera for good measure.

"All right, then. Security out." But they weren't, and both she and Tristan knew it.

Amelia picked up the file that lay next to Tristan's and came to him so she wouldn't have to speak loudly. "Dara Frost," she read. "She was sentenced to life for a series of bloody murders. Seems she called the police with some information that led them to one of the victims. He was already dead, and there were no clues to point to the killer. Except her call." She closed the file. "The chief of police testified against her, then pleaded for the jury to spare her life. No one really believed she did it, but the people were screaming for blood. And hers was the most readily available."

Tristan felt ice settle into the marrow of his bones. She'd seen it. She'd looked into a serial killer's mind because she couldn't keep it from happening. And now she was far too close to far too many of them, with no mental guards to keep out their sick thoughts. How did she survive without going mad?

She doesn't belong here. He hadn't realized he'd spoken out loud until Dr. Chase tilted her head, studying him curiously. "No, I suppose she doesn't. But there are a lot of us here who could make that claim. What should be doesn't change what is." Her tone didn't tell him whether she was talking about him, or herself. "I hope you're not planning to make a crusade out of this. It's not worth it to stick your own neck out for someone you don't even know."

Tristan was nobody's puppet. What the doctors did to him, they did only because he allowed it. Dr. Chase, for all her sage advice, had her own agenda when it came to him. Her research was dependent on his full cooperation, and until now, he'd given it without qualm. That she would stoop to this kind of manipulation was as low as it was unexpected. Which meant that Tristan shut down. "Perform your experiments, Doc. The sooner you're done, the sooner I can get out of here."

Amelia sighed, smart enough to know when it wasn't worth it to stay on a subject anymore. She pulled the ready kit close again and became all business. "It's an intravenous treatment to stabilize your fluctuations in strength. It should make outbursts more controllable." The serum was already prepared and she measured an exact amount in the syringe before she injected it into his arm. "The side effects should be mild. A little headache and muscle soreness. Nothing a guy like you can't handle."

– 4 –

29th day of the 3rd Blood Moon, just after midnight

Dara stared up at Hunt's bunk in the darkness. Her chest felt painfully clear, the way it usually did after she'd cried for a long time. She'd been in the middle of the best chapter when she'd felt something she couldn't even name. For a second, Dara had been so connected with Hunt, it had been like she wasn't in the cell, reading a book, but there with him, wherever the hell he'd been.

She'd seen through his eyes, felt her hands cramp—just as his had—her chest going tight until she couldn't breathe. For that instant, Dara had literally shared a single mind with him, but she still hadn't gotten any of his thoughts, just raw emotions.

And those emotions had scared her.

Dara could feel the fury making his jaw lock; felt the awful wrath he'd kept just barely leashed. Joined with him, she'd feared for her life.

So this was what he'd been hiding from her. A wolf in sheep's clothing, helping her, teaching her, making her think he was safe. But he was even worse than the others—he was locked in the cell with her!

What had set him off like that, she'd had no idea. Her biggest concern at that moment had been whether he would bring all that rage down on her once he got back. She'd been frozen for a long time after the connection broke, overwhelmed, sorting through the flood of information so she could let it dissipate. She'd had to do it, and quickly, so she wouldn't be paralyzed and left to his mercy when he came back.

Dara had forced herself to wade through the anger, shock, and disbelief to the underlying nuances of what had happened to him, and found something that scared her even more than his rage.

Fear. What could a man like him fear so much that it would bring him to such a state? What could he have found out that would make this kind of reaction a natural response? In this place, after who knew how long, after whatever he'd done to get in here, what could he possibly have to fear?

Did she even want to know?

Don't think about it, she told herself. *There's enough for you to worry about already without adding the unknown to it. Just close your eyes and sleep.*

Easier said than done.

Dara took a deep breath and closed her eyes. But after being so tense all day long, she couldn't make herself relax. Every time she managed it, she thought about that instant of connection. Her breathing became faster, and she had to concentrate to slow it down again. Of course, as soon as she started thinking about breathing, she couldn't relax, because if she did, she'd remember that her breathing had been off-kilter and then she'd be right back to near-hyperventilating again.

Frustrated and tired, Dara resorted to the one technique that never failed her: her mental happy place. She put everything from her mind and imagined herself sitting on the battlements of a medieval keep. It stood in the middle of a vast open plain, a dirt path cutting its way from the front gate to forever, through a field of tall grass that moved like ocean waves in the breeze. In the north and east, a thick forest framed the plain. In the west, the ocean lay indomitable.

There were torches lit on the battlements and the whole scene had the feel of calm before a great storm. She could feel a war brewing; that usually wasn't part of her world. Somewhere to the south, where she'd never imagined anything beyond what she could see, battle drums rumbled in the night. The drums turned to thunder as clouds gathered; Dara could just make out their dark, oppressive outline.

A wolf howled at the big, round moon. Others joined it and Dara, in her mind, threw her head back and howled with them.

She smiled as sleep slowly seeped into her, taking her from the cold, dark prison to that place and time where she felt at peace.

Tristan had to make himself uncurl his fingers. His hands had been fisted ever since he'd returned to his cell. All he remembered from the way back was men looking at him strangely as they stepped out of his way to give him a wide berth. He didn't give a shit about any of them.

And then Dara had been there, with her wide eyes and her luscious lips parted on a question as he'd barged in. He'd never given her a chance to ask anything, instead closing himself off in the bathroom corner. Only after a long time of splashing cold water on his face had he returned to his bunk.

That's where he'd been ever since, pretending to sleep. Tristan had never been one to prowl and pace restlessly but, by God, this week was about to drive him to it. He opened his mouth wide to relieve some of the soreness in his jaw, then lay perfectly still and simply listened.

Thump-thump—his heart beat. *Thump-thump, thump-thump.*

And then the sound receded and a vision took shape. It was so vivid and sharp that at first he thought he was dreaming. But his mind was too alert to be asleep. Tristan's chest became tight as he looked around.

He was in a different world, one that was too picturesque to be real, even if it seemed thousands of years removed. It was a castle. The sun was setting, and a silhouette of a woman sat high up on the battlements with her back to him. She looked relaxed, but there was a subtle tension in her spine as she gazed out over the castle walls at something in the distance. Tristan couldn't see what she saw from his vantage point, but he could hear the echo of drums.

Wolves howled in the distance, and so did she. Her voice was eerie, like some strange song; a haunting, sorrowful melody that seemed natural in this world.

The vision changed slightly, becoming foggier and more like a dream. A pyre burst into flame, sending thick smoke curling up toward the starry sky.

The woman rose on the battlements and walked past him. There was pride in her step, dignity in the way she held her head up high, and despair in her shining gaze as it settled briefly on him.

Tristan's eyes snapped open. His heart was racing, and his fingers were once more curled tightly, crushing his blanket.

Below him, Dara stirred in her bed, a soft feminine shift of her head on the pillow. She made a sighing sound, and his vision clouded over again.

She was dancing around the pyre, so close that when she extended her hand, it brushed the flames. Her hair was wild; her skirts lifted and floated around her. Her movements were fluid, graceful.

She danced as though with joy, but there was that sadness on her face when it was illuminated by the flames, a look that told him she was dancing to convince herself that she was happy. And from the tears glittering their way down her cheeks, he surmised that she was failing.

Tristan shook his head, banishing Dara's dream from his mind. He must have relaxed his guards, otherwise he never would have seen any of it. That would make it the second time in twenty-four hours that his control had slipped.

It was a sign.

No matter how strong he thought he was, this place was driving him out of his mind. He never would have allowed outer stimuli to affect his mind this way if he was completely sane.

Satisfied with that conclusion, he relaxed and stretched out on his bunk.

Before he could settle in comfortably, a silent alarm went off in his mind. *Danger!* He scanned his surroundings, looking for possible threats, but everyone was asleep.

Everyone except Blanc.

Tristan swore. The bastard was headed this way, just as he'd said he would. If Tristan didn't think of something fast, Dara would have a nasty awakening, in more ways than one.

Think. Think. Think!

Blanc was coming closer. He was quiet about it, too, even in his mind, whispering his thoughts. The guard didn't want the others to know he was about to make use of one of the prettier inmates—he didn't like sharing any more than Tristan did.

A few more seconds and Tristan would be able to see the guard approaching. Not enough time for a plan. Not nearly enough time to search Blanc's mind and find the one thing that would make him forget about Dara for the moment and turn to something else. Tristan could wake a couple of prisoners and incite a fight, but not quickly enough. He could fight the guard and risk a full-out intervention, getting his ass royally kicked in the process, but that would make things even worse for Dara. The less attention drawn to her, the better.

Tristan didn't bother analyzing why he was so protective of her, or why he even cared. Maybe it was her dream affecting him like this, but he was now absolutely certain that Dara didn't belong here and he wanted to protect her. He had to do it, to prove to himself that he wasn't one of *them* yet. Dara was a woman facing impossible odds and any man worthy of that title would try to help her.

More than that, she was a telepath and he didn't want to give up a potential—he gritted his teeth at the term—friend.

Tap, tap, tap.

He could hear Blanc's boots no matter how softly he walked. The guard was almost there. A few more steps and he'd reach the cell.

Tristan closed his mind to him, but not before catching a glimpse. The man was deprived, living light years away from his wife, and he meant to take it out on Dara. She reminded the man of his old college crush and he wanted to seize a missed opportunity.

Tap, tap… tap.

No more time to think.

Tristan threw back his blanket and moved without thinking. He slid off his bunk and onto hers in one fluid motion. His body hid hers from sight completely.

As his weight settled on her, she woke, her eyes open wide but unseeing in the darkness. Tristan put a hand over her mouth to keep her quiet. "Don't make a sound," he whispered into her ear, so close, his lips brushed its delicate edge.

– 5 –

She was suffocating in the darkness, unable to breathe—not because of the big hand covering her mouth, or the body on top of hers, pressing her down—but because air suddenly didn't exist.

…gonna have me a good time tonight, oh yeah. 'Bout damn time, too—shithole can drive a guy out of his fucking mind… just a little game to start… fucker better not give me any more grief…

Dara balled her hands into fists, her entire body tensing in fear. Images flashed through her mind's eye; she was lost in them, unable to see what was real and what wasn't. In the night, in the nightmare, phantom hands grabbed at her; invaded, hurt. Her eyes watered.

Fantasies. Sick, sick thoughts. Anticipation. Hungerlustsexsexsexgonnahaveittonight. I will. I will. Willwillwillwillwill…

Dara bucked, thrashed, tried to escape her own mind. It wasn't him. It wasn't the man on top of her thinking those things. It was the one outside.

Security officer Alexander James Blanc.

Coming closer. Closer. Step. And one more. Drooling for her. Groping himself.

…sweet piece of assssssssssss…

Dara cried out, the sound muffled by Hunt's hand over her mouth. She bucked again, but it felt as if the entire world was pinning her down. She didn't gain an inch. Terrified, she fought harder. *—Let go!—* she screamed in her mind. Needed to run.

—Nowhere to run,— Hunt replied, trying to calm her.

—Then I have to hide!— Dara could feel Hunt in her mind now, heard the sound of his breath and felt compelled to match it. Inhale, exhale. In and out. It hurt, as if the air was being forced in and out of her lungs.

—Hide in your mind,— his voice said. "Go somewhere else," he whispered to her, and with no other recourse, she grasped onto the sound. Followed it out of the terror. Ran toward something else. Anything.

She fell into another mind—Hunt's.

Heart thumping quickquickquickquick. Breathe slow—about to lose it! No! Won't hurt her. Pain at the base of his/her skull, washing over him/her. Head pounding with it. Muscles tensing. No! Growling. Low, animalistic; fury and wrath manifesting in sound. Will kill the fuck first. Snap his neck and feel the bones break.

Dara couldn't fight that maelstrom. She cringed and cowered, her body going tense, wanting to curl into a ball, but unable to move.

He sensed her then. Thoughts quieted, a soft vacuum around her where nothing made a sound. She was in a black fog, but it was warm, and the fear faded. She could breathe again.

—Don't be here,— he thought, and she knew he was speaking to her. Next to her ear, he whispered, "In your mind. Don't be here. Go somewhere else." She was already moving, leaving; being pushed—pulled?—back to herself. *—Think of something other than him. Think of your castle, and the bonfire and dancing.—* Dara squeezed her eyes shut and let it happen. Before the noises and nightmares could claw at her again, she built her castle around herself, the walls rising toward the sky. Armies were at the door; she could hear them yelling and ramming the gate. They wouldn't get through. She would not let them.

And there was something else… something just outside her walls, keeping the intruders away. She could sense it, but couldn't name it.

Oh, yeah. Game on… The guard's voice leaked through, unchecked. And with it, fear made her shiver again.

A bow appeared in Dara's hand. Fear turned to resolve. Not by her doing. Some other power guided her. She raced up the stairs to the battlements and beheld her enemy. One man. Just one man stared back up at her. He had the face of the guard, Blanc, and the voice of legions.

One man. One man…

One man you can fight.

Dara put an arrow to her bow, drew it back, and let the arrow fly. Bastard would sprout a field of them by the time she was done.

She couldn't see or hear what was going on around her physical self, but she could still feel Tristan on top of her. Dara knew he had to make this convincing enough to make Blanc back off. He shifted over her, mimicking the movements of sex. He grasped one of her wrists, brought it up to the edge of the bed over her head where her other hand rested.

In her vision, Dara was fighting back; she was winning.

—*That's it, lass,*— Hunt praised, and a sense of triumph filled her.

Until his perceptions somehow slipped into her consciousness and she heard the doorway zap as the force field disengaged. Blanc was inside the cell. Her inner vision clouded and she lost hold of her castle fantasy. There was no more castle. She was back in the cell and she was… Hunt. Dara saw through his eyes; heard with his ears.

"Fuck off," he spat, faking a groan.

Blanc sneered and drawled, "I'll have my turn. I can wait."

She felt his indecision. Hunt could watch two minds, but he couldn't affect both. It was either stay with Dara and shield her, or risk taking on Blanc.

He stayed with Dara.

Reality faded again into a fractured version of her fantasy, but Hunt's voice trailed behind. *"If you make me stop, you'll regret it."*

A savage voice, full of hatred and aggression. Dara squirmed beneath Hunt, her illusion giving way again, this time to her own perceptions. The guard was less than three feet from the bunk. Too close. An involuntary shiver ran through her. She knew Hunt felt it, and his control—which seemed to be volatile at the best of times—slipped a little more.

—*Dead bastard standing!*— he hissed all around her.

Dara heard the angry growl that built up in his throat, softened at the last moment so that it came out as a sound of pleasure. Blanc would never know how close he was to being ripped apart. Dara knew, and it made her brave. *Enemy of my enemy is my friend.* As far as friends went, Tristan Hunt now looked indestructible. She stopped fighting, made herself relax beneath him. His muscles bunched and his hold on her loosened, readying to let go completely and turn on Blanc.

Better to crush the guard's skull than her wrists…

Dara let go of her vision, needing to see this through. Tristan seemed to be waiting for something. He was keeping up the pretense, moving over her like they were really having sex, but his mind was elsewhere.

"Hurry the fuck up, will you?" Blanc demanded. "I don't have all night." Dara had opened herself to other minds again. She could sense him shifting his weight to the other foot. He rearranged his crotch, blatantly fondling himself in the process as he watched the two of them on the bunk. He was working himself up into a lather. All this was just turning him on even more.

Dara made a sound and quickly retreated, somehow closing herself in a loop between her own mind and Tristan's. She felt the aggression, the need to rip the guard's head off then and there. But Tristan breathed through it, pulled his lips back into a smile that she could feel. A vicious snarl. He groaned again. "Ah, but I do," he informed Blanc with easy arrogance, thrusting his hips forward for emphasis.

Dara gasped. Not with fear, but shock. Tristan's hand pinned both of hers, but his grip was gentle. His breath teased her hair at her temple. She was trapped, completely at his mercy, and she… *liked* it.

Enemy of my enemy is still dangerous.

He moved over her and, despite all reason, her body responded. What was wrong with her? She should be terrified—she *was*. She could still sense Blanc in the cell, but with Tristan shielding her it seemed as if he wasn't even real.

And Tristan! Dara could feel his muscles bulging, a terrifying reminder of what he was capable of. Yet he wasn't hurting her.

He didn't frighten her.

Tristan moved, and her back wanted to arch, even though there was no room for any kind of movement. The blanket imprisoned her legs and she wanted it gone, wanted to cradle the body over hers.

What was this, some kind of mind control? Dara recognized Tristan's presence in her mind, shielding her, soothing her. But her thoughts were her own. He wasn't manipulating her into feeling this way. —

Won't hurt you,— he was saying, and all she wanted to say back was, *Touch me.*

This wasn't normal. How could she be turned on?

And then his hand was gone from her mouth and he was kissing her. Her mind filled with a confusing vision of incomplete shapes and sharp sensations. Fantasies coming to life in the spur of the moment, unfinished but all the more potent because of it. Dara felt weightless in that instant, drunk. She felt him suck in a breath, and felt his surprise mirror her own.

Tristan shifted just a little, kissed her briefly, just a small taste, observing the change in himself. His mind was calm, focused—the burst of rage was gone, but the strength remained. He was completely in control of his body for the first time since this whole mess with the experiments started. Not only that, there was nothing else invading his thoughts. There were no voices slipping through his shields; they held without any effort on his part. It was as if he'd lost his telepathy in that kiss.

But he hadn't.

He shared Dara's mind as easily as if the two were not separate at all. Tristan felt her surprise and confusion, and he shared it. He knew she sensed him in her mind, as he sensed her in his, but the feeling was not unpleasant.

His mouth moved over hers, his tongue slipping between her lips to seek the warmth beyond. She matched him, kissing him back for a moment of complete abandon. He felt her fear dissipate as she let go and simply felt. Tristan released her wrists and twined his fingers with hers. He moved over her again, this time in a long, slow thrust.

Her lips were as sweet as honey. Tristan kissed her harder, deeper, coaxing and demanding a response. Soaking it up like long-lost sunshine. He let go of one of her hands to get beneath her shirt, craving the feel of her skin.

As soon as she was free, she grabbed his hair and threw a leg over him to keep him in place. Tristan smiled against her mouth and curled his hips languidly. *Greedy little thing.* Her shirt came up to the edge of her bra, but would not move farther, unless he gave up the feel of her breasts rubbing against him every time he moved. *Won't.* He contented himself with caressing her side and back, drinking up the little moaning noises she wasn't even aware of making. Reveling in the way she raised her hips to meet his next thrust.

Sharing her mind, he savored every reaction. Dara could scarcely catch her breath, and she didn't want to, afraid he'd stop. Tristan thrilled to know he'd brought her to this. She let herself go completely. There were no shields or barriers between their minds, and he was feeling what she felt; got his own pleasure returned to him, amplified.

They were both dizzy with it and craving more. Her leg around him was clenched so tight, trying to make him do more, but he wouldn't.

—*Why?*— she demanded desperately. Dara rocked her hips to his, wordlessly urging him on. It was all he could do not to give in.

Tristan lost track of time and everything else, caught up in that kiss, wanting it to last forever. Had anything ever felt this good? Dara arched to him, and he shuddered. *Too far. Too fast.* She didn't care about that now, drowning in a mad swirl of adrenaline and lust, but she would in the morning.

She did it again and he wanted to take the invitation—*Christ*, how he wanted to. *Just take the free pass, forget about everything for a while.*

How was he any different from Blanc?

Tristan shuddered and broke the kiss, then dropped his head to the pillow next to her, cheek to cheek. He could feel her heart beating against his so fast, but her mind was completely open. Completely trusting. She squirmed beneath him, and he clamped his hand down on her leg. "Hold still," he said.

"Don't want to," she said wickedly.

Telepath, Tristan reminded himself and raised his head to look her in the eye. She could see his mind just as he saw hers, but she couldn't see the full distinction between the two. She knew he didn't want her to hold still either, and it was changing her own feelings. But it wasn't her. Beneath the intensity of this was still a kernel of fear. She was still frightened and, in trying to escape it, she embraced the one thing that could overcome it. Lust.

Dara *needed* this.

Though she might end up hating herself for it in the morning.

– 6 –

Dara stared up at Tristan, meeting his green gaze. She was so close, her body aching, weeping for release. For him. She didn't understand it and didn't want to. It was just the two of them now. The guard was gone. Out of patience and out of time. There was nothing keeping Tristan from finishing what he'd started.

But he wouldn't. He looked as confused as she felt. With her mind merged so completely with his, she shifted her focus and looked at herself through his eyes. What she saw surprised her. She… fascinated him. In Tristan's eyes, she was a creature of grace. He saw everything, good and bad, blended in a way that yielded something utterly beautiful: her.

He saw her as a ray of light and color in this dark place. A breath of fresh air, scented with—she blushed—ecstasy. Tristan regarded her as a treasure that was all his own. To admire and gain strength from, to keep safe from other, greedy hands.

The discovery was so unexpected, it took some of the edge off the frighteningly intense lust of a second ago. She still felt drawn to him, but it was… different. Astonished, she looked deeper. That she even could, spoke more than anything about how rattled both of them were about what just happened. Dara wasn't above exploiting it a little.

She let herself fall into his gaze, into his mind.

There were shadows and ghosts, faces from memories, distorted like reflections in funhouse mirrors. Whispers and voices blended together around her, incomprehensible words in a language she'd never heard before. As she slowly adjusted to her surroundings, she realized there were... pathways like vague, dark alleys all around her.

It was a maze of sorts. Each path would lead to a different place; different memories and perceptions. Easy enough to follow. And so easy to get lost in.

For the moment, she simply soaked in what she could. She could hear a sort of rhythm to the strange voices. They were memories, but not of people. It was something Dara recognized easily—passages from books. Poetry? Not quite, but very close. So the man had read a book. And it *seemed as though these passages held some meaning for him, but she couldn't tell why.*

More faces appeared, these with sharp teeth and hollow eyes. They disappeared just as quickly, leaving behind residual anger and disgust. She turned away from them, shuddering in mind and body. To hate someone that much...

Dara heard a woman's voice somewhere, and frowned. She turned to follow it.

Tristan must have realized what she was doing, because he started to retreat. The pathways dissolved one by one, cutting off her options, including the one she'd chosen.

Reality began bleeding into her vision...

Dara was back in the cell, but there was still a connection between her mind and Tristan's. She didn't want to let this go yet. There was a kind of relief in sharing minds; knowing that he was like her and understood.

Knowing that he'd just put himself at risk to protect her, when he knew nothing about her. He hadn't asked her to trust him. Not in so many words. Tristan probably just figured she didn't have another choice. He might be right. But right now, trusting him didn't seem like the lesser of two evils anymore. It seemed more like salvation.

As the pleasant calm began to fade, it started to become frighteningly clear to Dara that there might be fates worse than death and insanity in this place. It hadn't really sunk in before. She'd thought that if she just kept her head down, stayed invisible, she could get through this. Well, there was no staying invisible now. Even the illusion of safety inside this cell had been stripped away. She had nothing. No safe harbor.

Except for Tristan. Even if he was a giant gamble she would most likely lose, there was nowhere else for her to turn. Dara was afraid that if he left now, she wouldn't be able to move past this horrible feeling of being completely exposed. She'd panic, and stay panicked for a very long time. Maybe forever. Maybe she would try her luck and walk through the shielded doorway.

She needed him to distract her, at least for the time being.

Dara slid her fingers into his hair again, molding them to his scalp, and pulled him back to her. Tristan made a rough sound that reverberated in his chest and he settled his weight more fully on top of her, sliding an arm underneath her shoulders to pull her even closer. His mouth took possession of hers, devouring, conquering, seducing his way to her very soul.

Before, he'd been distracted, caught up in the moment. Now Tristan took his time, leisurely tasting her, slowly stoking her desire to a flame that burned much lower than before, but so much hotter. Their tongues touched and danced, teasing and light, then deep and hot. Dara couldn't remember what kissing had been like before him anymore.

Certainly not like this… *nothing* was like this. She was being possessed and she loved it. She reveled in the feeling, in being able to touch someone and be touched without driving the other person away. There was a certain sense of awe and power to see his thoughts and memories, and in the knowledge that he knew what she was seeing and he let her. Dara wanted to know him—his mind, his past… everything.

She slowly slunk back into his mind once more.

Tristan groaned and pulled away, resting his forehead on hers. He could feel her hot breath on his mouth and wanted to kiss her again. And keep kissing her. He didn't trust himself to move yet; didn't want to give up what they had. He didn't want to sever the connection between their minds. Tristan *liked* her in his mind. He liked it too damn much, and that was a problem.

He couldn't afford to get close to her, not when one or both of them could be dead in a very short time. This brief little escape from reality couldn't happen again. This place… stripped away every last ounce of humanity out of a person. Bled them dry until there was nothing left but rage and madness. Some fought it with everything they had, and still lost. Others just silently let it all slip away.

Tristan had given up so much already. Maybe too much. But he recognized that there was a line, a point of no return. There was something he'd held back for years, had nurtured and protected it; let it lie sleeping so others wouldn't be tempted to exploit it. Something about Dara was waking it to life.

If he gave in, if he took the risk and lost…

He couldn't. Far too much was at stake. But it surprised him how much he was bothered by that decision.

Dara was unmoving beneath him, her mind still searching his for anything she could find. Curious as a cat. "You could have asked," he told her. He probably wouldn't have answered, but it was a hell of a lot easier than snooping in someone's brain.

She didn't reply. She had no idea how open she'd left herself. Tristan knew almost everything about her now.

She was a librarian. Or used to be, before all of this. Lived in a small apartment in the middle of a nondescript neighborhood. No friends to speak of, just a handful of relatives who never visited. Dara was alone not by choice, but because getting close to anyone meant opening herself up to madness. She loved books because the people in them were safe. A writer could allow her a peek into someone's mind without overwhelming her. Showing her only what she needed and wanted to see. Dara buried herself in stories, living life to the fullest through words on a page or screen, pretending it was real.

She thought her mind was broken and believed she'd never have even a fraction of the happiness she read about. There was a deep loneliness inside her, but an equal measure of joy—thousands of small moments she'd wrenched out of the most mundane things in life, building them up on each other until they balanced the sadness and started to resemble something like peace. Or at the very least, contentment.

They were more alike than Dara realized.

But she was much too inexperienced to do that kind of gleaning.

Even the little effort she exerted now to spy inside his mind would make her head ache like the devil in the morning.

For both their sakes, he made himself move. Shifting with minimal effort, he raised himself off her and slowly put his shields up. Dara was gently expelled from his mind and, despite the aching emptiness her presence left behind, Tristan forced himself to shut her out completely. By the time he hopped up onto his own bunk, he was in a foul temper again. And sore as hell, to boot.

But when he closed his eyes, his dreams weren't filled with Dara's soft body beneath his, but that damn empty castle of hers.

- 7 -

3rd day of the 4th Blood Moon, 3028

"Again. Try it again."

Dara glared at Tristan, clicking her teeth together. She'd been *trying* for the last seven hours and the task wasn't getting any easier. *"Again, again,"* he kept telling her, *"push. You have to push your mind."* She'd like to push *him*. Right into the force field in the doorway. The man was insufferable! He was relentless, as if it mattered whether she learned to do it or not. "Just give me a second," she told him, daring him to comment.

They didn't talk about what happened four nights ago; they hadn't even mentioned it since. By some unspoken agreement, they'd decided to just forget about it and move on. Yeah. She wondered how that was working out for him. For her… not so well. Dara might have become something of an expert at compartmentalizing during the day, but she dreamed about that kiss almost nightly. And it didn't help that she always woke up in the morning to the sight of Tristan hopping off his bunk half-naked and stretching that gorgeous body of his.

Which four nights ago had been pressing her into her bunk, while he'd kissed her breathless.

She still blushed to remember it. Not from embarrassment that it had happened, but because she may have just found someone she could have sex with, without the potential side effects. At least of the psychic kind. It was a giant pink elephant in the room that they refused to acknowledge, but all Dara wanted to do was kiss it.

Er… *him*. Kiss *him*. Again. Longer.

Tristan rapped his knuckles on the floor. "Head in the game, Dara."

And then there were the consequences of that night to deal with.

The monumental headache, which had caused her to deplete all of her assigned painkillers already, had been just the beginning. In the last few days, her life had narrowed down into a routine: wake up, ogle Tristan (she could swear he swaggered around shirtless on purpose just to remind her of what he wouldn't allow her to have), go to breakfast with him, daydream about something very erotic and extremely ill-advised (as he was a telepath, after all), train her mind, shower in record-setting time, come back, train some more, sleep, dream about Tristan.

"I have a headache," she told him, stalling for time.

It was a problematic routine.

Problem one: showers. Dara had used to enjoy soaking under hot running water. Now her goal was always to get in, get done, and get out, without confrontation. Twice now she'd tarried long enough for the other women to catch up. The first time, she'd gotten odd looks, but left when they'd decided to approach her. The second time, a fight among the men had distracted them long enough for her to escape.

She was officially on the map now. Whenever she walked into the cafeteria these days, people noticed. Hence, her "out" time had gotten cut down even more. Sometimes she got so claustrophobic in the cell that she couldn't breathe.

Problem two: food. Since her outing, Tristan had become glued to her side. It was her amazing good luck that he (A) seemed to be feared and/or respected by the others, and (B) he was determined to keep her safe. If someone got too curious or friendly or verbal or close, one look from Tristan Hunt made him back off. Far off. This was usually followed by another hasty retreat into the cell.

Dara didn't really know why he even cared. Her foray into his mind hadn't offered any clues as to his character, only a jumbled mess of images she couldn't unravel. Maybe he was trying to redeem himself. Or maybe it was one big mind game to get her to believe he was really her friend before he attacked.

He had to know by now that she would possibly… probably—okay, most likely—be open to round two with him on that bunk. At times, he looked at her with so much fire in those intense green eyes of his, Dara thought she might go up in flames. Other times he just stared off into space and his shields lowered just the smallest bit. Just enough for Dara to catch a hint of something that made her breathing quicken. But most of the time Tristan was his usual hard-nosed self, headstrong and curt; the ever-present grumpy, sleep-deprived bodyguard.

In any case, she was grateful for his protection. The unfortunate drawback to this was that Tristan was more paranoid than even she, which meant less food time, ergo less food for Dara.

And problem number three: training. Case in point, right now.

"You'll have an even bigger headache by the time we're done. Now do as I say."

Did the word *no* mean nothing to him?

"Perhaps you misunderstood me," she said tightly, balling her hands into fists. "I've had enough for the day." At first, the realization that he was like her had been a comfort. It explained why she couldn't read him and provided her with an ally. Now it was an annoyance. Tristan was like a gadfly always buzzing around, mostly in her head, driving her insane with his little tests and exercises. She felt all of ten years old again, learning to spell absurd words that she would never need to use in real life. Dara had never asked for this *ability*. She hadn't wanted it then, and she didn't want it now.

Unfortunately, it didn't work like a muscle. She couldn't lose it by not using it and Tristan was a relentless teacher. Her training was almost round the clock. She was hungry and she was exhausted, and she wanted to just shut him out and sleep.

He didn't care one bit.

Tristan stopped playing with a balled-up piece of paper and lowered his knee to stretch both of his legs out in front of him on the floor. His back was to the wall, and his legs were so long that his feet hid under her bunk. He raised his head to look her in the eye.

It infuriated him that she kept resisting his teaching methods. The woman had so much potential and refused to utilize it. With any other skill, Tristan wouldn't have given a shit. But this wasn't something she could afford to neglect. She was putting both of them at risk by leaving herself vulnerable.

She continued to piss him off, not because she was incapable—the woman might actually be a stronger telepath than Tristan—but because she was in denial, deliberately making an idiot of herself, hoping it would all go away on its own.

Tristan didn't suffer fools very well.

He let himself into her mind to drive his point home.

Dara tried to stop him, but her shields weren't strong enough to even slow him down, and trying to do so only gave her a real headache. He did it on purpose, crawling around in her mind like a snake, coiling and shifting, making her feel as if he were rearranging her brain.

Finally she stopped her feeble attempts to get him out and let him do as he pleased. He made sure it hurt. Tristan didn't have to be felt at all if he didn't want to be; he could hide in someone's mind, crouched in a dark corner where the person didn't feel anything more than maybe a niggling memory of something he couldn't quite recall. It was a potent power to wield and he was trying to teach Dara how to develop her own skill to his level.

Tristan tortured her a little longer before he withdrew, allowing her to take a breath. "I wasn't even half trying," he told her quietly. She had no idea how important it was for her to harness the power of her mind. Tristan knew better than most what a toll it took to be a telepath and not be able to control the things his mind did. Dara was going through the same thing and still she refused to try using that gift to her advantage. Her resistance was hurting her even more, and pissing him off in the process. He released a tense breath. "I'll say this again. Try to hear it this time. You *need* to strengthen your defenses."

"I've been doing perfectly fine with the ones I have so far," she snapped, massaging her temples. Her hair fell forward, hiding her face. It was like a glossy lure to wrap his hand in, tilt her head back, and kiss the resistance out of her. Tristan banished that thought instantly.

"And why do you think that is?" he asked through clenched teeth. —*Look around you, woman. Rapists. Killers. Psychopaths. One sick mind next to another in this place, crammed together like sardines. Have you heard a single sick thought since you got here?—* He spoke in her mind, knowing full well the guards had plenty of eavesdropping devices in the cells. There were video and audio feeds—not a moment in this prison went by unobserved.

Until now, their conversation might have seemed strange and random to the eavesdroppers, but they would find some way to rationalize it. It wasn't like the prison was filled with titillating discussions of classical literary works. Some craziness was expected. But if one word about telepathy escaped either him or Dara, it would all be over. They'd either spend the rest of their days as lab rats or sedated out of their heads until some judge somewhere decided to grant them a death sentence.

The first option was a lot more likely. So Tristan carefully selected his words before he spoke, because both of their brains would get fried if he didn't.

Dara wouldn't look at him. He knew she hadn't even thought about it before; that she had simply assumed the thoughts she was hearing and seeing were just more of the usual. The fact that there was a distinct lack of *sickness* in them hadn't even registered in her mind. Until now he'd been willing to let her believe as much. But there came a point when ignorance turned into a hindrance.

—Who do you think has been shielding you from them? You certainly couldn't do it.— He leaned forward to stare her down. "So here's the deal. Either you do as I tell you, when I tell you, or I cut you off and let you deal on your own. Consider carefully, Dara," he warned. "My way might be hard, but it's nothing compared to the alternative." Then, "Chess is not that hard to learn."

The thought of his threat alone terrified her into compliance despite everything, as he knew it would. Dara bit her lip and looked back at the chessboard. It was both the cover and the exercise. They were playing *through* each other. Tristan had the black pieces, but Dara played them, sending him the instructions on the next move telepathically, then moving the white pieces the way he told her to. It was getting progressively harder. Now, Dara had to focus and push past Tristan's shields to make herself heard and put up her own shields to turn down the volume of his voice in her head.

She squared her shoulders and contemplated the board.

Assured she would finally cooperate, Tristan sat back down.

Dara sighed, resigned to another head-pounding day. She glanced wistfully at the white knight, rook, and three pawns neatly laid out beside the board. He was winning.

Something occurred to Dara. If she couldn't get through his shields, why not go around them? She pictured a closed door in her mind to represent his defenses. A good thief would have lock picks. Dara had nothing but her wits. There was nothing around the door except empty space, so she slipped around it as quickly and quietly as she could and thought him her next move. *—Queen to G5.—*

Tristan raised an eyebrow in surprise, but though his mouth twitched to smile, he shook his head and made the move she indicated. "Check," he announced.

"Mighty sneaky of you," she noted, not unduly proud of herself.

"Focus," he replied sternly, "it's your move."

Without any other warning, the attack shuddered through her shields.

They held.

Dara focused on not letting him through, even when he intensified the assault until her head felt as if it would implode. Her shields gave way slightly, but not enough to allow communication. She looked at the chessboard, not really seeing it as she massaged her temples again, pressing harder this time to alleviate the pain. The board was her way of grounding herself.

Then a high-pitched sound pierced her mind and she jerked back on her bunk, hitting her head against the wall. Her shields shattered, one and all, and she heard the next move. *—Knight to G5.—*

Dara straightened when the sound faded away and glared at Tristan. She leaned down to move the piece, taking the white queen off the board.

"Good one," he said, his mouth twitching. *—Quid pro quo, lassie.—* The smugness in his mind-voice made her glare. "I thought I had you there."

"Call it divine intervention. My muse kicked me hard this time." She dropped her gaze to the board again. It was either that or throw something at him. Her head was pounding and it was damn difficult to see her next move from the *other* side. She bit back a sigh, resting her chin on her knees. "Your move," she said, closing her eyes. It took a little effort, but she managed it. She looked through his eyes, a ghost in his mind, careful not to make a move or a sound to alert him to her presence. It was a double task—keeping hidden and still managing to do what she was there to do.

Tristan wasn't making it easy. He wasn't even looking at the chessboard, but a place just beyond it, making the pieces out of focus. Was he doing that spacing-out thing again?

The doorway zapped open, startling her. She jumped, both mentally and physically, and Tristan's gaze snapped up to lock with hers. His face was blank, but there was surprise in his eyes. "You—"

"Dara Frost." The man at the door was tall and lanky, his hair slicked back with either gel or grease. Dara didn't want to guess which. He wore a white coat and was reading something on his electronic notepad, not bothering to look up. "You are reporting to the med lab."

"For what?" she asked, frowning.

The man looked up at her, his dark eyes sharp but uninterested. "No questions. Follow me."

"She's busy," Tristan told him, using his most persuasive glare on the doc. If Dara were in the doctor's place, she would have backed down.

The doc didn't. "Not your call, buddy," he told Tristan flatly. "Miss Frost here is overdue for a physical."

"What physical? I don't need one."

The doctor speared her with his gaze. "Follow. Now. Or I'll call the guards."

"We'll finish the game later," Hunt told her at the same time as he spoke in her mind. —*Just relax. Keep your shields up. Don't let them see what you know.*—

"All right." She nodded apprehensively and stood off her bunk. "No cheating."

The doctor turned impatiently and led the way down the catwalk to a corridor. There was an elevator at the end and they took it, going down. The man didn't say a word to her. He didn't even look at her, and Dara was grateful to be ignored. When the elevator door opened, they went down another corridor, this one sporting large glass windows that provided a view into the labs.

They passed five of them. The first two rooms held prisoners seated in odd chairs while doctors stood at their sides and wrote something down. The next two were empty, immaculately clean and sparkling white. The last one was being cleaned of blood.

Dara looked away hastily, shutting out the sight of it. She resisted the urge to glean information out of the doctor's mind. He'd seen her look inside and was probably thinking both the real explanation and a fake one he'd have rehearsed for just this type of situation—when a prisoner saw something she shouldn't have. People did that often—thought of the things they couldn't say, reminding themselves of the secrets they had to keep.

There was no trace of a body in that lab, so it was probably nothing. But her heart was racing and it was becoming difficult to keep her breathing even. It wasn't nothing. *Something* had happened in there. She didn't want to know what it was, but in this case, not knowing was worse than finding out.

Before she could convince herself to try it, the doctor opened a door and waved her inside. Dara hesitated, but one look at the man told her it would be better if she didn't piss him off. She went inside.

He didn't follow her. Instead, the door closed behind her and she was left inside the lab with no supervision or instructions. She wiped her moist palms on her thighs.

"Dara Frost?"

Dara faced the woman at the lighted keyboard to her right. She was a slight woman; not small, just thin. Her hair was as blonde as Dara's was black, and her features were elfin rather than elegant. There was a mischievous spark in her blue eyes that was muted by her glasses and a great deal of professionalism. She approached Dara with an outstretched hand. "I'm Dr. Amelia Chase," she said with a friendly enough smile.

Still apprehensive, Dara shook the offered hand carefully. "Why am I here?"

"Please," the doctor said, indicating the chair. "Have a seat; I'll explain everything."

Dara sat, placing her hands on the armrests. They didn't feel right. Everything in the lab looked shiny and new, gleaming clean, but the texture of the armrests was strange. She pressed her fingers into the material and felt along the grooves. But as soon as she recognized the shape, she snatched her hands away. They were handprints, pressed into the tough material with an incredible force.

Some of her fear must have shown in her face, because the doctor smiled at her reassuringly. "There's no need to worry. This is just a routine physical for our records."

"I already had a physical," Dara told her. "I was scanned just after they sentenced me back on Prime Gama." The public outcry had been too great to hold the trial on Earth. They'd removed the proceedings from the public's eye and deprived Dara of any sympathy votes she might have received. Prime Gama was mainly a military base, so anything and everything they did there was apathetic and efficient. She'd been out of there and on her way to New Alaska in a matter of days.

"I know," Dr. Chase replied easily. She made no move to begin the physical while she spoke, giving Dara her full attention. It made her feel like a child, but it was better than having things done to her body without her consent. "But we don't exactly trust the bureaucrats on Prime Gama. There's a saying among us MDs: if you want practice, go to Earth. If you want the appearance of practice, go to Prime Gama." She grinned then, but Dara didn't get the joke.

"Never mind," the doctor said. "I suppose it's a medical thing. We have better machines here. More precision and accuracy. That's why we examine each person when they arrive."

Dara frowned. The doctor was only telling her half the truth. If what she'd just told her was true, then Dara should have been brought in for a physical a week ago. Facilities as well-run as this one didn't have such long delays.

The woman seemed to realize that her lie wasn't very believable; she half-rolled her eyes and shoved her hands into her coat pockets. "The point is, we want to make sure the records we received are accurate. You'd be surprised at the mistakes we've found in the past. One of the men came in with results that said he was genetically a whale at the time the scan was performed. This is just a precaution."

Seeing Dara was not about to say anything, Dr. Chase smiled and went to her computer screen, tapping on it several times to bring up a three-dimensional image of Dara in midair. The likeness was projected between the two of them. It rotated and changed, displaying the different structures and organs of her body. "Here we go," Dr. Chase said distractedly, looking at the computer screen and not the scan. Her fingers moved rapidly over two keyboards and she looked at two different screens as she typed.

Hurry, hurry, hurry. Before it saves. The stray thought slipped past Dara's shields. "What are you doing?" she asked.

"Modifying the scale and precision of the image," the woman said, sounding as if she had memorized the response from a manual. "Every body is different, so the gradient has to be adjusted."

Dara frowned, getting a sense that the doctor's mind was multitasking.

An alarm beeped, and they looked at the scan in unison. There was a flashing light where her uterus was. Dr. Chase tapped on the screen a couple of times and the scan zoomed in on the area, zeroing in on her ovaries, which now flashed red.

"What's going on?"

The doctor typed in some formulas, then came to Dara and pushed a button on the back of her chair. It shifted and stretched out while it rose, creating a gurney. Another keypad came hovering toward them from the corner of the lab and stopped in front of the doctor. "I'm sure it's nothing. But I still need to check to make sure."

"Make sure of what?"

Dr. Chase spoke as she typed one-handed, passing the keypad over Dara's abdomen. "The chemicals are all in balance, so that's not the problem. Your hormones are working fine…"

"But?" Dara prompted impatiently. The image was still flashing red close by and it frightened her. Was something wrong? She didn't feel anything wrong—and shouldn't she know these things? Women knew when they were sick, didn't they? "Doctor?"

"I'm afraid there is nothing I can do," Dr. Chase said and pushed the keypad away, allowing it to hover back to its place. She set the seat upright again so that they were face-to-face. "There are no eggs in your ovaries."

Dara reeled. "W-what? How is that possible? Are you sure?" Her head spinning, she grasped the armrests again and this time, her fingers slipped into the large grooves without hesitation. She suddenly wished she could sense something of the person who had made them. In a moment of weakness, she let her shields drop.

Dr. Chase nodded, but Dara could sense dishonesty in her. "You were born with dysfunctional ovaries. They are basically just a mass of cells that failed to develop properly. You won't be able to have children."

Liar! her mind shouted with absolute conviction. But even as she knew that the doctor was lying, she also felt her anxious determination. There was a reason for what she'd just told Dara. Without looking deeper into her mind, Dara couldn't tell what that reason was, and she didn't dare take the risk. Instead, she slowly raised her shields again and made herself relax her grip on the armrests.

It took her a while. She was still learning how to do things like this, and she was so freaked out, she couldn't concentrate on the process. Part of her wanted to demand answers, pry them from Dr. Chase's mind. Dara had to fight with herself not to do anything stupid. Tristan would kill her if she exposed them.

"I'm truly very sorry," Dr. Chase said.

"Can I go now?" Dara had to get out of here this instant. The walls were beginning to close in on her and the doctor's voice was echoing in her head. It was a bad sign. She was losing control. *Focus,* she told herself, but it was impossible. Her shields were slipping again and without them, she didn't know how deep she'd get into the doctor's mind if the woman touched her. Couldn't tell if she'd want to stop it, let alone whether she'd even be able to. Her mind was like an open sore; a single touch would be agonizing to the both of them.

When Dr. Chase tried to touch her to offer comfort, Dara flinched and snatched her hand away.

All at once, she felt the faint presence of Tristan. He wasn't quite there, but remained a weak projection of his telepathic self. It was enough to give her something else to focus on. Dara grasped onto that fragile link and slowly built her defenses around it, shutting herself off from the outside world. Another headache built up behind her eyes, but if she looked queasy, the doctor would take it as the reaction to the bad news she'd just received.

Dr. Chase nodded. "Yes, of course. We're done here. I'll be sure to update your file and get you assigned to me as your primary physician. I don't usually see women, since there are so few of them in Wolf block, so this should be a nice change for me. Is that acceptable?"

Dara all but jumped out of the seat, about to run out and in any direction she happened to turn, as long as it was far from here. But she stopped at the question. "You're asking my opinion?"

"Of course," Dr. Chase said kindly, and smiled. "When you are in here, you are first and foremost my patient."

Have to get out of here! "Then it's acceptable," Dara said and nodded. "Which way out?"

– 8 –

Tristan turned the page in his book and cursed. He had no idea what he'd just read. He looked at the bathroom shield again, for at least the thousandth time in the last two hours. And it didn't help that he'd turned his back to it; he seemed to have a compulsive need to look.

Dara was still in there. Had been since she'd come back from med lab. Not a word or a thought. She'd just closed herself away and refused to come out. Tristan had even tried to look into her mind, but apparently she'd learned how to lock him out.

So he'd stopped trying, telling himself he was giving her space.

The cells were open for the daily five hours of "out time." Most of the men were in the gym or in front of the TV—where Tristan should be. But instead of availing himself of the pool for an hour or two, he had opted to stay here and pretend to read, just in case some stray decided to cause trouble.

It used to be there wasn't a single prisoner who would voluntarily enter his cell without express invitation, but today he'd sensed at least six guys pass by with more than a little curiosity. Tristan had no doubt that if he wasn't there, they'd make themselves right at home. So he'd placed himself between the doorway and the bathroom screen and brooded.

That protective streak was really beginning to piss him off.

Seemed he couldn't go anywhere these days without someone thinking his cellmate was fair game. He'd found himself in the surprising position of needing to reclaim his place among the other inmates. As if taking in a female cellmate—like he'd had any choice about it—had made him an outcast and fair game. What was it about this woman that made all order in his life evaporate?

He'd even taken some time out of his routine over the last few days to do the stupidest thing he could: make it clear to a few men that Dara Frost was not to be touched if they valued their extremities. He couldn't have signaled a weakness more clearly. Instead of using his influence to get something for himself, he was undermining it to help a female. If he didn't get cornered by a gang this week, he'd call it good.

Today when Dara had gone to the med lab, he'd made his way to the gym. He hadn't even gotten halfway there before he'd passed a group of men talking about her. Tristan had known what he was doing, even as he'd caught a couple of them by their throats and slammed them up against the wall. He'd *known* it, damn it! And still he would not have been able to stop himself if he'd tried. Disgusted with himself and this protect-the-little-woman shit, he'd skulked back to his cell, not in the mood for exercise anymore.

He'd made it here just in time to feel Dara lose it.

Whatever had happened to her today, it had shaken her badly. She'd come back even paler than usual, moving like a marionette on strings, eyes wide as saucers. Bad news notwithstanding, they were supposed to be a team, damn it! Maybe he hadn't made that clear enough. Maybe she still hadn't grasped the concept that whatever happened to one of them happened to the other. For Christ's sake, they as good as shared a mind!

Tristan tossed the book away and pushed off the floor. He faced the screen and silently counted to five to give her one more chance. Nothing happened. He reached out with his mind and encountered her shields. His hands balled into fists at his sides. "Dara," he called to her.

No answer.

"Damn it, get out here."

Nothing stirred.

"*Dara!*" He banged his fist against the shield. Of course, it made no sound, but the force was enough to create a faint outward ripple. "Don't make me force you."

The shield retracted like a solid curtain and Dara came out, brushing past him without meeting his gaze. She was still firmly in flight mode, headed for the doorway, completely heedless of what was on the other side. *Oh no, you don't.* He caught her arm and turned her around. "You're not going anywhere. Not until you explain."

"Let go of me," she said, remaining as tense as a caught mouse.

"Not a chance. Tell me what happened."

"Can't you just… guess?" she taunted, raising a challenging eyebrow. The brave front would have been more convincing if he couldn't feel her shivering.

"Not without making us both… extremely uncomfortable." She was resisting the telepathic link. He'd destroy her mind if he tried to force it. "*Talk* to me," he said instead.

"No," she said, yanking her arm out of his hold. Her head had to be hurting again, trying to keep him out of her mind, and out here, there was no escape from him. At least the impulse to flee seemed to have passed. Dara wasn't an idiot. She knew what was outside this cell was far worse than what was inside it. So instead of bolting out the door, she sat on her bunk and gave him her back, seemingly determined to ignore him.

"You still don't get it," he said, baffled by the realization. "No, you act like you do, but you really don't. Try to wrap your irrational female mind around this concept: I am the only one on this planet whom you can trust."

Dara laughed; a scornful, bitter sound. "Then my situation is sad indeed, if the only one I can trust is an inmate of the highest security prison known to man. Housed, I might add, in the block reserved for the worst of the most dangerous criminals. Sure, pal, let me just whip out the cookies and hot chocolate and tell you all my deepest, darkest secrets. I just know you'll keep them safe forever and ever."

Tristan silently watched her sitting there for a moment. Her hair was more out than in the clip she'd restrained it with. Sitting the way she was, hugging her knees to her chest on the bunk, she looked even more vulnerable now than she had the day she'd arrived; a scared little mouse trying to hide in a cave crawling with hungry vipers. Now that mouse had come far too close to a viper's fangs.

The urge to put his arms around her and tell her he'd keep her safe almost overwhelmed him. He stamped it down. It would do her no good if she didn't learn to keep herself safe. And he had a feeling Dara wouldn't believe him anyway.

"There are snakes," he said quietly, "and there are bears in this prison. The snakes are the ones who have ice in their veins. They kill and torture for the thrill of causing pain. They slither from place to place, live in shadows and stare out of them to choose their prey. And they have no remorse. A snake only gets caught when he gets too greedy. Picks a prey too prominent to be overlooked. The bears…" He trailed off. The bears kept the snakes here in line. But she wouldn't believe that. She still thought the guards were the law. Hell, the guards were the worst of them.

Tristan picked up the book he'd tossed away and tore out a random page, crumpling it into a tight ball. He sent it flying out the doorway, over the catwalk, and down into the abyss. "A soldier killed my parents when I was ten. A boogeyman in a Shadow blue uniform."

He felt the frown in Dara's mind when she timidly asked, "Shadow? As in…?"

"Be good, or the Shadows will get you," he finished the dire threat every parent used to get bad children to behave. If only they knew the truth… "He invoked his right to be housed in our living quarters. We had no choice but to let him in." To refuse a soldier shelter or food was punishable by imprisonment. "Bastard stuffed his face at dinner and wouldn't shut his mouth. Asking my parents whether they were supporters of the Union. Whether they were ready to contribute to the effort and give their son into the service. When my parents didn't jump at the offer, he tied my father to his chair and made him watch as he raped my mother. Over and over again." Ten pages came loose in his grip and he balled them up so tightly that his nails bit into his palms.

"And when she was dead and he was so weak he could barely stand on his feet, he took out his gun, put it to my father's head, and pulled the trigger. I was closed away in my room. They thought it would be safer for me. Thought if something happened, I would be safe locked away. But I wasn't." —*I was in my father's mind. Saw it all through his eyes. And when his brains exploded all over the floor, I screamed.*—

Dara made a small sound, but would not look at him. Her hands fisted in her lap. He knew she'd heard him in her mind. He'd felt her shields give way. Now they were up again. "He found me there," he continued. "Took me with him to the front. 'Congratulations,' he'd said. 'You've been given the privilege of serving the Union to better mankind.'" Those words would never leave him, so long as he lived.

The book in his hands ripped in two. How he wished the bastard was alive so he could get his hands on him again. "I trained in their army, built up my strength, learned how to work every weapon ever invented. Mastered techniques outlawed on seventeen planets.

"I discovered my mind was the greatest weapon of all." And what a weapon it had turned out to be. Once he'd learned to channel and control it, there'd been nothing to stand in his way. Men had tried to hide the soldier, protecting their own. Snakes writhing in their nests. The harder they'd fought, the more determined he'd become. And the more they'd suffered.

"It took me twelve years, but I found him eventually. There wasn't much left of him by the time I was done. But the others, an entire outpost of sadistic sons of bitches just like *him*... I made them piss themselves in fear of the shadows they lived in."

"T-that's why you're here," she said.

If only it were that simple. "No," he replied. "I am here because I gave myself up. They wouldn't have caught me otherwise. After the soldier was dead..." He shuddered at the memory. Blood everywhere, covering him from head to toe, and still he'd known they would never be able to link him to any of the deaths. *That* had made him sick to his stomach—the thought that after everything, he'd become one of them. A monster walking around with blood on his hands and no one to point a finger at him.

Tristan looked at his hands and they were bloody. He dropped what was left of the book and shook his head to chase the memory away. He wouldn't go back there again. Not ever. His hands were shaking when he forced himself to look at them again, but this time, there was no more blood.

"I was finished. No more need to hunt. Snakes get greedy. Bears only kill to survive." That night had nearly killed him. Grief aside, he'd *felt* the bullet tear through his father's head. Only the thought of revenge had kept him going. And so he'd thought he would trade one nightmare for another. But neither nightmare had ever gone away.

"Why are you telling me this?" Dara hugged her knees to her chest and tried very hard not to focus on the gruesome picture his words had drawn in her mind. Try as she might, though, she could not rid herself of the image of him as a little boy, huddled in a dark room all alone.

She was still shivering occasionally from the news Dr. Chase had delivered. Though she was certain it was a lie, Dara knew there was something else, far worse, that the doctor had kept from her. She was scared, a state of mind that made it all too easy to put herself in Tristan's place, hiding from a monster while it destroyed his parents just beyond a locked door.

Dr. Chase was not the monster in Dara's case—she was the door.

This place… now she knew how it worked. The incarceration was nothing. That was merely putting a wild beast in a cage. What truly broke its spirit were the tortures of the mind. The looks that promised unimaginable pain. The secrets only hinted at, the things that poked at the beast and taunted it without ever revealing themselves.

No matter how much she tried to resist it, despite the brave front she put up, it was fear that would finally break her. Fear of the things that hid in the darkness of her captors' minds.

"Why confide in me?" she asked when he hadn't replied.

"Because, sooner or later, you will get out of here. But things in this prison will get much, much worse for you if it doesn't happen sooner rather than later. And when they do, I may be the only one within a hundred light years who can help you."

What happens to one, happens to the other, he thought—to her, or to himself?

"Worse how? And why do you talk like there's no more hope for you?" *Duh.* Maybe because he'd killed God knew how many people—soldiers. The better question was, how he was even still alive?

He laughed. "Dara, I just told you that I am a trained killing machine. If anything, this place gave me an upgrade. You really think they'll ever let me surface again?"

"They might," she mumbled, but she didn't really believe her words. Crimes like that didn't usually get forgiven. For a civilian to harm a politician or a soldier was treason. But he hadn't been executed. Maybe there was still hope. "You lasted this long; don't give up now." If Tristan was all that stood between her and whatever the bad stuff was, then she needed him to stand strong. "Self-pity is very unattractive," she told him.

Tristan shook his head and hopped up onto his bunk. "If I ever get out, it'll be to a place far worse than this," he said above her. —*They might be gracious enough to hire me on as a government assassin.*—

Dara took the clip out of her hair to play with it. A month ago she never would have thought evil like he'd described could exist outside of books. If Tristan had gone to the authorities, would they have helped him?

No. Brothers-in-arms always protected their own. Most likely the soldier's crimes against Tristan's parents would have been covered up, and Tristan would have just been locked up that much sooner. Wasn't that almost exactly what had happened to her? Justice had died a quiet death long ago.

—*The doctor,*— she said after a while. —*She said I can't have children. But she was lying.*—

Tristan felt some of his tension ease. *She found a loophole, then.* He hadn't meant for Dara to hear, but she did.

—*A loophole? In what?*—

—*It's better not to know,*— Tristan said. He sure as shit didn't want to be the one to tell her the whole truth.

Dara sighed, a feminine sound of frustration, and for a moment Tristan didn't feel as if he was in prison anymore. He'd forgotten how much he'd once enjoyed the simple things in life. The sound of rain hitting the roof. The sweet smell of a woman. The joy of simply having a conversation without having to choose his words carefully for fear of exposing his abilities.

At that moment, he felt almost… normal. Just a simple man, spending an evening with his woman. He imagined her lying next to him, nestled against his side. He'd have his arm around her, fingers sifting through her hair.

The image wasn't sexual. Instead, it gave him a measure of peace and deep contentment. Both so foreign to him, he didn't know what to do with them.

He was changing. The latest treatment might have tempered outbursts of strength, but there were other changes that were not so easy to control. His senses were sharper now whether his strength increased suddenly or not. Whispers from cells across the abyss were now as clear as if he was right there, a fly on the wall. He could see things from so far away, it felt inhuman. And the scents... Tristan doubted he would ever rid himself of Dara's.

But the most disturbing changes were with his instincts. His id was gaining supremacy. The other prisoners were no longer just a nuisance. They were trespassers on his territory. Someone baiting him into a fight was a challenger, and resisting the urge to fight to the death was becoming more and more difficult.

The only thing that seemed to help was Dara's presence and *that* inspired entirely different instincts. It put him in an untenable position. Although any contact with her seemed to temper the beast growing stronger inside him, it also intensified his possessiveness of her. Tristan didn't know when, but at some point, he'd begun to think of her as *his*. His cellmate. His woman. And that became dangerous when it bordered on obsession, as it was beginning to.

Which meant that not having her around drove him up the wall. He worried. *Worried*, for Christ's sake, about a woman he'd met little more than a week ago. And when he didn't worry, he raged, irrationally and insanely jealous of any other male even looking at her.

But when it was just the two of them, it felt like his right to be near her, to touch her and taste her. He wanted to bury his nose in her hair and just breathe her in; he craved her scent more than air. And he wanted to—he frowned, trying to identify it. Sex was too tame a word. What he felt was more possessive and animalistic than anything he'd ever felt before. Tristan needed her to recognize that she was his, needed to put some kind of claim on her.

The need to stake his territory baffled him.

Tristan punched the pillow, then tossed it to the foot of his bunk when it stubbornly refused to remain disfigured. The problem wasn't the serums and the experiments. What really drove him up the wall was that after years of solitude in this prison, he was forced to spend almost twenty-four hours a day with a woman he *liked*. It was a purely male response. He probably would have had the same reaction with any other female.

So why was it that since she got here he'd felt at the same time more human and more animal than he had in years?

~

His heart slammed against the wall of his chest, knocking the breath out of him. Dizzy with the urge to protect, he jumped down from the tree and landed on all fours. It felt natural to him.

Lifting his nose to the air, he sniffed. He was looking for her. *Because she was in danger. He could smell her fear, and it made him crazed. Whatever was threatening her had no scent. It was a void where something* should have been and it felt... wrong.

The city was abandoned. Transports stood out like tumbleweeds in the desert; white drapes billowed out of open windows and artificial lights flickered at all levels—but nothing living moved. Nothing stirred in the night, and he wouldn't have cared if it did. With single-minded determination, he loped through the empty streets, reveling in the feel of it. Running free. Hunting.

His mate screamed nearby, and he shouted in response—but it came out as an animal roar. He ran faster.

Turn the corner. Run to the end of the street.

Jump over an abandoned transport.

Another corner...

And then he saw them.

She was backing into a corner, frantically looking for a way out. There was none.

He growled and launched himself onto the man pursuing her. Instinct took over and he bit into the fiend's neck with relish. He tore at the flesh, ignoring the ache in his teeth and claws as he buried them in the attacker's body.

But he didn't die.

*The killing rage subsided, the bloody haze cleared, and he saw his prey covered with his own blood, flesh torn open at the neck and chest—*laughing. *He didn't make a sound, but it was no cough that made him shake like that. The man—the thing that didn't smell like anything, not even bleeding out on the ground—opened his purple eyes and kept on laughing as he pulled himself up to sit. His head fell back against his shoulders without the neck's support, and still he laughed.*

Still down on all fours, Tristan backed away toward his mate, shielding her with his own body, wanting her far away from this.

The monster before him laughed and laughed, and then he leaned forward and his head flipped back to its normal position. But it was no longer the purple-eyed puppet that stared at him.

It was the soldier.

Tristan jerked awake and struck out blindly at the wall. Something sharp bit into his hands, and he uncurled his fists, horrified to find sharp, inch-long claws pulling out of his palms. Even as he watched, his nails retracted and dulled back into their normal shape.

He clenched his fists again to stop the bleeding and jumped down, landing on the balls of his feet without the smallest sound. He was in the bathroom before a single drop of blood could fall to the floor.

It was there that he caught a glimpse of his face in the mirror. Hair streaked with light brown, slitted yellow-green eyes, sharper cheekbones… and fangs.

Christ, what was happening to him?

– 9 –

6th Day of the 4th Blood Moon, 3028

There were seventeen TVs in a room acoustically designed to deliver sound only to those people watching the individual movies. Each TV had an area that seated forty people.

And all of them were playing slasher flicks.

Wonderful. Just what Tristan needed—a werewolf movie. And a bad one at that. He should have gone to the gym instead.

Ah, but there the pool's sensors would have detected traces of blood, and then he'd be in deep shit indeed. Because the docs would want to know what he'd impaled his hands on.

He kept his hands in his pockets to hide the marks on his palms. The claws had gone almost clean through, tenting the skin on the backs of his hands, but not quite long enough to pierce it.

At least the good thing—if it could be called that—was that he was healing rapidly. Mind over matter? Hardly. It was just another part of the exciting New Alaska chemical gift package. The fun never stopped.

"Word on the block is you got yourself a sweet young thing in that burrow of yours."

Anthony Sinclair. The man was as wide as he was tall, and that was saying something, since he was as tall as Tristan. Disgusting slime-ball of a human being, he forced the weaker prisoners to wash those parts of him he couldn't reach in the shower. And still he smelled like regurgitated molding sewage.

He plopped himself down into a chair, making it creak dangerously under his gargantuan weight, while his long greasy hair swept the floor.

Tristan almost gagged. He turned to leave the other way and found his path blocked by Switch.

"Yeah," the scrawny guy agreed. "That's what we heard." He was the human equivalent of a hyper weasel. His hair was spiked, and he had dark circles around his crazed eyes from lack of sleep—his assigned treatment. Sinclair and Switch were joined at the hip. Wherever Sinclair went, Switch followed like a lapdog. He had no choice, really. At barely five-foot-four, he was the smallest of them all, and his life literally depended on Sinclair's size. Parasite.

Tristan sat back down. No point fighting them here. He might get one lucky punch in before the guards rained down on them, and then he'd have to wait until the next ambush to finish it. Might as well save himself the trouble. But even while his mind decided this, his body went on alert, muscles tightening to ready for attack and senses sharpening to catch the smallest change in the environment.

"Word on the block is Sinclair is using your head as a vibrator," he said to Switch. "Should I believe it? It would explain those brown spots around your eyes. And your hair is sort of a shitty color."

Switch's expression turned wrathful, but before he could lash out as he was prone to do, Sinclair put a massive hand on Tristan's shoulder and turned him to face his armpit. "No need to fight," he said pleasantly, ever the businessman looking to deal first and crush the opposition later. Often that was literally what he did. "I'm sure we can come to some sort of agreement."

Tristan winced sarcastically. "I don't know, Blubber. I've had some bad experiences with whales before. They always find a way to renege."

Sinclair's chuckle jiggled parts of him in a ripple effect, releasing new and exotic scents from skin folds that hadn't been touched by air in years. "That mouth of yours is gonna get you killed one night," he said. "But I'll take it as a compliment this time. Whales do have the biggest dicks in the whole animal kingdom, don't they? And that's why we're here to talk to you in the first place. It's not nice of you not to let your plaything enjoy it."

"Damn waste is what it is," Switch added, nearly salivating. It was a well-known fact that Sinclair didn't exactly share with the little guy. Instead, Switch got the leftovers. Apparently that was more than enough for him.

Tristan stayed firmly out of his mind, refusing to catch even a glimpse of his memories. "Sounds like you've had some experience in that area." Not missing a beat on the eye twitch the rodent had suddenly developed, he addressed Sinclair. "I'll tell you what," he said, disengaging himself from the sack of lard and his horny hamster. "When I get tired of her, I might give her the option of striking out on her own. But you should know she's getting a little addicted to me."

Sinclair waved that away easily. "Not to worry; I have ways of curing those pesky little addictions to pleasure."

If Tristan had hackles, they'd be standing on end now. "First come, first serve, Sinclair," he said, trying to rein in his temper. "She was given to me—to *my cell*. And nobody is touching her until I am through." Then he smiled, though it felt more predatory than pleasant. "We are all civilized human beings, after all, not wild animals." *Not yet.*

Sinclair nodded in complete agreement. "If we don't have class, we don't have anything."

Said the man who'd eaten his victims alive, with expensive silverware.

"Gentlemen, always a pleasure. Enjoy your movie."

He took his time leaving, taking controlled breaths in hopes that it would keep him from changing outwardly. Instead of calming him, the ritual merely served to expand his lungs until he thought his chest would burst. The sudden flood of oxygen made his nostrils flare and his eyesight sharpen even more. His jaw ached even though he wasn't clenching his teeth. A bad sign. It was, he found, a precursor to fangs.

Just a few more feet. Just a little longer.

He was almost at the elevator when his speedy escape was thwarted.

"Tristan?"

Great. What now? He didn't slow down. If he could just make it into the elevator, he'd be fine. But he had to get there first.

Amelia hurried to catch up with him. "Let's talk, shall we?"

"Not in the mood. Some other time."

"Now."

Surprised by the sudden assertion of authority, Tristan stopped in his tracks. What was this? A backbone? The cutting comment died before he could utter it. He glanced at the elevator in indecision but ultimately nodded, following her to one of the observation rooms. The experiments never ceased. Prisoners were under the microscope at all times, even if they weren't doing anything except watching TV.

"What's this about, Doc?"

She took off her glasses to polish the lenses, a sure sign she was upset. "Why don't you tell me?" she countered. "Sensors in your cell's sink recorded traces of blood two nights ago, and there was no record in the database of a fight."

"I cut myself shaving."

The mechanism didn't work that way, and they both knew it. No sharp blades of any kind were allowed anywhere near the prisoners. That meant no cuts.

Apparently Amelia decided to humor him. "Then why are you wearing at least three days' worth of beard now?"

He shrugged a shoulder carelessly.

"If you don't tell me what's wrong, I can't help you."

Tristan didn't say anything.

Amelia took a breath, as if she was losing patience with him. "Let me put this another way. You can tell *me* voluntarily, or you can tell someone else under duress. But one way or another, they will find out. In your place, I'd at least try to minimize the cost."

"It was a paper cut," he said, impatient to get out of there. He had Dara's scent in his nostrils as if he was hunting without having realized it. His muscles ached to move, ached to run as fast as he could and feel the freedom of it. He needed that sense of abandon now if he hoped to get out of this situation without killing someone.

His conversation with Sinclair and the rodent refused to leave his mind as quickly as so many others before had. This one had hit far too close to a sensitive subject, and for the first time he could actually believe Sinclair would do exactly as he pleased, whether Tristan agreed or not. But if it came to a showdown between the two of them, there was no doubt in Tristan's mind that he would win. He couldn't allow that sludge bucket to get anywhere near Dara.

This little chat with Amelia was slowing him down, and that wouldn't do.

"I have never seen you read a book. And the amount of blood was indicative of a much larger injury."

If she didn't release him soon, he'd turn on her. The thought made him fight harder for control. Amelia was a friend, probably the only one he'd ever had here. He didn't want to hurt her. He looked at the floor, searching with his enhanced vision for patterns that weren't there. *Take your mind off things. Breathe. Dara is safe inside the cell, probably with her nose buried in a book.* His lungs contracted somewhat, allowing him to take slow breaths and calm down. Even his jaw stopped aching.

Amelia shoved her hands into her coat pockets. "Come on, Tristan, this isn't a joking matter. Tell me what happened."

Tristan frowned, finally calm enough to pick up on emotional cues. "It almost sounds like you're worried about me, Doc."

Her eyes lost some of the impatience, but now they looked haunted. "One of *my* subjects starts bleeding without apparent reason? Yeah, I'm worried."

Her mind was a slide show of images she'd internally classified as "Sach's Study." One after the other, she was mentally flipping through them with incredible speed, and yet each image was painfully clear. Head shots of people who had bled out of their eyes and noses. Countless others who had bruised and bled internally until their skin had burst. Internal scans of subjects showing absolutely no distinction between organs. The images sickened him.

Something Dr. Sach was testing was killing the prisoners.

Amelia was worried because she and Sach sometimes shared subjects without informing each other. And Sach no more knew what was causing the "life cessations" than he knew how to fix it. Hell, they didn't even know if it was contagious.

"Nothing to worry about," Tristan assured her. "There was a cause. I just don't particularly feel like sharing it." There was nothing deathly wrong with him; it was just unnerving. If anything, he was having symptoms completely opposite to those her mind had stored away. His body didn't refuse to heal; rather, it healed more rapidly.

His answer didn't seem to reassure her. She kept looking at him as if she could read the truth in his expression.

Tristan narrowed his eyes. "There is something else bothering you. What is it?"

Amelia shook her head, her gaze briefly touching on the monitoring strips in a silent message: *Not here.*

"So can I go now?"

"In a moment," she said, pulling out her digital chart. "Your vitals are a little out of the ordinary, but nothing that would concern me. Have you been having any psychological problems?"

He raised an eyebrow. "You mean, am I going crazy? You think I'd tell you if I was?"

"Nightmares. Anxiety. Restlessness, depression, that sort of thing."

"Yes."

"Which one?"

He snorted. "Doc, I'm in a prison. I've had all of them at one point or another."

She glared at him over the frames of her glasses. "Fine. You can go. I can see you're not about to cooperate any time soon."

He nodded and turned to leave. But he paused at the door. "Doc?"

"Yes?"

"That DNA recombination study you tried on me last year… did you ever find out why it didn't work?"

"You mean why you never actually took on animal traits?" Amelia shrugged. "On a scientific level, it was impossible from the beginning. Forgetting the fact that in order to make it work, we'd have to have changed every cell in your body individually—"

"You had that solved, didn't you? Don't tell me you didn't consider viral studies for this. Get a virus aggressive enough and you can reengineer it to deliver any mutations you choose. The government's been doing that for years."

Amelia sighed and nodded in agreement. "They have been. And they've only seen a five percent success rate, and even that was among young children on chemotherapy." She gave him an arch look. "That means fewer cells, most of which are being killed off by the chemo."

Her mind was an open book. She didn't approve of those studies, even if there were consent forms that the parents always signed with the full knowledge of what would happen to their children. To her, a child was not a lab rat, period.

"But you did use the virus on me, right?"

"Yes. The final results showed that it had spread successfully to the majority of your body, but the mutation didn't take." *Thank God.*

Once again, a slide show of images assaulted him, these of patients only slightly better-looking than the previous ones. These were dead for reasons he couldn't tell. Several of them had distorted faces, with flat noses and split upper lips, the beginnings of a snout. They were those who'd been on the verge of changing shape and their bodies could not deal with the stress to the tissues. When he saw a woman who had brain matter dripping out of her nose and ears, he firmly shut it all out.

Amelia was talking again. "The two DNA strands were incompatible with each other and chromosome treatments only managed to suppress one or the other in earlier trials. You were lucky you didn't sustain any damage."

Tristan was hearing two voices despite the shields he put up. His telepathy was slipping in a way it had never done before. *It might have been brought to a dormant stage, but it will be in his genes forever now,* Amelia was thinking, and he knew what she meant. The first viral load had been too stressful for his body to take so they'd had to abort the experiment early. They'd had no idea how far it had truly spread because subsequent treatments for the side effects had hidden the virus's progress.

Dormant? Not a fucking chance.

"I truly don't know why it didn't take," she told him with a shrug. "Although I did have this theory once that what we lacked was the right catalyst. Emotional change triggers the strongest physiological reactions in all humans; I thought perhaps this might work the same. I guess I was wrong." *Wouldn't be the first time.*

Whatever the trigger was, it had worked its magic. Tristan felt different, not only physically but psychologically as well. It was as if his personality had split in two and only half of it was human. His base instincts were gaining strength and becoming an entity of their own.

There was a beast growing inside him, and though it was still *him*, it had a mind of its own, without reason, functioning on the simplest of principles: *guard what's mine.*

At the moment, it was biding its time, stirring occasionally and raising its head to growl without fighting for control, but Tristan feared that someday soon it would take him over and he had no idea what would happen when it did.

"Are you sure you're okay?" Amelia asked, and he realized he was frowning.

"Fine," he said, eager to get out of there. Chances were good that Sinclair wouldn't move from his seat for a good long while, since it took so much effort to stand, but Tristan wanted to be back in his cell anyway. He had to find a way to control this, and do it so no one found out. For that, he might need Dara's help.

That'll go over well, he thought. He could just see her reaction when he told her that not only was he a telepath, he was also an engineered mutant with super strength and heightened senses who, on top of it all, had the ability to change his shape. Sure. Why not? Women dealt with things like that every day.

"Thanks, Doc, I truly enjoy our little chats."

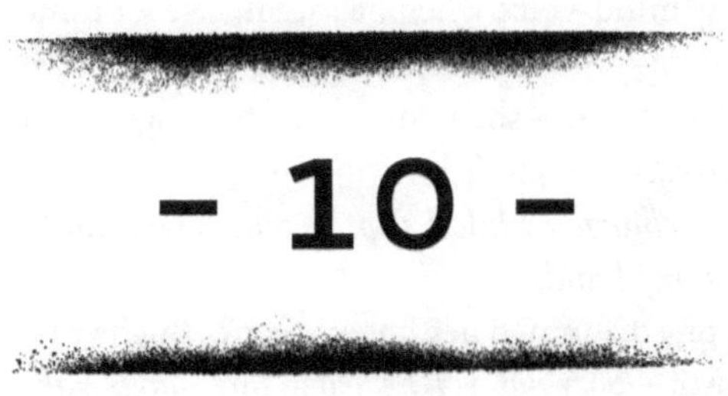

– 10 –

Dara stared at the bunk above her, mouth hanging open. —*You're pulling my chain, aren't you?*— Animal DNA? Viral experiments? What? This wasn't some sci-fi movie with mad scientists… although, admittedly, there seemed to be plenty of those around.

—*Then why is my story so difficult for you to believe?*— he challenged.

—*Are you kidding me? You mean there are experiments being done on the prisoners here, and one of them was meant to change you into an animal?*—

—*No, it was meant to give me the ability to change into one at will,*— he told her in a tone that said he was losing his patience. —*An animal wouldn't do them any good. But a shape-shifter? Think of the possibilities.*—

—*Even if I buy into this whole thing, which I don't, where is your proof? You think that just because you had a nightmare, that you can change your shape now?*— Was he finally losing it? Hell, he'd been here long enough for it. Dara herself was already feeling edgy and claustrophobic in this prison, and she hadn't been here all that long.

She heard him heave a sigh and shift, and then he leaned over the edge of his bed to look down at her and show her his hand. Raising an eyebrow, she sat up. "What am I supposed to be seeing, exactly?"

Tristan frowned and looked at his palm. —*I had holes almost clean through my hands four days ago.—* There was a frustrated sort of wonder in his mind-voice when he said it. "Never mind." *—But they were there.—*

—And, let me guess,— she said, leaning back against the wall. *—You did it to yourself.—*

—Exactly. I changed while I slept... somehow... and my own nails made holes in my hands!—

"Oh-kay." She drummed her fingers on her thighs a few times, then laid back down. *—So, what, you healed in three days, without a mark?—*

—Forget it.—

—No, no, keep going. It's a good story; I'm waiting for the punch line.— It was a strange feeling to be teasing a man as potentially dangerous as Tristan Hunt, especially when he was so obviously on the edge. But the fact that he still refused to acknowledge what had happened between them that night was making her crazy, and she wasn't above taking it out on him. As off-balance as she was in this place, he was making it a hundred times worse.

Tristan still looked at her as if he'd like nothing better than to rip her clothes off and make her his own personal playground. Whenever he did, Dara tensed, waiting for him to do it, wanting him to. And every time he got that frustrated jaw twitch and turned away instead.

He'd been spending a lot of time in the bathroom corner.

And where did that leave her? Tormented by dreams so erotic they woke her every night on the verge of an orgasm she couldn't allow herself, because Tristan would know. He knew already and chose to do nothing. Bastard. It was all his fault they were doing some elaborate dance around each other—in a room that barely allowed them to breathe without getting in each other's way!

Now she was hot and bothered, and out for revenge. It was somewhat cruel and maybe a little evil, seeing as how he seemed to be genuinely upset right now, but there was no avoiding the truth.

He deserved it. As a matter of fact, she was starting to appreciate her own power to drive him mad. A well-timed word or look and she could simply watch steam rise from his skull. If his voice now was anything to go by, Tristan was very close to spontaneously combusting. In no time he would be running frantic circles around the cell with his hair on fire.

Dara managed not to laugh at that thought, but she couldn't keep from grinning. A vivid imagination was a godsend in this place.

—*I would think that when a person spends so much time with her head up in the clouds, she wouldn't be so quick to label something as impossible,*— he said tightly. He must have glimpsed the images in her mind. And in true Tristan fashion, decided to ignore the important stuff and focus only on the burning hair.

"That is weak, Hunt," she retorted. Since he wouldn't let her broach the subject either, she had no choice but to play along. For now. —*I may be a dreamer, but I'm not stupid. And you can't prove anything, so…*—

—*I can prove it, but not without getting myself permanently installed in a man-sized rat maze.*— He hopped down from his bunk to pace. —*Do you realize how much trust I am showing by telling you this? How about you trust* me *a little in return?*—

That was true. He'd just about handed her a weapon without knowing whether she would run with it or turn around and shoot him. She propped herself up on one elbow to watch him. He looked trapped, like a cornered beast. Something told her that the smallest provocation might make him snap and do something stupid. Like hurl himself at the force field he was contemplating so intently. She didn't like seeing him like that. It didn't bode well for either of them. Without him to watch her back, she was a sitting duck, and what if someone else got assigned to her cell?

To distract him and draw his gaze away from the damn force field, she racked her brain for some conversation thread. —*You said your senses are heightened,*— she tried. —*Can you control* that?—

—*Yes,*— he said without pausing his step.

—*Do you just see and hear everything all the time?*— If so, she didn't know how he could stand it. Add telepathy into the mix and the result was understandably a man on the edge. Talk about sensory overload!

—*No. I can control it easily enough when I'm calm.*—

—*And when you're not?*—

A silence. Then, —*I don't know. Worst it's ever been, I grew fangs and claws and my hair changed color. Oh, and I could see in the dark and hear your heartbeat from ten steps away like a drum right next to my ear.*— He stopped to look at his hands once more. —*I don't know what causes it to get worse. Most of the time I can bring myself back under control and it's only my senses that go berserk and I get... stronger. But I felt the animal inside me. It's strong. Maybe stronger than I am. If I ever lose it...*— He started pacing again.

That she could believe. She'd felt him grow stronger before, felt his struggle to control himself. —*It probably works like telepathy, then,*— she guessed, trying her best to sound matter-of-fact about it.

—*You just have to practice.*—

"Will you stop that? You're making me seasick." But it was the idea of him losing control that was making her sick. She didn't exactly believe he was able to turn into an animal, but what if someone provoked him and he unleashed that strength? Telepathy posed a threat to its bearer more than anyone else, but physical strength?

And what if he couldn't stop himself?

—*Practice has to help. Practice control. If you can manage to get ahold of the small changes, like the sensory overload, the bigger ones should become easier to deal with.*—

He stopped and turned on her. —*Practice... You of all people tell me this?*—

Dara shrugged. —*It's what you always tell me, isn't it? Practice. Push. Control your mind or it will control you.*—

—*It's not that simple.*—

Another double standard? Was he kidding? —*Oh, please explain to me how it magically happens that when I don't want to do something, you make me. But when it comes to you, all of a sudden there is a logical and compelling reason why you can't.*— She couldn't wait to hear this.

He raked his hands through his hair and made a sound like some sort of animal. —*Woman, every time I'm near you I...*—

Dara held her breath. —*You what?*— Would he say it? Would he finally admit to something?

Tristan looked at her and his eyes flickered. —*I don't know up from down. No, that's not... I don't care which way is up. I look at you and... God, I can see your pulse throbbing in your neck. I can hear your heart beating faster. I could track you anywhere by just your scent. And you have no idea what that does to me.*—

Dara blinked. Or tried to, anyway. She watched his chest rise and fall; he breathed as if he'd just run a mile, and the growling noises that rumbled from his chest made her shiver. She was mesmerized both by what she saw and by what he told her, and all she could come up with as a response was an inane, —*I smell?*—

Tristan's mouth twitched with a small smile. He sent her a brief impression, a dizzying feeling, like getting drunk off fumes. It was disorienting, but at the same time, she knew exactly where to find the source—and she wanted to find it so badly that it hurt to keep still. —*That is maybe a fraction of what I feel,*— he said. —*Is that what you want me to practice?*—

She couldn't answer. It felt as if she'd just gotten a shot of aphrodisiac straight into her veins. Her body clenched, aching. Her nipples throbbed to be suckled; her hands curled into the blanket, wanting to touch. The man she knew could ease her was standing not two feet from her and she was too far gone already to even try getting off the bunk to go to him. Dara had never felt something so powerful and instantaneous. The shock of it left her breathless, hot in her clothes. She licked her lips to bring some moisture to them, but that wasn't what she needed. She needed friction.

Two steps brought Tristan to her bunk, and he dropped into a crouch to bring their faces level. —*Here's practice for you, then,*— he said, looking her steadily in the eye.

Dara had to stop herself from reaching out to him. So close she could feel the heat his body exuded, and she craved it. She remained tense and unmoving as she watched his eyes start to change. Their color faded gradually from green to gold, and his pupils elongated like a cat's. In the dim light, his eyes glowed, and she stared without blinking. It was the most amazing thing she'd ever seen.

Tristan's mouth quirked, and this time he gave a wry smile. "Breathe, Dara."

She didn't. —*What can you see?*— Could he see what that little glimpse had done to her? What it was still doing to her? Dara felt completely drugged, but although the intensity of it was staggering, the feeling was nothing new. Tristan hadn't made her want him. He'd just made it impossible to ignore any longer.

—Everything,— came the answer. *—I hear everything, too. Breathe. Your heart is beating too fast.—*

—I-is it just your sight and hearing that's affected?—

Tristan's fingers curled around the edges of her mattress. All of his senses were affected. His clothes abraded him so much he thought he would rip them off just to find some relief. His own hair brushing his neck was almost too much to bear. Dara's scent was everywhere around him and he could almost taste it. Her arousal made him desperate to sate her. *—No,—* he told her.

He was losing control. Reason retreated, giving instinct free rein, but this time he didn't feel claws lengthen. Instead, his fingers itched to touch. To feel. Everything.

Dara reached out, her fingers brushing his brow, his temple, down to his cheek. *—Your face is changing,—* he heard her say. *—Does it hurt?—*

He heard his own growl, a purely animal sound no human vocal cords could produce. Did it hurt? *Christ, yes.* He was in agony just keeping still under her touch. Her fingers brushed into his hair, sifting through it, and he almost purred. Was his sight changing again? She hadn't been so close to him before.

But it wasn't Dara who'd moved. Without meaning to, he'd slid his hand forward to just beside her hip and shifted his weight on it in a slow, fluid motion, leaning closer to her. He never blinked as he watched her face. Her heartbeat quickened, and she was breathing in little gasps. Her pupils went wide, her cheeks became rosy, and her lips… Ah, it was a beautiful sight to behold them plumping the slightest bit and parting just a little.

He'd dreamed of this. Seeing her like this. Feeling her tremble beneath his touch. He'd imagined the feel of those lush lips on him so many times he'd lost count. In his dreams, he'd had her on all fours before him as he slammed into her and bit her shoulder in a frenzy. He'd seen her riding his cock in complete abandon, as wild as he felt. Tristan had felt her go down on him in his mind so many times he could almost believe it had really happened.

Dara thought he was trying to forget their kiss. She had no idea.

But this wasn't a dream. This was real.

And then he was tasting her. He knew she would welcome him if he pressed, but he stayed himself, remaining half-poised over her where she leaned back against the wall. For now, he was content to be kissing her. It felt like nothing he'd ever experienced before. His entire being hummed with energy, but it was somehow different. Aggressive, yet gentle at the same time. Persistent, but patient. He was fully in control of his strength, though his senses were running amok, and he instinctively knew he would never harm her, no matter how much he changed or how much control he lost.

The beast in him had free rein now, banishing reason completely, and yet it did not rule him. At least for the moment, beast and man were one and the same, equally intent on one thing: Dara.

He touched her hair and it slid like so much silk through his fingers. But it didn't compare to the feel of her skin. Tristan felt her slender arms encircle his neck, and another growl fought its way up his throat. Tristan had tried like hell to do the honorable thing and keep his distance as much as this cell allowed—and she hadn't made it easy. Just watching her get up in the morning, tousled and sleep-warmed, was enough to foul his mood for the rest of the day. Dara was his most private torment, and trying to resist her was becoming a futile effort.

He had no chance fighting his instincts now that he had her like this again.

With an impatient tug, he got her lying beneath him, stretched length for length on the narrow bunk. He kissed her deeply, searching for every single taste of her to commit to memory.

Dara moaned, her fingers curling into the fabric of his shirt. He tore it off in an instant, eager for her touch. *Yes!* she cried in her mind, and her knees rose off the mattress to create a cradle for him. He did not take the invitation, keeping that part of himself away, though he wanted nothing more than to thrust into her and let her peace seep into him.

Finally! Dara arched, stroking her hands up and down his torso, loving the movement of hard muscles under her touch. She raked her nails lightly down his back and had the pleasure of hearing him groan, as if that had felt incredible. *Just don't stop,* she silently willed.

He couldn't change his mind again. Just the thought of it made her dig her nails in a little harder.

Never. Neverneverneverneverneverner... Tristan grabbed her ass, pulled her up tighter against himself. Raking his hand down her thigh, he hooked her leg around him again, the way it had been that night. His shields were breaking down and Dara could tell that he did this from memory, reliving it, changing the script. Making it go right this time.

She thrilled and rolled her hips into his thrust. His strength was enormous but so carefully leashed, and his drugging kisses left her breathless and yearning for more. It was messing with her head, the way his hands were never still. Dara felt them everywhere, petting her entire body all at the same time. In some hazy corner of her mind, she recognized that her perception was skewing, incorporating his thoughts as well. She felt what he was doing and what he *wanted* to do. It made her lose all track of time, space, and direction, and she could do nothing except feel.

Tristan tore his mouth away from hers. She moaned at the loss, but then she felt his lips on her cheek, by her ear—*Oh, God*—just below. He nipped her neck playfully, then pressed his open mouth to the spot to soothe it. Dara raked her nails over his back as far as she could reach, wanting him closer, *needing* to feel him everywhere.

His tongue traced along the neckline of her T-shirt, then his teeth nipped again, this time catching the fabric. It tore so easily, Dara gasped, her knees closing on his hips in reflex. He groaned and curled his hips in a long, hard thrust against her. It brought the heat of him precisely to the right spot, making her shiver.

—*More!*— she demanded, clamping a hand over her mouth to smother a cry. He did it again, squeezing her breasts at the same time. He kissed the fingers covering her mouth, licked the crevices between them, coaxing them aside. Dara had to bite her tongue to keep quiet, but then he was kissing her again, and she fisted her hand in his hair to keep him there.

God, she could come like this. With just this. She was so close, her body trembled for release. Tristan pinched her nipple through her bra, rolled his hips, then settled his weight atop her and rocked against her, intensifying the friction. She could feel the climax coming, held her breath in anticipation. But just before she could have it, he pulled away.

Dara cried out, tugged at his hair in retaliation, tightened her legs around him to get him back, but he would not be moved. Not again!

Tristan braced himself on his forearms to make sure he wouldn't crush her, as small as she was, and thrust against her in a slow, languorous caress that had them both gasping for breath. Her arms around him tightened, drawing him closer, and he happily obliged, dropping his head to her chest. A quick tug with his teeth and the front clasp of her bra popped open, baring her breasts to his hungry gaze.

More beautiful than I imagined. Perfectly plump with dusky nipples beading for him, begging to be licked. He took one into his mouth and suckled, teasing the hard bud with his tongue. Her soft cries were music to his ears. Dara was trying to muffle them, keep as quiet as she could, but it only made him want to hear more. He wanted to hear her scream for him in ecstasy. Tristan wanted her to remember this night for the rest of her life, because he sure as hell would.

Tristan sucked her hard, nipped her gently, then licked and kissed in delight until she squirmed beneath him. He knew she was on the brink again, but he wouldn't give her the satisfaction just yet. —*Sensory overload? By the time I'm done with you, lass, you'll know what that means,*— he promised and shifted to lavish her other breast with the same kind of attention.

—*Why don't you lose the pants, and then we'll talk,*— she replied saucily, straining against him, trying at the same time to bring her breast to his hand and her pelvis harder against his. His laugh turned into a groan. —*My timing,*— he told her and filled her mind with images of what he would do. Just as he'd imagined them time and again.

He would keep her on that edge as long as he could. Hours, maybe. Until her body craved his touch more than air. He would taste all of her, again and again, tease and torment until she begged for him, ordered him to ease her. Tristan wanted her wild and out of control; he wanted her demanding and greedy for what he could give her. By the time he was done, she would know he was the only one who could bring her to that desperate state—and he was the only one who could then sate her. Completely.

Tristan wanted this night seared into her memory so that she couldn't keep from thinking about it every time she looked at him. He wanted her to hunger for him as much as he did for her. He wanted her to *need* him.

Dara writhed even more. —*Oh, God, Tristan, please! I need you now!*—

—*What do you want, Dara?*— he asked in a devil's voice. —*This?*— He shifted his weight to gain more leverage and thrust against her. —*Or this?*— Shifting again, he kissed her sternum and trailed his tongue down to her navel, dipping inside briefly. The front of her pants opened easily and he kissed her even lower, in the crease of her hip, but still not where he knew she needed it. His mouth watered for that intimate taste, but he denied them both, waiting for her answer.

—*Yes,*— she cried again, both in his mind and out loud.

But it wasn't enough. —*Yes what? What do you need, lass? Say it. Tell me what you need.*— His voice was different, deeper. He didn't care.

—*Anything,*— she panted, and he no longer knew whether he heard her in his mind or not. —*Everything. I want all of you.*—

—*Yes!*— His ego shouted in triumph. Sweeter words he'd never heard before in his life. *Anything,* she'd said. Freedom to do with her whatever he wished. Falling over her once more, he slipped his hand into her pants and nearly came then and there to find her wet and wanting. The first thing he wanted…

Dara cried out when he touched her clit. His clever, cruel fingers stroked while he bent his head to her breast again, suckling her in perfect rhythm to them. —*Are you ready to come for me, sweet Dara?*— she heard him say just as one of those fingers dipped inside her just a little, then retreated at once. He stroked her again, bringing her so close… but he was still only teasing her. Her entire body was tense, straining for what he held just out of reach. She reached for his cock, just barely brushed it with her fingertips before he pulled away with a groan. —*Not yet.*—

"*Now,*" she cried. He was torturing her on purpose, wanting her completely wild and screw the consequences. And, damn him, it was working. Dara would do just about anything for him to screw *her.*

Or at least let her come. Just once. "Please!" She couldn't take this much longer.

His finger dipped into her briefly, retreating just before she could climax.

—Tristan!—

He groaned again. "I love the way you say my name," he purred into her ear. As if to reward her for it, two of his fingers slid into her, thrusting against the most perfect spot nature had ever granted a woman, and she nearly screamed, rising off the bed, held down by Tristan as she finally, *finally* came. And it went on, and on, hard and merciless, just like his teasing had been, her body squeezing his fingers inside her, weeping for his cock.

Tristan hushed her cries with his mouth, taking her breath and giving her his own as sensation washed over her, so intense, her vision went dark for a moment. He continued to stroke her, knowing precisely when and how to keep pleasure coursing through her in waves.

Their minds as one, Tristan felt what she felt, reflected it back to her like a cascade of pleasure. Another orgasm followed right on the heels of the first one, and Dara heard him curse harshly. Every pleasure, large and small, they shared. In that dizzying loop between their minds again, Dara felt the pleasure Tristan got through her. He could feel her orgasm, as if it was his own, but didn't ejaculate. Through him, she sensed him touch her and feel the impact on his own skin. Her thoughts, as scattered as they were, guided him, and the more she felt, the more it affected him. There were no more secrets, no more barriers between them. All of him was exposed to her, just as all of her was his to explore, though Dara was too far gone to focus on that.

Before the last of her pleasure had ebbed away, he replaced his fingers with his cock, filling her completely and it felt almost like relief. Dara cried out at the same time as he gave a harsh growl-groan. *—God,—* he said in her mind, unable to form the words in voice. *—Wet... hot... So. Damn. Tight.—* She felt it along with him, along with her own pleasure. He held himself still, seated deep inside her, relishing the feeling, the connection. Dara tightened her legs around him. Tristan's body dominated hers completely. He was twice as large, a hundred times stronger, and yet she felt powerful, herself. This wasn't just sex to either of them. —*You feel like…*—

—*Heaven?*— she supplied at the same time as he finished, —*Home.*—

Tristan's golden feline eyes glowed feral and intense when he lowered himself so close to her their lips nearly touched. He held her gaze as he thrust steadily, deeply into her, as far as he could go. He rocked his hips against her, altered his angle slightly and kept moving in a steady rhythm. Dara's eyes became unfocused. Her nails trailed over his back again, and he arched into the caress, silently demanding more.

Too much. Too close with her. But it felt. So. Good. He kissed her roughly to let her know exactly what she was doing to him.

—*Mine now,*— he growled, both in her mind and against her lips, and his words made her come again. Her body squeezed his cock like a fist, milking him, and this time he let himself go, too, sharing in her pleasure in perfect harmony, her clenching heat drawing more and more pleasure out of him. It was far more intense than anything he'd ever experienced before, and it wouldn't let up, shuddering through both of them in endless cycles until his arms couldn't support him anymore and he lowered himself fully over her.

Dara welcomed him, tightening her arms around him to hold him even closer. Euphoria continued to hum through his body even after the last of the intense sensation faded away and, sharing her mind, he knew she felt the same.

The lights went out long after their bodies had cooled. Still entwined with her, still joined, Tristan was reluctant to move. He nuzzled her shoulder where it met her neck, scattering nibbling kisses over the elegant length of her throat while she stroked his shoulders and back. It was deeply satisfying in its own right, just to be this close. Just to be touching her.

For this one moment of perfection, he would have gone through hell again, endured everything he had. If he'd known this would be what he would find, he'd have welcomed every nightmare, *thanked* the soldier for taking him from home. Even in this place, even after everything, he sent a silent prayer of thanks to whatever deity would listen for sending Dara to him.

His body replete and his senses buzzing, he rolled with her until she was draped on top of him. She raised her head off his chest to look at him, and her heavy-lidded gaze and sleepy smile made him feel like a god. And when she kissed him in her sweet way…

Ah, God. This was heaven.

Before he could do the smart thing and retreat to his own bunk, sleep claimed him and, with Dara in his arms, sighing softly, he had never been more content to let it.

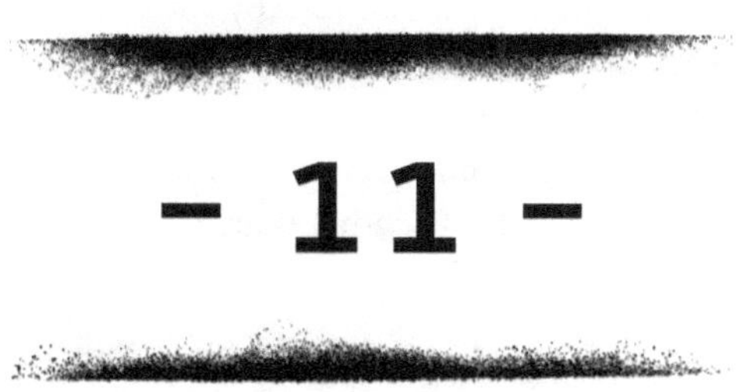

– 11 –

9th day of the 4th Blood Moon, 3028

Dara woke up cold, alone on her bunk. It was still dark. Where had Tristan gone? Shivering, she drew the blanket tighter around herself and curled up in it. It was odd. After the day and night she'd had, Dara had thought she'd sleep well past the morning alarm. She was still tired, but her mind was awake. Why?

She sensed him, then, the guard named Blanc, and a chill passed through her. Fully awake, dreading another confrontation, Dara bit her lip to keep quiet and channeled her mind to listen.

He was far across the open space, two levels above her. A small relief. He was speaking to someone, whispering something about markers and payment. His mind was busily sorting through all kinds of things Dara had no wish to see. There were deals, and deals within deals. Payments and debts—he'd double-crossed someone in the past. That was what the other guy now had on him. She frowned, trying to make sense of it. Both men were talking around the issue, without saying anything directly. It was confusing, and looking into their minds didn't help, either.

Trying to keep track of his thoughts and the conversation at the same time was impossible. She wanted to know what they were talking about more than what they were thinking, so she let that go for now. Not that she could block it out completely—she was hearing the conversation telepathically, not physically. Anything she got came with a trickle of background and images.

Blanc was talking to a prisoner. Dara could sense him looking around every so often to make sure no one was watching. He was standing in the one place where the security feeds wouldn't catch him, and he couldn't stay there long, otherwise it would look suspicious. This prison was vast. Too many prisoners, too many places to keep an eye on. The surveillance team usually just kept a general eye on things, not looking anywhere too closely.

It was a system flaw that Blanc exploited. Right now, he was in the clear. Whoever he was talking to was willing to make a deal, and the only way things could get fucked up was if someone in the surveillance room decided to listen to the audio feeds. He couldn't give them a reason to do it.

Blanc didn't like being there, but he had no choice. The man wanted something, and Blanc was cornered. If he refused this, bad things would happen. He couldn't risk it. To him, this was damage control, pure and simple.

Dara's frown deepened, and she tried shifting her focus a little to look into the man inside the cell. His mind was very different from Blanc's. Completely clear of any clutter, almost as if he had tunnel vision. As if he didn't concern himself with anything. Even this pris-on didn't bother him. What he wanted from Blanc, and the fact that he couldn't get it—*that* bothered him. His ego was bruised. He was supposed to be the big boss of this place, and he had to ask a *guard* for *permission* to do this.

There seemed to be a time element to it, too. They didn't have much longer to do whatever it was the prisoner wanted. He had information, something he shouldn't, and soon his chance would be gone.

The guard finally relented. *"Tomorrow night,"* he said.

"Why not now?"

The lights came on. *"That's why,"* Blanc replied, and walked away. Dara stayed with him until the elevator door closed behind him. She couldn't see past that barrier.

"It might be time I taught you how to hide," Tristan said from above, his tone grave. He was all business again and she just knew there was another grueling day of practice and testing in the works. While it was nice to know that Tristan was so eager to take up the fight, Dara knew from experience that he would be utterly merciless about it.

The siren rang through their block; the wake-up call. Dara groaned and sat up. She didn't want to go anywhere. Couldn't she just curl back up and pretend to sleep? Or possibly *actually* sleep?

Tristan hopped down from his bunk. "We stay here," he said as the doorway zapped open. "You don't mind skipping a meal, do you?"

Dara was famished, but shrugged. "If it was anything worth eating, I would. It's not." Tristan wouldn't deprive her of food if it wasn't something important.

"Good," he said with a nod. Not a smile, no "Good morning, last night was great," nothing.

"Grouch," she accused. And last night *had* been great. With all the craziness of this prison and Tristan's revelation, the mind-blowing sex should have been the straw that broke her. Instead, Dara had never felt so… normal. And content. Not in her entire life. She could learn to really love that feeling. Maybe…

Could she seduce him to get that feeling again?

"Always," he said, and she couldn't tell whether he meant her words or her thoughts. She opted for the latter, which significantly improved her outlook on the day to come.

She darted around him and closed herself in the bathroom corner before he could stop her. —*Ha!*— Dara grinned triumphantly.

—*You'll pay for that,*— he said, his shadow looming large just outside the screen.

She sent him a mental image of her sticking her tongue out at him. His response made her knees turn to jelly, and she had to brace herself against the sink to keep from melting to the floor. Tristan was taking over her mind. Her vision darkened until she could perceive only what he allowed, what he showed her. She felt his touch, as if he was physically there with her.

His ghostly hands roamed over her body, cupping her breasts, teasing her nipples, then moving down while his mouth brushed over her shoulder, the side of her neck. Her fingers curled around the sink when he touched her abdomen, then lower, dipping into the curls and stroking, stroking…

He flooded her mind with memories of the night before, bringing her instantly back to that moment just before his cock plunged into her. She could feel it even now, the slick head circling her entrance, teasing while he stroked her clit. Images, sensations. Dara felt him as if he stood just behind her, her back to his chest, but he wasn't really there to keep her upright. She had to do that herself. Of course, he knew exactly how difficult it was. He made it even worse.

Stroked harder, faster, kneaded her breasts, caressed her body; once again, she felt his hands everywhere. His mouth, too.

The onslaught, the sensory overload, became too much. Dara cried out as she came, still clutching that damn sink and shivering from head to toe. She knew he could feel what she felt. Knew it, because he reflected it back to her, amplifying everything. Prolonging it.

When he finally released her, withdrawing his mental touch, she reached out a shaky hand to turn on the water. —*That wasn't fair,*— she told him.

—*Maybe not,*— he allowed. —*But was it good?*—

And that was when she realized something. A playful Tristan was dangerous. He made her forget where she was and why. He made all of it not matter, made her not care that she was on a planet far from home, locked deep underground with legions of sociopaths, killers, and rapists. He forced her to drop all of the guards she'd spent a lifetime putting up—as feeble as they were—and destroyed those he'd taught her to build, and Dara was left naked and exposed, forced to rely on him completely. And she took what he gave her, because she was greedy for it. Anything to help her pretend everything was happy and nice; that this was just another normal day, in her normal life, with her not-so-normal boyfriend.

But it was all an illusion. By giving in to it, she might as well blindfold herself while she waded into a pool of sharks. Dara was just setting herself up for disaster. Sooner or later, she would be caught on her own without him there to protect her. It was just a matter of time.

It crushed her to see the illusion shatter. Plunging headfirst back into reality, she now felt more vulnerable than ever before. She should never have opened herself up like that.

Needing some distance to regroup, Dara closed herself off from Tristan and took her time washing up. When she came out again, Tristan was pacing, his jaw clenched. "Don't do that again," he told her as he went past for his turn in the bathroom. *—You can't shut down like that.—*

The screen closed behind him, leaving her bewildered. *—I can't have privacy in my own mind?—*

There was a metallic groan on the other side. What had he done? *—It's not about that.—* He sounded the same as always, but Dara sensed she'd… hurt him somehow.

—Then what's it about?—

—You need to keep alert. When you shut down, you may as well have made yourself deaf and blind. The cell is open; anyone could have gotten in. What if I wasn't here?—

His words made sense, but it wasn't what was bothering him. Dara decided to push. *—If you weren't here, I wouldn't have had to do it.—*

He was silent. She'd surprised him.

—I'm not used to sharing my mind with another person, Tristan. It's like the ultimate invasion of privacy. By now you probably know everything there is to know about me. To the last detail. Do you know how weird that feels?—

And that was another thing she couldn't get over. Tristan knew her better than anyone she'd ever known, because he had access to her most secret thoughts. *She'd* done that. She'd allowed him entrance, when he hadn't done the same. She still had no idea who Tristan Hunt really was, because every time he'd opened up, Dara had been too busy enjoying his body to even glance at anything but his surface thoughts.

So stupid! she berated herself.

Dara took her comb and dragged it ruthlessly through her hair. She felt like crying. Because of one mindless decision, because of one stupid phone call, she'd lost everything. *Everything.* Even her mind wasn't her own anymore.

The screen opened and Tristan stepped out. He rubbed a hand over his smooth jaw, looking at her as if he was at a loss for words. "You know me," he said.

"Do I?" she retorted. "Enlighten me, then. Are you the boy, still huddling in the dark? Or the stone-cold killer, tracking down his target, regardless of who stands in your way? Or the scholar who reads dead languages?" *That* hadn't escaped her before. The voices in his mind that sounded like gibberish, the memorized passages, they were in languages so rare most people didn't even talk about them anymore. "Or are you someone completely different and I just haven't figured it out yet?"

"Maybe I am all of those things." He sounded dejected, as if admitting what he had been, and what he might be, was shameful, but he was doing it anyway, to put her at ease. His shields lowered a little more, as if in invitation.

Dara didn't go snooping. She recognized this might be her chance to learn about him, but something held her back. She was… afraid. Of what she might discover.

Tristan sighed, but didn't shut her back out. She got the impression that he didn't want to. He *liked* this connection between them, liked sharing her mind and thoughts. It probably hadn't occurred to him how one-sided he'd made it.

Made, because he was the more skilled telepath. He set the rules and Dara wasn't strong enough to challenge them. Yet.

The surprise came when he lowered his shields even more. Because he did it *for her*. It mollified her somewhat that he was making such an effort. He was meeting her halfway, or at least as much as he was able.

It still didn't change what was.

—I know what you did,— he said. Of course, he'd read her mind. *—I know you dreamed the murder and called it in.—* There was a quiet assurance in his mind-voice, as well as curiosity. *—I don't know why. You had to know they'd suspect you. So why* did *you call it in, Dara?—*

Dara dragged the comb through her hair a couple more times in those angry brushes that snagged and broke the strands, while he watched and winced. How to answer? Waking up in the midst of that horror, still seeing the blood all over the walls—she could see it coating *her* walls for a moment—hadn't been nearly as bad as the realization that the dizzying back-and-forth between killer and victim had been real.

Empty hunger, compulsion, anticipation.

And in the next instant seemingly irrational paranoia. A person just walking home from work, sensing that he was being followed. Then darkness. More fear. Heart racing so fast it was a hum.

And in contrast, the *other* heart beating strong and steady. A perverted sense of pleasure from the chase, the hunt.

The knife in his hand—her hand. But it wouldn't be used. Not yet. The muffled scream.

The kill—he took his time. Building up the anticipation.

The pain—it was everywhere. Hot, searing. Endless.

The blood—all around her, soaking her.

The solemn quietude afterward that lasted only a few moments before restlessness took over and the thirst for blood built up again.

She'd sat there in the dark, shaking, crying, fighting for breath. Part of her mind had still been torn between the two of them, the one now dead and quiet, and it had sickened her.

—He was gone,— she told Tristan, *—but still close enough to be caught. If they just got there fast enough. They didn't.—*

The victim had been screaming in her mind; his invisible mouth open wide, silently screaming and screaming. A sound not heard but felt. She couldn't make it stop. It wouldn't stop.

—I had to do something.—

She hadn't thought. She'd just picked up the phone and dialed the police. She'd been wheezing and sobbing as she'd told the officer on the line where the dead body was. *"It'll still be fresh,"* Dara had told her, fighting down a wave of nausea. *"The killer just left."*

Another drag of the comb. This time, Tristan took it out of her hands. "Are you PMSing or something?" he said out loud while he mentally brushed her memories away.

"Hunt!" Her reproach carried no weight at all.

He smiled crookedly, but his eyes were serious. *—Time to get to work.—*

—What exactly are we working on today?—

He sat on the floor to face her. *—Skewing perception. Sounds easy enough when it's just one or two people, but when it's a room full of them, it gets a little tricky. And you won't be able to fool machines.—*

Dara took a breath to get rid of the bad feelings and memories, and sat down on the floor. "Yoga hour?" she teased.

He glared at her. "Never needed meditation before you got here, woman."

She grinned. "Eyes and mouth closed," she said primly.

He cast his gaze upward. "Finally!" Then, in the privacy of their minds, wickedly added, —*Later on we can try that downward dog thing.*—

~

Two hours later, they were in the entertainment room and Dara's palms were sweating. She was on her own, with Tristan all the way at the other end of the room. If this went wrong, she wasn't sure he could get to her in time. *Don't think about it,* she told herself. *Focus.*

Skewing perception, it turned out, was a lot like projecting one's thoughts to others. Only it was a *lack* of thought that she had to project, and she had to do it to everyone simultaneously, and never let up, or the illusion would break. Tricky, tricky.

Dara cleared her mind and pictured the room. She gave it every detail she could see, with the exception of empty space where she actually stood. Tristan had told her to start simple, just make them not want to look there. But for her, affecting the will involved a lot more effort than affecting perception, so her way was how she was doing this.

Once she had the image ready in her mind, she held it for a moment, solidified it, and cast it out over the room like an invisible net. It settled over the men watching TV, and those playing video games, and everyone else around. Some of them frowned—there were always those minds a little stronger than others, not so easily affected—but they soon returned to what they'd been doing. Not many people chose to investigate an anomaly; most just attributed it to their imagination. That worked to her advantage now.

When she was confident she could hold the illusion, she gave it motion. Her picture turned into a movie, and she matched it to what she and the others were doing. Now, when she moved from her spot, that empty space she'd painted over herself moved with her. It took a moment to get it just right, so the two moved identically, but once she got the hang of it, she had to fight down a satisfied smile.

She ambled to the other side of the room, toward Tristan. He was sitting in the last row, in the corner of the last section where some kind of horror movie was playing. Except when she got there and tried to touch him, her hand passed through his shoulder and he dissolved into nothing.

Caught off guard, Dara's illusion failed, and she froze, afraid to move an inch.

—*It works both ways,*— he told her.

—*I lost it,*— she said, looking to see if anyone was watching her. If they saw, she was as good as dead. Where the hell was Tristan?

—*Don't worry,*— he said. —*They can't see you.*—

A small relief, but not enough to make her relax. —*Where are you?*—

He sent her an impression of a smile and challenged, —*Find me.*—

Another test. Damn it. She should have seen it coming.

She started making her way back out, cautious but quick, because while she could affect the prisoners, the doctors and scientists watching them would notice something was wrong if a room full of men *didn't* look at the only female in attendance. But while she walked, Dara thought of Tristan and looked for the link between them. She moved on instinct, searching by mental touch rather than trying to see through his eyes to pinpoint his location.

It was like combing through a snarled mess of strings. Each one was a thought or a memory, things these men had on their minds that connected to others. Among all of them, she had to find the one that belonged to Tristan and trace it back to him. Dara was improvising with this; she'd never tried to do anything like it before.

Of all the threads, only one felt warm to her. It wasn't quite a feeling, just a distinction she recognized. She locked onto it and turned down a corridor toward the elevators. She was grinning now. *I'm tracking!* she thought excitedly, exercising just enough self-control not to break into a run.

All of a sudden, Tristan was in her mind, hissing in a breath. —*Dara, stop,*— he said tensely. —*Turn around* now.—

—*No way. I am coming for you now, buddy boy.*—

—Dara, don't!—

The elevator opened. It wasn't empty.

Dara stopped in her tracks at the same time the man looked up and saw her. He was a wiry sort, slim but still muscled, the way acrobats usually were. He wore a prisoner's uniform, but on him it looked moneyed somehow, as if he was modeling the outfit instead of wearing it day in and day out. He had dark blond hair, expensively cut and meticulously combed, and sharp brown eyes that missed nothing. By all accounts, he was handsome, but the way his mouth curled up when he saw her gave her the willies.

"Dara Frost, right?" he said, and even his voice was different from everyone else's here. Cultured. Arrogant, but engaging at the same time. He'd be a wonderful singer.

Dara stifled a shiver. "How'd you guess?"

His smile widened, and she tried to figure out what bothered her about him. "You're kind of hard to mistake," he said and came out of the elevator.

She backed away for every step that he took toward her.

"Skittish, aren't you?" He stopped and held his hands up. "I'll stay here, then."

His eyes. That was what bothered her. His eyes were beautiful, but cold as ice. Sharp and calculating, as if he was measuring her to see how far he could go before she'd bolt.

The elevator closed behind him, called by someone else. *Damn.* "That's okay, I wouldn't want to keep you," she said, keeping her voice calm and even. "I was just heading back." She'd almost said *back home.*

He glanced over his shoulder. "Looks like you just missed your ride."

—I'm coming,— Tristan said in her mind.

Dara made herself shrug. "It'll be back at some point."

"Allow me," he said and went back to push the call button.

"Thank you. I can wait for it by myself."

He flashed that handsome grin again. "I'm sure you can. But you see, there is a problem." He stepped closer again.

Dara retreated, racking her mind for some way to get him to back off. Her thoughts must have shown on her face.

As if she'd just proven his point, the guy raised an eyebrow. "I take a step, and you run. If I tried to walk past you, you'd be by the far wall before the elevator could even get here."

"I'm sure I could manage."

"If you're looking for Hunt to protect you, you'll be sorely disappointed. He's not in his cell." Another step forward. This time, Dara's retreat was a little smaller.

—*Keep him talking.*— Tristan's voice was different. She stilled for a moment, analyzing the cues. He was pensive, stalking and pacing inside his own mind, impatient to get to—*him*. He was restless to get to the other man, a challenger. No, not that. Nothing so equal to him. Dara frowned, trying to narrow it down.

The man was a target. Prey. This was a hunt to Tristan, and he was so intent on it, Dara shivered. Tristan was losing it. If this guy was still here by the time Tristan reached her, there would be a fight. Or worse.

—*I can handle him,*— she said in reassurance, but even to herself she sounded nervous. —*Relax. Take a breath.*—

"You assume much," she told the stranger who, for all his charm and good manners, still hadn't introduced himself.

He ignored that. "You'll also be disappointed if you think his protection will last. Hunt cares for nothing. He'll cut you loose eventually. Knowing him, it won't take too long."

Tristan's pacing stopped. All of that restless energy stilled and concentrated. He was furious; a predator poised to strike.

—*Tristan, please,*— she said. —*I can't do this if you lose it.*—

If he heard her, he gave no sign of it.

The man took another step.

Dara held her ground, held his gaze, and said nothing.

He smiled, this time slow and intrigued. "How interesting." He was close enough that if she allowed it, his thoughts would leak into her, just by being near.

She lowered her shields gradually, little by little. Tristan was protesting. He fought himself for control, trying to stop her, but in his current state, Dara overruled his wishes easily. She needed a target if she was going to strike.

The man's name was Clay. In his mind, it was a flourish of a signature. He considered himself an artist. That signature was a mark he left on all of his victims. A memento for them to remember him by. *Women. Stunning women. Bloodied women. Robbed of their beauty.* "You and I," he was saying, "we don't belong in this place." *Scarred bodies. Broken spirits. Shattered minds. And that signature—a permanent mark on their skin. They would never be rid of it. They would never be allowed to forget.*

"You and I," Dara said, her voice shaking. She was livid for those women, and mourned them. They had no one to fight for them. Many had since killed themselves—something he considered a great affront. "We have nothing in common."

People approaching. Dara brought her shields back up.

"One day, you might come to think differently. You could be my masterpiece, Dara. What I could do with you—"

"You never will," she told him.

Footsteps behind her. Elevator coming closer. She stepped back and to the side to let him pass. The move seemed to anger him, but he composed himself again when he glanced at the group of guards approaching them. "We'll talk later."

The elevator stopped and opened. Dara could feel Tristan's heart racing as if it was her own. She turned her back on Clay as he went past the guards, politely bidding Dr. Chase a good day. Tristan's eyes were glowing again, trained on the bastard's back. As soon as the door was open enough to allow him through, he charged forward.

Dara had no choice but to step into his path. If he killed Clay now, in this state, they'd both be dead. —*Look at me,*— she ordered, heartened when he stopped before he ran her over in his pursuit. His body shook with barely leashed aggression, but he held still. She was so proud of him, it hurt.

She hadn't intended to send him that thought, but he caught it nonetheless. His answer was wry and wordless, more of a feeling than a coherent thought. "I've been looking for you," she told him. —*Come back to me.*—

Only then did he look at her. "You okay?" His voice was still gravelly. He had to clear his throat a couple of times to get it under control. But he did it.

"Fine," she assured him, managing a small smile.

"Dr. Chase," Tristan said without looking away from Dara. "What's with the entourage?"

She was safe, he kept telling himself, but the aggression, the bloodlust refused to subside. He needed to drag her back to the cell and hide her; make sure no one came close to her again. The presence of others kept him on a razor's edge. It didn't bode well for any of them. Tristan dragged his gaze away to take in the potential adversaries.

"Actually," the doctor began, making a visible effort to compose herself. Something was up. "We were just on our way to get you two."

"Get us?" Dara repeated. "For what?"

"Let's go to your cell to talk," she said. She didn't wait for them to follow—the guards took up the rear, so they really had no choice but to get into the elevator after her. The moving metal box could comfortably hold about five people. Now they were sharing it with five others, including four burly guards.

Tristan kept next to Dara, shielding her from the others. He didn't touch her outright, but kept close enough so he could brush her shoulder or lean in close whenever no one was looking. It wasn't enough. Nowhere near. But their present company didn't allow for more. So he forced himself to breathe through it, letting her scent pull him back to sanity.

The guards were armed. When they stepped out of the elevator, the doctor and her two subjects were sandwiched between pairs of them as they cleared the way in front and kept it clear from the back. They flanked the cell from each side as the three of them went inside.

"We're leaving," Dr. Chase said without preamble. "Tonight, or tomorrow morning at the latest. I still have some packing to do, but as soon as I am done, we're out of here."

Tristan could feel Dara starting to reach out to Amelia's mind. He laid a hand on her shoulder to strengthen their telepathic connection and blocked her. —*Don't look,*— he told her. "You're bailing?" he asked Amelia.

"The thing I told you about is scheduled to start in two days. I did what I could, and Dara is safe, but there's no way to tell how the study will affect everyone after it's done. The captain of the guard is already beefing up security. I think he's expecting trouble."

"How'd you get them to let you go?"

In no way was I about to stay here, he heard in the doctor's adamant mind. She would have moved heaven and earth to get the hell out of this place. Amelia sighed, rubbing her forehead. "I put in for a transfer to Niren Colony. They wanted my research. I told them they could have it if I could take a subject with me." *Warped research,* she thought.

He pursued it a little deeper and found she'd sabotaged her notes long before this, anticipating their move. Clever, clever woman. She knew what the authorities would do with her work. Though her situation now was lamentable, she'd become a doctor to help people, not hurt them. Now she'd made sure no one would be able to recreate and bastardize her results, possibly ever.

She'd demanded her only semi-successful DNA recombination patient—Tristan. He was the only one who had survived the initial introduction of animal DNA, and she had legitimate reason for wanting to continue monitoring him, which was the only reason they'd even considered it. Apparently they'd ultimately agreed because he hadn't caused any trouble in the last few months. And because they wanted Amelia's research too much to refuse.

Tristan was getting transferred out on good behavior. *Better than in a body bag,* he thought with a careless shrug. Still…

"I'm not leaving," he told her.

Amelia stared at him for a moment. She glanced at Dara, then at the door to see if anyone was eavesdropping. "No, you don't understand, Tristan," she said quietly. "We're *all* leaving. Dara, too."

Dara put it together faster than he could. She shuddered and swayed back. If he hadn't been there, she would have fallen over. He put his arms around her to steady her, but he couldn't reach her mind past the thick fog of sheer terror that suddenly clouded it. "Oh, God," she whispered, and he could feel her grow cold. "He's killed again."

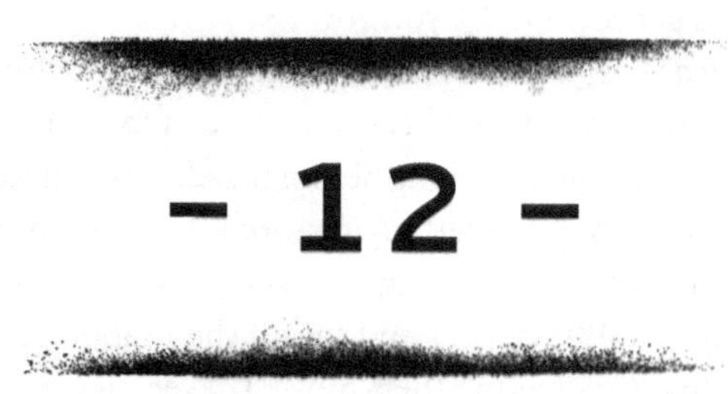

- 12 -

One hour after lights out

Half of the guards stayed behind after Dr. Chase left, but Dara didn't believe the illusion of safety for a second. She was on edge, scared and pissed off and, if the silent treatment she was getting from Tristan was anything to go by, he was in little better shape.

It was probably her emotional state he was picking up on and tuning into. *He* certainly had nothing to be on edge about. He was getting transferred to a place that would be like a holiday resort compared to this.

But for Dara, the story would be quite different. She'd thought this was bad—and it was—but she had a feeling that her life was about to take a swan dive into something worse.

Because the killer had struck again.

Because she'd given the police detailed information about the last murder, and because she'd done it minutes after the fact, from across the city. They couldn't hold her on the murder charge anymore, but they would drill her mercilessly to find out how she'd known what she'd reported.

And what if she slipped up? What if they found out she was really a telepath?

Better for them to think she was an accomplice. If she cooperated and helped them find the real killer, they might even be lenient on her accessory to murder charges.

But that meant she would have to look into his mind again. Deliberately this time. To convince them that she knew something, she had to *know* something, and the only way to find out was to make contact again. It exponentially raised her chances of getting caught—by the killer, as well by as the authorities. At the moment, she didn't know which scared her more.

—*You're not ready,*— Tristan said. —*Nowhere near ready to do that.*—

She knew that, of course. There were too many what-ifs that she might not even realize until it was too late.

—*Would you really be so willing to try it?*— he asked.

—*No. I wouldn't* want *to do it, but I may not have a choice.*—

—*There are always choices!*—

—*Yeah? Then give me an alternative. How would you explain to them what I knew?*—

Silence.

—*Then teach me what I need to know.*—

—*It would take more time than we have.*— Though they were both going to the same colony, they might end up in completely different camps. His crime was far worse than hers, but even without that, she had something the officials wanted. They would want her isolated for the interrogation.

Just that word *interrogation* made her shudder. Just how far would they go to get information out of her? This little stay in New Alaska was enough to give her a pretty good idea about the value placed on human life in prisons. Depending on how badly they wanted to catch this guy, how guilty they thought she was, and the value they placed on what she knew… she had no idea what to expect. But she was pretty sure it wouldn't be anything good.

—*You're right,*— she told him. —*Let's just sit here and stare at the walls. That's a much better way to spend our last few hours here.*—

—*You're asking me to teach you how to stay silent in another's mind for extended periods of time, despite external stimuli, while gleaning information* and *not getting caught. Any one of those would take years to master. You want to do it in a matter of hours?*—

—*I can at least try.*— What other choice did she have?

He was silent again, his thoughts buzzing behind an almost-transparent veil he'd cast over himself. He did that a lot now; he didn't want her to see what he was thinking, but didn't want to block her out completely, either.

—*We do this my way,*— he finally said. —*You enter my mind, and no one else's. If you do it right, I won't know you're there, so I'll need some sort of sign.*—

—*I can do that.*—

—*This won't be easy, Dara. No matter what happens, you cannot flinch. You have to go on as if you're you, but in my mind, you have to be like a ghost.*—

—*Fine. Let's do it.*—

He was still hesitant, but he'd do it. They might never see each other again, and even though Dara had already learned a lot from him, there was still a lot more she needed to learn about her abilities. After tonight, she would have to learn it on her own. But this, he could still do, and as far as teaching went, Dara knew that Tristan wasn't one to let an opportunity pass by.

—*Let me know when you're in.*—

No more instructions. Dara closed her eyes and imagined herself as smoke. Nothing but mist in the air. In that form, she could go wherever she wanted. She floated up toward Tristan's bunk and settled silently over his mind. Her consciousness seeped into his, contracting slowly, carefully, into something so small that—she hoped—he wouldn't be able to perceive it.

When she opened her mind's eye, she saw what Tristan saw. He didn't seem to react to her presence at all, and if he noticed, he gave no sign of it. She knew that if he noticed, he *would* give a sign of it, so she relaxed a little. This at least she knew how to do. Now would come the hard part. She gave a small wriggle in his mind to let him know she was there, then settled quietly again.

Tristan slid off his bunk, graceful as a cat, and faced her where she sat with her eyes closed. It was pitch-black in the cell, and still he could see her clear as day. He cupped her cheek. "Open your eyes, Dara," he said. She was an apt student. He couldn't find her in his mind, though she was there. But now she had to react with her body as if it still housed her mind. It was near impossible for humans to pull off, the ultimate in multitasking—thinking of two different things at the same time and comprehending them.

He didn't expect her to be able to do it on her first try, but if this was their last night together, then he wanted to make the most of it. After tonight, he had no idea what to expect. How would the animal part of him react to her absence? In the past few days, whenever she hadn't been in the same room, he'd walked a razor's edge of control. He'd felt both the compulsion to find her and the aggressive need to lash out at whomever he decided was keeping her from him—which meant anyone in his way.

Dara thought he spent all this time teaching her because he wanted to help her. In truth, he couldn't leave her, because he had no idea what would happen to him if he did. Tristan had a bad feeling that he wouldn't be able to see her walk away, without doing something violent. Without her there to ground him, he knew that the animal would take over. His mind would change, and his body would become stronger, out of control. His senses would overwhelm him, and he wouldn't be able to stop himself from changing completely, even if it ended up killing him like so many others in Dr. Chase's study.

Tristan had to make Dara stronger, expand her range as far as it could go. He could meet her halfway if necessary, but he needed her always within contact range.

Dara's brows drew together. She was trying to do as he asked.

Tristan brushed his mouth over hers. "Open your eyes," he whispered against her lips.

The gentlest of quivers in his mind was the only indication she was struggling. A normal person would barely notice. Then she opened her eyes, and he watched them shift rapidly back and forth, as if she was dreaming. Her breathing became uneven as she struggled to keep her focus on both her mind and her body.

A warm glow of pride filled him to near bursting. She was still and steady, looking a little confused, but otherwise perfectly normal. He kissed her, because he couldn't help himself. She responded, hesitantly at first, but a moment later, her small fingers slid into his hair, her nails gently raking over his scalp. Tristan shuddered, feeling himself change as he focused on her.

How had he gone so long without this? Her taste was addictive. He could kiss her forever. Already he scented the sweet honeydew of her arousal, and it maddened him. Tristan wanted to feel the heat of her skin next to his, to feel her tremble when he touched her. Just like every other time he'd had his hands on her, the strength of his reaction to her threw him off-kilter, made him clumsy. He wanted to tear her clothes off to be rid of them, but realized that in this state, he could hurt her doing it.

And Tristan didn't want that. Never that. He'd used his hands to hurt and kill before. With Dara, he only wanted them to bring her pleasure. Never pain. Though it took all the willpower he possessed, Tristan gentled himself, reminding himself that this was a test.

What a perfect way to test her, he decided. He deepened the kiss, tasting her, committing everything to memory, saving it for later, when he might not have her soft and warm in his arms. She wavered slightly in his mind once more when he laid her down on her bunk, and then held steady, meeting him physically, touch for touch.

It was a game now, to see how much outer stimuli she could handle before she faltered in her task. Tristan was not about to make it easy on her. He set to her clothes, kissing and nipping every new inch of skin he revealed. Her shirt came away easily, and he nuzzled her stomach, taut with tension until she relaxed. When he divested Dara of her pants, her breath became shallow. Tristan took his time caressing the length of her legs. She had a pair of them just long enough to hook and lock around him. He couldn't wait for her to do that again.

When he got to her underwear, like a feline with a new plaything, he nuzzled her breasts, nipped at her through her bra, then traced the outlines with his tongue, feeling her heartbeat quicken against it. He held her close, soaking up the feel of her hands roaming over his back and her legs squeezing around him.

"I… can't…" she breathed, her brows drawing together again. She was losing it, becoming restless in his mind. Tristan could feel how much of an effort she put into this, fighting herself for control. It was no more than he'd done every day since she'd arrived. Dara *needed*. So much, it made her ache. How long would she be able to deny herself?

How long would he let her? The beast in him craved her pleasure, even more than its own. It drove him to obey her body's commands. She spoke them so clearly, telling him where she needed to be touched, how she wanted him to kiss her. Tristan was so attuned to her now, he didn't need telepathy. But he made use of it to intensify every touch, to make her crave him so much she couldn't breathe without him.

Still a test, he reminded himself. To Dara he said, "Focus," then thought of something that made him grin wickedly. "And if you want to play, play through me."

Curious to see if she would do it, hungry for her to do it, Tristan nipped her earlobe, then strung open-mouthed kisses down her throat. Dara moaned, but bit her lip to keep quiet. She arched to his mouth, arms looping around his head to bring him back when he pulled away to look at her. His hand caressed her back down her spine, making her arch more, then returned back up her front to cup her breast. *Good idea,* he thought, and proceeded to massage the soft mound, rubbing his face over the other at the same time.

He sought her nipple and suckled her hard, grazing it with his teeth just enough to make her shiver.

Another small lapse of concentration, and he found her in a part of his mind he hadn't expected. For no more than a second, he stilled to realize she'd directed him without his knowledge. Part of him thrilled to be managed like that. And another part of him was eager to show her who was in charge here.

Dara had only seconds to realize she'd been found out, come to terms with it, and regain her focus before Tristan's hand slipped into her panties. Her hips bucked up into his touch, and she bit back a moan, trying to hold her place in his mind. It was making her crazed, having to keep focused, when all she wanted to do was let go and touch him and be touched. She was managing to do two things halfway, when she wanted so much to do just one thing wholeheartedly.

She couldn't even direct him now, because he knew what she was doing. His fingers teased, spread her moisture all around, but wouldn't touch where she wanted him the most. Dara thrashed her head left and right on the pillow, not even breathing for fear she would scream. His teeth caught her nipple, and she dug her nails into his back. She felt him groan deep in his chest, wordlessly demanding more.

As if in reward, he stroked up her clit, then down all the way to her entrance, dipping in briefly, but not enough. Never enough. So she squeezed her legs around him and raised her hips to his next stroke, managing to take him deeper. Tristan cursed, releasing her breast to rest his forehead against her chest.

"If you keep doing that," he rasped, "this will be over before it even begins."

"God," she breathed, "then just *begin* already!"

She felt him smile against her, his mind filled with pure male satisfaction. He reveled in her reactions, loved seeing her so desperate for him. He *wanted* her this wild, so he could be the one to sate her, too.

Well, there were things *she* wanted, too. And she would not be denied. Not this time. Dara wanted to taste him. She subtly inserted an image into his mind, of her hands on his cock and her tongue stroking the underside, her breath teasing the head, so close to touching, but not quite there. She showed him how she would lick the slit and suck him into the heat of her mouth, hoping to provoke him enough to release her from this stupid lesson.

Tristan paused and shuddered, breathing hard against her chest, and Dara smiled.

And then her panties were gone and his mouth was on her, and she had to cover her own mouth to keep from crying out. She nearly dropped out of his mind right then and there, and clutched the blanket beneath her. Her own fault to have the tables turned on her. Tristan wasn't about to be outdone. He kissed her as he would her mouth, tongue delving in while he clutched her thighs to hold her immobile. She couldn't move, not even to rock against his ravaging mouth. All she could do was take what he gave.

And give he did. Tristan feasted on her, teasing more moisture out of her before licking it up like his favorite dessert. He was voracious, as if he couldn't get enough of her, and within moments, Dara was on the edge, so close to coming, her body clenched rhythmically in readiness.

She sensed everything along with him. Tristan was single-mindedly focused on her, on teasing and soothing and tasting, and all of it brought him more pleasure than he even realized. All of it she could feel, and it stoked her own desire to impossible heights.

Too much. It overwhelmed her. She lost her focus and betrayed her presence in his mind, no longer able to keep hidden. Tristan made a rough sound and, almost as punishment, thrust his fingers into her and sucked her clit at the same time. Dara came with such force that only Tristan's hold on her kept her from rising off the bunk.

Now *he* was in *her* mind, feeling what she felt. He shuddered as he finally released her to crawl over her. He still hadn't taken his clothes off and the feel of coarse fabric over her sensitive skin made her shiver. They brushed chest to chest as Tristan shifted his weight over her. She didn't know when she'd managed to lose her bra, but the feel of his shirt rasping over her nipples made her hips buck against him again.

Tristan groaned and tore his shirt off, then pulled her against him skin to skin while he thrust slowly against her, building the pleasure up again. His teeth, sharper now, brushed over her shoulder, scraping, then nipping. When she gasped, he soothed the sore spot with drawn-out laps and kisses. Even his mind in hers felt different now. Dara wasn't as out of control as she'd been the first time. Now she recognized how open he was and could even understand a few things. He was more animal than man now—wild, focused on taking her, yet also on bringing her pleasure. It was like a game, but far more intense.

There was the thought that she was his—his to claim, his to take care of. His to keep. No, it wasn't a thought; nothing that clear and delineated. It was more instinct, rooted so deep she wondered if he even realized it was there, or just took it as a matter of course. Some part of him had to know that it was irrational, even pointless, but right now, that silent claim on her guided every move he made, every unsteady caress he delivered and every hungry kiss he stole. Dara knew this version of Tristan would be confused if she tried to tell him something that went against that instinct. She found it… endearing.

…endearing… Tristan heard, so focused on the physical that he hadn't paid attention to the mental connection until now. Endearing? Well,

he'd put an end to *that*.

He could feel her growing wet again, even through the fabric of his pants between them. With a last, lingering kiss to her throat, Tristan raised his head, wanting to see her face when he thrust into her. Freeing his cock from his pants, watching her eyes grow unfocused while he thrust against her a couple of times, his cock slipping up and down between her slick folds. Then he plunged deep and took her cries into his mouth.

Home. He was home.

His heart thudded in his chest, feeling as if it wanted to burst out of him and into her. Nothing in his life could ever compare with this. Here, being with Dara this way, Tristan felt indestructible and weak at the same time. It made him shudder, a little uneasy, but there were no words to describe the rightness of it. He never wanted to leave.

They breathed in unison, for each other, exchanging air in a dizzying cycle. When Dara exhaled, Tristan inhaled, wanting every part of her, even her breath. He thrust into the welcoming heat of her, feeling her arms clutch around him and her legs squeeze to hold him close. He could feel her heartbeat against his chest and part of his mind worried that he was holding her too tightly. He couldn't make himself loosen his hold even a little.

He plunged deep, then stayed, circling his hips against her. Tristan could feel her close in on the edge and he pushed her over, prolonging her pleasure with slow, even friction. Her nails dug into his back; he wouldn't stop, guiding her body smoothly into another orgasm. She bit him, muffling her moans against his shoulder, and it made him come so hard, his vision darkened and his breath exploded out of his lungs. He wanted to shout, to roar her name to the sky, but couldn't make a sound.

Instead, he contented himself with holding her as tightly as he dared and continuing to slowly move within her, reluctant to see this end. "Never get enough of this," he said, and it was as much an admission as it was a command.

"Won't," she replied, the sound echoing in his mind over and over again.

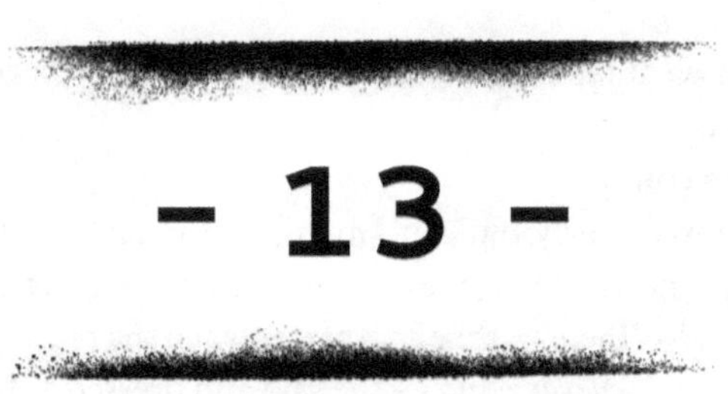

– 13 –

—*I guess I failed,*— Dara said later, trailing her fingers in slow patterns over his chest.

—*I'd have been insulted if you didn't,*— he replied. Even to his own ears, his voice drawled like a contented purr.

She shivered in her own mind. "I'm scared, Tristan."

He pulled her closer and nuzzled her hair. "I know."

"Lie to me," she said. "Tell me everything will be okay."

"No."

He'd expected it, but it still hit him like a blow to the gut. The disappointment. The hurt. She wouldn't have believed it, just wanted to hear the words so she could take at least one full breath without her heart pounding out of control. She'd wanted an illusion to hold on to; to be taken care of, even if it was just for a few seconds.

And Tristan had just reminded her that she had no friends here. *That* was what she believed. Always had, though she'd been distracted from it a few times. Tristan wanted to tell her otherwise, but it would have been nothing more than an empty promise. No matter how much he wanted her—*Christ, how he wanted her*—the situation was beyond his control. Once they left this cell for good, he wouldn't be able to protect her anymore.

All that time she'd spent in his mind, his thoughts and memories, she still had no idea. Tristan couldn't tell her now. It would make no difference if he did. They stood at a crossroads and no matter how much he wanted to hold on to her, Dara's road led where he couldn't follow.

An alarm went off in his head. *Whispers in the dark, enemies conspiring. On the move.*

They were coming.

Tristan moved slowly, but in his mind, he was anything but calm. —*Get dressed,*— he told Dara, moving away from her to get off the bunk.

—*What's…?*— There was the stab of fear when she picked up on what he was sensing. —*Never mind,*— she said and dressed as he'd told her.

Tristan hoisted her up onto his bunk. "Last night," he said aloud. "You can have the top bunk." In her mind he warned, —*Stay still. Hide. Anyone comes close, you're not there. You're asleep on your own bunk. Got it?*—

"Thanks, I guess." Despite the calm of his voice, Tristan's eyes were flickering gold. —*What are you gonna do?*—

—*You leave that to me. Just make sure you don't slip up.*—

The guards were gone. They had to be changing shifts, though it was more likely that someone had called them off. There was nothing to stand between them and the two approaching except that force field.

Dara pulled her knees up to her chest and breathed to calm her mind. She focused on the cell and changed the picture until she appeared to be asleep on her bunk. It had been one thing to do something like this during the day, but now in the dark, when her heart was racing with fear, Dara had a hard time concentrating. Her body was screaming at her to run or hide, find something to use as a weapon, anything but just sit there and wait. An evolutionary defense mechanism was now making her panic.

Tristan had lain down on her bunk. Dara used him as a focal point and lowered the illusion of her over him. It took her three tries to do it while keeping herself hidden. What Tristan was doing, she couldn't tell, but she could sense the two men approaching.

Merely registering the thought processes, she recognized the mind attached to one man. Blanc. He was the one who'd let the prisoner out and was now leading the way to her cell. She merely skimmed over the surface of his mind to get to the other one.

Her illusion wavered when she determined his identity. It was the same man Blanc had been talking to last night. And after today, she had a face and name to put with the mind: Clay.

Dara clutched the blanket until her fingers felt like they would cramp. She couldn't panic now. She and Tristan were in a tiny chamber, about to face two men, one of whom would be carrying a gun and possibly be eager to use it. All they had going for them was the element of surprise. If they lost that because of Dara, it wouldn't matter that they were both getting transferred out. They might not even make it through the night.

So she forced herself to focus. She solidified the image in her mind and then carefully, oh so subtly, laid it over Blanc's and Clay's minds, just as they were coming into view. Like a child afraid of monsters, Dara wanted to close her eyes and pretend it made her invisible. She could hear their footsteps nearing. Could sense what they were feeling, and she couldn't block it out, not without letting go of the illusion she'd created.

Anticipation glowed around Clay like an aura. Excitement, focus on the task that was to come. The artist was coming, and a blank canvas was awaiting him. Annoyance. Blanc's measured gait was too slow. Hurry the hell up! Calm… calm down. Just one chance. Only one. Have to do it right.

What he wasn't factoring into the equation was Blanc. *Saw her first,* the guard was thinking. *Will get my dues. Let him out, debt paid… now I get to play. First come, first served, you fuck.*

The doorway zapped open. Dara clutched Tristan's pillow to her chest, with the edge just covering her mouth. Fear made her want to shrink into a tiny ball. She made herself as small as she could, but it wasn't enough. If the illusion didn't hold, she was dead. This time, she knew it for certain.

There was movement in the cell, shadows closing in. Dara closed her eyes to block it out.

Muffled sounds, a commotion; a fight. Someone hit the top bunk, and she started so badly that she lost control of her illusion.

The gun went off, and Dara screamed. More fighting. She could hear someone being slammed against the wall, the sound of fists on flesh, grunts and growls. She scooted back against the wall as far as she could go and made herself even smaller.

Pain was leaking into her mind from all three fighters, and her body shook with it. It was impossible to block out. She could tell that Clay was down, though she didn't know whether he was just unconscious or dead. And Blanc wasn't doing too well, either. Dara could sense that Tristan was hurt, but there was a haze in his mind, a killing rage that shielded him from the pain. He couldn't feel any of it, so Dara didn't, either. He had closed himself off—no. Not closed off. He was so focused on killing the guard that nothing else could get his attention. Dara could still reach him, but he wasn't listening.

His thought patterns were different. Base instincts were taking over—survival above all else. *Protect the female—my pack, my mate. Destroy the challenger, by any means necessary.* Right now the only means at his disposal was his own body. His strength alone could kill so easily, but the more control he lost, the more his outward appearance would change. She'd seen his eyes glow in the dark, seen his face change until he was barely recognizable. What would happen to him if it went too far?

Running footsteps outside the cell. The guards were coming. She was just about to warn Tristan when she was pulled off her bunk. Dara screamed and fought, but Tristan's hold on her was unrelenting. He shoved her into the bathroom area and closed it off after her, leaving her completely alone, shaken and frightened, still shivering uncontrollably.

Dara stared at that flimsy barrier, willing herself to see what was on the other side, but there was no light. She couldn't even see shadows. Couldn't hear anything out there, either. She banged her fists against the shield, needing to be there next to him, to make sure he was all right. The shield barely registered the feeble disturbance.

Someone shouted for the lights to be turned on. When light flooded the cell, Dara could see Tristan's shadow loom large just on the other side of the barrier. He'd taken a stand in front of it to shield her.

Dara placed her hands on the thing, pretending that he was leaning against it and she could feel him through it. She closed her eyes to see through his. He was focused on more intruders in his lair and distracted enough to let her through. Blanc and Clay were on the floor. There were three armed guards in the cell, two aiming their guns at Tristan, one checking Blanc's vital signs.

Dara ignored all of that and focused on Tristan's mind. She molded her consciousness to his and slowly, gently, started bringing his own memories to the fore. He was still on edge, a hair trigger ready to go off and slaughter anything in his way. Which included the guards. Dara had to be his control now; she had to get him calm somehow. The alternative was unacceptable.

If she could just distract him long enough, maybe the diversion would help him return to himself. This was the worst possible time to start experimenting with her telepathy, but what choice did she have? They were in enough trouble already.

—*Tristan? Talk to me.*—

"He's dead," one of the guards said, and she had no idea who he was talking about.

—*Tristan, please.*—

"Randal," another said, and she could tell he was talking to someone who wasn't in the room. "Do you have the feed cued? I see. Call Dr. Chase. Tell her the flight plan has been moved up."

—*Tristan!*—

—*I'm here,*— he finally said, and Dara sagged against the sink.

—*What's going on?*—

The bathroom opened and Tristan grasped her hand to pull her out to his side. There was blood staining his shirt under his arm and his hand was slick with it. "Oh, God, you're hurt!"

—*Leave it. It's fine.*— He spoke in her mind, because he didn't trust his voice. Dara looked up and just stifled a gasp. For a split second, he didn't look anything like the Tristan she knew. His hair had become lighter, streaked. His face had changed drastically; it was now animal-istic, with his nose flattened and his mouth bulging with fangs, the upper lip curved, almost split like a cat's. And all over his skin, stripes appeared and faded like tattoos. It was all there one moment, then almost gone the next. All that remained constant were his golden eyes.

The guard talking on his com unit nodded. "Got it." Then he turned to the two of them. "Someone tampered with the video feed."

His voice startled her out of her shock. She struggled to get some sort of handle on the situation and failed miserably. Dead men on the floor, at her feet. Blood everywhere. *Oh, God,* it was like that night all over again. The guards were looking at her, and she shrank from their gaze. Tristan's hand tightened on hers, keeping her with him. It was warm around her chilled fingers, but wet and sticky with blood—and she couldn't even tell whose it was! But she knew he was hurt badly. Dara grasped onto that. One crisis at a time. *—Fine? You're bleeding all over the floor!—*

"And you think Hunt is responsible?" Dr. Chase pushed her way into the cell. "Excuse me," she said authoritatively and came to crouch by Blanc.

—Quiet,— Tristan told Dara. Still on point, assessing the situation with a predator's eye.

Dara watched Dr. Chase's movements. It brought the dead men into her field of vision again.

"No, ma'am," the guard said. "We got the feed back online just as Blanc opened this cell. We know foul play was involved."

Dr. Chase pressed her fingers to Blanc's neck. After a moment, she said, "He's dead."

"Yes, ma'am. The prisoner as well."

The *prisoner* lay in a broken heap next to Blanc. His arm was twisted at an awkward angle, and his neck was crushed and broken. His head was turned almost two hundred degrees from normal. And the look on his face was an eternal testament to the pain he'd felt before he died. The doctor didn't even bother checking him. "Then why did you call me and not the cleanup crew?" she demanded.

Dara turned her face into Tristan's shoulder to block out the sight, but she could still see them in her mind. *Too much. I can't do this again!*

—H-how badly are you hurt?— she asked him, trying desperately to focus on something else. Tristan was alive. She clung to that knowledge for all she was worth.

—I'll live. Trust me.— He wasn't getting any better, keeping his attention on everyone else. His strength gave Dara courage enough to peek at the scene again, firmly ignoring the bodies on the floor.

The guard who had first checked the two men answered the doctor.

"The guards you ordered to be posted here were called away. We don't know who gave the order, but it's obvious that it was someone on the security team. Probably Blanc. There is protocol to follow here, ma'am. You posted the guards because you expected trouble, and you were proven right."

"But you don't approve of such use for the security team, right?"

"There's many of us who don't, ma'am. But we get that certain prisoners are also valuable test subjects."

"And some aren't even supposed to be here," Dr. Chase said, indicating Dara. That brought Tristan's bleeding side into her view, and she nudged Dara away to examine him. Tristan growled—actually growled—but let go of Dara's hand.

Dara squeezed herself into the space between the bathroom and the bunks, feeling utterly exposed and vulnerable.

While she checked his wounds, Dr. Chase said, "I doubt either of these men came here tonight for a social visit to Hunt. This is a gunshot wound." She tapped the wall where Dara always got books, and typed something onto the touch screen. A compartment opened underneath it, and Dr. Chase took out a med kit. "Sit," she told Tristan, then addressed the guards. "So what's the protocol to deal with this?"

—*See?*— Tristan said. —*I told you I'd live.*—

Dara didn't reply. Only turned her face away and pressed herself tighter against the wall.

Tristan finally turned his head to look at her, his features drawn in a frown. —*Dara?*—

Dr. Chase set to cleaning his wounds. Dara was so shaken she didn't have the sense to shield her mind. She was picking up everything around her. From Dr. Chase, she heard Tristan would be fine. It did nothing to reassure her, not when he still looked like he might bite into someone's neck if they made a sudden movement.

The guards were tense, uncomfortable being in the cell with a guy who'd taken out two men like an animal. They were scared of him— and with good reason.

Tristan's mind was the loudest. He was still in fight mode, tense every time Dr. Chase touched him. He couldn't see Dara clearly where she'd hidden herself, and it frustrated him. His mind was in turmoil, needing to protect her, but he sensed how fragile she was so he struggled to pull back from the brink. For her sake. Each time he failed, it infuriated him and set him further back.

"Your flight plan has been moved up," the guard closest to the door said. "The shuttle is fueled and ready for takeoff whenever you are. You and the prisoners will be escorted to the launch pad, and we'll be increasing our security measures to make sure you arrive safely and without mishap at Niren Colony."

"Very good," Dr. Chase said, all business. "Have someone bring my luggage to the launch pad. There are two suitcases and a box waiting by the door of my room. And make sure they get there in the same condition I left them, or we will have a problem."

"Yes, ma'am," the guard said and left.

"As for you two," she said to the remaining guards, "call the cleanup crew and clear the way to the launch pad. Tell the pilot we're on our way."

– 14 –

Dara was shaking. Her arms tight around her chest, she tried desperately to stop the shivers, but it was like being hypothermic. Her body automatically did what it needed to do to survive and her mind had no say in the matter. And the more she tried to hold still, the worse the shaking became.

Part of her mind recognized that she was going into shock. Or was already in shock. Something like that. But the rest of her didn't give a shit what was going on, because it was hell all over again. This might as well be the night she'd seen the murder. Only this time it was worse. This time, she hadn't dreamed the events—they had actually been happening around her.

Her mind was on spin cycle, perversely replaying everything over and over again, and each time with more details that her imagination filled in. The faces of Blanc and Clay started to look more demonic than human, their sneers sharper, colder. Their hands turned into claws, and their postures hunched. Bogeymen coming to get her.

And then the fight. *Oh, God…* Dara clutched her head to keep the memories back. They were black shadows, ghosts in her mind. Things that could reach out of the darkness and tear her to pieces, but each time she tried to fight back, her hands passed through the shapeless things like mist. She couldn't defend against that; no one could.

The others were talking—the guards and Dr. Chase. But Dara couldn't hear them past the din in her head and the noise the prisoners were making. The rest of the prisoners had awakened when the lights were turned on, and now they were going insane watching Tristan and Dara be escorted out.

They were screaming, shouting, throwing things against the force fields and each time something vaporized, it emitted a brief flash of light. There were hundreds of those flashes going off all around her, and Dara flinched at each one, her gaze darting back and forth. It was making her dizzy and disoriented.

She was having trouble breathing, and she was tripping over her own two feet as the guards led them across the catwalks and the bridge to the main exit. There were three guards in front of her, two between her and Hunt, and four more after Dr. Chase. *Too many people. Too much noise.* Dara was on the verge of screaming her head off.

Then they were past the exit, in the cool tunnel, and when the gate closed behind them, the noises hushed. Dara slowed her step, shaking so badly she feared that any longer and her legs would simply give out. They felt about as steady as toothpicks.

The guard behind her nudged her into motion again. "Keep moving," he said, and somewhere behind him, Dara heard Tristan growl low. He was handcuffed to a chain belt, but she doubted those flimsy restraints would even slow him down if he decided to stop playing nice. For a moment, she wished he would.

As if in answer, she sensed him tense against his bonds, hands curling into fists, gaze fixed on the guard behind her.

"Go!" the guard barked when she still hadn't moved.

Before anyone else, even Tristan, could react, Dr. Chase shoved her way past a guard to get to the one who'd shouted. "Enough," she hissed low, glaring up at a man easily twice or three times her size. She gave him her back and faced Dara, her eyes assessing the situation rapidly from behind her glasses.

When she laid a hand on Dara's shoulder, it was like opening the floodgates. Dr. Chase put a calm face on things, but inside she was all chaos. Her mind-voice wasn't just echoing, it was multiple. And all were talking over each other.

—had to fight tooth and nail for him, and now some jackass shot him up—

—fought like an animal—

—didn't help; she's in shock anyway—

—so close to a body bag—

Thank God, I'm finally getting out of here!

Dara flinched, moving away.

Tristan swore.

"She's in shock," Dr. Chase said, keeping her voice low and even. "Get me a blanket and a glass of water."

"We have to keep moving," the guard at the front said.

Dr. Chase ignored him. "Dara?"

Her voice was still echoing in Dara's mind and others were starting to leak through, becoming more agitated with the delay.

—wanted escort and now she won't move—

—can't believe Blanc and Clay—

Hell, she's sweet on the eye; I'd probably do her. But not—

—fucking shuttle is—

—bastard got what he deserved—

She shook her head, slowly easing away from all of them until her back hit the wall. They didn't try to stop her; there was nowhere to run.

Lil' thing is losing it. Can't blame her...

Her legs gave out then. She slid down to the floor, knees to her chest, and started rocking back and forth.

Great. Now we'll never get out of here.

She'd expected her body to stop functioning. But what she hadn't expected was the steady stream of tears. Dara wasn't crying. There were no sobs, though her breaths were choppy. The tears filled her eyes silently, blurring her vision, and slid down her cheeks one after the other. Her eyes became unfocused; the voices faded into a hum. Darkness settled over her, but she was still awake, still aware of what was happening. Only now, it was in a world that she wasn't in, behind a dark veil she couldn't cross.

And on her side of it, the shadows were gathering...

Christ, he couldn't stand this! Two guards and Amelia were between him and his female, and she was fucking *crying*. Each tear cut through him, far worse than the bullet had, and he couldn't do a goddamn thing. Tristan couldn't reach her, physically or mentally. She was so scared, the fog that he'd encountered earlier was nothing compared to the thick blackness that was hiding her now.

It was killing him that he couldn't touch her. His claws were digging into his palms, his wrists somehow straining against the handcuffs, and he could feel them slightly giving way. There would be deadly consequences to his breaking loose, but he was beyond giving a shit about that now. Tristan was so focused on getting to her, shielding her from the others, that he didn't even notice he was moving until one of the guards stepped in his way to stop him.

Over the man's shoulder he could see Amelia stoop down in front of Dara and touch her shoulder again. The little sound of distress she made was like a dagger straight into his brain.

"Back off," the guard warned him.

"Let me take her," he growled, without letting Dara out of his sight. He couldn't. If he looked at the guard, he might just tear the fucker's throat out with his teeth for getting in his way.

Amelia looked at him, clearly calculating the options here. He read her mind easily. She knew Dara wouldn't let anyone touch her now, and without touching her, they wouldn't be able to get her to the shuttle unless she was sedated, and Amelia didn't want that. Somehow they needed to get her moving.

She gave a tight nod and said to the guard, "Release him."

"Dr. Chase—"

"I take full responsibility," she cut in. "Release him."

Heart in his throat, Tristan waited tensely as the guard took for-fuck-ing-*ever* to unlock the handcuffs. He knew the man was just dragging it out in hopes that Amelia would change her mind and stop him, but that infuriated him even more.

As soon as he was free, he shoved past the guard, ignoring the nine firearms that immediately trained on him. Amelia, thankfully, got out of his way before he had to make her. He knelt down in front of Dara, his legs bracketing hers and took a good look at her face. Her expression was blank, her eyes trained on nothing, as if she'd completely checked out, but those tears kept coming in steady streams she seemed completely unaware of.

It scared the shit out of him.

"Dara," he said, hoping his voice would keep her calm.

She didn't respond, and Tristan nearly lost it at the silence that answered him. He fought to keep calm for her sake. Tristan carefully brushed the pad of his thumb over her cheek, catching a tear as it fell. Her breath hitched in a broken gasp, and he could happily have cut off his own hand. "Come on, Dara, I need you to focus for a little bit."

When even that didn't work, he ruthlessly cut through the darkness in her mind, seeking her. Following nothing but instinct to find her.

And find her he did. A small girl, a child, huddled in a forgotten corner of her mind. She was weeping softly, her face hidden against her up-drawn knees. She was flinching every so often as that darkness reached out time and again, invading her space to lash at her. The stuff of nightmares was haunting her, hurting her. It raised every protective instinct he possessed—and a few he hadn't until now—amplified a thousandfold.

Tristan shaped his presence to envelop her, using himself as a shield against those shadows. His mind firmly locked with hers, around hers, Tristan scooped her up in his arms, and relief made his knees quiver when she didn't resist him. "Move," he told the others impatiently.

The guards fell back into formation surrounding them and picked up their speed. The hallways passed so quickly, even if he'd wanted to, Tristan wouldn't have noticed. They passed Herb's front desk, and without sparing him a glance, Tristan sensed the clerk gaping at them. He faintly heard the man say, "What the fuck happened?" but it seemed he didn't expect an answer. Good thing, too, because none of them slowed long enough to give one.

—*Hang on, baby. We're almost there.*—

Amelia fell behind to sign the transfer protocol for all three of them, and a guard witnessed while Herb authorized it. It all took no more than thirty seconds with Amelia's efficient command of the situation, and then, before Tristan knew it, they were at the launch pad.

Once again, the guards flanked the entrance as Amelia led the way inside. Another team of guards waited there, this one trained for transport difficulties. They had a bunk ready—someone must have sent word ahead—and two seats for them, one with built-in restraints.

Only one cabin. Easier to keep an eye on things that way. Tristan didn't mind. At least he'd be able to keep Dara in sight.

"We may need to sedate her," Amelia told him softly. She didn't want the others to overhear.

Tristan gauged Dara's state of mind. She was completely traumatized, scared and in shock. She had no control over her own mind, and right now, he couldn't think of a way to bring her out of it slowly. Much as he hated doing it to Dara, he hated the thought of her suffering all the way to Niren Colony even more. The sedative might just be enough to restart her mind and keep her calm enough in her dreams so Tristan could dull her memories for her. "Do it," he said.

Amelia grimly fished out a syringe from her med kit. When she turned to them again, she met his gaze briefly, as if she sensed that this was a dangerous thing she was about to do. At his sharp nod, she injected the sedative into Dara's arm. The tension left her body almost immediately, and a brief spike of panic stabbed through him.

"Put her down here," Amelia directed.

He made sure her heart was beating strong and steady before he complied. Gently, slowly, he laid Dara down onto the bunk, wincing when her brows drew into a quick frown of protest as he released her completely. Her sleeping mind was at peace. He could have withdrawn and left her to rest, but he didn't. Tristan watched as Amelia raised the bunk's edges to make sure Dara wouldn't slip off during the trip. He should be with her. He should be the one making sure nothing happened to her while she slept.

As if reading his thoughts, Amelia touched his arm, making him flinch. "She'll be fine," she assured him.

Tristan wasn't so sure. At a guard's urging, he took his seat and placed his arms and legs into the restraints. They locked immediately, securing him in place. But at least he could still turn his head to look at Dara.

As soon as Amelia was seated and strapped in, the pilot began the launch sequence. The shuttle rattled as it took off through the launch tunnel, and then there was a brief, blinding flash of light as they emerged aboveground. Within seconds they were out of the planet's orbit, and the window screens darkened to protect against the four suns' glare.

Once they passed the worst of it, Tristan had an unobstructed view of the stars. There were colors he hadn't seen in years, except on a TV screen. Beautiful pinks and purples, greens and blues swirling together, gases colliding and forming new things to fill up the empty space.

It should have been a glorious sight, or at least a great feeling, to finally be free from that underground cave. But there was only the impatient worry that made him seek Dara's sleeping form time and again.

And the devastating, desolate realization that this was just a taste of things to come.

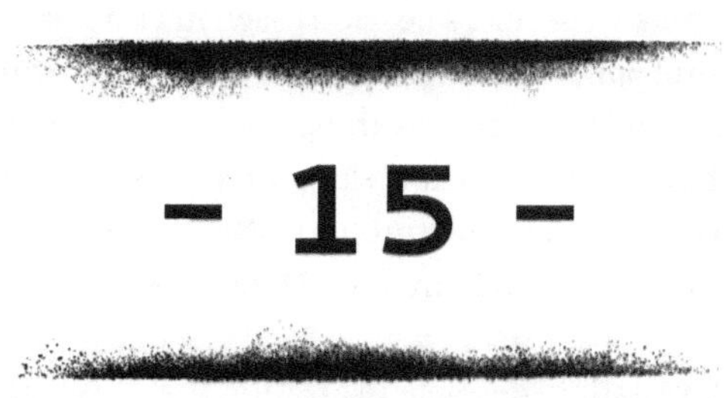

12th day of the 4th Blood Moon, 3028

When a good thing comes along, grab it. Dara's mind was still fuzzy from the tranq, and everything felt like a dream. As far as she was concerned, that was exactly how it was going to remain—a very bad dream that didn't really happen, so there was no reason to freak out about dead bodies, or prisons underground on a faraway planet.

The occasional shiver that passed through her was now an acceptable nuisance compared to the incapacitating shaking from that dream place where she was not going to go again. Ever.

Here, she could see the one solitary sun shining just outside the window. The door was made of wood and plastic, and the bureaucracy was a flourishing piece of art.

Dara was sitting before an empty desk, in a plush, worn chair next to Hunt (unrestrained and sitting in his own chair), because the clerk in charge of checking them in had stepped out to get something authorized. They'd been sitting here alone for a good half hour now. After the nightmare of the past weeks, this felt absolutely surreal and dreamlike, and Dara didn't quite know how to deal with it.

She kept shooting covert glances at Hunt. He hadn't said a word to her since wishing her a good morning when she'd woken up after they'd landed on Niren Colony. Frankly, with security as lax as it was, she was surprised he hadn't even twitched toward the direction of the door. With his… special abilities, he could be out of here and off-world in a matter of minutes, and no one would even hear about him ever again.

There were cookies set out on a plate in the middle of the desk. What kind of prison warden offered his prisoners cookies?

—Lass…—

She shook her head. *Firmly in deny-and-repress mode.* And she was almost done convincing herself everything was normal. If she got distracted back to that-which-she-was-forgetting, everything would come crashing down again. She couldn't take that chance. Dara couldn't handle another meltdown right now. Not when things were starting to look up.

Stubbornly refusing to be ignored, Hunt slinked into her mind with a soft brush of fur against the inside of her brain and curled up like a cat, seemingly relaxed, but she knew he was watching everything she did and thought. For some reason, it soothed her. He wasn't asking anything of her; he was just there, just in case. He was her security blanket now. Dara wasn't sure she could give that up even if she wanted to.

And that scared her. At some point, sooner or later, they *would* be separated, whether confined to this planet or not. And what would she do when she didn't have him to pick up the pieces anymore? Because the likelihood of her falling apart was rising gradually the longer she was in this unbelievably complicated situation.

But that didn't pain her as much as the fact she was automatically assuming he would even care, when he probably couldn't be bothered.

Hunt shoved to his feet—both physically and telepathically—so fast, she flinched. Dara watched him pace back and forth in front of the window, but for someone who hadn't seen sunshine in years, he seemed strangely fascinated with the floor. He was staring at it fixedly, without blinking, and the muscles in his jaw were bunching and jumping in rapid succession. She assured herself that if anyone watching the security feed noticed his eyes glinting briefly gold, they'd attribute it to a play of sunlight.

"Something wrong?" she ventured, feeling unaccountably guilty for his outburst.

"Just stretching my legs," he replied shortly.

Was he going to ignore her now? While he was still grousing and grumbling in her mind? —*What's* up *with you?*—

—*Leave it.*— That was a growl more than a verbal command.

Dara shrugged. —*Fine.*— If he didn't want to talk about it, she wouldn't push him.

—*Insufferable cow.*—

—*Hard-headed jerk-off.*—

His mouth twitched.

In her mind, he now felt almost more animal than human. His shape, when he chose to have one, was vague, but it was huge, and four-legged and furry. With a human mind and consciousness, but animal reactions.

Another concern of hers was purely for him—he was changing, in more ways than even he seemed to realize.

—*I feel it,*— he said, stopping before the window. —*The change.*— There was a painful moment of hesitation in which Dara discovered he knew more than he was telling her. He didn't know how much to tell her, playing a careful balancing game—trying desperately to reach out to her, needing someone to trust, and not wanting to overwhelm her with the scary details.

She contorted herself in her mind into a shape to match him and put her arms around the great beast, burying her face in its fur. His physical body went still as a statue in front of that window, while in her mind, the beast's giant head moved ever so carefully to rest against her shoulder and back. Dara felt the growl-purr rumble in his chest and it rocked her frame with pleasant warmth.

They were looking at each other, gazes locked, but not seeing. In that place of darkness and blind shapes, brilliant green grass grew beneath them, cushioning and soft. The landscape formed as if painted by an artist, stroke by stroke; hills and valleys, meadows filled with flowers, clumps of trees here and there, their branches heavy with leaves and fruits until they nearly touched the ground.

A forest in the distance appeared to her from a bird's eye view, dark and ominous-looking, but it didn't frighten her. The beast she clutched looked out at that forest and sighed almost with longing, and she knew it was his home. The blackness above her gave way to a sky bright with the sun, and clouds vaguely shaped like pictures from a storybook floating across it on a mild breeze.

It wasn't only Tristan's doing. Both of their minds simply decided to add elements of what was missing, and somehow they blended together to form one cohesive world. Dara knew it was complete now, and would hold even when she wasn't there. They'd created a sort of hideaway, like a secret universe only the two of them would ever know about and be able to reach. And they'd created it in that dark corner Dara vaguely remembered from before. There were no more shadows here now, only sunlight and warmth and safety.

The door opened, admitting the administrator, and the two of them finally broke their stares. "Sorry about that," the man said, adjusting his glasses as he read from a paper file. When he looked up and saw Tristan by the window, he half frowned, but hid his unease well.

Tristan casually turned his face up to the sun, and his shoulders rose and fell with a heavy sigh of contentment. Dara could feel the warmth of it on her skin, as if it was her standing there.

"Enjoying the sun?" the administrator queried, making his way to his desk.

"I am," Tristan replied, making no move to return to his seat, deliberately making the man uncomfortable to have a convict at his back.

"Well then, let's get this over with." He spread the file on his desk, next to an already opened one, and made a great show of checking both against the computer screen readout. "I see here that you two have been cellmates in Wolf block. Given the circumstances, that must have been very traumatic for you, Miss Frost."

"Not at all," she replied. When both Tristan and the administrator each raised a skeptical eyebrow at her, she shrugged. *Not about to remember.*

"Well, in any case," the administrator continued, "rest assured that every effort will be made in making you comfortable here." In his mind, she saw what he meant. It was like watching a promotional video for an exotic vacation destination.

There were no cells, only picturesque bungalows with all amenities in an almost idyllic environment. The only restriction was a sort of curfew when all prisoners had to be "at home" for lights out, and the bungalows locked down for the night. The only way off this planet was a launch pad, which was locked and guarded day and night, making it the most heavily guarded thing around, not the prisoners themselves.

There was no comparison between here and where she'd just come from.

"Thank you." she said when the administrator seemed to expect some sort of reply. She wasn't really sure what to say.

He inclined his head graciously and started typing something. "As for you, Mr. Hunt," he said, then looked over his shoulder to find him still standing there. "Excuse me, but the protocol is me sitting here and you over there. I really must insist on it."

Tristan moved, but he took his time about it. When he sat—covertly moving his chair the slightest bit toward Dara's—the administrator straightened in his seat, finally comfortable behind his desk. He even smiled. After some more typing, he continued, "As for you, Mr. Hunt, Dr. Chase has requested your presence in the med camp. You will be under her supervision and care. I hope that agrees with you."

"It doesn't," Tristan said flat out, surprising both Dara and the administrator.

"I'm afraid I don't understand," the suit said.

Of course he didn't. Tristan already had the layout of this place in his mind. The suit had as good as provided him with a map. He now knew that not only was the men's camp separated from the women's, but the med camp was even farther removed from both. As far as days went, prisoners were free to socialize any way they wished, but at night it was solitary confinement. He liked none of this.

The suit had it in his mind that Tristan would be a lab rat rarely, if ever, leaving the med camp to interfere with the "rehabilitation" of the other prisoners. If that was what Amelia expected from him, she had another think coming. "Is Dr. Chase aware of this arrangement?" he asked the suit.

The man checked his files and his computer screen again. "As far as I am aware, she was the one who made them."

Lie.

"Have you been apprised of her research?"

"Not of the details, no. My knowledge does not extend very far beyond you being the main subject of it, but I believe it has something to do with your genetic makeup. Therefore, observation is necessary."

"Close," he said, knowing it would placate the guy to think he knew something that wasn't necessarily his to know. "It has to do with genetics, as they pertain to behavior. Social behavior, to be more exact."

The suit frowned and checked his files again.

—*What are you doing?*— Dara asked. She had that look on her face that said she didn't understand but was doing her damnedest to figure it out. It meant she was finally returning to her old self again. The relief he felt made him want to kiss her.

The suit cleared his throat. "This is something I would of course have to check with Dr. Chase."

"Of course," he agreed.

"What about me?" Dara chimed in. "Dr. Chase is my doctor, too."

"Ah, yes, well, unless you are also part of her research, I have been instructed to set you up on the south side of the women's camp. The area borders a lovely lake."

Tristan leaned forward in his chair and caught the man's gaze. "Are you sure that is a good place for her?" he asked, adding as gentle a push as he was capable of to get him thinking and talking.

The suit nodded, as if hypnotized. "It is the closest to the med lab, which should be convenient for Miss Frost should she need medical care." Just across the lake. A ten-minute swim, as opposed to a twenty-five-minute run from where Tristan would have been placed at the outside border of the men's camp. If the med camp was as lavish and untended as the rest of this colony, then perhaps this arrangement was good enough.

"She's not really a prisoner, you know."

Still not moving of his own accord, the suit nodded again. His voice, at least, sounded normal. The only anomaly in his behavior was that he was unable to look away from Tristan. "Yes, of course. The usual security procedures will not apply to her. The house she's being assigned to will remain unlocked unless she chooses to lock it."

And Tristan could talk to Amelia about his own confinement. *Per-*

fect. "Then I suppose that will have to do. You can go on and finish what you were doing."

As he sat back, the suit shook his head to clear it and frowned at the computer screen, typing commands in rapid progression while they waited in silence.

—What was that all about?— Dara asked.

—Just making sure everything is as it should be.—

—Meaning…?—

He gave her a smile in answer.

"I saw some woods as we were landing," Dara said. She couldn't have seen anything, having been unconscious, but it was a nice cover.

"Yes," the suit said. "Around the med camp. What about them?"

"Are there animals in them?"

"The usual variety, I should think. Rodents and small mammals, some birds perhaps. Are you a zoology enthusiast, Miss Frost?"

"I just want to be sure I don't get devoured on my way to see Dr. Chase."

The way she'd said it brought all kinds of images to Tristan's mind. He reciprocated by sending them all back at her. He could hear her breath catch the slightest bit and her heartbeat speed up. Her scent grew stronger where the heat of her blush intensified it and he had to focus on not crushing the armrests he clutched.

"I can assure you that has never been reported to happen."

—Not yet,— Tristan added.

"That is… r-reassuring." When the suit gave her a look at her odd tone, she cleared her throat. "How much longer?"

The suit consulted his computer screen. "We're done, actually." He closed both files and set them neatly aside, then pushed to his feet. "I can escort you both to the supply dorms to get everything you'll need and then to your new homes. If you'll follow me."

No guards fell into step in front or behind them. It was a little unnerving after years of constantly being watched. As prisons went, this one was a luxurious resort, not a correctional facility. And as long as the government was willing to fund it, Tristan was not going to complain.

They took a winding, graveled path to the supply dorms, a grouping of buildings with signs over doors advertising what they held: Apparel, Groceries, and Supplies. After visiting them, he and Dara each received two large boxes of clothing and a basket of fresh and frozen foods, neatly packed as if from a department store. They were each given a trolley as well—a hovering platform with a handle—to carry everything to their bungalows. They were told that these three dorms were open five days a week in case they needed anything, and then the suit led them down another garden path to the women's camp.

Tristan could already tell the men's camp wouldn't look anywhere near this good. Here, the women had planted colorful flowers; some even had vegetable gardens. There were clotheslines hung with freshly washed clothes—which he couldn't understand since there was a laundering system set up for the entire camp—and lounge areas both in the sun and under the shade of trees.

"It's calming," Dara told him.

"What is?"

"Washing clothes by hand."

"You mean you've done it?"

She smiled in that bright, innocent way, making his chest contract around his heart. Sunlight suited her. "Once or twice when I was a girl, at my grandmother's house." She showed him images of a place much like this one, with children running around, chasing each other between curtains of drying bed sheets. "It takes your mind off other things. And it makes the clothes smell nice when they dry in the sun."

He believed her.

"Here we are," the suit said, stopping in front of a bungalow at the end of the path. Beyond it was a stretch of green grass, and then the lake with a beach and a small wooden pier. "Welcome home, Miss Frost."

Her smile faded, and she hesitated, looking to Tristan.

He couldn't think of anything to say. Not wanting the silence to stretch on too long, he settled for, "I'll see you in a bit."

"At Dr. Chase's discretion, of course," the suit added with a ready smile. Tristan nearly punched him.

—*Watch that temper,*— Dara told him. —*And let me know as soon as you get there, okay?*—

—*Will you miss me, little Dara?*—

She blushed prettily. —*I'll get by.*—

It wasn't the answer he wanted to hear. It bothered him more than it should have.

"See you soon," she said for the suit's benefit.

—*Tonight,*— he promised. With a tight nod, he turned to follow the suit around the lake, schooling himself not to look back. Instead, he closed his eyes and looked through Dara's as she fumbled with the doorknob and entered her bungalow. Her vision was blurred, but she squeezed her eyes shut a moment, and when she opened them, the tears were gone.

"It seems the two of you have gotten quite close," the suit remarked, distracting him. From his tone, he didn't seem enthusiastic about the notion of *close.*

"Given a choice," Tristan said, focusing on making his voice even, "who would you rather *get close* to, a woman like Dara, or the psychopathic serial killer next door?"

The suit opened his mouth to say something, then closed it again, changing his mind. He didn't need to say anything. Didn't need to look over his shoulder at the now empty doorway of Dara's bungalow. Tristan could see inside the man's mind and knew he harbored romantic notions about Dara.

Romantic, because they were so different from the sickening thoughts he'd seen in the minds of men who'd seen her in Wolf block. But no less disturbing. "I suppose you have a point," the man finally said.

Though Tristan knew the suit was too timid to act on what he was thinking, it still pissed him off, and he tightened his grip on the trolley's handle, nearly crushing it. The rest of the way he spent watching the ground he walked on, memorizing the route so he could find his way back. With her scent, he could find her anywhere, reach her over any terrain. It was heartening to know he'd be able to find her so easily.

With that thought in mind, he opened all of his senses to the landscape and let it tell him stories of what secret treasures it held. When they reached the med camp, it was an almost happy Tristan who met Dr. Chase at the doorstep of his new living quarters. The beast in him had found a playground.

But as soon as they reached her, Tristan knew something was wrong. It put him on guard, his good mood diminishing rapidly.

"Thank you, Mr. Hillcroft," Amelia said to the suit, "I can take it from here." She didn't even look at Tristan. He nudged at her mind to investigate what the hell was going on, but for once, the good doctor was locked down tight.

"As you wish," the suit said. "Welcome to Niren Colony, Mr. Hunt. Dr. Chase, I leave him in your capable hands."

Amelia waited until he was completely gone before she turned on her heels and marched into the house. "Come in," she said, and her tone was all professional detachment.

Interesting, he thought as he followed.

The house had a similar layout as those in the other camps. There was a bedroom, kitchen, and bathroom, even a sort of living room. Small, but compared to his previous accommodations, a mansion. Right off the bat he noticed the distinct lack of camera feeds. No doubt there would be some in Amelia's lab, but it looked as if every courtesy was being extended to him. For the moment.

So why did Amelia have her panties in such a twist? "What's going on?" he inquired.

"We need to talk."

He almost groaned. That never boded well. "All right," he said and set everything down in one corner to be unpacked later. He took the groceries to the kitchen to be stored in a refrigerator. Tristan didn't want anything to spoil. His culinary expertise was limited to boiling water, but eating raw food was better than eating spoiled food.

Amelia was staring out the living room window when he met her there. "Have a seat," she said without facing him.

"I think I'd rather stand," he said, just to be contrary.

Finally, she turned to him, her sharp eyes trained on him. "You know, it's started occurring to me lately that there should be a biological reason for chem-resistance. I mean, sure, bugs do it all the time. Find a way to kill them and they adapt to be resistant to that poison."

"Makes sense."

"But, you see," she continued, as if she'd caught him in a lie, "mammalian anatomy is much more complicated than an invertebrate's.

Our systems are more evolved, each interconnected part serving a specific and precise function. There's always a reason for everything, and it always has to do with the internal, rather than the external."

"I'm… not following."

"You don't adapt one part of your system to deal with one specific external stimulus. You adapt the entire system to deal differently with a *number* of external stimuli."

"Are we talking human race, here, or me specifically?"

Amelia sat on the couch and leaned back, studying him again in that unnerving way of hers, as if she was trying to figure out all of his secrets. "Good question," she said.

"All right, you're being cryptic. That's not like you. What's going on?"

"I came into possession of the security feed from the night of your attack."

Fuck.

"I can see from the look on your face you're beginning to follow my train of thought. Perhaps you should take that seat now."

He did. "What did you see on it?"

"I saw that you lied to me. Or, more precisely, misled me. I was under the impression that, aside from your musculature and sensory perception, nothing had changed after the DNA treatments had been stabilized."

"What the hell was on that feed?"

"To the untrained eye, nothing," she said, and Tristan relaxed a little. "Security was already aware of your heightened senses, so the fact that you seemed to be aware of people approaching was taken as a matter of course. They also knew about your speed and strength, so the outcome of the fight had been a foregone conclusion. I only had a hunch, must have noticed something that others would not. And then I had to slow the feed down to almost frame by frame, and magnify a great deal to see that you had fangs. Big enough to begin altering your facial structure."

"I didn't feel anything at the time." It was true. He'd been so focused on ripping into his prey, he hadn't felt any pain at all. And there must have been pain when bones rearranged themselves. Tristan just hadn't noticed.

"The point is," Amelia said, leaning forward, "that you've just thrown a variable into the equation I thought I'd already disqualified as a participant, and I want to know why."

Tristan raised a brow. "You think I did this on purpose?"

She rolled her eyes. "No, that's not what I meant. I meant that your body started changing for a reason. I'll have to do some tests to figure out what triggered it." She chuckled without humor. "Unless you know, and feel like telling me?"

Tristan had a feeling he just might know. But he wasn't about to tell her.

"I didn't think so. So tell me, was that the first time you'd changed?"

He considered the repercussions of the answers he had to give and the possibility of her asking for them. Saw no harm in this one. "No."

"Would you mind being a little more specific?"

"That time with the blood in the sink," he said.

She waved him on.

Tristan shifted in his seat. "My hands changed. I grew claws."

"What were you doing at the time?"

"Sleeping."

"Dreaming?"

"Yes."

"About what?"

"I don't remember."

"You're lying."

"It was some kind of a nightmare. I woke up and punched the wall. My claws stabbed into my palms."

He could see the wheels turning in her head as she watched him a while. "Was it fear- or anger-initiated?"

"What's it matter?"

"Just answer the question, please."

"Both."

Again she paused, as if debating what to say next. In an unguarded instant, he caught the direction of her thought. *Fear is triggered externally. Without the trigger, there is no reaction. Better option—he's safe here. Anger is more unpredictable. Can't account for internal variables.* "How long did it take your hand to heal?"

He hadn't exactly been timing it. He gave his best estimate. "Hours for the skin to close completely. After a day or two there wasn't even a scar left."

She seemed impressed. As well she should be. An injury like that, one that had damaged muscle, tendon, and bone, should have taken at least a week, if not longer—with extensive medical treatment. Without it, under normal circumstances, he'd probably never have regained full use of his hand.

"I'd like to take some blood for testing."

"I'm at your service, as always."

"Once I get more information, I'll be able to estimate the progression of the mutation so far, and in the future."

"You think I'll change more?"

"It's too early to tell."

"You're lying."

She sighed in frustration. "You forget, I didn't expect you to change *at all*. I don't know enough about what's happening to you to give you a prognosis at this time."

"But you know enough to judge whether it will get better or worse."

Amelia curled her hands around her knees, clearly not wanting to say too much. "In previous studies, anyone who's gotten to this point progressed rapidly to a full physical change. None of them survived long enough to be studied." *They died in their dreams,* she was thinking.

In her mind, she was putting together case after case of people having died during sleep. A body at rest would not have reacted. The proper catalyst had to be some kind of sensory or emotional stimulus. Ergo, all of those people were killed by their dreams. Good or bad, it didn't matter. The change was what had ultimately killed them.

And because they'd all been in their beds at night when it had happened, no one had been able to monitor them.

"But none of the previous subjects have been chem-resistant. It could be that that's the difference. Maybe your chemical makeup is slowing this down, giving your body time to adjust, like a child that's still growing."

She made it sound almost like a good thing, but postponing the inevitable was still not preventing it. He could still die; only the timeline was different.

Thinking out loud now, she continued. "Or maybe it works like a vaccine. We introduced a foreign virus into your body, and your chemical makeup is working to integrate it into your system. With a regular immune system, you'd just create antibodies to fight off the infection. But what if, instead of that, the infection becomes a part of your system and somehow works *with* your body instead of against it?"

"So what you're saying is, you don't know."

"Not *yet*," she said. "But the equipment here is almost better than back on New Alaska. A few dozen tests should give me plenty of data to analyze. If, of course, you cooperate."

"Why wouldn't I?"

"Why, indeed," she returned. "Tell me, how is Dara doing?"

Danger! Trick question! "She's still shaken up," he said, considering his words carefully.

"Of course; I would be, too. How is she taking the separation?"

Tristan shifted in his seat a little. "Didn't seem too broken up about it. Why?"

"And how are *you* taking it?"

"Okay, what are you up to now?"

Amelia shrugged. "It's merely a psychological phenomenon that occurs sometimes. Prisoners tend to form strong bonds with their cellmates and display some difficulties in coping with change when they are separated."

"We haven't been cellmates long enough to get psychologically attached." Psychically, though…

"I didn't say it was a psychological bond. I said it was a psychological *reaction* to separation. The bond, by all accounts, is very much emotional. For example, you've been without a cellmate for—how long was it?"

"Ten years," he grated.

"That is a long time without a friend."

"You overestimate my need for social connection."

"Do I? I don't think so. Everyone needs some kind of social connection. Everyone on New Alaska had some sort of friend—and I use that term loosely. But you seem to have purposely alienated yourself from everyone around. Almost as if you were punishing yourself." Again, she gave him that analytical look.

"You've interacted with those people. Tell me, which one of them would you choose to get friendly with?"

"Dara Frost," she said without hesitation. "Which is why I find it difficult to believe that having met someone *normal*, and spent time with her in very close proximity for weeks, you don't feel separation anxiety now that you're not together anymore."

"Are you done with your romantic musings yet?" he snapped, quickly losing patience. "Because there is a private shower just behind that door with my name on it." More likely, he'd be going for a swim in the lake, but she didn't have to know that. Or any of what she was asking about now.

Amelia's brows went up in surprise, and she leaned back again, looking at him as if he'd sprouted a second head. Which, given his current chemical state—or physiological, whatever the hell it was— might actually be a possibility. "Interesting," she said. "I never said anything about romance."

Ah, shit. "Twisting my words now?"

"Come to think of it, on the feed from that night, I saw that you had switched bunks with Dara at some point." She prudently didn't mention what she might have seen on that feed *before* that. "Did you suspect they were coming for her?"

He'd known it. He'd seen it. Tristan said nothing now, just held Amelia's gaze, hoping to make her drop the subject and get the hell out.

Her expression softened. "Your eyes are changing. The same way they did when I told you about the new study."

Tristan looked away, shocked that the mere idea of Dara in any kind of danger could cause such a reaction in him. He hated being so far from her. Anything could happen, and he'd never get to her in time. And it pissed him off that he was apparently completely transparent about it.

"I'll leave," Amelia finally said and pushed to her feet. "I just have one last question before I go." Because she seemed to be waiting for it, he looked at her again. "Were you dreaming about Dara the night your own claws stabbed through your hands?"

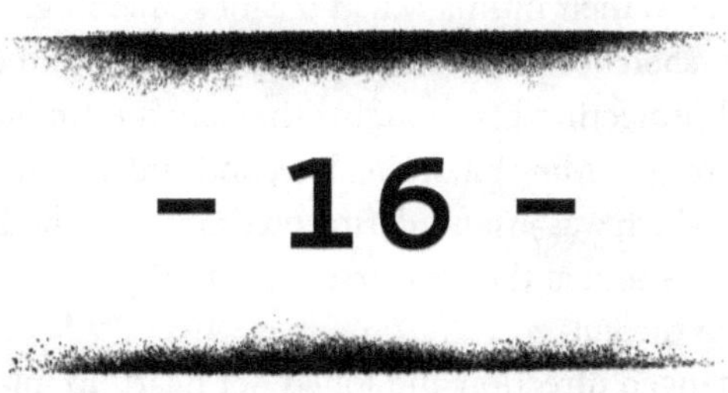

- 16 -

13th day of the 4th Blood Moon, 3028

He didn't come. After he'd promised he would come see her, he hadn't shown. Dara didn't really know what to think about that. Or about the sharp stab of disappointment she'd felt when she'd woken up this morning, all cramped up from having slept in the armchair. *I fell asleep waiting for him…*

I freaking fell asleep there, waiting *for him!* And the bastard hadn't shown.

No explanation, not even a notice. He'd actually pulled a whole new mental trick Dara might pay big bucks to learn. Every time she'd tried talking to him across their link, it had felt as if she was talking right through him; and if he'd heard a thing, he'd given no sign of it.

It… *hurt.* Which surprised Dara, and then it pissed her off. She knew how attached people could get in intense situations, but she'd thought she was stronger than that.

Oh, who was she kidding? Dara was a wuss. Always had been. Running away and hiding was her MO. She'd even been running away from herself, her abilities, before Hunt had forced her to face them.

The one thing she hadn't run away from was this whole mess with Tristan. Possibly the one thing she'd had legitimate reason *to* run from.

The sad—and by that, she meant *pathetic*—thing was, it would have always come to this, regardless of anything. It had only been a matter of time. Dara had known Tristan would cut her loose. But she'd actually believed their intimacy had meant something.

Obviously, she'd been mistaken. Tristan had to be far better at controlling and projecting his thoughts than she'd estimated, because she'd fallen for that *Mine* bit, hook, line, and sinker. She still wanted to believe it, which was just bordering on desperate—he'd thrown her over for his freedom at the very first opportunity.

A punch in the gut.

Which changed direction and jolted her heart up into her throat where it couldn't beat.

And it hurt.

So she was ignoring *him* for a change.

This morning, when she'd realized what he'd done—or rather *hadn't* done—she'd put up her strongest shields and built them up to withstand a telepathic bomb blast. There was total silence in Dara's brain and it felt… righteous. Maybe a little lonely, but really, normal people went through their whole lives with only themselves in their heads. *I better get used to it.*

Breakfast this morning was a lovely bowl of fresh berries, a far cry from the colorless, shapeless, tasteless goop of the weeks previous. She was determined to enjoy every last morsel. She sat at her very own table, windows open to let in the sunlight and fresh air, which carried with it a hint of lake. The audio system played a song she didn't know but happened to like, and she tapped her foot to its rhythm, wriggling in her seat as she popped a big red strawberry into her mouth. Her eyes almost rolled back in her head with pleasure. *Heaven.*

The authoritative knock on her door completely shattered her idyllic reverie.

Dara glared at the door. If Hunt thought she would let him in after standing her up, he had another think coming. She pretended not to hear and picked out a raspberry.

It was poised on her lip, about to roll down onto her tongue and be squished against the roof of her mouth, when the knock came again. "Go away!" The raspberry went into her mouth, but her ire made the taste disappear down her throat before she'd even had a chance to relish it.

And the knocking continued!

"I said go away, Hunt," she shouted. "I don't want to see you right now."

"Miss Frost," came a muffled voice from outside—a *strange* voice.

Apprehension gave her gooseflesh, and her hands balled into fists on the tabletop. "Who is it?" she called back, not moving from her seat.

"My name is Agent Calen. I am with a special cases agency based on Earth. I'd like to speak to you for a few minutes, if you don't mind."

Shit. Oh, shit! For a split second, Dara started dismantling her mental shields, sheer panic making her reach out to the person she'd come to rely on in these types of *very bad* situations. But she stopped herself, straightening in her seat. She couldn't rely on Hunt. He wouldn't always be there; he wasn't keen on being there *now*, as he'd demonstrated last night.

Still, he had taught her a lot. And Dara was nothing if not an apt student. That she even *had* shields now spoke volumes about how far she'd come.

This was a golden opportunity for Dara to prove her mettle, and show everyone that she could take care of herself. She would see the agent, spin some lies, feign exhaustion/insanity/PMS, and send him on his way thinking how lovely their chat had gone.

She hesitated only a little getting to her feet. Padding barefoot across the spotless floors to the door, she even wriggled her toes a little, enjoying the feel of not having to wear shoes again for fear of what she might be stepping into.

She stalled again as she reached for the doorknob. *What if I can't do it?*

Another knock startled her into moving again. Too late to pretend she wasn't home. "I'm coming," she said, swallowing her apprehension.

The door opened.

On the other side, half-in and half-out of the shadow cast by the awning, stood a man about six feet in height, with immaculately combed hair, wearing a nondescript suit and shined shoes. His hands were at his sides, relaxed, but giving the impression that he was standing at attention. There was a certain alertness to him, an energy that belied the easy smile on his face. Dara supposed he was even handsome. In a plastic, I-am-ruled-by-the-government-and-they-buy-my-underpants sort of way. Just looking at him gave her a wedgie.

"Good morning, Miss Frost," he said.

Dara was surprised she wasn't getting any sense of him, no tidbit of information—and then she remembered her shields. She left them in place for the moment. "Agent…?"

"Calen," he supplied. The introduction was followed by the classic reach into his pocket, the showing of the badge. Count *one, two, three* seconds. The badge holder closed and returned to the pocket. Practiced movements she'd seen a lot in the days preceding her trial and incarceration. Back then, she'd answered every question they'd asked, telling them the truth, in as much detail as she could recall without embellishment and without revealing she could read minds.

Back then, she'd been naive and trusting.

Her current circumstances were swiftly—some might say brutally—curing her of that affliction.

"Can we talk for a moment?"

Dara stood aside to let the agent in. He smiled again as he passed her, as if he was trying very hard not to frighten her. The back of her head itched, and she scratched at it while his back was turned.

Calen waited politely while she closed the door. He didn't make himself at home, didn't commandeer a seat on her couch, or at the table, where her half-eaten breakfast was laid out. His gaze moved over the surroundings, taking in everything with a casual glance. Dara was almost 99 percent certain he would be able to recall the smallest detail of her new home.

Not that there was much to see; she hadn't really unpacked yet. Too busy waiting for the bastard who hadn't shown.

Bastard.

It bore repeating. *Bastard!*

"Sit, please," she invited, because he was still standing and it made her nervous.

"Thank you," he said, taking a seat at the table, across from her bowl. "I seem to have interrupted your meal. Please, continue. This won't take too much time."

Dara shrugged and sat down to her fruit bowl. As she happily munched on a handful of blueberries, she slowly lowered a layer of her shields. That itch at the back of her head returned. Only this time she realized it was on the inside of her skull. *What the hell…*

"So what is it you want to talk about?"

"I assume you know why you have been transferred to this facility," he said conversationally. "There's been another murder, in the same style as the one you were accused of committing. It would seem to prove your innocence."

That was a very careful choice of words. "*Seem* to?"

"There is, of course, a process. Procedure to follow. We need to gather as much evidence as we can in order to vindicate you completely."

She needed to see into his mind. Another layer of shields came down. The itch became nearly unbearable. What *was* that? She picked through the assortment of berries in her bowl to give herself time to examine it. With each layer she shed, the itch got deeper. It was as if…

Ice settled deep into her bones.

It was a probe!

She opened a doorway in her shields, rebuilding her connection with Hunt. For one frantic instant, she forced her mind to meld with his, shoving her perceptions at him. He jerked from sleep, sitting up, now wide awake.

—*Delay!*— she heard before Hunt slammed the doorway shut again and added a good number of his own shields around her.

Son of a bitch! It had never even occurred to her the government might already have telepaths on the payroll—much less that they'd bother sending one after her.

"Miss Frost?" Calen said. "Are you okay?"

Would you *be okay if someone was trying to root through your brain with all the subtlety of a sledgehammer?* "Fine," she said. "It's just…" *Just what?* "I guess I just wish they'd put up this sort of effort before I was sent to New Alaska." *Excellent save!*

"I apologize. I wasn't on the case then. If I was, I can assure you it would have been."

I'll just bet. That itching intensified. If she didn't want him to catch on, she'd have to let him through. It was a risk, but what else could she do? So she… shifted her shields to gradually expose her memories of the murder she'd dreamed, hoping it would feel to him like they were merely resurfacing. A few stray images of New Alaska, but nothing more than a glimpse, and nothing connected in any way with Tristan.

Act normal, Dara reminded herself. She picked another strawberry from her bowl and popped it into her mouth. She didn't even taste its juices. Nearly choked on it as she swallowed. Where the hell was Tristan? She was in way over her head here!

"Look," Calen said, his probe receding. Had his face paled? He'd definitely leaned back farther in his seat, as if he was subtly trying to get away from her. "I can't imagine how tough the last few weeks have been on you. Especially since we've been informed that you'd opted to be placed in Wolf block. A foolish choice, I think."

Hazy memories surfaced, sharp emotions welling in swift succession. Dara frowned, making an effort to push them back. No time for nightmares. She forced a careless shrug. "I like wolves."

He considered her for a moment. "I've dealt with a number of cases like yours," he said carefully. "Much as I hate to admit, our legal system leaves something to be desired. There have been cases when a person was accused of a crime they hadn't committed. Sometimes the accused themselves begin to doubt their innocence."

He paused there. It wasn't a question, but he was definitely fishing for an answer. The safest course of action was probably to play into his preconceptions. "I suppose that makes sense," she said, more into her bowl than to him. "The lawyers can be very convincing with their facts."

Calen nodded, as if he'd expected this. "Was Wolf block meant to be a form of penance? Are you a religious person, Miss Frost?"

"Are you, Mr. Calen?" she returned, meeting his gaze. She considered taking a risk, testing his mind. If she stayed very still, she might be able to pull it off.

"Religious? I suppose. My parents took me to church as a child. Before the government closed religious sites in our city. The priest was… relocated after that."

Keep him talking. If he's distracted, he won't notice. "I've never been in a church. What's it like?"

"Dark," he said with a small smile. "But in a comforting way. The windows were stained glass; not much sunlight got through. But the candles made up for it."

She imagined a door while he talked. A plain door in the middle of nothing. As she'd done with Tristan once, Dara shaped her consciousness into mist, slipping quietly through the keyhole into Calen's mind. She had to be careful. If he caught her, she was as good as dead.

As she saw herself through his eyes, through the veil of judgments he'd already passed over her, scenes from his childhood drifted all around her like ghosts. She made her face smile and blink for his benefit, encouraging him to continue while she slowly acclimated herself to the pathways of his mind.

It was different from the way Tristan's mind felt. She couldn't explain it, couldn't pinpoint the difference, but it definitely felt foreign. Like entering another country where they spoke English. The language was the same, but the landscape and customs were completely alien. She made her form spread out slowly, carefully, over as much territory as she could, simply absorbing whatever she found and storing it away to be examined later.

Dara had to be fast; she couldn't get greedy. The longer she stayed there, the greater her chance of being discovered. When she thought she was about to reach her limits, she retreated, flowing back into herself. "Sounds almost magical," she said, and had to clear her throat to stop sounding so mechanical.

The smile remained on Calen's face, but his eyes turned hard as he leaned forward again. "Why don't we do away with the pleasantries, Miss Frost? You know something you're not telling me. I cannot tell you how ill-advised that is."

She frowned. "Whatever I know about what happened, I already told the investigating officers and the court."

He nodded, not looking the least bit convinced. "I should tell you that I have been authorized to extract information from you any way I can."

At this, Dara raised an eyebrow, swiftly sorting through what she'd managed to get from him. Unfortunately, it seemed she'd gotten nothing of use. "What does that mean? Torture?" Again she opened a channel to Tristan and passed on everything she'd gleaned, then closed the link. She got the sense that he was nearing, but he'd stopped momentarily, surprised by what she'd given him.

"If it comes to that," Calen said.

"I really don't like pain," she confided. "Especially because I am a woman. We seem to get more than our fair share of it, if you know what I mean."

He ignored that. "How did you know a murder was occurring?"

A trick question. But he was very subtle about it. All hard-faced and intent, as if he was asking something she'd already answered a dozen times, but wanted to catch her in a lie. "I didn't. I knew after the fact."

"Were you at any time during the past three months in contact with the murderer?"

Define contact… "No."

Calen's gaze flickered over her face and posture to spot a lie, and Dara couldn't be sure if he saw anything. She couldn't feel his mental probe anymore. It worried her a little. "How did you know anything at all, then?"

"A dream. It felt very real. Maybe some sort of premonition? But about the past… if that makes any sense." She brought her nightmare to the surface of her shields in case he was still broadcasting and she just couldn't feel it. Shouldn't he know she was blocking him? Maybe he wasn't as strong as he thought.

The door opened with enough force to make her jump. "Hey, Dara," Tristan called, "you coming? The water's great."

Calen raised an eyebrow. "Friend of yours?"

Friend, ex-lover, guard dog, the scary thing with huge fangs that stalks people at night…

"I am very sociable," she told him, then to Tristan, she said, "Come in, there's berries."

He was at the table instantly. "I love berries," he said with a grin for Calen's benefit. He may as well have been another agent. His charm was all a mask. Underneath it, his sharp mind missed nothing.

"Are you who I think you are?" Calen asked him.

Tristan shrugged, taking a handful of berries and throwing them into his mouth one at a time. "I don't know who you think I am," he said between bites. "These are good." He took another handful.

Calen looked Dara over speculatively. "Hmm. Sociable, indeed."

Dara took offense at his tone. Instead of talking to the agent, she addressed Tristan. "You want to sit?"

He shook his head. "I don't want to ruin your chairs. I'm all wet from the lake."

It was only then she noticed that, except for his bare feet, he was fully dressed. Soaked through and making a puddle on the floor.

"Were you pushed into the lake?" Calen asked.

Tristan turned his gaze on the agent. "People don't push around a man like me."

"I'll keep that in mind."

What was it with men and their thinly veiled threats of excessive violence? "Are we done here?" she demanded of the agent.

"I got what I came here for," Calen said cryptically and got to his feet. "You are… a remarkable surprise, Miss Frost. But you're not as subtle as you think." He straightened his immaculate suit. "Get comfortable here, Miss Frost. It'll be a while before you'll be allowed to leave. Especially if you don't cooperate."

"You know, it just figures that a government operative would pick on someone who can't defend herself," Tristan said. "Why don't you try your tricks on me? See what happens."

"No, I have no ties to the government," he said offhandedly. "I am an acquisitor, Mr. Hunt, if you'll pardon the crude metaphor. I have a shopping list and, well, let's just say you're not on it. For now. Someone will be in touch, Miss Frost."

"What the fuck did you do?" Anger overrode the sheer terror that had fueled him on his way here. The agent was gone and now there was no one to focus it on but Dara.

"Where were you?" she demanded at the same time, shoving at him.

His jaw ached like the devil, and his fingers itched like there was an army of ants digging their way through his flesh. It was all Tristan could do not to bare his fangs and pin her to the ground. "Are you out of your fucking mind?" he snarled. "Weeks I spent teaching you, training you. I leave for *one day* and you throw it all away with one monumental fuck up. Do you want to die?"

"How the hell was I supposed to know they'd send a telepath?" She shoved at him again, which just stoked his rage. "If you'd been here, maybe you could have warned me. I'd have been better off if I'd never met you! Then they would have just chalked it up to dumb luck that I saw anything at all."

He heard the growl in his mind a split second before his head started splitting like a log. The pain was blinding. He roared, clutching his head to keep it from exploding, and all the while his claws dug into his skull. Dara's fright barely registered as his back bowed, making him bend forward. His muscles tightened until he thought they would tear like his clothes, popping stitch by stitch.

Through the thundering of his heart and the roar of pain inside his head, he heard his breaths rumbling in and out of his lungs like a giant bellows. He didn't even try moving his jaw; it felt wired shut, but he knew it was because his fangs had changed before his face could.

Then his face did change, and he screamed. And the sound was more animal than human.

The shifting and tearing and breaking inside him brought him to his knees, his body rearranging into something else. He didn't have time to be afraid. The pain consumed him, blinding him to his surroundings and deafening him to everything, even Dara's frantic voice inside his head. Tristan had the impression of her terror and the scent of her nearness, but that was it.

Then he felt her arms around him and it was agony far beyond what he was already feeling. He was two seconds away from shoving her off him, no matter the consequences, when he felt her in his mind. She muscled her way inside, took advantage of his inattention and forced her will on him, taking control when he could not. She filled his mind with pictures of green fields, a forest in the distance, spurred him on to run there, run where he was safe.

Tristan obeyed, because it was the only thing he could do. He ran. With ground-eating lopes, he fled for those trees, aching for the sweet coolness of shadow and dew. And each time his paws met the ground, he saw himself a man. Eyes glowing golden, fierce, body larger, stronger, but human. Dara didn't let the pain touch his mind, though his body writhed, tormented.

Then the blinding sunlight was gone, and he was in the trees. The pain began to subside, leaving a dull ache he could at last control. Tristan forced himself to breathe slowly, evenly, though his ribs felt broken. He focused on that coolness in his mind, in the forest, filled the places around him with giant trees and snarls of enormous, twisting roots, perfect hiding places. He put birds in the trees, and insects hissing and chirping on the ground. Their songs muted the drum of his heartbeat, eased the pain in his head.

He felt his fingers changing, contorting back to their normal shape, and there was no pain in that. His fangs receded, dormant once more, and with them gone, his face changed back, and he could finally flex his jaw.

Tristan was back. On the floor, shaking uncontrollably, with Dara's arms still around him and his fingers digging into her to hold her there. He didn't dare open his eyes, fearing what he would see in hers when she looked at him.

After analyzing his blood, Amelia had tried for hours on end last night to trigger a change in him, using everything from sensory stimuli to chemical injections. Nothing had worked. Nothing had so much as altered his senses. What was it about Dara that had this effect on him?

He could already hear people approaching at a run. No doubt the ruckus he'd made had attracted an audience, but he knew Amelia was among them, probably with an EMT or two.

He was going to need them. The new patch he'd been fitted with would have transmitted throughout his change, and Amelia would have every detail of it saved in her notepad. Tristan could save her the trouble and just tell her what happened. Except that he didn't feel much like talking at the moment.

Christ, how was he still breathing after that?

As his head slowly stopped spinning, he became more and more aware of his immediate surroundings. Dara was shivering against him. He was cold in his wet clothes, on the hard floor, and… he smelled blood.

A group of people forced their way into the bungalow.

"Get my kit!" Amelia ordered, coming toward them.

"What the hell have you done to him?" Dara yelled. She was crying, and Tristan couldn't even sit up by himself to try to comfort her. He wanted to tell her he was all right, but couldn't manage to get his mouth working properly. The beast he'd become inside his mind was no longer capable of human speech.

Strong arms lifted him onto a stretcher. Hands pried him away from Dara. They were all talking, thinking at the same time, and he couldn't make sense of it. Dara was arguing with Amelia. A team of four orderlies were cataloging his physical state in their minds, thinking the same thing in different orders, confusing the fuck out of him.

And then they were outside, and the glittering sunlight warmed his chilled flesh. They were moving fast toward Amelia's labs, through the forest where the quick flashes of light between tree limbs made his eyes want to roll back in his head. Tristan reached blindly for Dara. She was there, he could hear her, feel her in his mind, but she was on a different platform behind him.

Once again, they emerged from the forest, from shadow to sunlight to cool darkness as he was brought inside the facility. Once more, the flood of voices washed over him, more people coming close, watching, talking, debating.

His eyes fluttered open for a moment as the tranquilizer jabbed into his shoulder.

Before he passed out, he saw Dara on a stretcher not five feet from him, her arm in bandages, soaked with blood.

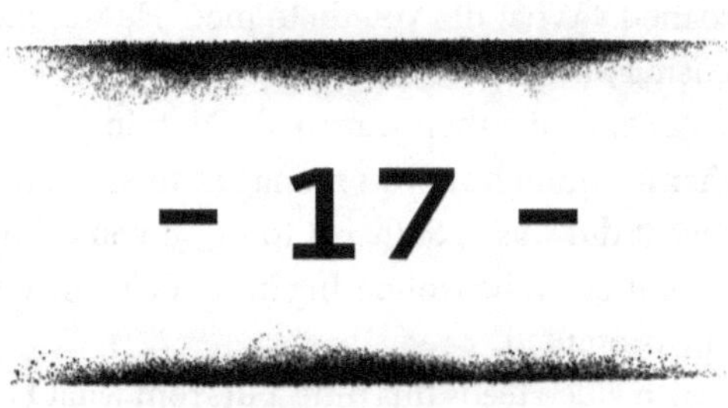

- 17 -

15th day of the 4th Blood Moon, 3028

It was dark when he finally came to his senses and opened his eyes, and for a moment, Tristan thought he'd gone blind. He fought his way through the thick fog of grogginess and tried to sit up. He couldn't. Baffled, he twisted his wrists inside the restraints. His legs were bound up to his knees and he could feel a band stretching across his chest.

He pulled sharply with one arm and broke the restraints, muscles screaming. It hurt too much to do the same with the other, so he felt with his free hand for the release mechanisms. "Lights," he croaked, but his voice wasn't loud enough. His mouth was parched and his throat was sore. Tristan moistened his lips with a sticky tongue and tried again. "*Lights.*" They came on instantly, piercing needles into his head through his eyes. "Low," he said. The lights dimmed.

Free of the restraints on his upper body, he tried to sit again. He had to twist to his side and do it by degrees. By the time he'd started working on the bands over his legs, Amelia came in, a tranquilizer in her hand.

"Are we suspending civilities between us, lass? Has it come to that, then?"

"How are you feeling?" She pocketed the syringe.

"Like I was run over by a shuttle." *Repeatedly.*

Amelia came to help him with the restraints and adjusted the bed so he could sit up and lean back. "We've had a trying couple of days."

Tristan groaned. "What did you do to me?" He was having a hard time just focusing his mind to form a sentence.

"Nothing," Amelia said, then amended, "Nothing else. You started a physical change. Somehow you managed to stop and reverse it, but the damage it did was… Suffice it to say, if you didn't have your regenerative abilities, I'd be wondering how you're alive right now."

"Tell me," he prompted.

"There were no video feeds this time, but from what I could gather from Dara—"

"Dara!" Tristan straightened so quickly, a rib that had just healed cracked again. "Where is she? Is she okay?"

Amelia pushed him to lean back again. "She's fine. She's resting from the surgery, but the damage wasn't as bad as it looked."

He brushed her hands away.

"Tristan you can't—she's sleeping. You need to rest!"

Tristan was already hobbling out the door. "So either help me or shut up."

She didn't help. But she followed close behind, and he didn't need to see inside her head to guess what she was thinking.

Tristan followed his instinct, dragging his feet down one long corridor, then another, leaning on the wall for support when his knees buckled, until he found her. There was a large window into her room; he could see her on the bed, bandaged, with tubes stuck in both arms. She was sleeping, but he could tell how weak she was.

"From what I could gather," Amelia said, "you changed about halfway. It was mainly in your upper body, mostly your head and chest and arms—it seems to progress downward, which would appear to confirm my theory that the trigger must be perceived. And it's also why you can walk now. Your legs weren't affected as much."

"Damage?"

"Torn muscles, broken ribs, dislocated joints, massive internal bleeding…"

"Not to me," he said. "To her."

"Dara sustained some muscle strain and a number of deep cuts. She was trying to hold on to you is my guess, even when your body mass increased beyond what she could handle. When you reached out to her, your claws cut pretty deep. One of the claw marks was millimeters from her lung. A single deep breath and it could have been punctured."

Tristan staggered back.

"Tristan, she'll be fine. I'm more concerned about you. You kept… changing after we brought you in here. We had to keep you under for almost two days now."

I'd have been better off if I'd never met you!

Christ, lass, I'm sorry.

He turned and started back to his own room. "So what's next?"

Amelia hesitated. "What do you mean?"

"Don't play coy, Doc." He attempted a smile, but doubted she was fooled. "There's probably a million new ideas in that head of yours. So where do we start? A new serum to control the change? More chemicals to make me invincible?"

"No. No more serums."

Tristan stopped, hearing something in her tone. "Explain."

"I told my superiors that you died. With no more viable subjects, I can shut down the experiment. Not that anyone besides me cares whether other people would be hurt if I kept going, but the higher-ups agreed it's time to cut their losses. I'm sorry, Tristan. I believe the risk is just too great to continue."

"It's even greater if you cut me loose!"

Amelia had that look on her face, the same one she'd had back when she'd tried to explain that he'd been infected with a mutation virus. She was considering her words very carefully before she spoke them. "There is…nothing more I can do. On a chemical level. The damage has been done, your DNA is changed, and there is no way to stop or reverse it. The only controlling factor left is the strength of your mind."

"What do you mean?" he said slowly.

She gently ushered him to keep going. "I told you, the trigger must be perceived. It might be emotional, but emotions are triggered by something, too. A memory. A sight or sound. If you can anticipate the trigger, control your emotions, you might be able to control whether you change or not. But that's something I can't help you with."

"And if I wanted to learn to harness it? Learn to control the change so it doesn't kill me?"

"I would strongly advise against it."

"I don't have that option. Too many memories."

He was still looking at his hands, seeing claws that weren't there, covered with Dara's blood, when Amelia's hand covered his. "It could kill you."

Tristan focused on his hand, willingly remembered Dara's fear. His fingers changed, nails darkening, sharpening to claws. He did it slowly, keeping careful control of his body, not moving an inch. His hand ached as it transformed, but it was nothing compared to the pain he'd felt before.

It didn't shift fully into a furry paw, but when Amelia turned his hand over, he could see the pigment of his skin changing to what the fur would look like. Stripes. "You said it yourself." He tried not to flinch when Amelia squeezed the pad of one of his fingers to bring out his claw to its full length. "The controlling factor is the strength of my mind."

"That is only a small part of it."

"Then we do it by degrees."

"Do you think you can control it that way?"

"I have to," he said fiercely. His past hadn't killed him. Wolf block hadn't killed him. He sure as hell wouldn't let something like this bring him down. Just another skill to hone and perfect. Just like telepathy. Besides, it was only his body. As long as no one fucked with his mind…

Tristan almost turned back to go to Dara. The more of the animal he let out, the more it made his body want to go to her. His rational mind knew there was nothing he could do for her except cause more pain, and that for her safety he had to stay away. But his primal instincts, already off the charts where she was concerned, were starting to rule him more and more, commanding him to stay with her, watch over her. Guard her. What would happen if he lost control? If he gave it up to change completely?

"Tell me, Amelia, do you have a cage?"

- 18 -

17th day of the 4th Blood Moon, 3028

The nurse's name was Andrew. He'd been in and out of Dara's room several times a day since she'd come to after her surgery, checking her vitals and bandages, asking if she needed anything for the pain, if she was hungry or thirsty. He was sweet. But he wouldn't tell her anything about Tristan and refused to let her see him, or Dr. Chase. The patient was not allowed to see her own doctor.

Still, she could let it go for now. Dara had spent enough time indoors that what she needed most was to get the hell out of this bed. She needed to walk, go outside into the sunlight. The one window in this room was a pane of glass with a breathtaking view of the hallway. Being here all by herself made her feel like a corpse on display.

Of course, when she told him this, Andrew had informed her that she was on strict bed rest for a couple more days, and besides, it was raining outside and had been since yesterday. Truth was, Dara didn't care. She'd happily stand beneath the thunderclouds, shivering in the rain, as long as she could breathe fresh air. She'd had too much darkness these past weeks. Too many walls closing in on her and doors slamming shut in her face. She was starting to feel claustrophobic again. And this time it was worse, because the only thing standing in her way was a nurse.

They'd removed one of the IVs from her arm. Now all she had

to deal with was the one that supplied her with fluids and a steady stream of painkillers. Dara could feel where she'd been hurt. Suffice it to say, there would be scars. Dara didn't care. She wanted to know how Tristan was doing. Having witnessed firsthand what New Alaska had really done to him, she couldn't stave off the welling worry.

Was he hurt? Was he even still alive? Human? What was he thinking? Her head felt far too fuzzy to attempt any kind of connection and questions like those could drive her mad very quickly. So she kept her mind firmly on things she could handle. Like rain.

Dara sat up and swung her legs off the bed. Her knees nearly buckled. A head rush coupled with the painkillers was making her weak, but she held on to the edge of the bed until she found her balance. There were slippers neatly lined up by the little bedside table, and she stuffed her feet into them because the floor was cold; it was the kind of artificial cold that made her shiver even when the rest of her was comfortably warm.

Taking hold of the IV stand on wheels, she leaned on it just a little going out of the room. A long, brightly lit corridor stretched left and right. She had no idea where she was, but opted for going left. Another corridor was a dead end, but a door mercifully opened to a third, at the end of which she could see a wide doorway leading outside. She headed straight for it.

Andrew hadn't been lying. It was pouring rain, the grounds flooded with it. Dara shivered again and this time it was a pleasant feeling. She caught a few drops on her palm, and then boldly stepped into the cold shower. Within moments, she was drenched and freezing, her breath misting before her. She adored every second of it; let it cleanse her mind of bad thoughts.

She was alive, and she was healing. She'd get through this. And Tristan was strong. There was no point in worrying about him at all. If there was one thing she was certain of, it was that Tristan was a survivor.

When a ray of sunshine pierced through the clouds as the rain subsided, Dara thought this was as close to Heaven as she could imagine.

The patch on the inside of her left wrist started blinking a little red light. Dara counted the seconds—forty-five—until Andrew found her. "Are you crazy?" was the first thing he said to her. "You're days after surgery!"

She grinned at him, her teeth chattering too much to speak.

"Dr. Chase will kill me if she finds out about this."

"I'll t-tell herrr I knocked y-you out-t."

"Funny," he retorted. "Have you had enough freezing cold rain yet?"

Dara nodded with jerky movements.

"Would you mind getting back inside, then?"

"'K-kay."

Andrew had to help her up the three stairs back inside, and he kept an arm around her for support over the shined floors that were dangerously slippery in her wet shoes. He only left her side for a moment when he ducked into a dark storage room and returned with towels. One he wrapped around her shoulders, the other he tossed over her head and ruffled her hair like a little kid's. "If you get some kind of complication because of this, I am so blaming it on you."

He was leading her back to that windowless room again and something in her rebelled. Dara stopped moving and refused to take one more step. She'd had enough of dark, depressing places to last her a lifetime. That room might as well be underground as far as she was concerned. Dara wasn't going back there. Sunshine, fresh air—those were the things that healed one best. They were essential to Dara's recovery. The rest was just medical crap.

She glanced furtively behind her at the rain she could still see outside. It was just drizzling now. Dara cast a pleading glance at Andrew, hoping he would catch her meaning.

He groaned. "Now she wants a room with a view."

Yes! Andrew was smart. She liked him.

"All right, come on," he said with the strained patience of someone who was being put out on her behalf. "Let's get you dried. I need to check your bandages. Again."

Andrew took her to a room with sliding doors leading outside onto a deck. Free access to anywhere she wanted to go. It even had a bathroom attached, where he herded her as soon as they entered, to dry off and change into clean clothes. He made her talk to him while he stayed out in the room, to make sure she was all right.

Dara was still cold when she came out, but the bed was blissfully warm, and it didn't take long at all for her to stop shivering, even with her hair still wet. After Andrew changed her bandages, he said, "I need to let the doc know you moved—I mean *were* moved to recovery. You stay put."

"Will do," she said, but despite her efforts to match his serious face, her mouth twitched to smile.

Andrew scowled at her before he left.

He'd left the sliding doors open just a couple of inches, and Dara could still smell rain in the air; even her soaked hair carried the scent. She imagined that the walls were made of stone and, instead of a hospital gurney, she was lying on a big, soft, four-poster bed, with gossamer curtains pulled aside, a fireplace in front of her, and colorful tapestries all around. The glass window became an arched opening in the wall, big enough to serve as a doorway.

Dara yawned. *So tired…*

She let her eyes drift closed, lulled to sleep by the gentle sounds of nature.

~

Two days had yielded results. Tristan had managed to force his body into submission, and with the help of some serious painkillers, he'd changed by degrees, always reverting back to human. It was exhausting. Amelia stayed with him to monitor him the first few hours, then ordered him to take a break and eat something. He didn't. Every time she left the room, he tried again and again, going further each time.

The first time he tried to push his limits, he cracked a couple of ribs.

The second time, he pulled his hip completely out of the socket.

The third time, he sustained brain damage and had to be knocked out for hours. That was when he'd figured out that if the shift started at his head, his head had the most potential to kill him. He had to change the flow of the shift so it started at his feet.

The fourth time, he managed to change his feet and legs up to his hips without injury.

The fifth time, he grew a tail. That was a freaky couple of hours.

The practice had another advantage: Each time Tristan shifted, even partially, it hurt less and less. It was as Amelia had said—it all depended on the strength of his mind. And that was one more thing he had working in his favor. His focus was absolute. Pain, hunger, exhaustion… nothing touched him while he worked. Even at night, when he collapsed in a shivering heap on the mattress they'd put on the floor inside his cage, he continued shifting his hands and feet, small things he could now do easily. He didn't trust himself to fall asleep.

At midnight, when Amelia came to check on him and discovered he wasn't sleeping, she knocked him out again. Tristan was too weak to stop her. He dreamed of rain washing down his body, pooling at his bare feet and soaking the ground until it turned to mud. And he woke up shivering with cold.

Today was the last stage. He hadn't told Amelia, but he figured she guessed it by the look on his face. He'd successfully shifted parts of his body; now it was time to change completely. Tristan didn't even touch the breakfast Amelia had brought with her, unsure of how his body would react to a full stomach in a different shape.

"Ready to practice?" Amelia sounded nervous. She had her electronic notepad at the ready, and a tranquilizer at hand, just in case.

Tristan sat down on his mattress and took a deep, bracing breath before he began. He shifted his legs first; easy enough. His hips and spine were a little more problematic. He could feel his spine elongating, like someone was stretching him out and it was… not a comfortable feeling to have.

"Good," Amelia said. "Now reverse."

He didn't. When his ribs began to pop and crack, he gritted his teeth against the pain. It was bearable. For now.

"Tristan, stop."

He couldn't. Too far gone now. Fur grew, itching until he wanted to roll around to scratch every inch of his skin. His upper body changed simultaneously, arms shifting, hands becoming paws, face and head groaning as his skull expanded unevenly to become something else. Tristan forgot to breathe as splintering pain shot through his head and neck. His lips pulled away from his teeth. They weren't human anymore.

It was done.

As the pain slowly dissipated, Tristan breathed a sigh of relief. He'd done it.

His tongue felt different in his mouth, and the mattress felt different beneath his paws. His claws were dug into it. When he tried to lift a paw, the mattress came with it a few inches, then tore beneath its own weight, leaving nothing but cloth stuck on the tips of two razor-sharp claws.

His head tilted at the sight. He flexed his paw, and the claws retracted beneath fur and flesh, releasing the cloth. When his gaze settled on Amelia, she was staring at him wide-eyed, the tranquilizer clutched in her hand. He heard her heart racing; she was barely breathing. Tristan could scent her emotions—surprise and a light tang of fear.

Even the smallest physical cues were so much clearer now. Her perfume, her own innate scent. Tristan picked up on something that puzzled him until his instincts deciphered the message: She was in heat. Or, as humans would call it, ovulating.

He wanted to laugh, and it came out as a strange bark-growl.

"Holy shit," he heard Amelia whisper from ten feet away.

You got that right.

Tristan pawed at the air above his head, getting used to his range of motion. He got to his paws clumsily, picking up each in turn, unused to the feel of standing on all fours. His new body felt foreign but somehow familiar. If there was such a thing as DNA memory, Tristan felt like he was remembering what the tiger had learned. He might not have learned how to walk or run on all fours, jump, swim, or hunt, but the tiger had. And its instincts were now Tristan's.

He stretched, feeling his muscles and bones settle into place as they should be, and it was almost pleasant. He swished his tail far left, then far right, until he caught it in his jaws. His human mind explored every nuance like a little kid with a new toy. His animal body emitted a rumbling growl, almost like a purr, but far more dangerous. Tristan wanted to run. To test what this body could do.

But Amelia was still staring at him, and he could smell her growing fear. Of him, and for him. "Can you understand me?" Her voice was soft, trembling a little.

Tristan nodded as best he could. He approached the bars of the cage and rubbed his head over them, pawing at them, asking in the only way he could to be let out.

"Can you change back?"

He considered that. Having come this far and lived, he wasn't keen on attempting another change right this minute. He was tired of the in-between. The shift was painful, but once he was completely in the new body, there was no more pain. And while Tristan was still like this, he wanted to go exploring. He yawned big and shook himself out, regarding Amelia through the bars.

She swallowed nervously. "I don't know what that means." After a moment, she tore her gaze away from him to look at her notepad. "It took you twenty-two point four nine minutes to change. Your vitals are fine. Some bruising, but nothing major. It's 11:17 now." She looked at him again. "I'd like to run some tests, but frankly I'm afraid to open the cage."

Tristan made a gruff sound. It was still him, wasn't it? Although he was starting to get a little hungry, he wasn't about to sink his fangs into human flesh. He wasn't *that* far gone. So he lay down on his side to put her mind at ease. When she still hadn't opened the cage, he sought her again with his inquisitive gaze, moving nothing more than his head. Though, to be fair, it felt enormous at the moment.

He felt movement along the floor, minute vibrations of approaching footsteps, and caught a foreign scent. He was on his feet—*paws*—instantly, sitting up at the cage entrance, his gaze fixed on the door.

It opened in seconds and a male human in a nurse's uniform came in. He started at the sight of a huge tiger in a cage inside the medical facility, and Tristan tasted his surprise and fear on the air. He made a face, not liking it at all. But beneath that odor, he caught the scent of something familiar.

The nurse spoke to Amelia softly, yet Tristan was still able to make out some of his words. His mind made sense of them at the same time he identified the familiar scent.

Dara!

He reacted without thought, launching himself at the cage, frightening the two on the other side even more. His call came out as a roar. The cage was inescapable—he'd insisted on it. Now his instinct overrode his common sense and he attacked the cage again and again, trying to claw himself out of it and knowing he couldn't.

The nurse fled.

Amelia was yelling something at him, but Tristan wasn't hearing anything. He'd scented Dara. He'd heard another male talking about her. He wanted the fuck out of this cage! Wanted to tear that little shit apart and take her somewhere else. There was a forest just outside. He could hide her there.

When he couldn't escape the cage, Tristan started pacing, sniffing at the concrete beneath and around him, looking for a way to dig himself out. He even clawed at the floor to see if it would give. Not even a little. All he managed to do was dull his claws. With no other way to vent his frustration, he attacked the mattress. Bits and pieces of material exploded all around him as he tore into it with claws and fangs. There was little left but fabric and synthetic snow by the time he was finished.

He could see Amelia from the corner of his eye, standing at a distance. She was too afraid to approach the cage to knock him out. Tristan wasn't hearing her words. He pawed at his own head, shaking it out, trying to get himself under control.

A strong mind. Stronger than instinct. He had that, but wasn't willing to utilize it when his instinct made so much more sense. Tristan fought it. He thought of Dara, the pain he'd caused her with the same claws that now raked at the floor. He turned his paw to look at the underside. Forced himself to see, to remember the damage he'd done to her pale skin, her frail body. The sound he made was as much a whine of pain as a tiger was capable of.

Tristan fought the beast he'd become, forcing it back inside, struggling for control of his body. The beast had no words to speak with, but it comprehended what he was trying to do. Understood, but fought back for dominion. The man couldn't protect her. The beast could.

The beast hurt her! he shouted back, and the tiger in the cage roared his denial. Tristan grasped at the last strands of his sanity, squeezing his eyes shut and ignoring everything else but what he needed to do to change back to his human self.

If the shift to tiger had been painful, the shift back was doubly so. His concentration was broken up with instinct screaming for him to do something else. He bled through it, limbs shifting, joints popping and sliding back where they belonged. His body was shrinking and it felt as if he was trying to squeeze himself into a space too small. He ignored it. By the time he was human, Tristan was once again rendered motionless, a shivering heap of misery on the floor of a cell littered with the remnants of a mattress.

He couldn't speak, couldn't lever himself up to sit. His muscles felt weak and strained. His jaw might as well have been wired shut. Tristan felt caged by more than the bars separating him from Dara. He was imprisoned by a body that could never hope to be as strong or as fast as the one he'd just left behind. It frightened him, the feeling of utter loss that made his human heart shudder inside his all too human chest.

Amelia approached then, one hesitant step after another. She came to the cage bars and reached through to touch his face, then sought his pulse at his neck. "Your heart is beating too fast," she said. "Can you move?"

Tristan tried. The agony robbed him of breath, but he managed to shift his weight so he could sit with his shoulder against the bars. That was as far as he could get without help. He knew he'd just offered himself up to the tranquilizer, but Amelia seemed reluctant to use it.

"Here," she said, pushing clothes at him.

He eyed them, gave her a doubtful look, but tried anyway. It took five tries and twenty minutes just to pull pants up over his hips, and by then he was beyond even attempting to pull the shirt over his head. But the effort it took gave him a chance to get used to his human form again. His breathing evened out and that crushing vise around his heart eased a little. He needed to see Dara. Touch her. Assure himself that he was still human and could feel normal in his own skin.

Amelia entered the cage to help him to his feet. She wasn't strong enough to support him by herself, so he tried not to lean too much of his weight on her narrow shoulders. Somehow they managed to make it to the gurney, and Amelia hooked him up to an IV for the time being. She talked to him while she worked, keeping his mind occupied. He was tired, but didn't want to sleep. He ached, but didn't want to be lying down like an invalid.

When he tried to get up, Amelia threatened him with the restraints again. Tristan didn't mind those as much as that damn tranquilizer. So, naturally, that was her next threat, and he had to relent.

Forced to bed rest, Tristan focused his wearied mind on the link he'd forged with Dara. He could feel it tremble, a fragile thread of awareness between them. He sought her, not to talk—he couldn't manage that much—but just to feel her with him. He needed her to make him feel human again, not an animal, not a science experiment, not a convicted murderer.

For years he'd teetered on the edge of losing his mind; had fought tooth and nail not to succumb to the madness that had ruled him. And he'd succeeded. Tristan had trained his mind to do what he never thought it could do. And when the animal had taken a foothold inside him, he'd fought that, too. He'd tried to control the beast, tried to learn how to harness its strength as relentlessly as his mental abilities in order to save his humanity.

He'd managed to nearly destroy it instead.

Tristan felt Dara start at the contact he managed to establish. She hesitated and shrank a little with residual fear and pain. His eyes felt wet and the beast inside him howled wretchedly. He remained at a distance, close enough to sense but not to touch, leaving his fate to her mercy. Tristan was painfully aware of one truth: her judgment was the only one that mattered. She was the only salvation he had left.

And if she shunned him now, whatever vestiges of humanity he'd managed to recover would forever disappear.

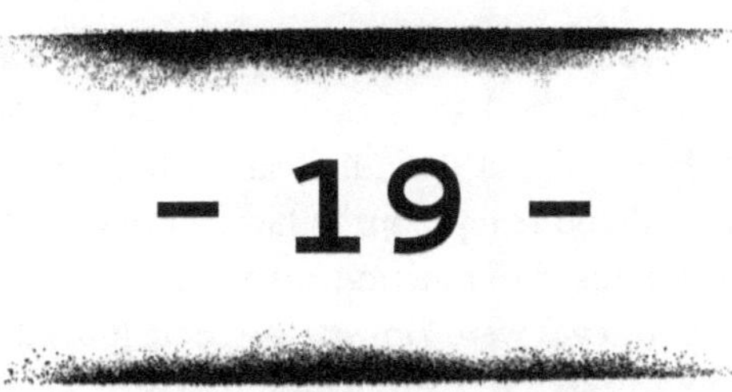

– 19 –

18th day of the 4th Blood Moon, 3028

"Safe to assume that Dara is the trigger, I think," Amelia said as he came to. Tristan didn't remember her knocking him out, but he'd somehow slept through the rest of the day and night. There was a clock on the wall just behind her that said it was 11:12 in the morning. "What is it about that woman that's got you so twisted?"

"Agents want her," he said thickly, levering himself up to sit. His entire body was one giant bruise.

"I know," Amelia said. "A couple of them have come by yesterday, asking about her. I told them the patient was in no condition to talk to anyone. What's going on?"

"Nothing that concerns you."

She made a sound that may have been a chuckle if it wasn't so bitter. "You're kidding, right? She's interfering with my experiment. Hell, by this point, she's more in control of it than I am. That concerns me."

"The *experiment* was shut down, remember?"

"Only officially," she returned, and they stared each other down for a moment. Amelia looked away first, blowing out a frustrated breath. "Look, I'm not an idiot, okay? I know you're holding something back from me and I know it's probably the key to whatever the hell is happening to you to make you the first-ever viable shape-shifter. Why can't you just tell me?"

One thing to mess with my body… another to mess with someone's mind.

He wasn't aware he'd spoken aloud, but he must have because, Amelia being Amelia, she had an opinion about it. "The body can't exist without the mind, but the mind can without the body. Is that your logic? Would you really want to have a mind if your body for whatever reason refused to function anymore?"

Tristan knew his eyes were glowing when he looked at her again because she moved a step away from him. "Leave it," he said, imbuing the command with as much persuasion as he dared.

Amelia shrugged, but it was not as easy a gesture as she wanted it to be. "I'll connect the dots eventually. I could probably ask those agents and they'd tell me. They don't care who knows what, as long as they do what they're told."

"Amelia," he said in warning.

"You've been protecting her from the first," she said. "Did you know her before New Alaska? Is that why?"

"No."

"Then why? What is it about her that makes her so special? What could one woman possibly possess that could turn a man like you so thoroughly inside out in a matter of weeks?" *And why wasn't it me?*

Tristan went still, staring. Speechless. Was his mind playing tricks on him? He hadn't heard anything—hadn't tried to—since he'd started his new training routine. But that one thought had been so loud and insistent in Amelia's mind, he'd somehow heard it without ever meaning to. He thought a few seconds back to make sure she hadn't said it out loud, but Amelia was much too careful for that.

"What?" she all but shouted. "Why are you staring at me like that?"

He chose his words carefully. "You sound… jealous, lass."

"Do *not* call me that."

"All right," he conceded and made himself unlock his muscles. The bruises were healing rapidly and with some food, he'd be back to his old self in an hour or two. But this new revelation disturbed him. How could he have possibly missed it?

"And don't be ridiculous. I'm not jealous. It's just that I don't get it. The two of you are point and counterpoint. You have nothing in common."

"Maybe that's it, then. She is what I'm not."

Amelia fidgeted. "Maybe," she said. "But my point was, there is obviously a connection. So maybe I should bring her in on this."

"No."

"Don't think I don't know why you went off like that yesterday. If Dara is the trigger, then she's also your internally external source of control."

"First, that makes no sense. And second, no."

"It does too make sense, and I *am* going to ask her. If she agrees, she's in."

"Amelia, she's been hurt enough," Tristan forced himself to say. Damn it! He didn't need a devil's advocate in this. He was doing a fine enough job of it already. The only reason he wasn't stalking through the corridors to find her was that he was weak.

Amelia pulled up a tray of breakfast, busying herself while she formulated a diplomatic response. "Consider that there is something special enough about her that agents have taken notice. Decide which is the bigger threat to her: you or them. And then keep in mind that, as long as she's here, she can't be there. You'll be able to keep an eye on her, and I'll keep an eye on you to make sure no one gets hurt."

Tristan eyed the food. His stomach was growling for it, but he was swiftly losing his appetite. "Moot point," he said. "She won't agree." She hadn't reached out to him. He'd have felt it if she had—even deeply unconscious he'd have felt it. He met Amelia's gaze. "And you will not force her."

"No," she said. "Force is not my style. You have my word that I won't try to force Dara to do anything. But I will do my best to try to persuade her."

"Persuade me to do what?"

Tristan closed his eyes, shuddering at the mere sound of her voice behind him. And even while his mind screamed for her to run, his arms wanted to reach out to pull her to him.

He curled his fingers into the edge of his bed, crushing metal to stop himself.

Wuss. Wimp. Weakling, pushover, sissy, and her favorite word of the day: *IDIOT!*

All night long, Dara had tossed and turned. She hadn't slept a wink and it was all because of him again. Because, no matter how much he'd freaked her out with that half-morph to deadly Big Cat with lethal claws, no matter how much he'd hurt her with them, she'd still wanted to run to him—and she couldn't even run!

Because the truth was, she'd rather take her chances with him than on her own.

Yes, he'd abandoned her. Yes, he'd attacked her in the throes of whatever his malfunction was. And yes, he was a heartless jackass who wouldn't give her a second thought as soon as he got this under control and his life back together—which, Tristan Hunt, being who he was, he would manage sooner or later, and it would probably be sooner.

Dara knew all that.

And still, she wasn't running the other way.

When she'd felt him yesterday, she'd nearly drowned in his anguish. It had occurred to her, in those terrifying minutes during which she'd waited to see if he would dump it all on her and crush her with the weight of his mind in such torment, that just as he was the only one within light years who might be able to help her, she might just be the only lifeline Tristan had—*anywhere.*

How could anyone expect her to walk away from that? Her—Dara Frost. The idiot who'd called the police and had gotten herself thrown into jail because she was trying to help someone who was already dead anyway.

She was a fool.

And it sucked, because if all this wasn't happening around them, Dara might actually enjoy being with Tristan. Heaven help her, she might actually *like* him.

So that was why she was now standing here, in the jeans and T-shirt she'd made Andrew get for her, with her arm in a sling and a thick sweater draped over her shoulders. And the sad thing was, this was the first time in days that she'd been able to breathe without feeling as if the walls were closing in on her.

Dr. Chase looked like a kid caught stealing candy to have been heard talking about Dara, and Tristan wouldn't even look at her. Was it possible for a person to be *this* much of a glutton for punishment? "Good morning," Dr. Chase said. "How are you feeling?"

"Okay, I suppose. What did you want to persuade me to do?"

Dr. Chase looked at Tristan, and there was a silent battle of wills. Dara wasn't sure which of them won, but Dr. Chase came around Tristan's bed toward her. "We were discussing the possibility that you might be able to help us in this study."

"You mean the animal thing?" *Whoa.* "You mean you want to turn me into one, too?"

"No, not at all. Nothing like that. It would just be a small, peripheral, really minor role."

Dara looked around for something else to focus on so she could think. Her gaze caught on the cage at the end of the room. "The pillow doesn't look like it fared well."

"It was a mattress," Dr. Chase corrected.

"Oh," Dara said weakly. Not something so easily disintegrated into snowflake-sized pieces. Good to know. "So"—she had to clear her throat to find her voice again—"what would you need me to do?"

"She thinks you're the trigger," Tristan said, twisting to face them. But he still hadn't looked at her. "She wants you to be here when I change, so I have something to focus on." His tone told her he wouldn't do it in her place.

"It's really not as dangerous as he makes it sound," Dr. Chase said quickly. "We already know he can't get out of the cage, so as long as you stayed outside of it, you'd be perfectly safe."

Tristan snorted. "Yeah, just don't stand too close."

"Tristan," Dr. Chase rebuked, glaring at him.

He glared right back at her.

"You'd be helping both of us," the doc said.

"You could get killed," Tristan returned.

"You know you'd never hurt her."

"Don't you dare make her that promise," he snarled viciously. "You have no idea what I could do."

"Neither do you," Dr. Chase yelled right back, undaunted. "That's precisely my point!"

"Stop it, both of you!" God, it was like listening to five-year-olds. Dara rubbed her forehead to stall a blooming headache. "I'm not a bone for you to fight over, so just stop it. And let me decide."

"Don't be stupid—"

"Dr. Chase," she said, ignoring him for the time being, "are you telling me he's already changed fully?"

"Yes, that's right. He assumed another shape for fifteen minutes and twelve point seven one seconds, not counting the actual trans-formation."

And he'd survived. One of his worst fears was finally allayed. "So what is your professional opinion of his state of mind during that time?"

Dr. Chase had clearly been ready to tout the success of her experiment before Dara had even finished speaking. To say that there'd been little physical damage to Tristan—things Dara could see with her own eyes. She'd probably even prepared a speech about it to convince her. But the doctor hadn't expected to be asked about his mental health, and she hesitated. Casting a quick glance Tristan's way, she shoved her hands into her pockets. "For the most part, the subject appeared—"

"The *subject*?"

"—in full possession of his senses, the same way he is now." Tristan looked incensed to be interrupted, but Dr. Chase took her cue from Dara and ignored him. "He was cooperative as usual, and seemed comfortable enough in his new shape to try testing it somewhat. As much as the cage allowed."

My God, he'd done it.

Dara was amazed, listening to Dr. Chase. Tristan had changed into an animal, all on his own, then changed back, and he was still in one piece.

He won't need me now, she thought, and a stab of regret made her wince a little. But she mentally shook herself and tuned back in to what the doctor was saying.

"He even looked playful, now that I think about it. In the interest of full disclosure, I should say that he had a… brief episode of aggression, but it didn't last long. He got himself under control without interference from me and changed his shape back."

That was a very detailed briefing in which Dara learned absolutely nothing about what she wanted to know. So she turned to Tristan. "Your turn," she told him. "Tell me what you're thinking."

Finally he looked at her and in his eyes, Dara could see the anguish she'd felt in him yesterday. "You saw the mattress," he said simply, but his gaze spoke volumes more. "That could easily be you." It made her want to hug him to her breast, not just for his comfort, but also for her own.

"Are you basing that on the added strength you have as an animal?" she asked, needing more detail. Conversation to distract her from other, more complicated things. "Do you think you will hurt me that way? Or is there another reason?"

"*Rational* is not something I had a grip on yesterday. Despite what Dr. Chase might lead you to believe. I could hurt you without meaning to. Or I could do it with very clear intent. You wouldn't climb into a cage with a wild animal. You shouldn't do this."

"You don't trust yourself."

"Look in the mirror, Dara." He sounded as if he had to force himself to say the words. "Look at what I did to you, and I wasn't even fully changed then."

For some reason, that pissed her off. "So let me get this straight. It's okay for you to be the big tough guy, stepping in whenever you feel like it"—*protecting me from everything, including myself*—"but not for me to return the favor?"

Tristan flinched at her mental touch. There was surprise; he hadn't expected her to talk to him like that. She was hit by a wave of relief so immense it made her sway on her feet. And on that wave, words. Many and varied, overlapping and echoing.

—*Don't deserve you. Needyoucraveyoudreamyou… My life.*— The last rang out as clear as bells and made her shiver. There was so much emotion behind those words; he couldn't have fabricated that.

As drawn as she felt to him, Dara now understood that she could multiply that feeling a hundred times, mix it with a decade of loneliness, self-doubt, self-fear, and desolation, and she wouldn't come close to what he was feeling. There were no words to describe it.

Maybe she wasn't such a fool to stake so much on this thing between them.

"What would be the point of me having kept you safe, if now I end up ripping you to shreds?" he said aloud.

Before Dara could come up with an answer, Dr. Chase chimed in, giving her a reprieve to collect her thoughts. "Oh, now you're just trying to scare her," she said.

"I can be persuasive, too," Tristan told her pointedly.

"You're being deliberately dramatic! That's not fair. I gave her the facts."

"Yeah, conveniently leaving out some pretty fucking major ones. Like the fact that she might be the trigger because she's the target!"

"I gave my professional opinion based on my observations—"

"Professionally worded bullshit, and you know it. If you want to be the professional, *objective* scientist you pretend to be, then show her the video. Show her how *not* in possession of my senses I really was."

"You're an asshole, you know that?"

"And you're a manipulative bitch. Dara, if you had any sense, you would run far away from me. And hope to hell that I don't catch you."

And still, even trying to scare her, there was an underlying message: Don't go.

Well, that did it.

The bickering was giving her a headache and Tristan was confusing her. There was only so much of this crap that Dara was willing to take. "I've decided," she said to put a stop to it. "I'll do it. Whatever it is." Tristan had given her the chance to take her life back. She owed him this.

Dr. Chase smiled triumphantly.

Tristan stared. He pushed to his feet resolutely. The patch of purple on his bare torso that almost encompassed it made Dara cringe. How much pain he must be in. "It doesn't matter," he said. "I won't do it." This time he meant it.

The sight of his body so bruised made her heart squeeze. She wanted to do something to help. Kissing the wounds away only worked metaphorically. But if she could help him master this so it didn't hurt anymore…

Dara hated seeing creatures in pain. "Do you remember our chess games?" she said thoughtfully.

Tristan glared in answer.

—I simply won't give you a choice.— Dara smiled, suddenly eager to pull the tiger's tail. "Payback's a bitch."

He swore and came to her swiftly, grasping her shoulders, careful with the one he'd clawed. "Dara, be smart about this," he said, his voice fierce, almost desperate. His eyes were glowing. "No one knows what I'll be capable of. Not me, and definitely not Dr. Chase. It was my first time changing and I was weakened because I'd been trying it for two days. I'm not now. If I get even stronger, I might be able to get out of that cage."

She saw his pupils change, felt his need to lean close and breathe her in—a need he was keeping in check because Dr. Chase was in the room. "Then I'll just have to be in the cage with you," she told him recklessly.

Tristan released her as if she'd burned him and backed away again to the bed. There he sat, and there he stayed, tense and silent while Dara and Dr. Chase discussed the details of what Dara would be expected to do. He even shut himself off telepathically.

It had taken him nearly half an hour to change completely, the doc told her. Dara couldn't even imagine the pain he must have gone through. The huge risk he'd taken with his life.

It was just like her telepathy. Tristan had opened the door with this complete shift, and now it was a chaotic new ability that could get activated at any moment.

If Tristan didn't learn to control it, it would destroy him. She knew he wasn't about to give up on this, but if she could somehow ease the process, Dara would try.

One way or another, he was going to learn how to change his shape at will and only at will. And he'd learn to do it painlessly.

"I think I'm ready. Let's get to work."

Tristan met her gaze, his eyes cold as ice. In that moment, cut off from his mind, Dara thought he might actually hate her.

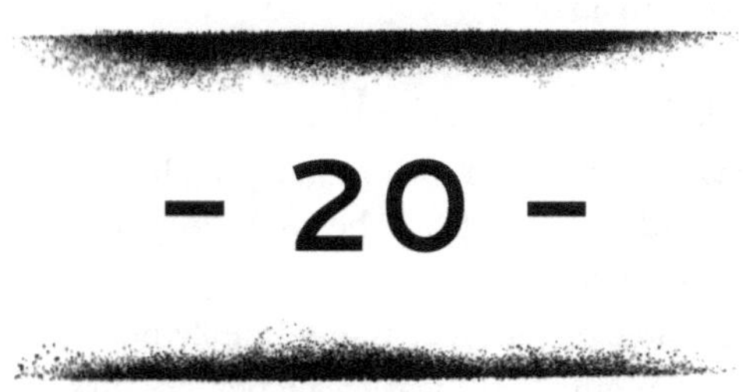

- 20 -

19th day of the 4th Blood Moon, 3028

"How long was that?"

"Nine twenty in and fifteen two out."

—*It takes you longer to shift back to human. Why is that?*—

—*If you knew how much this hurts, you wouldn't ask.*—

—*I know how much it will hurt if you don't get it under control.*—

Tristan glared daggers.

"Let's take a break," Amelia suggested. Tristan could have kissed her feet. "Eat something, relax for a while. If you're up to it, you can go outside. I hear it's nice today. Not that I'd know."

Tristan stabbed his legs through the pants he'd had the good sense to take off today before he'd started shifting. His body felt weak, but the pain wasn't as intense as he'd made it sound to Dara. If he'd known what a relentless, merciless tyrant she'd turn out to be, he would have tried a lot harder to chase her away.

When Amelia opened the cage, he all but ran out of the lab and into the sun. It felt like heaven on his skin, and he wanted to roll around in it and forget he'd ever been human. He hadn't seen the sun in days. Barefoot, he took off into the forest, seeking solitude. The ground was covered with dry leaves and, warmed by the sun, it smelled sweet and musky. His instinct told him to get that scent on him. Easier to hide that way. For a moment, that sounded like a good idea. Better the forest than the sterile lab.

At the outside edge of the forest, where it gave way to a clearing and then the lake, someone had raked the leaves into piles. Tristan couldn't resist. He threw himself onto one of those piles, tossing the leaves into the air until they rained down on him in a shower of bright colors. He let them fall where they may, linked his hands behind his head, and watched clouds move across the sky.

Contentment as he hadn't known since he'd been a child filled him and, like a cat sunning itself—which, he supposed, he was now—he let his eyelids droop and put everything else from his mind.

He could get used to this. It wasn't so bad having immense strength and the instinct to frolic in leaves, as long as there was no one around to hurt. He stretched and yawned, feeling like the king of the forest. This was his domain, and no one could challenge him here. He liked that feeling. For once, embraced it, along with this new tiger sense. Maybe if he didn't fight it, it wouldn't hurt so much.

It was worth considering. There were advantages to being a tiger that went beyond heightened senses and a really awesome tail. Just the way Dara looked at him when he was a tiger was worth all the pain he went through to change.

Tristan had expected her to freak out like Amelia had. But once the shift was complete, Dara always came right up to that cage and put her hands on him, like he was just some giant domestic cat she was petting. And it felt so damn good.

But it made him forget he was so much bigger and stronger than she was. She took his paw and rubbed her cheek over it, and Tristan held his breath, his claws too close to her slender neck. Just shifting his weight could put him off balance enough to lean on her too much. He constantly had visions of seeing her with her chest ripped open. Dara had faith that he was safe. And he couldn't make her leave, so he walked on pins and needles around her, hoping he wouldn't prove her wrong.

It was always both a relief and a chore to change back to human when his ten minutes of playtime were up. They timed it—Dara and Amelia. Tristan got ten minutes to catch his breath, with Dara petting him, and then she moved away and told him to change again. And just to be able to feel her hands on him again, he did. Because once he was fully human, she was right there, checking him for injuries. Brushing his hair aside, like he was some terminal patient.

He got water to drink, a bite to eat. Then his twenty minutes of rest were up and Dara went right back to Amelia's side and told him to change to tiger again. He hated both of them for it. Hated how much he wanted to do it right, just so he could see Dara smile at him with so much pride shining in her eyes.

Tristan scented Dara long before he heard her. He didn't move, waiting to see what she would do. But when she stopped at the forest's edge and didn't come closer, he opened one eye to look and cocked his head to beckon her closer. Part of him almost wished she would run away. He wanted to feel the thrill of chasing her. Delighted in imagining what he would do to her once he caught her.

She was wearing those form-fitting jeans again today and a deep green sleeveless top that covered her shoulders, but left the bandages on her arm exposed. The sight of them made him tense, the contentment he'd felt until now fading. She'd tossed the sling away yesterday because it had annoyed her, but he knew it still caused her pain to move her arm around. Hands in her back pockets, she came forward slowly, as if waiting for him to change his mind. He watched the sway of her hips, a low growl rumbling in his chest. He'd dreamed of this. Being free of the underground hell, watching Dara in the sunshine, with nothing around but open space. He'd craved the freedom of it, but more than that, he'd craved the peace of her presence in it.

"I thought you'd be sick of me by now," she said, lowering down next to him.

Sick of being in the same room and unable to put his arms around her. Sick of the incessant spying that kept him from stripping her down and tasting her skin again. *Sick of anything that keeps me from her.* "Not yet." He put his arm around her and pulled her to his chest, careful of her shoulder. Nothing would ever smell so good as her hair. She'd left it loose today, and Tristan put his face into it and breathed in as much as his lungs would allow.

Dara smiled against him and snuggled closer. "You do the strangest, sweetest things."

It would have been perfect to just lie there in the sun with her and let the hours pass by. He wanted more than anything to have enough peace of mind to do that; to not worry that he might shift if he fell asleep and crush her, or wake up with his arms empty of beautiful, brave Dara. But there was something he needed to do, and he dreaded it so much, his hands shook when he began to carefully unwind the bright white bandage from Dara's arm.

A long white patch covered her wounds beneath the bandage. It adhered to her skin with an ointment that sped up the healing process and kept the wound from getting infected. It covered nearly the entire back of her upper arm, from shoulder to elbow. He'd done this to her.

"It's not too bad," Dara said.

Tristan didn't believe her. She was tense in his arms and tensed even more as he began to slowly peel away the patch. The doctors had used another kind of adhesive to stitch the wound closed. It was a clean, straight cut about seven inches long and he had no idea how deep. He could tell by the shade of red that it got deeper the farther down her arm it went. One claw mark. Because her arm was too thin to have been marked by the others. But there was a red welt along the side where his claw had scraped her.

His chest couldn't hurt more if he'd stabbed himself in the heart and twisted the blade.

"It's already healing," Dara told him, but nothing she said could relieve the guilt. "Please don't look like that. It's nothing, really."

Nothing. Compared to the marks he knew he'd find on her back, this *was* nothing. *Millimeters away from piercing her lung.* He'd nearly killed her.

Dara's fingers brushed into his hair, tugged him down to her. Tristan followed, touching his face to her shoulder and neck while she soothed him. But he pulled away. "You shouldn't be comforting me, not after what I've done." He kissed the wound, wishing he could give her his regenerative abilities, and bandaged her back up. It wasn't as neat as the doctors had done it; she'd have to have it redone when they returned to the med camp.

Dara made an annoyed sound and shoved at him, rolling with him until she ended up straddling him. "I think I've had just about enough of us feeling sorry for ourselves," she declared and kissed him deep. No holds barred, no shy peck on the lips. She kissed him like nothing else mattered, and Tristan was lost.

He slapped his hands over the sweet curves of her ass and brought her down on him, shamelessly grinding against her until she moaned. She squeezed him with her knees for leverage and rubbed her breasts against him. He could tell she wasn't wearing a bra—the straps would have cut right across her wounds. That thought stung a little, but he brushed it away, just enjoying the feel of her against him. Too long without touching her.

Christ, he'd missed her!

Thought faded away beneath an onslaught of heat and lust. As it slowly took him over, it crossed his mind that perhaps Amelia's question might be valid. Just what was it about Dara that affected him this way?

She grinned against his lips. —*I'm the woman you always dreamed about having.*—

—*Is that so?*— he purred back. When he slipped his hands inside her jeans and discovered she wasn't wearing panties either, his hips bucked and his mind shouted triumphantly, *Hell yeah!*

~

It was a grim Tristan who walked back to the med camp with her. Whatever goodness they'd managed to soak in along with the sun's rays, he seemed to be losing it again, little by little, with each step he took. Dara knew what he felt; she was in his mind almost constantly. He detested returning to the cage, but didn't trust himself outside of it anymore. She'd have to break him of that.

They walked in silence, and Dara loved how he kept her hand in his, even while he brooded over his dark fate. He wasn't even aware of it, as if she were an extension of him. She loved that when she wriggled her fingers, about to slip her hand free, he got a look on his face as if it didn't make sense that she'd want to.

Dara just prevented herself from teasing him about it.

Back in front of the lab, someone had set up three chairs and a table laden with food. Amelia was just coming out, followed by an orderly toting a giant umbrella. They'd switched to first-name basis, coming to a mutual agreement that the intimate arrangement required for this particular experiment made titles somewhat redundant. She smiled at them, but it seemed a little too eager to be truly genuine. "I thought we could eat out here. I miss the sun."

"Fine by me," Dara said and snagged a seat in the shade. Her pale skin didn't tan very well. She took up a fork and dug into her lunch right away. Apparently, sex in the grass made her hungry. She slanted a covert glance at Tristan to see if he'd caught that thought. His mouth twitched as he watched her eat, and sipped his drink. His eyes said he wasn't hungry at all. Or, if he was, it wasn't for food. Dara shivered and flushed, ducking her head before Amelia could see.

"Do you like it?" Amelia asked her. "I had it made special. Duck in orange sauce, and mashed potatoes."

"Is it a French recipe?"

"I have no idea."

Dara sighed. "It tastes French." And by French, she meant *good*. The meat all but fell off the bone with the sauce as a perfect, sweet backdrop for it, and the potatoes were just fabulous. It was fancy comfort food, accompanied by sweet iced tea and crunchy bread sticks with *real butter*! "If I ever get out of here," she said, "I'm going to rob the first store I come across, just so I can come back here."

Amelia laughed, and Tristan grinned wide, clearly enjoying her delight a little too much. He still hadn't touched his plate. "Eat," she told him.

—I'd like to, but there are too many people around.— Making a face for Amelia's benefit, he ate. "Not bad," he allowed after a couple of bites. An understatement, if the way he polished it all off was anything to go by. His portion had been the biggest, and because he'd barely eaten anything all day, Amelia had another plate brought out for him.

Dessert was a large crepe folded over a pile of fresh berries and smothered in the most amazing chocolate Dara had ever tasted. "Oh my God," she said around a mouthful. "Where do you get this stuff?"

"Don't get used to it," Amelia warned. "This is a one-time thing. The higher-ups sent a sort of welcome feast for my arrival. But how could I not share?"

"You are a kind, generous woman," Dara said with feeling around a mouthful of fruit and crepe, with chocolate coating her lips.

Amelia smiled, accepting the compliment with awkward grace. Because she'd meant it, Dara pretended not to notice the brief glance Amelia cast Tristan's way, or the tense silence that followed afterward while all three of them busied themselves eating.

Someone came by to clear the table for them after they'd finished, leaving a fresh jug of iced tea and a bowl of berries. "I think that was the best meal I've ever had," Amelia said, finally dispelling the awkward silence.

"I love this bread," Dara said. "Do you know how long it's been since I had real butter?"

"This is nothing," Tristan said, tossing a small piece of bread on the ground for an inquisitive red squirrel. "There was a small bakery in Canada I went to once. They made bread like you wouldn't believe…"

They talked about food for the rest of the afternoon, until the sun went down and the evening dulled some of the day's heat. It felt like life *should* feel. A good meal shared with good friends, in a beautiful place in the summer. For those few hours, no one talked about prisons or experiments. They shared happy memories and joked as if everything was simple and perfect.

Dara was grateful for that afternoon. All of them needed a little easy downtime to pretend the last few weeks, or months, or years were behind them; that it was possible their future would be this carefree. For Dara, who'd never had friends she'd felt so perfectly comfortable around, this place and the time she spent here was something she couldn't hope to dream about once she was released to go back home.

In her mind, Tristan moved, shaping a memory. He embellished, added details he saw and felt. He created a picture and framed it, then tucked it away safely where she could always reach for it and be comforted.

—*Just a thought away,*— he said, and Dara didn't know whether he was talking about the memory or himself.

When the lab's external lights came on, it was time to go inside again. Back to reality, which wasn't as rosy as they would have liked.

They headed back inside, but Tristan, bringing up the rear, stopped at the stairs. And, because she was still linked with him, Dara stopped at the same time, one stair above him.

Amelia was a few feet away before she realized they weren't following and turned to raise a questioning eyebrow at them.

Dara turned to Tristan. —*Is something wrong?*—

He had a thoughtful, almost eager look on his face and didn't answer right away. "I think I'd like to sleep out here tonight," he said, surprising her.

"Out here… On the ground?"

He shrugged, looking up at the sky where stars were just beginning to wink into life. "I'll figure something out."

"Do you think that's a good idea?" Amelia asked, coming back.

He didn't reply, but the look on his face as he watched the stars told Dara he was desperate not to sleep another night in a concrete box. He was tense, on the verge of running off to wherever it was he needed to be, and she wasn't sure if it was the animal in him demanding that freedom. The man, too, had spent far more than his fair share of days without sunlight. She would have been surprised if he *didn't* want to be outside. Especially on a night like this, when it was warm and clean, and the breeze was nothing more than movement of air against the skin.

—*Do you want me to come with you?*—

Tristan dragged his gaze away from the sky to look at her. He slid his fingers into her hair to cup the back of her head and pulled her forward to press a kiss to her forehead. His lips felt hot. Feverish. "You go inside," he told her. "You still need to heal." To Amelia, he said, "Don't worry, I'll be back in the morning. I just… need this."

When he padded away, still barefoot, it was like watching a phantom melt into shadow. He never made a sound, never stirred a leaf or cracked a twig. And when he was gone, he was really *gone*.

Dara and Amelia exchanged a look, then each went her own way. Dara still had to return to her room in recovery. She had to be monitored for possible infections or complications. She showered as best she could without getting the bandages wet, opened the sliding doors all the way to let in the night air, and pulled the gossamer drapes closed to keep the bugs out.

Curling up in bed, she watched the drapes billow gently with the breeze. Aside from the drab white walls and the medical monitors built into them, this might actually have been a beautiful room. It felt romantic, if Dara imagined away everything except those drapes. She felt like a princess in a beautiful, exotic land. If she just went up to those drapes and pulled them aside, she could look out over an ancient city of clay houses and lit torches, smell sandalwood on the dry desert air.

Only it wasn't the desert beyond the drapes, but an enchanted forest. And instead of sandalwood, she smelled moss, earth, and summer. Dara listened to the sounds of insects and night birds outside, the hiss of leaves shivering on trees. It was a lullaby she hadn't heard since she'd been a small child.

Her eyelids became heavy, drooping, lowering, until they closed, and Dara drifted in that place between waking and sleep, where everything still registered in her mind but she didn't pay attention anymore.

It could have been minutes or hours. Enough time that when her eyes slowly opened again, she thought she was dreaming. Her ears heard, her eyes saw, but her body was heavy, tired, and unmoving. She was cushioned by clouds formed into bed and pillow, and she waited for something to happen.

It was the tiger who came to her. Melting out of the darkness like a shadow against the black foil of the forest, padding on silent, deadly paws, with magnificent grace. It nosed at the drapes, then ducked its head to pass through them, letting cloth slide over its back, and Dara could see its long tail swish left and right.

It came to her, a giant head rising above the level of the bed, golden eyes glowing. The heavy musk of its coat filled Dara's nose, but she didn't mind. Its whiskers tickled her cheek as its nose touched her chin and neck, and its breath was hot against her skin.

One enormous paw settled on the edge of the bed, claws briefly flashing out, then retracting. It brushed her covers down off her shoulder, and then that paw was a hand, lifting the covers as a hard body slid underneath them with her. Her eyes were closing again, but she felt an arm slide underneath her pillow and a leg push between hers.

Then she was nuzzling into an unyielding chest and that body curled around her possessively, protectively, long fingers clutching in her hair.

It was the best dream she'd ever had, and she said so in her mind.

Lips smiled against her temple, and Dara sighed, floating back into the dark abyss of dreamless sleep.

~

The streets were bustling, as they always were. There wasn't a single chair unoccupied, not one empty table. Even though it was the middle of the week, everyone was out tonight, celebrating. It was, after all, a great holiday. The anniversary of man's first success at occupying another planet. Sigma Day.

They were so loud, the thrum of the crowds was in his—her—blood. It echoed his heartbeat—her heartbeat!—in a way that made him so hot, he shivered. Their voices blended together in a symphony of cackling laughter and enthusiastic shouts, their clothes so bright it hurt to look at them.

But look he did.

He was starving for the sights, devouring each person who passed with such focused attention he was surprised no one noticed him.

But they wouldn't, would they? He was a wraith. A ghost among them. They didn't see him because they didn't want to see him. He reminded them of things they didn't want to remember. He was a walking testament to the government's stronghold on every aspect of its people's lives. They'd become cattle to the most powerful, the most intelligent, and the most cunning of their leaders.

It was convenient for him. A fox did not complain when he was locked in the henhouse.

Drinks were refilled, more food was brought out, and he crouched in the shadows, watching for a sign. There was always a sign. Whether it was a certain color or perfume, he always found what he yearned for the most. The powers of the universe were kind to him in that way. They were always clear in their instructions. He never had to guess and search for hidden meaning like those pathetic little fools, flocking in churches and looking for some grand design in all the wrong places.

He was the grand design.

Oh, God, no…

He was their hope.

A sharp pain in the back of his head made him double over. He stifled a groan and took deep breaths to keep from passing out. Count to ten. Breathe in and out. After a moment it passed, and he was able to straighten again. He leaned against the wall for the support his legs refused to provide. The ground was wet after last night's storm. He didn't want to end up sitting in the puddle.

As soon as the ringing in his ears subsided, he closed his eyes and listened for the hum of people again. He gave himself over to it; let it fill him to the brim. Only when he was part of the larger scheme of things could he recognize the signs. They stood out when all other stimuli ceased to distract him.

He swayed to the rhythm of life, soaking his mind in the endless prattle. His heartbeat quickened, and his palms began to sweat. He was close now.

After pushing away from the wall, he joined the throng, winding and weaving his way through the crowd the way a predator moved through tall grass.

Someone cheered, and he stopped in his tracks, his head turning toward the sound at once.

No!

The sign!

The crowds disappeared in that instant and he knew he'd seen the one. His soul leapt for joy at the discovery, but his mind remained focused.

Back into the shadows.

From there, he watched the girl hop onto a transport and raise her arms to the sky, a bottle in her hand. Her crimson top inched up to reveal glimpses of creamy skin as her hips swayed back and forth in a seductive rhythm she didn't seem to be aware of, lost in her reverie, her eyes closed.

He'd seen her before, keeping company with the dregs of society, kids who ran around with complete disrespect for anything sacred, even life itself. They drank, they took drugs, they fought constantly, and still he'd watched them—and her—and hoped they would redeem themselves somehow. It hadn't happened.

The siren brought the bottle to her pretty red lips and she drank, the liquid trickling down her chin and neck to her chest. One of the men in the crowd jumped up to the transport and put his arm around her, licking the trail of liquid up her chest. She didn't know him, the wraith was sure of it, but that didn't seem to bother her. The smile she gave the man was a sensual promise and an invitation, and he didn't hesitate to move in.

Yes, the universe had led him true once again.

Death shall come to those unworthy of life.

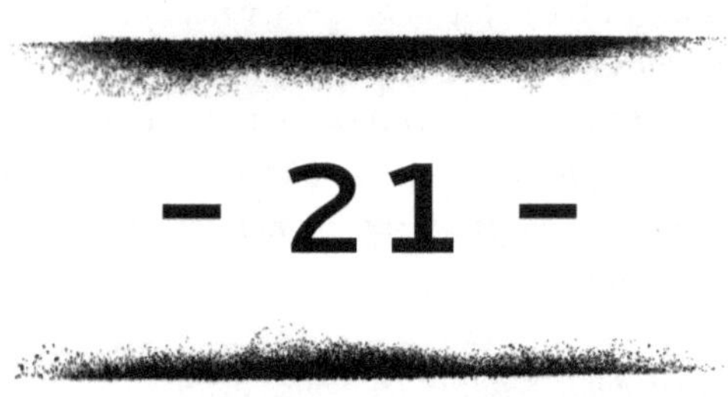

– 21 –

20th day of the 4th Blood Moon, 3028

Dara woke up screaming. With that terrible hunger still lingering in her mind, she screamed and screamed, reaching blindly for something real to hold on to. She was alone. The monitors were flashing an angry red, frantic lines snapping in spasms while a loud siren screeched from each one. She screamed for Tristan. She screamed at the murderer, trying to force him from her mind, but he was stuck there and she couldn't budge him. Like a moth circling an open flame, she mentally rammed him again and again, and each time she fell back more burned than before.

Her brain was splintering, shattering inside her skull. Her eyes felt as if they were bleeding, and she couldn't stop it. She couldn't stop screaming.

Dara didn't see more than flashes of white fabric, but she knew when nurses and orderlies rushed in, foreign hands grabbing her, trying to subdue her. They shouted for help, for tranquilizers. For someone to turn off the damn alarms. Dara fought them as if her life depended on it, because she had a feeling it just might. If they put her under again, if they forced her to dream, she wouldn't wake up.

She kicked, her covers flying, tangling her legs. She punched out blindly until someone grabbed her wrists and held them down. She bucked and arched, fighting their grip, fighting to escape them and herself, and nothing helped.

Someone came in with a syringe.

"*NO!*" she screamed, thrashing even more. She was exhausting herself, her heart racing painfully. Her bandages were slipping—she'd torn stitches. Dara didn't feel the pain. It was nothing compared to the daggers in her mind. Not a physical pain, but a frantic, hopeless rebellion against something she knew was coming.

She was losing herself to that nightmare, losing everything it meant to be Dara, little by little. It was like trying to stop a flood with paper napkins, and it terrified her, but she had to try.

She paid for it, drowning, sinking; fighting the whole way down.

Another orderly squeezed in close to her and leaned his weight on a forearm against her chest to hold her still. Two more were holding her legs. They were scared. Dara couldn't block out their fear, and it intensified her own. The weight on her chest was choking her. She was getting lightheaded, weak. Unable to draw enough breath into her lungs, her struggles eased, but the orderlies wouldn't move. They were killing her.

Dara's vision became cloudy, and she was glad for a reprieve from the sharp, stinging light. The fight was going out of her. It was a death sentence she passed over herself. A woman condemned, she turned her mind from impending death and faced her executioner. Looked in a mirror and saw her face contort and change into a mask of madness.

The murderer was an ordinary-looking man, with nothing to brand him as a psychopath except his violet eyes. They almost glowed, and he wore his brown hair long to shade them. She looked for a weakness; that's what Tristan would have done. Dara only needed one small thing to use against him and bring him to his knees.

And she found it…

—Don't look. Don't listen.— It was a sharp command she couldn't disobey. Her eyes squeezed shut; her ears began ringing. She perceived nothing. Unable to breathe, lightheaded and shivering, seeing nothing, hearing nothing, Dara was dying. It was about to be over and she was almost relieved. Her only regret was that she couldn't tell anyone about what she'd found.

Then the weight on her chest was gone, and she sucked in a huge, dizzying breath. Hands fell away from her; she could move again. She curled into a tight ball, pressing her hands to her ears to shut out the horrible sounds, but they kept leaking through. Things were breaking, shattering all around her. People screamed and yelled for help, but no one else entered her room. Fabric tore as something heavy flew through the drapes, and then came the thuds and thumps she was familiar with. Fighting. Bodies falling to the ground.

When everything fell silent, she felt the mattress depress behind her. A low cry escaped her as big hands grasped hers and pulled them away from her ears. Those same hands, hot on her freezing skin, then pressed against her head, and then Tristan was there in her mind.

He didn't take the demons away as he had before. He didn't shield her from their claws. Instead, he stood with her, sharing her pain. He purposely sought out her nightmares and dreamed them with her, watching, listening. Learning. Hunting.

He couldn't reach through her, couldn't find the murderer himself. But now he knew and, with images and feelings she could grasp, explained to Dara that somehow a connection had been established between her and the monster.

Only a few days ago, Dara had wanted to hunt the murderer herself. She'd thought about helping the police catch him despite the risk to herself, already sensing that she was probably the only one who could. Now she and Tristan both knew she'd been right. And there was no more choice in the matter.

The only way to get him out of her head was to find him.

And take him out.

Tristan bared his sharp fangs at the guards standing in the doorway with their guns pointed at him. Three more were at the balcony, picking up the unconscious orderlies. He dared them to try something. He didn't know how he'd managed it, but Tristan hadn't killed or permanently injured any of them, and the guards would find that out as soon as the orderlies were examined.

But if even one of the guards took a step toward him and Dara, if even one shot was fired, he'd slaughter them all. He could kill them before they even made the decision to react. Tristan opened all of his senses, listening for cues.

Christ, what is he?

Where the hell are the tranq rounds?

Their guns were loaded with live bullets. Tristan shifted to shield Dara with his body.

"Go find Dr. Chase," the apparent leader ordered, not taking his eyes off Tristan.

—no fucking protocol for this!

—I can take him out. No. He's too close to her. Fuck if it matters—

Tristan snarled at that guy, who started shaking, eyes wide with fear.

Got a pulse. Holy shit, this one's alive. The man who thought this was outside with the orderlies. He gave a silent signal to stand down, but no one moved.

Dara was shivering on the bed, her eyes still shut, even though he'd removed his command. She was scared and she had every right to be. Tristan was shielding her mind from everyone, but she still remembered their emotions when they'd all rushed her. She couldn't shake them off. And Tristan couldn't help her and protect her at the same time. He needed the rest of them gone. *Now.* He was seconds away from forcing them.

When Amelia pushed her way through the army of guards and took in the scene, she dismissed everyone from the room, efficient as ever. She smartly kept her distance, recognizing a potentially lethal situation when she saw it, but her tone was arch when she addressed Tristan. "I think maybe it's time you and I had that talk."

~

An hour later, the three of them were sitting in a greenhouse with plush furniture and carpets hidden among an oasis of exotic plants. The sun beat down on them; the air was thick and humid. Dara was bundled in thick blankets, with a cup of hot chocolate in her hands. She was nestled against Tristan's side and each time he shifted to move away, she made that small, desperate sound that made him want to kill something.

He did most of the explaining, because Dara wasn't up to talking, and she probably wouldn't say much even if she was. Even to him, talking about what his mind could do felt like a noose tightening around his throat. Tristan worked through it. Dara couldn't afford to hide anymore. She wouldn't make it through another episode like this one.

"You can read minds," Amelia said with a disbelieving look.

"Yes."

"That's why Dara went to Wolf block, and why you protected her all this time."

Tristan didn't like her tone. "We can sense each other."

"Have you been reading my mind?"

"Not exactly."

Her eyebrows inched up. "Just what does that mean?"

"It means that I haven't consciously made the decision to enter your mind and look. But your thoughts sometimes… leak through to me."

"Explain."

"There are more important things to talk about, don't you think?"

"No, I don't think," she said. "You're telling me that for years now one of my patients was a telepath who, for all I know, could have *seen* every last detail of my life in my mind. So you will explain yourself before we move on to anything else. You owe me that, Tristan."

"You don't even believe that yourself," he retorted. For all the things she'd done to him that could never be reversed now, risking his life again and again, he didn't owe her a goddamn thing. He'd never had the patience for hissy fits.

"Thoughts have a physical component," Dara said softly, her gaze locked on the carpet. It was the first thing she'd said all morning and it was all Amelia needed to shut the hell up. "Neurons firing electrical impulses create a… frequency. We can pick up on it. Most people's thoughts are just a hum; background noise."

"We build up blocks to shield against them," Tristan supplied. "The noise can be overwhelming if you don't learn how to mute it. It also depends on how strong a telepath is. The stronger the telepath, the softer the frequency he can pick up on, the longer the distance. Imagine being able to hear stray thoughts from everyone in the city where you live, whether you want to or not."

"But sometimes…" Dara shuddered. "Sometimes a thought is too loud to blend into the background. It gets through the shields and you can't ignore it."

"One thing to mess with your body," Amelia said thoughtfully. "Another to mess with someone's mind. This is what you meant." She leaned back in her seat, a bomb blast look on her face. "So exactly how strong are you?"

The question was directed at Tristan, but he answered for Dara. "Strong enough that she connected with the serial killer from here. He found another victim, Amelia."

"So what do you want me to do?"

Tristan met Dara's gaze briefly. She didn't know how to answer, but Tristan had an idea. He sent it to Amelia directly.

The doctor flinched. "Okay, that was really weird." She crossed her arms over her chest, hunching in on herself. She felt violated, Tristan knew. No more than he had under her examining eye all these years. "And you're out of your mind. There's no way that can work."

"It has to work."

"There are agents already after her," Amelia pointed out. "Even if I could somehow get you off-world, they'd be on us in seconds."

"I can hold them off."

Amelia pushed to her feet. "You're talking about aiding and abetting fugitives. You're asking me to give up everything—my work, my *life* to help you. And then what? Even if it works and you get the bastard, what do I do? Go into hiding? Run for the rest of my life?"

"You shouldn't have involved her," Dara said.

"Yeah, that's right. You shouldn't have involved me. And don't say I wanted to be involved. You kept this from me long enough; you should have known better now."

She was angry. For the first time since he'd met her, Amelia was genuinely pissed. Tristan considered manipulation, something he hadn't done since his hunting days. It would be easy. Amelia was ruled by logic. All he had to do was convince her mind that what he wanted from her was the next logical step.

It was a dirty tactic, and there was a chance it could go wrong in more ways than one. When he'd done it before, those he'd used had come out of the trance… damaged. He hadn't cared, as long as he'd gotten what he needed.

Dara leaned her head against him. She'd exhausted herself, but refused to close her eyes to sleep. —*This isn't her fight,*— she said. —*Or yours.*—

He ignored that last bit. —*I'll think of something.*—

Dara withdrew, moving away from him, leaving his side cold where they'd touched. "How long before I can go back to my house?"

"You did a lot of damage this morning." Amelia was making an effort to calm down. She kept her voice low and even, but her gaze kept shifting nervously to Tristan as if afraid he'd take a bite out of her brain. "I'd like you to be monitored for at least a day or two. But I understand that you're really anxious here. I can probably discharge you right now if you promise to take it easy for a couple of weeks."

"I would appreciate that."

"Do you want someone to go with you?"

"I'll take her," Tristan said. He wasn't letting her out of his sight again.

"You're not going anywhere," Amelia declared. "You can count yourself lucky those guards didn't make a sieve out of you."

"You can't stop me."

"No," she agreed, "but the ten armed guards outside probably can. You earned yourself a padlock. I now have direct orders to keep you restrained for the safety of others. And I've been told that if I can't keep you in line, you'll be on the next shuttle back to New Alaska. With the research officially suspended, I don't have any more leverage where you're concerned. Which means they can do whatever the hell they want. So you will be staying put from now on, unless I give you clearance."

"So give me fucking clearance," he growled.

"Meh," she said, shrugging a careless shoulder. "Don't feel like it." Her tone was light, but her gaze dared him to argue. She was done being nice.

"It's no problem," Dara said, uncurling from her seat to get up. "I can walk that far by myself."

"If I have to stay here, then you're not leaving, either." He made a grab for her blankets, but she let them fall away from her body and moved out of his reach.

"We live as we dream, Tristan," she said and her tone stopped him mid-step. "Alone. I'm… so tired of being pulled back and forth. You taught me to live with this. And you made me think I could depend on you, so I keep expecting you to come to my rescue every time something bad happens, but you know what? You can't be there. And I feel like an idiot every time things go from bad to worse when I just wait for you to show up."

He knew the look on her face: he had seen it many times before, had been the cause of it. It was absolute defeat. Tristan's hackles went up, the tiger rising to the fore faster than he could compensate. "What are you saying?"

"I can do this by myself." She moved farther away, her gentle presence fading from his mind. "I *have to* do it by myself, because no one else can do it for me." Only a ghost of her image remained in his mind now.

"Don't," he ordered.

"I don't have a choice."

She disappeared, but Tristan was still hanging on to her mind. He wasn't about to let her slip away. Everything inside him rejected the idea. "You think I made you depend on me? You don't think I depend on you?"

His grip on her was loosening. He was letting her go? No. He was being expelled. "You're stronger than you think." To Amelia, she said, "I'm ready to leave now."

"The hell you are!"

"I'll send a guard with you just in case," Amelia said.

Tristan lunged for Dara. Their link was severed. He had nothing else to hold on to except her. It was an instinct he couldn't fight. Panic overrode rational thought. Tristan couldn't let her go. She was his sanity. If she left…

Her cry of pain barely registered. "You stay with me, Dara."

Guards rushed in, shouting at him to release her, eager to fire the weapons they'd trained on him. He heard Amelia yelling at them and him, trying to reason with both and failing. Dara was struggling in his arms. Tristan felt her tears on his skin, knew he was hurting her.

With every last bit of control she'd gifted him, he fought the beast back. For her, he gritted his teeth until he felt them crack and forced his arms to loosen. He couldn't let go of her completely. Not with the tiger raging inside him, demanding he take her and run. To the end of the galaxy, if need be. Far enough that nothing could touch them. He could protect her. It was his right.

When his arms began to tighten around her again, he fought back twice as hard, until she was able to wriggle free. She was gone in an instant, and the beast in him howled furiously, still fighting for control. If he let it loose, everyone in the room would die. He wanted to let it loose. The battle with himself brought him to his knees.

It took three tranquilizer darts to take him down.

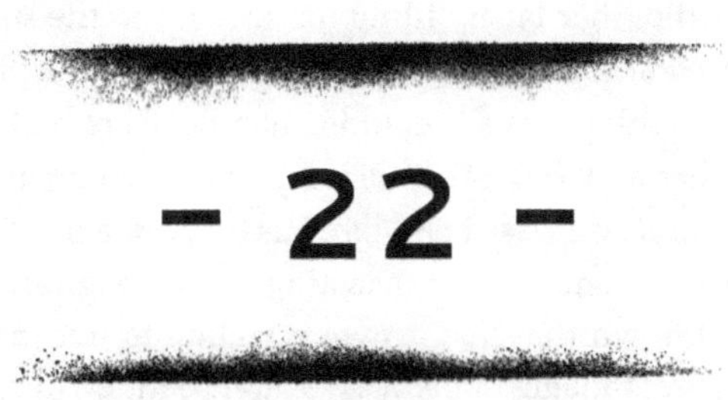

– 22 –

It was the hardest thing she'd ever had to do, to look on helplessly as Tristan fought so hard to stay human. She flinched each time a tranq round hit him and nearly panicked when he passed out. Without him in her mind, she felt the full force of the abomination that had taken root there. It sickened and terrified her.

But that wasn't why her heartbeat was like a punch to her ribs. Dara wanted to cry—for Tristan. To stay and be there when he woke up, to make sure he was all right and somehow assure him that she would be, too.

But already the guards were ushering her out for her safety. Dara's last sight before the door closed in her face was of Amelia bending over Tristan, checking his vitals. She choked back a sob and faced forward. *She'd* chosen this. Now she would have to see it through.

Cold, unsteady, feeling more lonely than she ever had before, Dara somehow made it through the forest to the lake. She kept her gaze on the glistening waters, unable to even face the place where she and Tristan had made love just the day before. It seemed like a lifetime ago now. A scene from some novel that never truly happened.

Where was the neat resolution? Where was the part where she rode off into the sunset with her hero? Where was her happily ever after?

Bitterly disappointed, Dara turned her gaze to her bungalow and frowned. It wasn't empty. Agent Calen was already waiting for her. She sensed him all the way from the lake. Something that might have passed for a half smile stretched her lips. She should have expected this.

She stopped on her lawn, lifting her face up to the sun for a few moments, pretending. For those precious seconds, she pushed from her mind everything that she couldn't handle. Dara had walked out the door on her and Tristan's little world. She'd closed and locked it behind her, but it still wasn't enough. His desperate need for her still beat at her shields and it was exhausting trying to ignore it.

Dara had known that he'd grown attached to her in some way. Tristan no longer thought of them as separate entities; in his thoughts, she was part of him, and anything that happened to her affected him, so he would do anything, fight anyone, even her, to make it so that nothing more happened to her. In his mind, his protecting her was equivalent to self-defense. And she'd gone along with it because it was just the sort of romantic sentiment she'd become addicted to, because it was so rare, she'd only ever read about it in books.

But there was a giant flaw in it. Dara had no way of knowing—because Tristan himself didn't know—why he wanted her so badly. He didn't bother thinking about it. In his mind, she was his, and that was the end of it. For all Dara knew, it could be just because she was the first woman he'd come into contact with since he'd been jailed. Or it could be one of those stress-induced things, where people in dangerous situations form a bond they wouldn't have otherwise.

It could be because she was the only one he'd confided in about everything and she hadn't turned him away, or because all the changes he was going through were confusing him. Dara just didn't know. It was far too big a leap of faith to simply accept it. The risk was too great for both of them.

We live as we dream. Alone, she'd quoted to him. *Heart of Darkness* had never seemed like such a fitting example. Odds were, Dara would turn into an even more twisted version of Mr. Kurtz in her final hours, breathing, "The horror! The horror!"

But good old Charlie Marlow had it right—there really was no way to compare experiences or share a life, not even with telepathy. Tristan had time to come to terms with it. Dara didn't.

So she put all thoughts of Tristan from her mind as well and just absorbed the feel of sunlight and the scent of fresh-cut grass, the sound of people happily in conversation not far away.

Then she opened her eyes, waved good-bye to the guard on the other side of the lake waiting for her to get inside, and walked up to her front door.

"Honey, I'm home," she called out, though the humor fell flat.

Agent Calen stood up from his seat at her table. A gentlemanly gesture. At least he was consistent. "I'll admit I was expecting a less cordial greeting."

"I'm sure you were. Sit, please."

"After you," he said, pulling out a chair for her. "I was told you've been injured."

She felt that probe in her mind again, light across the surface of her thoughts. "You're not as subtle as you think, either," she told him.

"I don't usually need to be," he said with an unapologetic shrug. The probe didn't retreat. Once he'd seated her, he offered, "Can I get you something to drink?"

"Let's do away with the pleasantries and get down to business."

"Fair enough." Calen sat kitty-corner from her, but turned his chair so he faced her.

"You want something from me. You need my help catching a serial killer."

"Our definition of *help* is probably a little different from yours."

She ignored that. "And I might be inclined to cooperate. *If* certain conditions are met."

"What do you want?"

Where to start? "I have… become aware of the reason why I am able to help you in this matter. Also, the reason why this is the *only* matter I will be able to help you with. And I know you're a man of your word. You don't give it often, but when you do, you keep it. So the first thing I want is your personal assurance that once this hunt is finished, the government will clear my record, let me return to my life, and not bother me again."

"I told you before, I have no ties to the government. They aren't involved in this issue, aside from PR."

"Then I am including whoever you do work for in that condition."

He raised an eyebrow. "That's a tall order. You really think we need you that much?"

"Yes."

Calen considered it, and without looking into his head, she knew what he was thinking. The killer was striking once every month, the victims seemingly random, but he was moving up the food chain. The public was scared. People knew the murders were still happening and pretty soon they'd start crucifying officials over it. "What else?"

"I assume you will need assurance that I can deliver the murderer."

"Naturally."

Dara nodded. "I will give you permission to scan me. I'll take down my shields and let you look. I don't need to tell you what you'll find. You'll know it when you see it."

"And your condition for this?"

"No one will bother anyone I know, no matter how interesting they might seem."

"By that, of course, you mean your friend Tristan Hunt."

"He is one of them, yes."

Again he considered her conditions. "Excuse me while I make a call."

"By all means."

While Calen went outside to talk, Dara checked the contents of her fridge. Someone had tossed out anything that might have spoiled while she'd been away. There was fresh fruit stacked in clear containers, juices and milk, even full meals. She took one out and put it in the oven.

By the time she brought it back to the table along with a glass of milk, Calen had returned, looking determined. "I can give you my word that your conditions will be honored," he said. "I've also gotten permission to get you whatever you need in the course of the investigation. If you keep your end of the deal."

"Believe me, Agent Calen, I'm not about to renege."

"At your leisure, then."

Dara wriggled in her seat, wincing, uncomfortable with the idea of a stranger crawling inside her head. "I've never done this before."

"You will feel slight discomfort. I was told it can be discomfiting, but I will try not to traumatize you too much."

She eyed lunch. "I probably shouldn't eat, then."

"Are you ready?"

Dara inhaled deep and exhaled slowly. "Yes," she said and lowered her shields. As soon as she did, she felt exposed. How quickly she'd gotten used to them.

Calen had all the subtlety of a stomping elephant. He didn't waste time, plunging in and snaking through her thoughts with incredible speed. *Discomfort*, he'd called it. Dara felt as if she'd taken a sudden drop, her stomach flipping and clenching. She felt her brain matter rearrange itself to accommodate another presence that didn't belong. Calen insinuated himself in her dreams and memories, as if he'd been there from the beginning, watching and listening. It was an invasion so complete that Dara could only hope she would still be herself after it was done.

She knew he could also feel physical sensations when he flinched and curled in on himself briefly. Embarrassed, Dara immediately thought of what else he might feel, and Tristan popped up in her mind.

He sucked in a breath. "Don't do that," he ordered in a harsh voice, steering away from visions of naked bodies twining together.

The instant he touched on what Dara had to show him, Calen stilled completely and she could finally take a breath. He circled the dark kernel of whispering voices and enraged screams, the incessant hunger and the emptiness that remained after it was sated. He examined the link that wasn't an actual link, but more of an invasion; a parasite that had attached itself to her mind. It was enough so she could go into it and… *be him*. Look through his eyes and hear with his ears.

Calen retreated slowly. He was shaking with strain across from her, his eyes tired and old. He looked as if he'd just fought a war single-handedly. As his presence faded away, his face disappeared from her memories again, leaving them untouched and unaltered, and her mind was able to settle back into place. Her stomach unclenched, the nausea subsiding.

It took a while for him to find his voice again. "To your knowledge, is he aware of the link?"

Like Tristan, he couldn't see through her to the killer. "I don't know. I hope he isn't." That was a scary thought.

Calen stumbled to the kitchen and pulled orange juice out of the fridge. He gulped it straight from the bottle, nearly finishing all of it.

Then he braced his hands on the counter, hung his head and stayed that way, just breathing.

Dara slowly brought her shields back up. Calen wasn't scanning or probing her anymore, and she had a feeling he wouldn't in the future, but she felt safer with them in place. Her stomach growled for sustenance, but rebelled at the thought of food. She was shaky and cold, and she missed Tristan like a phantom limb.

When Calen was finally able to stand on his own, he faced her and rubbed a hand over his mouth. The look on his face said he wasn't sure she was real and not a figment of his imagination. "I could go back on my word," he said. "You need this much more than we do. Seems as if that should be payment enough for your services."

"But you won't do that."

"No, I won't. Holy Christ."

"You should sit before you fall over."

He drew himself up. "When can you be ready to move?"

Dara started, surprised. Leave? She was just starting to get used to it here. *God, I'm an idiot.* It hadn't occurred to her that she'd have to go back home to do this. Back to her tiny, dark apartment on the fortieth floor, with a view of another apartment four feet from hers. Back to the city where the only green plants were on display in the natural museum and every city block was gray and drab.

She looked out her window at the lake glittering in sunlight, surrounded by grass greener than anything she'd ever seen. Leave this?

Leave Tristan?

The thought of him being locked in a cage—which she knew was where Amelia will have placed him, *for the safety of others*—was bad enough. His desperate need still beat at her, even as he lay unconscious, so deeply sedated that he shouldn't even be dreaming. Dara couldn't even imagine his reaction when he woke up and realized she was completely gone.

But she knew what he would do if he woke up and she *was* still here. *It'll get me away from him.*

And maybe that was what they needed.

"Tonight," she said. "I'll be ready tonight."

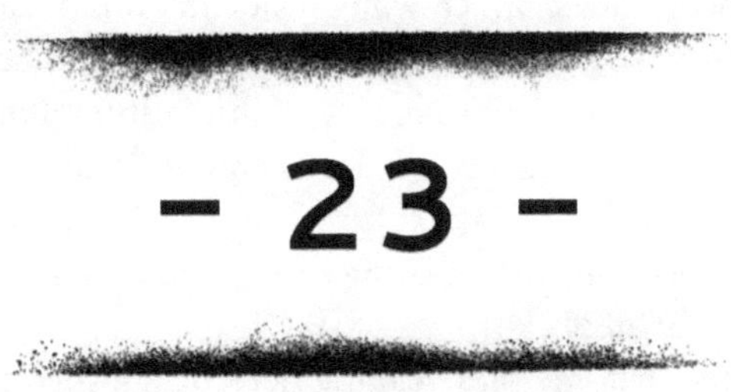

– 23 –

26th day of the 4th Blood Moon, 3028

It was raining. Had been for two days straight. On the streets of the aptly named Gray Dublin, in the forest of high-risers, that meant every street lamp was shining to lend some light on the dark day. The sewers weren't backing up yet, but it wouldn't be long. Already their aroma wafted through the chill air like a bad omen.

Dara shivered, huddling beneath her umbrella, lifting her feet out of the worst of the grayish brown water that poured along the sidewalks in small rivers. Her newly healed wounds itched so much, she wanted to scratch her back against the corner of a building. She refrained only because she didn't know how many people's DNA contributions coated it.

She was standing in front of a very official-looking building with no-nonsense tinted windows, all of them closed. In a few minutes, Calen would be meeting her inside to escort her to the Secret Society of Freaks, as she'd dubbed it, because it fit better than the official name. Dara had an appointment with Special Unit director John MacMurphy. It was special in that every member of the unit was a telepath.

Determined not to feel depressed, she walked up the stairs to the building's entrance and shook out her umbrella before she brought it inside after her. A helpful little old man took it from her and opened it near the heater to dry.

"Right on time," Calen said by way of greeting. He was still a gentleman in most things, but crawling inside her mind had somehow stripped him of his perfect control around her. He probably figured she'd seen worse than bad manners. "John is still talking to some recruits, but he reserved a room for us and he'll meet us there in a few minutes."

"Were you planning on me being among those recruits when you first came to see me?"

"It's not like that," he said, leading her down a surprisingly nice hallway. "Those people in there aren't trained telepaths. They're just scared kids, a lot of them drug addicts, who think they're losing their minds. A lot like you were a month ago."

"I never took drugs."

"You know what I mean. We give them the training they need to stay sane. We provide them with housing, food, clothes, whatever they need. We give them a purpose, a job, and a place to belong. That's not a bad deal."

"And in return, you ask them to look into thoughts so sick and twisted that they wish they'd never come here. How many have you lost so far?"

It was clear Calen didn't want to talk about this, but for some reason Dara didn't want to guess, he was humoring her. "In the first three years, about half. But times have changed. Back then, we were all just as lost. We learned by trial and error, and our rules evolved with us. Now, new recruits are only sent to scan nonviolent crime suspects. There are levels and ranks, but even at the highest levels, agents aren't *told* to go to places like New Alaska. They are asked, and can turn down any assignment they don't want to be involved with."

He opened the door for her and held his hand out for her coat. The room wasn't anything like the outside of this building. It was clean, but well used. Well lived-in. It looked like someone's home, complete with a kitchenette and bathroom. There was a plate of cookies on the table and a jug of milk. "What is this place?"

"This is where we train," Calen answered. "What did you expect, an interrogation room?"

The windows weren't windows here. They were screens showing a magnificent view of the ocean, waves gently breaking on the beach. All that was missing were the sounds.

"Considering joining forces with us?"

It was cozy here. But fake. The moment she stepped foot out of this building again, she'd be back in hell. Dara had seen heaven. She'd lived there for a while. To her, this was only slightly better than New Alaska.

Calen shrugged, reading the answer in her expression. "It was worth a try."

When MacMurphy came in, he wasn't what Dara had expected, either. The Special Unit director was a man in his late fifties, and the strength he'd had in his youth still showed in the proud way he carried himself. He had the airs of a rich man, but was dressed in worn jeans and a plain shirt with the sleeves rolled up past his elbows. His hair was dark gray and cut just a little long. All in all, a clear patriarch. Someone who was in charge and expected others to defer to his judgment. He bore the weight of that responsibility in his eyes.

"You know why you're here," he said without preamble.

"Yes," she said. She was here because the daughter of a prominent businessman—a man with political aspirations and ties to the upper levels of government—had gone missing, and in the three days since she'd been back, Dara hadn't been able to connect with the serial killer. There were five days left to the end of the month. If the killer had taken this girl, she didn't have long to live. Calen had brought Dara here so that MacMurphy could help her. Somehow.

"Good. Then let's get started." He motioned for them to sit and pulled up a chair for himself.

Dara chose the soft armchair and sat tensely, waiting for MacMurphy to give her directions.

"Jeremy has apprised me of your peculiar situation," the older man said. "Tell you the truth, it's not something I've seen before."

"Then how do you propose to help me?"

"We'll take this one step at a time. For now, just sit back and close your eyes. I want you to go to that place in your mind where you feel him. Just go there and get a sense for the way it looks, the way it feels. And tell me if you get anything."

Dara wanted to tell him that the thing had gone silent on her so there was no point, but she followed his directions, willing to try. She closed her eyes and turned her sight inward. It wasn't easy navigating her own mind. She kept seeing Niren Colony and everything she'd left behind. Tristan's face was ever present, both human and tiger. Even though he was light years removed, she still dreamed about him, as though he was still just across the lake. Dara did her best not to think about him during the day—and she succeeded some minutes more than others. But at night, when she slept, there was no shield to keep him out of her dreams.

It was unwise to dwell on the past. Especially now, thoughts of Tristan distracted her from her purpose here. But Dara didn't *want* to stop thinking about him. She'd held out hope that returning home, to the cocoon of her normal life, would be a comfort. She hadn't been prepared for the utter emptiness she'd felt since stepping foot back on Earth.

And it had nothing to do with the fact that no one had come to greet her, or that she had no one to call—not even her boss, since they'd fired her when she'd gotten arrested. It was because she'd walked away from something that could have been amazing. It might have been her happy ending, if she'd given it a chance.

Dara steeled herself against the sharp stab of regret, pushed Tristan from her thoughts, and focused on the task at hand. She knew she'd only be returning to all of it again as soon as she was done here, but for the moment, she couldn't dwell on how much she wished Tristan was here with her, or how much she wanted it to be his voice telling her what to do, rather than MacMurphy's.

Dara homed in on the source of the problem and approached it with caution. The alien thing in her mind had changed during her journey to Earth. She had no way to describe it except that it had become hard, like a nutshell. Opaque and black, when before it had been like a soft sponge of chaos.

She tested the waters a few times before drawing closer. The thing pulsed with bad vibes, but didn't give up any secrets. She touched the hard shell, looked for a seam of some sort, but there was nothing. Maybe it worked like a window and she wasn't supposed to go into it, but rather look through it.

Dara polished the surface and drew even closer to peer through the darkness. Black smoke curled and swirled in the depths of it; it felt far bigger on the inside than was possible, and she knew she was treading on dangerous ground. If that shell ever broke, if whatever was inside got out, it would poison every corner of her mind and she would cease to exist. Instinctively, she knew this. She described what she saw to MacMurphy without opening her eyes.

"That's good," he said. "We won't mess with it, don't worry. What I want you to do is see if you can move it."

Move something intangible with something else, just as intangible? And why would she want to anyway? It wasn't as if she could *move* it out of her mind. "I can't move it," she said. "It's not really there. *I'm* not really there."

"Imagine it moving."

She… tried. It was like trying to slap a ghost.

"You said it's not really there. *Make* it be there. It's your mind, Miss Frost. You make the rules."

Dara curled her fingers into the armrests. The black thing in her mind was both not there and more real than even she felt when she was this close to it. It was an impossibility inside her mind and rules didn't apply to it. MacMurphy would know that if it was in *his* mind.

"You can shape the world inside your mind. Shape yourself so that you have a physical presence. Then you can manipulate it."

Dara condensed her essence into a pair of hands. The thing was big enough—or she was small enough—that she could just get her hands around it. She placed her hands on the smooth surface and felt it change. It… tensed, as if it perceived that Dara was there and it was waiting for her to do something. She slipped her fingers underneath it and gently, carefully, tugged up.

The shell cracked, one long fault line along its length. There was a pale green light shining out of it, the black smoke still swirling, but only near the surface. Dara recognized the difference now. The smoke was just an illusion to hide what was inside.

Fear gripped her as that light stabbed through her mind, not with intent, but in a straight, unfocused line. She dropped the shell and drew far back.

"Miss Frost, what's going on? Talk to me."

Her awareness was split in three. Part of her was in the training room, hearing MacMurphy demand that she talk and feeling hot tears run down her cheeks. Another part of her was in her mind, watching the thing that had been nothing but a little black nut grow fangs and claws.

And still another part of her was with the killer, watching him watch her back.

~

Niren Colony

They'd kept him sedated for three days.

And on the fourth, the nurse came in five minutes late. There'd been no sedating Tristan after that. He was in his cage, naked. Not that it mattered. He kept shifting rapidly back and forth between human and tiger. He hadn't eaten in three days because no one was brave enough to enter the room to give him food.

Amelia didn't even dare approach the door. She was sitting in her office, watching the video feed on her computer, every muscle in her body tense, waiting for that cage to finally give. It would, sooner or later. It had been built to withstand attack, but not this constant onslaught of force. Tristan was alternating between throwing his enormous tiger body against the bars and prying at them with his human hands and amazing strength. They were already bulging and bent out of shape so much that, even if Amelia wanted to unlock the cage, she couldn't.

She silently timed his transformations. He'd reduced the time to two minutes, to a minute and a half. To sixty-five seconds. To twenty-two seconds. He was tireless. Mindless with rage she couldn't even comprehend. He no longer spoke, but roared his fury.

Except for Amelia and the handful of guards surrounding the building—their nervous fingers on triggers that would discharge live rounds—the med camp had been evacuated. Her superiors had broken off contact. They only talked to the gunmen now. Tristan was too unstable to transport. If he managed to get out, those men had orders to shoot to kill.

He knew it. That beast in the cage—whose last link to humanity Amelia had allowed to slip through her fingers—wasn't so much an animal that he didn't know what was going on. Oh, Tristan knew perfectly that Dara was gone. He knew—probably through Amelia—*why* she was gone. He knew how much time had passed, what had happened since he'd woken up, and what would happen when he got free.

He knew where the cameras were; he sought them out often, a terrible promise in his flickering eyes. She should run. There was a transport waiting to take her far from here. But like a captain unwilling to abandon a sinking ship, Amelia couldn't turn her back on Tristan. She'd done this to him. She'd created this monster and, even though it would kill her, tear her apart without mercy, she had to face it.

Amelia turned off the cameras, erased all of her files, destroyed all evidence of what she'd done, so that no one could ever repeat her mistakes. She shut down her computers and collected the satchel she'd prepared yesterday. There was a handgun resting on the side table by the wall. Amelia looked at it for a long moment before she picked it up and walked out the door.

The noise was deafening. Groaning metal, bangs as loud as a church bell, roars half animal and half human, and all of it echoing through the hallways until the entire building seemed to shake and shudder. Amelia braced herself by the door.

When she pushed it open, a half-man, half-beast stopped in his attack to stare at her with murder in his eyes—one green and one golden. He was snarling at her, but kept still, poised to strike as soon as she came within range. Not a mindless beast. She felt him in her mind, not scanning, but forcing his frenzied thoughts at her.

Her vision blurred with tears. He was panicking, too far away from his mate to protect her, and it translated to violence. Horrible, unimaginable violence that he unleashed on his prison for now. On his captors later. Dara had gone off without him, into danger, toward death, and he blamed Amelia.

She couldn't move a step farther, and realized it was because he was keeping her there. Cold fear gripped her.

—Not just a mind reader.—

The guards outside…

—No safer than you, even with their guns.—

The others in the colony…

—Irrelevant. Need out. Protect Dara… despite herself.— She didn't trust him, Tristan knew. She thought he would hurt her. *—Never!—*

Amelia's heart broke for him. *You love her.*

The beast stilled, in her mind as well as in the cage. *Surprise. Confusion. Images of Dara smiling in the sunlight. Warmth and comfort so far out of reach. Fear—for her—so deep, it obliterated coherent thought. Doubt. Could he harm her? Should he let her go?*

Another roar shook the walls around them. The beast in the cage became fully tiger and rammed the bars again and again. One of them snapped high up toward the top. Tristan turned human and pried at it until he'd bent it out of the way. It still wasn't enough to accommodate his large frame.

Frozen in place, shivering in the face of his rage, Amelia fought the compulsion he'd placed on her and unclenched her fingers from around the satchel. It dropped to the floor. "Y-you'll need that," she managed to force out through her clenched teeth. She couldn't unlock her jaw.

Again, the beast, more human than tiger, stopped in his assault and cocked his head curiously. Long fingers curled around a bar. Muscles bulged and strained. The bar broke above and below. Tristan forced his way through the opening he'd created, the jagged edges cutting deep. By the time he stalked toward Amelia, the tears in his skin were mended.

He came toe to toe with her, staring down through eyes changing rapidly between green and gold, huffing deep breaths against her hair. For long moments, he stood, unmoving. Thinking. Deciding.

When he bent close, Amelia squeezed her eyes shut, preparing to feel his fangs tear open her throat. It would be no more than she deserved.

But the bite never came. She waited tensely for her end, cringing, more afraid of dying than the after. She was so locked up that her body swayed back, and she had to take a step to keep her balance. Miraculously, she could. She could move again!

Amelia opened her eyes. Tristan was gone.

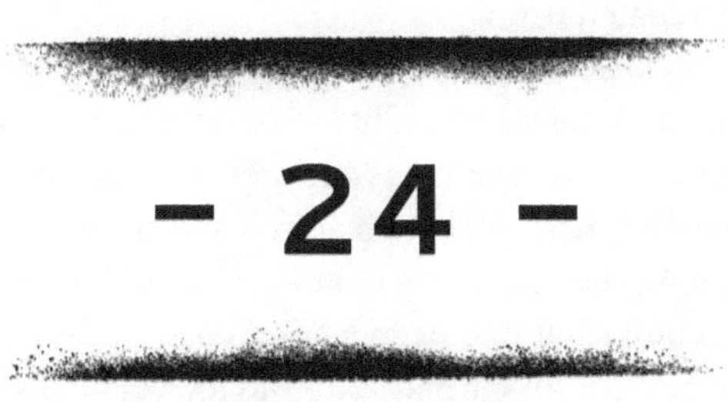

– 24 –

"He always kills on the night of the new moon," Dara said carefully. Everything she did now, she did carefully. There was a grenade in her mind with the pin pulled. She had no idea what might set it off.

"Yes, we know," the police psychologist said. He was a pretty boy, a year or two younger than Dara, and had been brought in by the skeptical chief of police to construct a profile. It was clear he had no idea what he was dealing with, otherwise he wouldn't be so eager to get the killer to *study* him. No one had told him yet that the killer wouldn't be coming in quietly, if at all. "It is a metaphor for the darkness inherent in our society."

"Excuse me," she said. "But you don't know shit."

The boy drew himself up, offended. Michael Allen Roseli. Graduate and PhD recipient of Athens University's very prestigious psych program. With honors. Star student, good boy who never got into trouble, never even skipped class. The only way he had to experience the bad side of life—without it messing up his perfectly carefree existence, of course—was through "studying" people who waded through its murky waters day after day.

Dara had a masters of lit from a little nowhere college. The only way she could have gotten into a school as good as Athens U had been to work there. She'd paid her college tuition by working in the digital library department of a university almost as good as the one Dr. Roseli graduated from.

She'd still been working there after graduation, right up until the day of her arrest. A quiet life, a solitary job, anything to minimize her contact with the outside world and the droves of people milling about in it. She'd met her boss once, to be hired and trained in her duties. After that, her pay had gone straight to her bank account. No human interaction required. It had been a good cocoon for her. Dara had loved her job because all she had to do was look at books all day long.

Dara used to envy the students who'd sent her reference queries there. Clever, lucky kids who got to learn from some of the best professors on Earth. Now, annoyed by this one's arrogance and stupid sense of entitlement, she realized she might have romanticized them a little.

"I understand that this is difficult for you," Dr. Roseli said, making his voice reasonable, but his eyes were still hard. "And you're directing your frustration at me because I'm the nearest available target. But I've studied the human thought process for—"

"I have been inside his mind," she said to shut him up. "All your theories and years of study don't even come close to what I *know* for a fact." The killer's light pulsed in her mind. With MacMurphy's and Calen's help, she'd managed to stabilize the crack somewhat, but there was no way to seal it. It gave her a glimpse of him, but only by exposing herself in return. And agitation of any kind seemed to make him… eager to pay attention. All Dara could do was keep herself calm and as far from that light as possible. "May I continue now?"

Like a petulant teenager, the psychologist leaned back in his chair and crossed his arms over his chest. But he shut up and let her talk.

"He is highly unstable. Killing is an addiction to him. He craves the thrill of the hunt, and the kill. His victims' fear excites him. But he's also very superstitious and needs to justify his actions as the *right ones*. He kills on the night of the new moon as a tribute to the universe. Because he's told himself that society is corrupt and he was sent to cleanse it, to the point where he actually believes it now. He hears… not voices, exactly, but some kind of directions from the universe that tell him who to take, where to kill them, and what messages to leave."

"Messages like these?" The boy opened a file on the computer screen table between them and spread out pictures of crime scenes from the last three months. Dara looked away, fighting a wave of nausea.

"Is this necessary?" MacMurphy said, stepping up.

"We have to confirm that the killer acts alone." It was a merciless attempt to put her in her place somehow. She was showing him up and his pride was bruised.

Dara made herself glance at the pictures. There was so much blood. It was everywhere. The messages were scrawled in it across the walls and floors all around the victims' bodies.

The first one read: *A lovely package hides maggots and rot inside.* The victim had been skinned from head to toe, exposing evidence of plastic surgery. There were maggots crawling all over the corpse.

The second read: *Money stolen buys everything a dead man needs.* The body had been cut open from throat to pelvis, the skin pulled aside. Dara shuddered and looked away; that was the one that had sent her to prison. She didn't need to see the pictures to remember what the victim looked like in the aftermath. The killer had poured molten silver down the man's throat. It had cooled and solidified and had replaced what used to be his trachea down to his stomach. Only echoes of his silent screams lingered in her mind now. Dara was grateful for that, at least.

The final picture was even more disturbing. The victim was a woman who had had her face peeled off, her breasts cut off, and her uterus removed. All the parts were arranged in a row next to her. The message said: *Pretty whore. Not so pretty anymore.*

The psychologist pointed out the first picture. "This used to be Layla Logan. She was a small-time actress. From what we could find, she'd had so much surgery, she didn't look like herself anymore." He pointed to the next one. "This man was Mason Duff. An investment banker who embezzled a fortune from his clients. It was even in the news, but the courts couldn't convict him due to lack of evidence." He moved the two aside and brought the third one forward. "Maureen Cunningham. Wife of the Three Oaks mayor. Her personal assistant told the police she came to Gray Dublin two or three times a month to cheat on her husband." The picture returned to the file, and the file closed. "Now you tell me, what kind of message can we expect over the dead and mangled body of Katie Grayson?"

"Death shall come to those unworthy of life," Dara said.

The psychologist looked to MacMurphy thinking, *Is she serious?* Even though he didn't ask the question aloud, MacMurphy nodded in answer. "What in the hell could that girl have done to deserve this?"

Dara met his gaze, because it sounded like Roseli was demanding an answer from *her*. "You want me to analyze the motives of a deranged psychopath? I thought that was your territory."

"You're the one who was inside his head," Roseli mocked.

"Boy, don't make me beat your face in," MacMurphy warned in a lethal voice.

She'd have to do it. Dara clutched her head, telling herself it was just a movie she was watching. She focused on the scene, not the killer; on what he saw, not what he felt. She made herself look at the young woman who might soon be reduced to a collection of bloody body parts. "The girl likes to party," she told the psychologist.

"And that's a crime?"

"In the killer's mind, it is, yes. She drinks, takes drugs… she makes a spectacle of herself because it's the only way she can draw attention to herself." Living in the shadow of her politically inclined father who, by all accounts, loved the media more than his own wife, the daughter was probably desperate for it. "I can't tell you where he's planning to kill her, but I can tell you that her body will be displayed in a very public place."

All that life, that deep yearning to be *seen*… the girl didn't deserve this. Dara had to stop him. And when her determination turned to anger and the foreign light in her mind pulsed, she directed that anger at the killer.

"Dara." MacMurphy touched her shoulder.

"What's going on?" the psychologist asked.

"Shut up," MacMurphy ordered him, then softened his tone. "Dara, look at me. Talk to me."

She couldn't. Every moment she spent protecting herself, she was condemning an innocent girl to a gruesome, torturous death. How could she let it happen and live with herself?

"Dara, don't do anything stupid, you hear? Dara? Dara…"

She let his voice fade away. Turned toward the light. She could feel the killer's eyes on her, eager, curious. It felt as if he was daring her to come out of hiding. At the moment, she felt very much like obliging him. She braced herself inside her own mind, hooked an anchor deep to find her way back, then launched herself at the light.

Dara felt the killer's triumph a split second before what remained of the dark shell shattered, and then she was inside his head. He was gloating. He thought he had her. She let him throw his untrained mental punches, took the pain and forced it to the back of her mind so she could focus. She didn't give a damn about his thoughts, though he screamed them at her, trying to drown her in his madness.

Dara didn't give him that satisfaction. Tristan had taught her well.

—*Dara…*— The killer was in her mind; she was hearing echoes of what her body perceived. He used her to spy. MacMurphy wouldn't give him anything, she knew. It gave her the confidence to do some spying of her own.

Except that the killer had closed his eyes. Furious that he would even consider denying her, she *made* him open them. Forced her way into that part of his mind which controlled his movements and pried his eyelids open. Dara wasn't subtle; she wasn't kind. He felt the manipulation, and it was painful. She showed him no mercy.

At last, light shone on the darkness and she was able to look through his eyes. Keeping tight control on him, she turned his head to look around. The room looked to be in the middle of construction. The walls weren't finished yet, and the floors were covered with plastic. There were wires sticking out everywhere. No lights were installed, but there was light enough coming from outside.

She moved his head even more, forcing him to turn his whole body or have his neck break. *There!* In the corner on the floor, a girl sat bound and gagged, her eyes covered. Her clothes were filthy. She had been beaten, and was shaking, frightened.

Dara was livid. She wanted to kill the bastard. Just make his heart stop and watch him writhe. But she couldn't, and he knew it. There was nothing around him to betray his location. If she killed him now, the girl would die of starvation.

—*Play a game with me,*— he invited. —*Tit for tat.*—

—Never!—

—Then she dies.—

He was moving inside her mind now, copying her movements, learning from them. He brought back her school memories, looking for anyone he could use against her. There were no faces in her past for him to latch on to. *There'd been no one to meet her at the shuttle station.* Dara hadn't expected anyone, but had hoped someone might care that she was free and back on her home planet. Even if it was just the media. The killer tried to exploit that emotional weakness, turn it against her.

Dara retreated quickly, slamming back to her own mind. If there hadn't been a clear connection before, there was one now. She shuddered at the feel of it, like a cold, slimy noose around her. Her skin crawled to have anything to do with him.

But he was *there* now, a tangible presence. And she could block him. Smiling darkly, in body and mind, she put up all of her shields, locking him out. Incensed, he battered them again and again, but there was no way he could get through. Dara may have opened a path, but it was *her* path, and she could close it any time. The killer wasn't a mind reader. That was the one thing the rest of them could be thankful for.

~

"That was a stupid, reckless, idiotic thing to do!" MacMurphy was driving her home.

"You should calm down before you have a heart attack."

"I should kick your ass out of the transport and make you walk back. What the hell got into you?"

"A serial killer," she answered.

A muscle ticked in his jaw, and his knuckles turned white.

"I thought you'd be happy. I got him out. All on my own."

"What you did," he said, gritting his teeth, "is expose yourself and put him on guard. He knows we're after him and can figure out where he is. What if he moves up his plans and kills the girl tonight?"

Dara wasn't worried about that. But she frowned, looking out the window. "Where are we going? I thought you were driving me home."

Not that she was looking forward to another cold night in her empty apartment that had started to resemble a tomb of late.

"You're not going home," he told her. "The psycho who killed and cut up three people was in your mind, probably knows where you live. I'm taking you to HQ and you'll stay there until this is taken care of."

"Your recruitment tactics are strange and unusual." Hugging herself, she pretended that the arms around her were Tristan's and it was his chest at her back rather than the transport seat. It was little things like that, minute actions, brief fantasies, that got her through the day.

"Fuck recruitment!"

Okay yeah, he is pissed.

"I don't give a damn what you do with your head, where you do it, or how. But you're on *my* watch now. And I sure as shit don't need more telepath blood on my hands."

Dara shut her mouth. This was the man who had been with the Special Unit since its inception. *He bears their deaths in his eyes.* Now she understood. Like a child reaching out recklessly to an open flame, she'd done something really dangerous without realizing it, and had scared him more than she had herself. Dara wanted to feel great about what she'd achieved, but the truth was she'd messed up.

She was the only link the police had to the killer. Dara hadn't yet told MacMurphy the worst part. Now, even more than before, they couldn't afford for her to take such risks.

MacMurphy pulled into the private parking lot and waited until the door had closed behind them before he unlocked the transport to let her out. He didn't wait for her, but stomped off inside, expecting her to follow.

Some of the recruits were waiting in the training room. This sort of thing had never happened to anyone in the unit, and they were morbidly curious about the outcome. Calen wasn't among them. MacMurphy had told Dara this morning that the agent had accepted another assignment off-world and wouldn't be back for at least a week.

The TV was on, three stations at the same time, but the audio only broadcast from one. She hadn't intended to watch, but the words *New Alaska* caught her attention, and she looked for the source of the voice. In the middle of the TV screen, a newsreporter stood in the glare of two of the planet's four suns, his eyes shielded by dark glasses.

As he talked, the camera cut away to show a photo inside the prison, looking down into the abyss, with levels of cells all around. A stock photo most likely. "…*reports are still coming in of violent outbreaks inside the correctional facility,*" he was saying, "*and the casualty count is still unknown.*"

Had there been an attempted prison break?

"*The officials are keeping a tight rein on the information they give the media, but we have learned from an anonymous source that various illegal experiments may have been the cause for this sudden event. The data we have received is sketchy so far, but we do know that extensive studies have been performed on the prisoners at this facility.*" The picture cut to something else, a video of a lab technician administering some kind of vaccine. It was clearly not from New Alaska, but they showed it for dramatic effect.

Dara felt something akin to vindication in Tristan's place. The news story would shame New Alaska, maybe even shut it down. It was a small revenge, not nearly enough for what they'd done to him, but it was a start.

The man's next words made Dara cold to her very core. "*We are receiving news so disturbing, it's difficult to believe. According to our source, the newest study on the prison's agenda, and the most probable cause of this violence, is what they referred to as a—quote, unquote—re-production study. We are still looking into exactly what this means*"—that was a lie, they already knew, she could tell by the sickened tone in his voice—"*but as of three p.m. local time, all experiments have been suspended pending an extensive inquiry…*" Dara stopped listening.

She was chilled to the bone, remembering the physical exam Amelia had so frantically forged. Tristan's relief that she'd *found a loophole.* He wouldn't tell her what it had all been about. She had a feeling he wouldn't have to now. Her memory of the night they'd left was hazy, mostly just flashes of dead bodies and sounds of fighting. But she remembered earlier, when Amelia and a group of guards had escorted her and Tristan to their cell. Security had already been expecting trouble.

Dara didn't want to dwell on it, or even guess at what might have happened after they'd left. It was too much. She never wanted to think about that place again.

"Turn it off," she heard MacMurphy order. It was a cue for the recruits to leave, but they didn't.

Dara pushed the whole disgusting business of prisons from her mind and tried to remember what was most important now: a girl's life hung in the balance. "I have to talk to you," she told MacMurphy's back as he headed for the plate of cookies. He hadn't looked at her since the meeting had broken up at the police station.

She could see his shoulder muscles bunching when he stopped in his tracks, and she expected him to start breaking things. When he pivoted to look at her, his gaze said: *Explain yourself.*

Dara swallowed nervously, looking around at the recruits. "Alone?"

She could read their disappointment, but one and all, they picked themselves up and filed out of the room. MacMurphy assumed a military-like stance with his arms crossed over his chest.

"Umm, you may want to sit down for this."

His shoulders slumped. "I'm not going to like this, am I?"

"No."

"Just tell me."

"I wasn't looking at his thoughts, but I picked up on some of them anyway. Katie is his last *message* to the city. In his twisted mind, all this was him trying to intimidate us into becoming better people. But we didn't listen. We didn't change. So once Katie's message is delivered, he'll be done with intimidation and rituals. He'll start taking people at random, every week, maybe every day. He won't stop unless we make him."

"*And you waited until now to tell me!*"

Dara flinched. Even those eavesdropping outside the door started humming with gossip. "I couldn't tell you in front of the police," she said in her defense. "You were there; you know what they're already planning. If we let the police get involved, they'll just make it easier for him to take people. He's *eager* for them to implement standard procedure."

MacMurphy punched the wall. "Fuck," he said emphatically. "It'll be like herding sheep to the slaughterhouse." He sat, looking much too old for Dara's peace of mind. "What do you suggest?"

"I think the Special Unit needs to be in charge of this one. I can show you what he looks like. Call in every agent and every favor you have. The more of us there are, walking the streets and looking for a face, the faster we'll get the bastard."

The recruits burst back inside. "Yes," the one at the front said. "We'll do it."

"Show us what he looks like," another added.

"We'll find him!"

"Give us a chance."

They were working themselves up into a fever pitch, shouting over each other. Then, as if they'd rehearsed the strategy, half flocked around MacMurphy to persuade him they were ready for this assignment, and the other half surrounded Dara, asking her to show them what "the bogeyman" looked like. It was sheer chaos for a few minutes. Stunned, Dara didn't know what to say, or even where to look.

She was hearing voices on top of voices, on top of thoughts, all of it a mishmash of raw emotion, determination, curiosity, fear, and eagerness. They had some idea of what they were trying to get themselves into, but no sense to turn and walk the other way.

Finally, MacMurphy raised his hand and instantly put a stop to it. The recruits converged back into one mass and sat on the floor facing him, waiting for instructions. They were young, teenagers and twenty-somethings with their entire lives ahead of them. Lives they were willing to put on the line to catch this guy. It was unfair, but this was their army. And even though Dara cringed at sending them out, they had no other choice.

"Dara," MacMurphy said tiredly, returning to what they'd been saying before the recruit invasion. "You won't be walking anywhere."

Outside the door, more recruits and full agents started appearing, coming in from all over the building to listen. It gave her hope, however fleeting, that maybe… maybe they were enough. Maybe, if they all banded together for once, the net they created would be sufficient to catch this guy. All they had to do was rethink their methods and completely reengineer the way the Special Unit operated.

"I know," she said. "You need me to look for him my way."

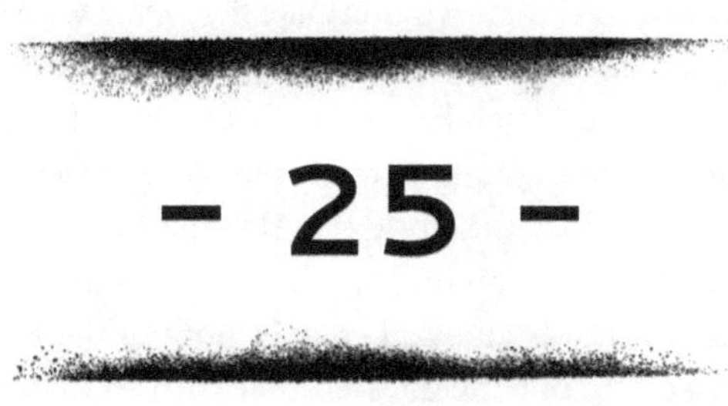

- 25 -

That evening

Dara had been practicing slowly opening and closing her connection with the killer for hours now and it was giving her a migraine. Mac-Murphy had assigned one of the agents to help her—a woman in her thirties, with a husband and three children. Her name was Eleanor, but MacMurphy called her Nell.

It was a pain in the ass because she couldn't practice on *that* link directly, unless she wanted *him* to get back into her mind. She'd had to create another connection with Nell and work with that. Dara didn't like her teaching style. Nell kept saying things like, "Good job. You're doing great," and, "Try again. You'll get it next time."

Very nice and sweet, and motherly. And completely useless to Dara. What she needed was clear directions; someone to tell her what she was doing wrong and how to do it right. Someone who wasn't afraid to be a little mean.

God, she missed Tristan.

If he was here, he'd be pushing her to get it right, not giving her the night off because of a headache. —*You'll have an even bigger one by the time we're done,*— he'd say. He'd give her an order, she'd try it, and ultimately find her own way of doing things. He'd be angry, but would praise her gruffly for getting things done. Dara needed him here so badly, she ached.

What was he doing now? Was he terrorizing the doctors? Did they have to sedate him again? He wouldn't like that. Dara wished she could talk to him. Had he heard about New Alaska? Did he even care? By now he probably knew she'd left and wasn't coming back.

Strangely lonely here among so many people who were like her, she turned the key to unlock the world they'd made. She didn't enter, just listened at the door a moment. Dara had no idea how this worked. She knew the world was an exact copy in both of their minds, built on their connection, but she guessed that with so many light years between them, they'd probably never encounter each other, even if they stood in the exact same spot.

Dara opened the door and stepped into the sunlight.

The grass came up to her knees and she ran her hand over the tops of the bright green blades. Colorful flowers popped up here and there, and to her left, the vast field dented and dipped, creating a lake. She built a small wooden pier and strolled down its length to sit on the edge and dip her bare feet into the cool water.

Dara had missed this place, missed the peace and contentment she felt here. It was like her happy-place castle—where she went to hide away from the world now more often than she cared to admit. The only difference was, one other person had access here.

The forest in the distance was as dark and ominous as before. There were creatures in it now, their voices so loud she could hear some of them all the way at the lake. She frowned at the thick thunderclouds that had settled over that part of her world. They rumbled and flashed with lightning every so often, flooding the forest floor with rain.

It worried her. This was Tristan's doing, a reflection of his state of mind.

In the next instant, she was in the middle of the field, going toward the forest: an unconscious decision, a need to see him. Sense him somehow. It became more and more strenuous the farther she went. Dara was approaching her limits. When she couldn't go any farther, she stopped and just stood there, watching the storm rage on and on.

This wasn't just a random tantrum. Had he lost his mind as he'd feared he would? Dara reached out, pushing her hand through air that felt thick as mud. Her touch rippled outward in every direction.

The moment a ripple touched the forest, the thunder quieted. The rain eased to a low hiss and the clouds lightened from nearly black to gray. Dara could feel eyes on her. Somewhere, in the depths of that forest, something was watching her.

There was no sound to betray movement, but a dark form melted out of the shadows like a ghost. It was large, but low to the ground. Dara tracked its approach by the movement of the grass. About halfway, the creature straightened to its full height, still dark and ominous, backlit by the setting sun.

He came to within fifteen yards of her, where he reached his limits. Dara gazed into the face of a creature she didn't recognize. His hair was wild, streaked like a tiger's fur. Dark stripes slashed across his skin like exotic tattoos, but on him they looked natural, like a tiger wearing a human skin. His face was altered, not completely human anymore. His cheekbones were sharper, more prominent. His eyes glowed in the dying sunlight, green and piercing. He had fangs, big enough to look threatening, but not enough to make him unrecognizable.

Then he moved half a step closer again, eyes intent on her. While Dara couldn't move any farther, he seemed to be expanding his limits by the minute. Another half-step. Then another. And the entire time, he didn't say a word. He just watched her, unblinking.

Closer and closer he inched that incredible, powerful body. He raised his hand, reaching out to her the way she'd done before, his fingers tipped with lethal black claws. His hand was turned palm up, beckoning. Dara felt compelled to reciprocate. She reached through that thick barrier of separation again, just touching one of his claws.

That small contact was enough for him. In an instant, she felt invaded, taken over, her mind at his mercy. He searched every corner of her soul, her every thought and perception, every emotion and dream. He did it so quickly, it was all over in a second. Before she could pull away, another half-step brought him close enough to capture her hand in his.

He still wouldn't speak, wouldn't allow her to question him, but when he got even closer, he brought her hand to his chest and pressed her palm against his beating heart.

And Dara understood.

Tristan wasn't stretching his limits; wasn't straining to reach her from light years away.

He was moving, bridging the physical distance to reach her mind. Already, he was close enough that their separate versions of this world were beginning to overlap.

He was with her now, sifting those claws of his through her hair. His face shifted, softened, became fully human, but his eyes never stopped glowing.

As the sun set, taking the last of its light with it, Tristan leaned down to nuzzle her temple and brush her cheek with his until their lips touched. When he kissed her, it was achingly slow and sweet, the beast gentling himself for her, doing everything he possibly could not to frighten her.

When he ended the kiss, Dara felt as if he'd stolen her soul. His arm was around her, holding her close, and when he released her hand, his heartbeat seemed to stay in the palm of it.

Stars were twinkling above them, drawing her eye. Tristan followed her gaze up to the needle-thin sliver of a moon above the lake. He cupped her cheek and made her look at him again. His eyes held a promise, an assurance. Dara felt protected here with him, insulated from everything else, but the knowledge was still there that tomorrow night, a young girl might die.

She couldn't let that happen. And so she slipped from Tristan's embrace, ignored the clouds darkening again, gathering just above her this time, and left.

Back in her room, Dara shivered.

"Who was that?" There was a young girl sitting cross-legged on the floor next to Dara's bed, staring at her with wide eyes.

"What are you talking about? How did you get in here?"

The girl scooted out of the way to let Dara stand and stretch her legs, but she wouldn't leave. "I don't know," she said. "I didn't see what happened, just felt it. He's like the prince from *Beauty and the Beast*."

Dara stared at the child. "How old are you?"

"Old enough." She didn't look more than ten or eleven years old.

"Why are you here?"

The girl shrugged and got to her feet to sit on the edge of the bed. "Nell sent me to check on you 'cause you weren't at dinner."

"Are you one of hers?"

She giggled. "No, I'm just Pixie."

A fitting name. For a girl with red hair cut short and sticking out everywhere. She had freckles on her nose, and her eyes were almost scary blue. She was just getting to that gangly period between child and woman when her limbs would grow before the rest of her, but there was something about her that Dara couldn't put her finger on. She didn't look awkward or uncomfortable in her own body, the way Dara had been starting to feel at her age. Some girls had all the luck…

"Well, Pixie, you can tell Nell that I'm fine. Now shoo."

Pixie's little shoulders slumped. "I was hoping you would tell me about the prince. I promise I won't try to steal him."

Dara's mouth twitched. "He's not really a prince. He's the villain."

Pixie perked right up. "Even better!"

Dara laughed. She couldn't help it; the girl was just too cute. But much too strong a telepath for her age. Pixie shouldn't be hanging around her, let alone *feeling* inside her mind. "It is way past your bedtime, kid. Go to sleep."

Pixie turned her head toward the door before the knock came. "Dara!" It was Nell. The woman opened the door, spared Pixie a glance, but then ignored her. "Someone sent a severed finger to the police station on Randal Street. It was in an envelope with your name on it."

Dara went cold all over. She wanted to ask, but didn't want to know. Didn't want the young girl in the room to have to hear anything about this. Pixie was quiet, still perched on her bed, but gave no sign that she was upset by this. Either she was too young to comprehend, or she'd seen worse. Dara hoped it was the first. Part of her wanted to send Pixie out of the room again; maybe she'd listen this time. But she knew it wouldn't do any good. She'd just find out another way.

"Was it… was it Katie's?"

Nell shook her head. "The fingerprint didn't match. He got someone else."

"Does MacMurphy know?"

"He's already sent a couple of agents over there. If anyone saw the messenger, they'll find him. He said you're supposed to stay put and not do anything stupid."

"Okay," she said numbly.

Nell scanned her lightly, and Dara was almost certain she didn't pick up on anything except shock. Assured that her student was in no shape to cause trouble, Nell left.

Pixie gave Dara a kind of studying look that a child her age shouldn't be capable of. "You're going to do something bad, aren't you?" she said. "John won't be happy. He doesn't like it when we do something we're not supposed to."

Dara breathed through her emotions, centering her mind. "I won't tell if you won't."

"But I should tell." For a moment, she had the same shadows in her eyes Dara had seen in MacMurphy's before.

"But you won't."

Pixie made a face, and the shadows were gone. "Fine," she said. "But only if you promise to tell me about *him*."

"Him?"

"The vile villainous villain who touches you like you're the most precious thing in the universe."

It had *felt that way, hadn't it?* "Fine. Now go."

Pixie shuffled her feet out the door. "Do you want me to wait out here, just in case?" At the look Dara gave her, the girl scurried off.

Dara closed and locked the door. If this went badly, she didn't want anyone else nearby. She sat on the bed and closed her eyes, opening the link to the killer. He'd been expecting her and didn't waste any time, shoving his consciousness through the door she'd opened, then lounging in her mind.

—*Who was it?*— she demanded.

—*Tit for tat,*— he replied. —*What will you give me in return?*— He sounded almost normal, but his voice was accompanied by a faint echo of dozens of other voices, things he heard on a daily basis. They were whimpers and sobs, sometimes screams, silent prayers and pleas for mercy, or death. It was like listening to hell. *Abandon every hope, all you who enter here.* Dara hadn't seen that warning the first time she'd seen his thoughts. It was too late now.

—*What do you want?*—

—*Oh, let's see… world peace, death to the so-called government, a litter of fluffy kittens, but I'll settle for something simple for now. I want your people off my back.*— One of the voices—and it sounded very much like an evil version of the one carrying on this conversation—chuckled as he spoke.

—*I don't have people.*— It was true; she didn't belong to any organization, and she wasn't calling the shots at the Special Unit.

—*Then whose side are you on?*—

—*No one's.*—

—*Ooh.*— He tittered, delighted. —*A rebel. I like it.*—

—*Yes,*— she replied dryly. —*The unaffiliated female. Run and hide.*—

His name was Brendon and the first initial of his last name was Z. She filed that away to be examined later.

Brendon Z chuckled. —*I have a feeling your sarcasm was meant to be ironic. Nonetheless, I run from no one.*—

—*But you hide from everyone.*—

—*Well, I'm not about to make it easy on you. What fun would that be?*— He was stretching himself, covertly reaching for things in her mind. Dara made sure he found nothing but smooth mirrors, reflecting his touch right back at him. It seemed to unnerve him. He recoiled from his own reflection, and she sensed his frustration and growing unease.

—*Whose finger did you cut off?*—

—*Now, my sweet girl, you know better than that.*—

"Oh, God! Help me!"

There was no one around to hear the terrified shriek. His victim was alone at the moment.

—*I answer one thing, and you'll think you can ask a hundred more. I'll tell you what. Because I'm such a nice guy, I'll give you one question. Ask what you want to know the most, and I'll tell you the truth. But I'll expect something in return.*—

He had no intention of giving her anything useful. This was a game to him, a small distraction from his own madness. Well, Dara was done playing. She shoved mental fingers into his mind and sifted through his thoughts, blocking out his screams. There was so much chaos, her mind felt sticky with it.

He often had episodes of uncontrollable rage, fits of madness during which he screamed at nothing, clawed at his own face. They were interspersed with periods of seeming lucidity, when the voices hushed slightly and he almost missed them. He remembered his victims, the moments before they died, their terror-filled gazes and their useless pleas.

Dara had to wade through all of it to find anything of use. It tainted her, made her feel as if she would never get that madness out of her mind. But she kept at it, keeping him off balance so he didn't have a chance to cover his tracks.

She found what she was looking for. Grabbed the knowledge and passed it on to Nell. To Brendon Z, she said, —*I don't play well with others.*—

—*That was a mistake, bitch,*— he said, his voice shaky. —*Just for that, I'll pay extra attention to my new guest. And I'll be sure to tell her she has you to th*—

Dara shut him out. She stumbled out the door, dizzy and disoriented, falling to her hands and knees, but she got right back up and hobbled in MacMurphy's direction. They didn't have much time. Brendon Z was probably already on his way out the door. If they had any chance of catching him, it was now.

MacMurphy met her halfway, looking as if he didn't know whether to hug her or strangle her. "Already sent a squad. You know, ever since you showed up, I've had this wonderful dream. It involves you leaving."

The light in the hallway blinded her. Her head was splitting open and images of Brendon Z clawing at his own face kept flashing across her eyes every time she blinked. It was just like that first time again, and Dara had a flashback to gasping for breath in her dark apartment, clutching the phone to her ear while she squeezed her eyes shut to block out the blood all over her walls. Knowing so much more about the killer now, she could still hear the voices he heard.

All of it was so overwhelming, the only thing she could think was: *They're going to get there too late again…*

MacMurphy caught her when her knees gave out. "Jesus, lady, how the hell did you manage to survive this long?" He picked her up, and Dara had to clench her teeth to keep from throwing up. The door opening and slamming shut again nearly ruptured her eardrums, but then it was finally, blessedly dark.

"Put me down."

"Will you relax? I told you we've got a team on it."

"That's what I thought last time."

She tilted away from him until he was forced to set her down. Dara sank to the floor, pushed away MacMurphy's helping hands. There was no time to waste. "Get in touch with your team. I say move, they move. No questions."

MacMurphy swore and moved away a little to do whatever psychic mojo he did to contact his people. His voice faded away as Dara retreated into her mind. Hours of practicing came down to this. One chance.

She lowered her shields by degrees, seamlessly dissolving one after the other. The indestructible wall became thinner and softer until it was little more than a gossamer veil over everything. Dara let it dissolve into mist that gently wafted away, leaving her with an unobstructed path to the killer. He hadn't noticed anything yet.

Dara pictured his mind as a screen with thousands of images. She selected away those that made no sense, internal musings of a psychopath. She screened out thoughts of revenge and violent scenes of what he planned to do to his victims.

Brendon Z was looking at something. Dara zeroed in on what he saw, stretching the image until she could see every detail.

Out of nowhere, Tristan's shields slammed down all around her so hard she nearly passed out. "*No!*" she screamed. He'd trapped her in her mind and cut off her connection to the killer. *Nononononono, not again!*

"Dara, what is it?" MacMurphy was there again, his hands on her, lifting her up. Her head was spinning so badly she couldn't tell up from down. "Talk to me!"

"He's in a transport, headed south on Leese Street." She described the type and color, and the buildings she'd seen him passing.

MacMurphy relayed the information to his agents. "Can you track him?" he asked her.

Dara shook her head. "I l-lost him." She didn't have it in her to try to get through those shields. Tristan had effectively shut her down—and taken away any chance they'd had to catch this guy.

"What? How did you lose him?"

"It's complicated." *Very complicated.* Tristan was close enough to mess with her mind again, which meant he had to be on Earth. Just the thought of it made her heart race with anticipation and dread. How the hell did he get here? Had he even left anyone alive back on Niren Colony? She moaned. "I think I'm gonna throw up."

"Here, get up," MacMurphy said, helping her to her feet. "Just breathe nice and deep, and imagine a pretty place far from here."

Dara glared at him.

"What?"

"Nothing," she said, her jaw clenched. "Did they find him?"

He sighed. That meant bad news. "No, he got away somehow. But they did find the woman who belongs to the severed finger. She was close by. A rookie picked up on her panic and led the cops to some back alley hostel. They're questioning everyone."

Dara inhaled and held her breath for a few seconds, fighting back the bitter sense of defeat. They'd saved one. And that *one* shouldn't even have been involved to begin with. Dara had no idea how strong Tristan's shields were and she was in no condition to fight them. Wouldn't be for a long time, if the way she was feeling now was anything to go by. When he lifted them—*if* he lifted them—would her link to Brendon Z still be there?

"I want to go home." She wanted to fall apart and cry. Preferably in a dark corner somewhere, without witnesses.

"I'll take you to your room."

"No, *my* home."

"Dara, I'm not letting you go anywhere alone, you understand?"

If there was something in this whole damn mess of a situation that she was 100 percent certain of… "Trust me, I won't be alone tonight."

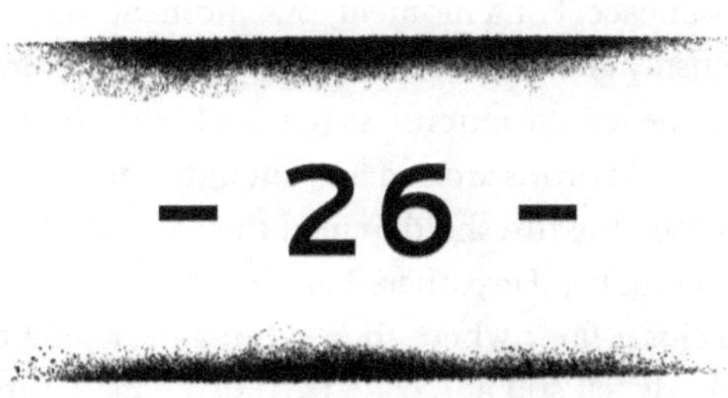

– 26 –

28th day of the 4th Blood Moon, 3028, just after midnight

Dara didn't ask how he got into her building, or how he unlocked her front door. When Tristan appeared in the doorway of her bedroom, she needed him to tell her just one thing. "Why did you do it?" She wanted to yell the question at him, but her head hurt too much. She was reduced to whispers. And that one came out sounding broken. Desperate.

She felt utterly betrayed and helpless. Her one chance to put an end to this, and he'd taken it away from her. A tyrant imposing his will on his subject. She should hate him. She should be scared of him. There was no way he'd been released from Niren Colony officially. How many bodies had he left in his wake this time? How many had stood in the way of him finding her?

Was Dara going to have even more blood on her hands now?

The thought sickened her, made her curl up tighter, until her muscles cramped.

But, looking at him, she somehow *knew*, without him having to tell her, that it wasn't like that. This time was different. He hadn't been hunting a villain, but his mate. She could feel the guilt rolling off him in tidal waves. Tristan would not cause her pain if he could do anything to prevent it.

Knowing this as surely as she knew her own name, the emotions that most overwhelmed her at the sight of him now were relief and a tainted sort of peace. For a moment, one moment too long, Dara let herself be selfishly glad he was there. Even with everything else going on, Tristan dispelled the emptiness that had been draining her. She craved the feel of his arms around her, but didn't dare reach out for it.

Tristan crossed the threshold, pulled the blanket off her bed, and wrapped it around her. He gathered her into his arms and picked her up from the closet floor where she'd sat in a near-fetal position for so long, her body felt stiff and cold. He didn't tuck her in, but sat on the bed with her in his lap.

Dara hated how good it felt to be in his arms again. Hated that when he rubbed his chin and cheek against the top of her head, she wanted to cry again and let him shoulder all of her aches and pains. She had no right to feel sorry for herself. And he had no right to try to make her feel like it was okay to break down when he was the one who'd messed everything up in the first place!

Tristan smoothed her hair and rocked her as if she were a frightened child. It made no sense, but Dara's headache began to ease. Her eyelids drooped. Dara recognized the subtle compulsion, but was too weak to resist it. She wanted to sleep until none of it mattered anymore. She didn't want to hold anyone's life in her incompetent hands. No one should have to shoulder that kind of responsibility.

When she forced her eyes open, her walls were painted red with blood. *Death shall come to those unworthy of life* was scrawled across her mirror. Dara flinched and turned her face into Tristan's chest. The voices were back again. Dozens of them, hissing through her mind like death carried on the wind. Hands trapped inside the blanket, she couldn't even cover her ears to shut them out.

"Shhh," Tristan soothed, settling his big hand on the back of her head.

All of a sudden, she felt a warm breeze cut through the voices, silencing them. She smelled fresh-cut grass and a lake. Dara peeked out cautiously and didn't see her bedroom anymore. She was sitting with Tristan on a lounge just outside her bungalow, looking out at the lake and the forest beyond.

"You are everything that's ever been good in my life," he told her, his deep voice rumbling in his chest at her ear. "You're all I have."

"Then, to save me, you sentenced a young girl to death." The sky above her darkened with ominous thunderclouds. A threat of storm, a hint, but not the storm itself. Not over her.

It was a wordless communication to make it clear that, for her, Tristan would have sacrificed anything. Whether she wanted him to or not. Where her safety was concerned, he would be relentless, merciless. Dara greedily took what he gave, for once feeling as if nothing bad could touch her, because he wouldn't let it. Even while she hated him for what would happen to Katie now, it seemed Dara was still the coward she'd been all her life.

A girl will die. Because of me.

Tristan tightened his hold on her, pressing his lips to the top of her head. "No, baby. Not yet."

His touch, his voice, made Dara feel precious, cherished. Protected for the moment from the things she didn't want to face. But she couldn't forget them, and Tristan didn't try to make her. "He got spooked," she told him. "He'll move up his plans."

"No, he won't. He has something to prove now. He won't do anything until he's good and ready, just to show you that he can. He'll want to see the stars above him before he makes his move. That gives us an entire day to track him." Tristan's voice was full of lethal promise when he said, "And I'm an expert hunter."

~

Tristan tucked Dara safely in bed. His little warrior heart. He left her dreaming about her castle, filled it for her with an army ready to do battle, but took away the enemy at the gates. It felt so fucking good to be able to touch her, hold her again, that he didn't want to leave the bed. By the time he made it to the bathroom, everything from the last week caught up with him, and his hands began to shake so much he could barely turn on the hot water for a shower.

Tristan wasn't sure exactly how he got here. He had vague recollections of waking up in the cage, sensing a terrifying void where Dara should have been. He'd managed to retain his senses long enough to find out that she wasn't dead, but back on Earth—*to hunt a killer without him*. He figured that must have been when he'd lost it, because after that, his memories were hazy.

He remembered Amelia showing up at some point with a bag and a gun. Then nothing but strange faces, staring back at him in frozen horror. Brief glimpses of stars all around him and a destination marked on the shuttle's flight plan.

He must have lost his mind a dozen times during the flight. Alone in a shuttle big enough to transport an army, the cavernous chambers filled with echoes of nothing. In that total isolation, Tristan had had nothing except the beast raging inside him. He thought… he thought he recalled mangled bunk beds, shredded mattresses, and warped metal scrap. His hands bloody, but healing. Tristan's rational mind hadn't stood a chance against that maelstrom. It had peeked out a few times, beheld the mindless destruction, and turned away.

He'd just barely stopped himself from destroying the shuttle's navigation systems. And even then, it was only because he'd begun to sense Dara again.

Having gone days without sleep, his body was now weak and starved, his mind exhausted from the constant internal battle. Tristan was almost sure he hadn't killed anyone but, given his landing, that wasn't a certainty, either.

As the hot water scalded him, he remembered the terrifying minutes when he'd entered Earth's atmosphere and felt Dara searching for the killer. Tristan could already feel how far beyond her limits she'd pushed herself. She'd have knocked herself into a coma if he hadn't stopped her. His claws dug into the shower wall, and he anchored himself with them when his knees became weak. Once again, he tested the shields he'd placed around her. They held strong.

He rubbed a hand over his chest. It had been feeling tight and choking him ever since he'd awakened in that cage. He'd beat his fists against it often in that shuttle, just needing to take one full breath. It hadn't worked. When he'd found her huddled in the corner, in the dark, he'd thought his chest would burst.

Tristan turned off the water and hurriedly dried himself. He didn't like not having her in easy sight.

But when he came out of the bathroom, she was still there, sleeping soundly, and the tightness finally began to ease by miniscule amounts. The fridge was almost empty, except for a few takeout boxes. Dara hadn't been staying here, but at that telepath central place, so she hadn't bothered to stock up on food. He ate what he could find, needing the sustenance, and tossed the empty boxes into the trash. They'd have to go out for breakfast.

This apartment was ridiculous. It had a warped triangle layout, and the kitchen opened into the living room on one side and the bedroom on the other. Sitting at the kitchen table, Tristan had a clear view of every corner of the place. He'd barely noticed when he'd come in, but now as he looked around, he wanted to smile. Only Dara would try to turn this bleak shell into a treasure box.

The walls were painted a drab gray, but she'd hung colorful pictures everywhere. He saw nature scenes, animals, even mythical beasts. There was no theme or design in her choices, just a mad attempt to fill the place with colors. Lots and lots of colors.

She had shelves of knickknacks, glittering jeweled boxes, picture frames, and crystal statues that reflected the light like diamonds. The plates and glasses in her kitchen were the colors of a rainbow, and there were vases everywhere, but no flowers. If she'd been living here, those vases would have been stuffed to cracking with blooms.

There was an electronic reader on her nightstand. Curious, Tristan picked it up and turned it on to see what she liked to read. He rolled his eyes. She'd added extra memory to the device and it held over two thousand books. The thing stored statistics about the contents. The books had ratings, kept count of how many times they'd been read, the number of bookmarks… The one with the highest rating had been read over a hundred times, and had seventy-nine bookmarks. If it were a physical book, it would have fallen apart several times by now.

Why would she do that—read the same thing over and over again, when she already knew how the story would end? Tristan had never been one to pick up a book just for the hell of it. But he'd been in others' minds when they'd read, marveling at how those stories came to life for them. To him, they'd always been just pages and pages of words. He read the story, but his imagination had to be lacking, because he never once saw the face of a character beyond the written description.

For people like Dara, those characters might as well be neighbors, walking down the street and living their stories, as real as they became for her.

Years ago, after he'd finished with the soldier and had hated himself so much he'd had a knife to his wrists every day, Tristan had been frantic to escape what he'd become. He had gone to museums and libraries, searching out people with the most vibrant imaginations. Books took too long. He'd needed a quick fix, to lose himself in what others saw in their minds and escape his own. The worlds he'd seen…

One of those people had been an elderly scholar of languages so old hardly anyone studied them anymore. The woman read ancient texts as if they were the morning newspaper, and Tristan had been baffled to realize that not only could he understand the language while he was in her mind, he still remembered it after he left. The hours he'd spent in her mind, part of one epic tale or another, had given him a modicum of peace he'd never thought to feel again.

When she'd died at the age of ninety-seven and taken away his sanctuary, Tristan had had two options: kill himself, or turn himself in. Ultimately, death had seemed too easy a way out.

Dragging his mind back to the present, Tristan memorized the title of Dara's favorite book and made a mental note to read it in the future.

He checked all of the windows and locks before going to bed. Even in sleep, Dara snuggled up to his side and laid her head on his shoulder. It was an amazing, terrifying feeling, suddenly having so much to lose. Tristan closed his eyes and passed through his own shields to settle into her mind. The tightness in his chest eased and he was finally able to take a deep breath, but he didn't get too comfortable yet. Making sure she was deep inside her dreams, he formed an empty room with a single door. It opened onto her path with this Brendon Z. Tristan couldn't get into his head, but he could draw him out here.

The killer had just begun to take down his guards, moments away from falling asleep. Tristan sent him a lure: an invitation in Dara's name. Brendon Z was just relaxed enough to accept, and his presence poured into the room like thick fog. There were things the killer was eager to say to Dara, but he soon realized she wasn't there, and his presence looked around in confusion, finding nothing that would normally be in a mind. Like thoughts.

But he found Tristan. —*Who are you?*— His voice was echoed by the desperate cries of his victims. Tristan didn't flinch. He had more than a few of those himself—and his were worse.

—*Your death,*— he answered, making his voice echo from all around. Then, because he didn't feel like talking to what amounted to the guy's back, he gave him a direction to focus on. —*I thought it was time we met.*—

Brendon Z chuckled, a scornful sound that came out shaky with unease. —*Right. Who are you really?*—

—*It'd be great if you could keep up. I don't want to have to go over the same thing again.*—

Brendon Z bristled with anger, insulted. —*What do you want from me?*—

—*When tomorrow dawns, I will already be on your trail. You won't know who I am, or where I'm coming from, but you will know when I find you.*—

—*And then I'll be shaking in my boots. You don't scare me.*—

Tristan smiled. He was muting his own presence, making it small and nonthreatening. And still, Brendon Z was shivering. —*Yes, I do,*— he said, growing slightly bigger and darker. To make things worse for the maggot, he hit the prick where it would hurt the most—his sense of purpose. —*You had a job to do. You failed, and innocents have suffered through your actions. The powers that gave you this assignment are not happy.*—

—*Y-you're bluffing! This is all a trick. That bitch is trying to scare me. Well, it won't work!*—

The shadow Tristan had been until now grew and stretched into an enormous thundercloud. It rumbled with shouts and pleas of men he'd reduced to weeping balls of terror. He added things he'd seen in others' minds, gave the memories teeth and claws to sink into his prey. With flashing glimpses of glowing eyes and sharp white fangs, he surrounded Brendon Z, drowned him in the thundercloud. —*Feeeeel meeee,*— he commanded on a hiss of air.

The killer screamed. Clawed at eyes that weren't there. Fled from the room to the safety of his own mind, but the nightmares followed him. He would dream them all through the night and wake up as scared as he'd made others feel.

Satisfied for the moment, Tristan brought his shields back up and dismantled the room. He sought Dara in her dream world, found her standing on the battlements, looking out over the lands. The gates were open to him, and he went inside and met her in the courtyard.

She was smiling when she dismissed the guards. Tristan let his mind relax, let her lead him into her own fantasies.

It was the best dream he'd ever had.

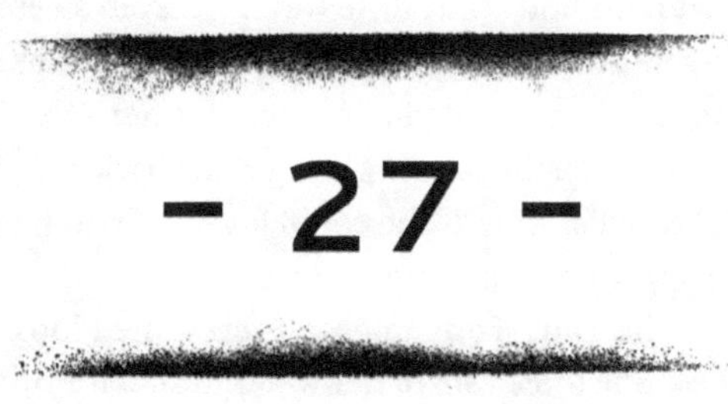

– 27 –

28th day of the 4th Blood Moon, 3028

They were going out to breakfast because Tristan had cleaned out the few supplies Dara had had. She took him to one of her favorite places. It was a rooftop restaurant with a view of the entire city, and on clear days, it was well worth the two-hour waiting time and the sky-high prices. Lucky for them she'd made a reservation before they'd left the apartment, so the waiter seated them almost as soon as they came in.

"So how does it feel to be a hundred and eight stories up?" she asked Tristan after they gave the waiter their selections.

He shrugged carelessly. "About the same it felt fifty stories below ground. But the view is better."

"You are a difficult man to impress," she grumbled, tearing off a piece of bread. She was still raw from the night before, but the worst of it had faded with the help of a good night's sleep and waking up in the arms of the most amazing, frustrating, incredibly intense, and fantastically hot man on the planet.

He'd looked at her with those heart-stopping green eyes of his filled with… something. He'd kissed her so tenderly, she thought she might die. And then he'd made love to her, holding her gaze the entire time. It had been the most intense experience of her life.

Tristan made her forget the fear she'd hugged to her chest falling asleep the night before. He was here now and left her no choice but to trust that he'd keep her safe. Just walking to the restaurant, he'd shielded her with his body the entire way. He'd even steered her away from strangers he seemed to have taken an instant dislike to. It gave Dara the confidence she needed to not fear for herself, which meant she could fully focus on the task of getting Katie back and stopping the madman in his tracks. Now, if she could just get Tristan to cooperate and show the appropriate amount of awe…

"No, I'm not," he said. "I am amazed every time I look at you."

Dara blushed. She took a sip of her water to stall for time while she thought of something to say. She'd had boyfriends before who'd said romantic things to her. It had disillusioned her more and more every time she saw in their minds that they didn't mean it. Romance was a game to most men, one small step above full-on manipulation, and all so they could get into a woman's pants.

So often in the past, her life had felt like a book she read. She knew the main characters' perspectives, their thoughts and feelings, their hopes and dreams. Only in real life, those thoughts never matched what came out of the characters' mouths. Tristan meant every word he said. If anything, his inner thoughts were even more powerful than he was able to express. Dara wanted to embrace it all, let the fates decide, and hope for a happy ending.

She thought… she thought she and Tristan might be happy together. Not here, but somewhere else.

Tristan took her hand and pressed a kiss into her palm. It throbbed with a heartbeat, not her own. *—We'll go wherever you want.—*

Their food arrived a moment later—plates stacked with pancakes and waffles, eggs and toast. They ate in comfortable silence, enjoying the atmosphere so far above the dark streets. Soft music played all around them, taking her mind off other, more unpleasant things. For the time being, it was just the two of them, eating breakfast in a nice restaurant like a normal couple would do on a Saturday morning.

Dara asked for the check, when her phone rang. She had a feeling it wouldn't be a pleasant call. She hadn't even said a greeting before MacMurphy demanded, "Where are you?"

"Eating breakfast," she replied. "Why?"

"Because I came to pick you up, and you're not home."

"Is something wrong?"

"Yeah, there's something wrong. You're meandering outside alone when there's a fucking serial killer on the loose!" She had to hold the phone away from her ear for that last part.

"One, I don't meander. Two, I'm not alone. A… friend came to town last night. I'm with him."

There was a long pause. "Would this friend happen to be Tristan Hunt?"

"Wow, you can read minds over the phone?"

"Dara," MacMurphy said carefully, "say good-bye and leave. Meet me at HQ."

She frowned at Tristan. "What are you talking about?"

"Jeremy returned this morning. He was on Niren Colony. I don't know what he's told you, but your *friend* is an escaped felon. He's dangerous, Dara."

"Is that true?" she asked Tristan without covering the mouthpiece. "Are you dangerous?"

"Terrifying," he said, green eyes sparkling briefly with flecks of gold.

She grinned. "Did ya hear that? I'm in good hands."

MacMurphy sputtered, and she pulled the phone away from her ear just in time to protect her sensitive eardrums from his yelling.

"Do you want me to talk to him?" Tristan asked.

"You'd give him a heart attack." She gave him her wallet and the check to pay, then stood up from the table and went to the edge of the patio. "John, is Jeremy with you?"

"Why, yes, Dara, he is. They sent him to apprehend Hunt and drag his ass back to New Alaska."

"Put him on, please."

The phone was passed on and Calen's voice came through. "Dara, you okay?"

"Perfectly fine. Now tell me what the hell is going on."

"There are a lot of people shitting their pants right about now. Your friend left a mess."

Dread settled in her stomach. "Any casualties?"

"Aside from a cage that looks like a tank came through it and a mangled security fence, thankfully no. He scared the shit out of some guards, but they'll live."

"And Dr. Chase?"

"She's fine. She quit and no one has heard from her since she left the colony, but she was fine the last time someone saw her."

Dara was relieved, but more than that, she was so damn proud of Tristan. Even at his worst—and she knew it had to have been really bad for him to wreck a cage that strong—he hadn't hurt anybody. For all his huffing and puffing about how dangerous he was, even when he'd had no reason to hold back, Tristan's only crime was some property damage. He was a good man.

—*I wasn't always,*— he said in her mind.

Dara wanted to argue that, but Calen was waiting for her to say something and right now, she was too all over the place to keep track of two conversations at the same time. "Well, if he didn't hurt anyone, then I don't understand," she told Calen. "What's the problem?"

"What's the prob—Dara, he's an escaped felon."

"Yes, I heard that. I mean, why are you coming after him?"

"I don't follow."

She balled her free hand into a fist on the railing. "Then let me clarify," she said. "You and I had a deal, remember? You gave me your word."

A pause. "I know. But the situation is out of my control now that he's broken the law again."

"Well then, get it back under control. Have John fill you in on what's been happening since you left. To remind you why you need me here."

Tristan was behind her, his hands on her shoulders, his mouth at her ear. "Let me talk to him," he said.

Dara considered all the ways in which *that* could go wrong, but finally surrendered the phone. "Don't give him any more reason to dislike you, okay?"

He smiled and kissed her. "I ordered some stuff to go. They should be bringing it out any minute."

"Perfect," she muttered. "Now I'm being dismissed."

But he let her listen in inside his mind.

"*Is this Hunt?*" Calen asked, sounding tense.

"Yes, and I assume you're the agent Dara met with on Niren Colony."

"*That's correct. Where are you?*"

"Keeping Dara safe."

Again, there was a pause. "*Damn it, a man like you, you could have gone anywhere, disappeared. Why the hell did you have to come here? You had to know you'd get caught.*"

In the face of Calen's bluster, Tristan remained unmoved. "Why do you ask questions you already know the answers to?"

Calen sighed and sounded defeated when he said, "*I guess I just need to hear it from you.*"

Tristan looked over his shoulder and met Dara's gaze. "I love her."

Dara's heart squeezed, even while pleasant heat warmed her entire body. The way he was looking at her... *Intense.* She felt more tears sting her eyes. *I love you,* she mouthed back, touching a hand to her heart. Tristan was her hero. She couldn't imagine a happily ever after without him.

His eyes briefly flashed golden.

The waiter came to drop off their takeout bags then, distracting her.

On the other side of the phone line, Calen blew out a breath. "*I know your story, man. I don't think that you're a menace to society, and I'm pretty sure you won't hurt Dara... again. I could almost be convinced that you're one of the good guys. But I don't know if I can convince everyone else.*"

"Tell them I can put an end to the killings."

"*Can you?*"

"Yes."

"*Then, as your reward, I suppose, you'd want your record cleared and, like Dara said, to be left alone.*" Another pause. Dara wished she knew what Calen was thinking right now. "*I'll see what I can do. It probably won't be much, but if I do manage to arrange something, understand that it will be contingent on you stopping this psycho.*"

"Understood."

"*Good. Put Dara back on the phone.*"

She met him halfway to the elevator with the bags. Tristan traded her phone for them and winked. "This is Dara, mind reader extraordinaire," she said into the mouthpiece, leaning her other cheek against Tristan, needing to touch him. He put his arm around her and squeezed her so tight for a moment, he almost lifted her off her feet.

"You keep dangerous company, lady," Calen told her.

Dara grinned. "No more dangerous than you are."

"I don't turn into a feral tiger when I lose my temper."

She shrugged. "Well, nobody's perfect. Don't let it get you down."

Tristan laughed, and then he did lift her one-armed off her feet to kiss the side of her neck.

They made arrangements to meet at HQ and hung up, but not before MacMurphy wrested the phone away from Calen again to threaten her with cruel and unusual punishment if she didn't come to her senses. In the background, just before he hung up, she heard Calen say, "Give it a rest, John. She's a wild child. You'll never rein her in."

Back on street level, Dara looked far up above her for a glimpse of the blue-gray sky. "This place is just depressing," she told Tristan.

He tugged on her hand to get her moving. "We'll get out of here soon."

They took a taxi to HQ. Tristan only half listened to Dara describing the sights. He didn't give a damn what she was saying. It was just good to hear her voice, carefree and excited. He paid attention when she pointed out the giant tiger statue in the middle of the square. It was roaring, fangs exposed, and one paw raised to slash out.

"What is it supposed to symbolize?"

Dara frowned. "I have no idea."

"It's a monument to the guy who built the zoo," the driver said.

"So where's the zoo?"

"Used to be right where you're looking. They tore it down years ago to make room for people."

Dara sighed. "Like I said. Depressing."

Tristan agreed. He didn't see the appeal of living here. It was a concrete anthill and, from what he'd seen on the news these last few years, the rest of Earth's major cities were no different.

The taxi pulled up to the curb across the street from HQ. Tristan already knew what to expect, having seen it in Dara's mind, but the sight of it still made him want to bare his fangs. He took the bags and crossed the busy street while Dara paid the driver. They'd be waiting for him and he wanted to talk to them, look them in the eye, before Dara got a chance to try to intervene on his behalf.

Tristan had a bad feeling about meeting so many other telepaths. From what he could tell, these people were more like a community than a crime-fighting unit. And he was an escaped felon about to walk into their midst. For their sakes, he hoped they had some manners and didn't get too curious. Sharing his mind with Dara was one thing. He didn't need others in his head; didn't want them there. He would be making that clear to them immediately.

Tristan was at the door, his hand on the handle, about to pull it open, when he got slammed with a wave of terror. It washed over him for a disorienting moment, then faded to nothing just as quickly. Heart in his throat, he dropped the bags and raced back down the stairs. He nearly got run over by at least half a dozen speeding transports, but he fought his way through traffic to the other side.

The taxi was already down the block, about to turn the corner, but the driver's mind was filled with mundane things. He wasn't involved. "Dara!" he yelled out loud and across their link. He didn't get an answer. He scented the air, looking for any trace of her. There was her fear, so thick it sickened him. His claws sharpened without conscious thought as he stalked the street, into a dark side alley, following that scent.

—*Dara!*— he called again, but met with only darkness. She'd been knocked out. And she'd seen it coming. He roared, wanting to tear the bastard apart so slowly. Brendon Z had no idea what he was dealing with.

The alley led to a dead end filled with overflowing dumpsters. The stench drowned out Dara's scent. It infuriated him even more. He hauled the heavy metal cubes away from the walls, gouging the cement, looking for any way of escape the killer could have used. Tristan searched the walls as high up as he could see, the ground for any indentation, a secret doorway—*something*. And every second he didn't find something, he changed a little more. Too many scents. Too much chaos. He couldn't sort through it fast enough, and the more time it took, the farther away Dara could be getting, and the wilder he became.

MacMurphy and Calen were at the edge of the alley, shouting something he didn't hear. They were too nervous to come any closer, not that he'd let them. Tristan dug through the garbage, praying that he wouldn't find Dara's dead body in the trash.

When his fingers encountered cold skin, he stopped breathing. He had to force his hand to move, to grasp the thin wrist and pull. He replaced the compulsion on MacMurphy and Calen with another, and they came running, digging out the trash on top of the body so he could pull her out. A woman. With a faint, stuttering heartbeat.

When the others had loosened enough trash, he tugged harder and pulled her out. She was cold, barely breathing, her clothes filthy and torn. Her face was bruised, her matted brown hair torn out in places. Katie Grayson.

"Call an ambulance!" MacMurphy ordered, checking the girl's neck for a pulse.

Tristan didn't see Calen leave. He didn't hear MacMurphy talking. Everything in him was focused on a small, tattered piece of paper that had been pinned to the girl's chest.

Tit for tat, it read. Dara was gone.

– 28 –

As long as he lived and breathed, Jeremy Calen would never forget the feeling of looking into the eyes of madness. And it wasn't even the serial killer. The look on Hunt's face when he stopped digging through trash… those three seconds in which Jeremy could *feel* everything inside Hunt just stop would stick with him for the rest of his days. He wouldn't have been surprised if the man's heart stopped beating. Couldn't imagine what he had to be feeling.

Could see what it did to him, though. His face *changed*. One minute he was like something out of a bad werewolf movie, half human, half beast, with huge black claws and fangs Jeremy could see all the way from the mouth of the alley, and the next he was completely human, baffled, terrified. It was almost as if even that tiger inside him had gotten scared into retreat.

A man like that didn't get scared.

Jeremy felt Hunt manipulating him, but he didn't give a shit. He jumped right into that dumpster with John, and when they cleared enough of the woman to see that it wasn't Dara, Jeremy didn't know which of them was more shocked.

Hunt didn't stick around for the ambulance to arrive. Jeremy was glad.

The paramedic said Katie needed medical care ASAP. She'd been hanging on by a thread. Even thirty seconds later, she could have been dead, suffocated by the trash piled on top of her, or just… given up.

She was taken to the hospital and her parents were notified.

But Jeremy and John had bigger issues. Now there were two psychotic killers on the loose, and they couldn't decide which one was more dangerous. One of them had traded Katie for Dara, that much was now clear. So, for all they knew, he wouldn't be looking for more victims until he was finished with her—and that thought made Jeremy sick to his stomach.

The other one, though, wouldn't stop until he found her. Leaving Niren Colony had been one thing. What would Hunt do? How many people would he plow through to get to his woman now that she was in danger of her life? Would he even be able to distinguish between friend and foe?

They had three agents and six more patrol transports out looking for him. It wasn't as if they had a chance in hell of finding him, but at least John felt as if they were doing *something*.

Jeremy closed himself in the training room to get away from the trainees and their incessant questions. They all knew something was wrong; something had to be, because Dara wasn't there. They knew about the new telepath, and that he wasn't there either, and they wanted to know what the hell was going on. Jeremy had no fucking clue.

Pixie crawled out from under the table where she must have been hiding. He hadn't noticed her before. "Dara made him mad," she said. Then she smiled impishly. "Both of them, actually, but the fluffy one likes it. The crazy one doesn't."

He snorted to hear Hunt referred to as the *fluffy one*. "What are you doing here?" He didn't have it in him to order her out. He'd missed his sister.

"You want a cookie?" She took one off the plate and held it out to him. "It's chocolate. Try it. It'll be good for you."

Jeremy took it, but didn't take a bite. "Pix, do you like it here?" Seven years ago, when they'd come here, there had been nowhere else for them to go. This place had become their home, the people in it their family. But as a full agent now, Jeremy spent more time away than he did here. He hated leaving Pixie alone, but told himself she was safe in John's care. Still, he knew she missed him when he was gone. He was the only real family she had left.

"You're worried that this isn't the best environment for me to grow up in," she said, reading him easily. She'd learned to talk from reading his mind like an open book. Not surprisingly, her first words had been curses.

"Is it?"

She shrugged, tossing herself onto the sofa next to him. "There's people like us here."

"What about the city? Wouldn't you rather be somewhere with grass and flowers? Maybe some trees?"

Pixie brightened. "I know what those look like! They're pretty."

His chest hurt. Pixie had never seen them for herself. She could only touch grass in the memories of others. Smell flowers through those who'd seen them bloom outside a hothouse. "How about you and I go on a trip? Would you like that?"

She turned to him with her whole soul shining bright in her eyes. "Really?"

He nodded, struggling to make a sound. "Really."

Pixie squealed and ran around the room like a dizzy little bee for a while, chanting, "We're going out, we're going out, we're going out! We're. Going. Out!"

I'm sorry I neglected you, he thought. *Christ, I'm so sorry.*

She stopped her twirling and ran for the door. "He's here! He's back!"

Cold fear twisting his gut, he crushed the cookie as he shot to his feet to stop her. "Pixie, no!" But she was already out the door, racing down the hall and around the corner where he couldn't see her anymore. He stopped breathing, and black covered his vision for a second when he rounded the corner. Jeremy grasped for the wall to keep from passing out.

His sister, the only person he cared for in his entire messed-up life, the small redheaded waif, was standing in front of a storybook monster, looking far up at his distorted face. Jesus, she was so small, the top of her head barely reached his stomach!

Hunt stood there, looking down at her with glowing yellow eyes, head cocked to the side as if he didn't know what Pixie was. Had he grown fucking *bigger*? His hair was streaked like tiger fur; shadows of stripes were on his skin one second, then Jeremy blinked and they were gone. His face was inhuman, his fangs enormous. His fingers were clawed again—*and his sister was two feet from him!*

"Bend down," she ordered, and Jeremy panicked, starting forward again.

But he stopped dead when Hunt's head tilted even farther to the side at the sound of her voice. Jeremy didn't dare make any sudden moves. Pixie would pay the price if Hunt got spooked. *—Christ, Pixie, get away from him!—* he thought to her. She wasn't listening.

And then Hunt did something so completely astonishing, it left Jeremy gaping. He got down on one knee in front of the little girl—dozens of grown-ups around, staring, frightened for her, not knowing what to do—and bowed his head so she could reach his hair.

Pixie ruffled his hair and giggled in delight, and when Hunt raised his gaze to her face again, he was *smiling.* But then Pixie stopped laughing, and Hunt's smile faded with the sound. They stared at each other for two full minutes without moving and all the while, Jeremy was frantic inside, ready to kill Hunt if he so much as harmed a hair on her head.

Hunt was the first to move. He slowly pushed to his full height, somehow gaining control of himself as he went, so that by the time he stood straight, he was almost fully human again, except for his eyes, and his claws, which he couldn't seem to change back. He held out his hand palm up, and Pixie put hers into it.

Then, with her hand clasped ever so gently in Hunt's, she turned to Jeremy, pulling Hunt along. "The fluffy one shall behave himself," she announced. "He promised."

Jeremy followed them tensely back to the training room, keeping an eye on Hunt the entire way. Pixie told Hunt to sit, and he did, and then she perched on his lap, as if nothing was wrong. "I don't think your brother likes you so close to me," Hunt said. He didn't sound anything like the voice Jeremy had heard over the phone earlier. More like the roaring beast he'd heard in the alley later.

Pixie sighed and rolled her eyes as if he was being unreasonable, but she scrambled off his lap and sat cross-legged on the floor by the armchair. She even cast Jeremy a pointed look, a silent command to sit. He placed himself between the two of them. If anything happened, he would protect Pixie. Even if it cost him his life.

"He took Dara," Hunt and Pixie said, as if with the same voice. "He'll hurt her. It's my—"

"—not your—"

"—fault."

"He'll hurt her as much as he can before he kills her," they said together again.

"Stop it!" Jeremy snapped. "Get out of her head."

Pixie blinked at him. When she spoke, it was with her voice. Hunt was silent. "He's not doing it, Jer," she said. "I am."

"Well, stop it," he commanded. "You shouldn't even be here."

"I *have to* be here," she told him, crossing her arms over her chest stubbornly. "Dara is gone and he can't focus without her. He needs our help. My—"

"—voice keeps the others away," they said together again.

"I'll fucking kill you for this, Hunt," Jeremy snarled, pushing to his feet. "Leave my sister out of this."

Hunt's face contorted again, his claws digging into his palms. He curled in on himself, clutching his head, visibly fighting for control. "I… can't track her. Here," he said brokenly, but alone.

Jeremy glanced down at Pixie to make sure she was okay. His sister's chin wobbled as she watched Hunt. Crying for the beast. "Pixie, get out of here. Go find Nell and have her make you something to eat."

"But I—"

"No buts. Go." If she was far enough away and occupied, she wouldn't feel Hunt's struggle anymore. It wouldn't hurt her.

Pixie left, closing the door softly behind her.

"Wouldn't have. Hurt her," Hunt said in a growling voice.

"You expect me to believe you? Have you looked in the mirror lately?"

Hunt shook his head sharply. "No. But I can see me. Through you."

Jeremy didn't even feel anything. He *should* feel something if someone else was in his mind.

If it was Pixie… came a stray thought. It was his, but not brought up by him. *If it was Pixie taken, and I couldn't find her…* "Stop it."

"Need to find her," Hunt said.

"And you can't track her."

"This place stinks. Too many scents. Can't find hers."

"Her mind?"

"Black. Unconscious."

John had told him what Dara had done yesterday. The killer knew Dara could get inside his head. He was crazy, but he wasn't stupid. Of course he would have knocked her out. If she wasn't conscious, she couldn't read his mind.

Jeremy paced to the cookie plate and back again. He looked at Hunt, who was now sitting back with his eyes closed and his jaw locked, barely hanging on. He returned to the plate of cookies and brought it back with him. "Have one," he said, rolling his eyes at himself. He was sounding like Pixie. "Chocolate will do you good."

One golden eye cracked open. A black-clawed hand uncurled, one bloody finger at a time. Hunt took a cookie gingerly but, like Jeremy, he didn't eat it. Probably couldn't open his jaw enough to take a bite.

"We'll find her," Jeremy said, making an attempt to be supportive. But with the vision of his little sister standing so fearlessly in front of Hunt, it was damn difficult.

"If we're too late…"

"We won't be."

"I'll kill him," Hunt said savagely and Jeremy's mind flooded with scenes of torture like he hadn't seen before, even in Dara's memories of the killer. This was Hunt's doing. What he was capable of, and what he would let loose again, just as he had before. Far too much had been torn away from him already. He wouldn't lose Dara, too. That woman's grace was all that stood between him and what he'd once become to avenge his family. He wouldn't hesitate to become it again if anything happened to her.

"When I'm done," Hunt said, "stop me."

Jeremy looked into his golden tiger eyes; Hunt wouldn't let him look away. He wanted something from Jeremy. Didn't need words; a nod would do. He wasn't asking for a cage, or a tranquilizer, because neither would stop him, and both of them knew it.

Jeremy nodded. Once. When he gave his word, he never went back on it. Both of them knew that, too.

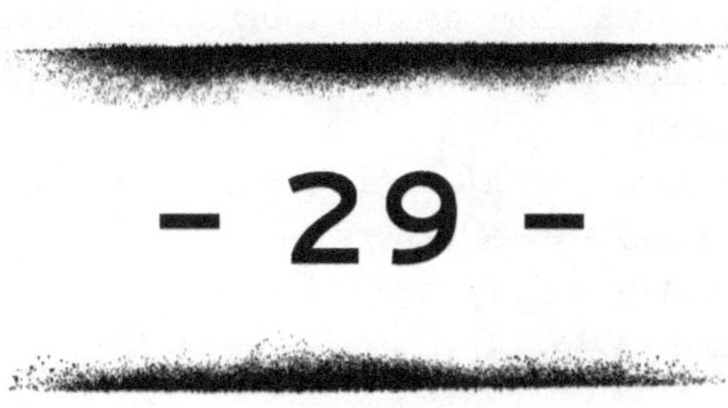

- 29 -

Some time later

—*Wake up... Wake up... Dara,* wake up!—

Dara couldn't open her eyes. She was blindfolded, lying on her side on a hard floor, with her hands and feet bound. As she dragged herself out of the fog and back to consciousness, she felt nauseated and could guess that the blow to the head she'd received had probably caused a concussion. Her body hurt. Her shoulder was bruised, and her hip and left her leg were numb.

—*Dara...*—

—*I'm here.*— Everything echoed in her mind. She felt dizzy, as if she'd just fallen down after spinning for an hour.

A wave of relief hit her, nearly making her pass out. She moaned in her mind. —*Don't do that.*—

—*Are you hurt?*—

She hesitated. —*Yes.*—

Rage.

—*Tristan, stop.*—

He pulled back the maelstrom of emotion, but stayed with her. —*Do you know where you are?*— His voice brushed away the cobwebs, but it couldn't stop the pounding pain.

—*No, but it's cold.*—

She felt him settle over her senses, gauging what she felt, what she heard and smelled. Dara didn't have his mutant nose. All she smelled was dust and cement. That meant nothing in a city filled with both. Tristan pulled up her memories of seeing Katie through the killer's eyes as a question.

—*Could be there. Can't tell.*— And even if she was, they still didn't know the location. —*What time is it?*—

He didn't answer. —*Can you sit up?*—

—*Not sure.*—

—*Try.*—

Dara pulled her knees to her chest and tried to lever herself up. Without the use of her hands, without knowing what was around her, and with the constant feeling of vertigo from the concussion, it was like trying to stand up on an out of control merry-go-round.

"Good morning." Brendon Z sounded like he was within ten feet of her. Dara stopped moving, and in her mind, Tristan stilled. "Took you long enough. I was beginning to worry that you wouldn't wake up in time."

"In time for what?" she asked. Her tongue felt thick in her mouth.

He grabbed her by her hair, tearing it out where it had stuck to her skull with dried blood. Dara cried out as he pulled her head up. "For the big finale, bitch," he said right in her face, his rancid breath scorching her.

The blindfold absorbed her tears. Tristan had retreated, but from a distance, she felt his rage and was glad he was shielding her from it. He was moving. Where, she didn't know.

"What's the matter? Can't use that clever little brain of yours?" He tapped her head hard with something heavy. "I was wondering if that would do the trick."

—*Breathe in deep, Dara.*—

She did. Except for Brendon Z's breath, she smelled nothing.

Brendon Z released her and she fell back, her head thumping against the floor. She nearly knocked herself out again. "You have five hours, bitch. If you're the praying type, now would be a good time to confess your sins."

Has to justify his actions as the right ones, she recalled. *Very super-stitious; use it against him!* The impulse was strong enough that she and Tristan might just have come up with it at the same time. There wasn't much she had going for her right now. She had to exploit any small advantage.

"No, but I'll hear yours," she said, fighting to sit up again.

Brendon Z laughed. "My sins? Who the hell do you think you are?"

—*Your death,*— Tristan said in her mind, wanting her to say it out loud. "The harbinger of your death," she said instead. She'd made it to an unsteady, half-sitting position on her hip, but it took muscle strength she didn't have now to keep herself upright.

The killer was quiet for a long moment. Then a hard, booted kick to her side sent her sprawling again. It knocked the breath out of her, and she coughed weakly, fighting the darkness reaching out to her. "My brain is full of demons," he said in a hollow voice. "One more makes no difference. Whatever you tried to do, it didn't work. Dragons don't fear mice."

Dara had no idea what he was talking about. "You know, you sounded a lot more rational in my head. How'd you even find me?"

He got in her face again. "Can't you read my mind?"

She attempted a shrug. "Can. Won't. I feel sick enough already."

She felt him draw back. "Imagine living with that sickness day after day," he said in that hollow voice. "Imagine not being able to escape the voices, the faces, not even in sleep."

"Is that…" No, she had to be hearing wrong. He couldn't possibly… "Are you seriously asking for my sympathy?"

"And if I am?"

Aaaand we're back to psycho again. Amazingly, Dara wasn't afraid. He wasn't a formless nightmare anymore. He was a flesh and blood man. A twisted monster, yes, but somehow far less fearsome than she'd imagined him. Now she had a tangible target. *Now* she could fight him.

Now, she only felt anger. That this sick piece of shit had dared to touch her… galling. "You conked me on the head, dragged me God knows where, and you plan to sadistically murder me and put my body on display. Hmm, let me think for a second. Here's what I think: fuck you, asshole."

Tristan read her intent the second it sprang up in her mind and lowered his shields around her just as she gathered her strength to force her way into Brendon Z's mind. He screamed again, and Dara vaguely heard him fall, but she didn't have time to pay attention. She looked for anything that might tell her where she was, but he knew what she was looking for and confused her with a flood of other places.

Shuffling noises came at her, then he hit her with that heavy thing again and again, trying to dislodge her from his head. Dara held steady, feeling bones break. He would kill her if she didn't stop, but he'd kill her later anyway. Anything she could find and pass on to Tristan was a chance that they might find her still alive. Bruises and broken bones healed. Death did not.

The killer was imagining his revenge again. He would make it last a long time for this, and for ruining his plans with Katie. He had a location already picked out—wide open and very public, and not far from here. He wasn't about to drag her too far. Dara pried the location from him, but got several others along with it.

When he hit her over the head again, Dara had just enough time to shove what she'd found at Tristan before she passed out again.

~

She woke up with no idea how much time had passed. She was still lying on the floor, it still felt and smelled the same, and her eyes were still covered. But now, on top of that, her head was splitting and her body was in so much pain she could barely breathe. Dara didn't even try telepathy.

Somewhere nearby, Brendon Z was muttering something to himself. She couldn't make out what he was saying, but the fact that he was so unstable he was talking to himself scared her. Was he even speaking English? She picked up on a rhythmic thumping sound and imagined him banging his head against the wall.

Shit, she was really in trouble here.

The thumping stopped, and she heard footsteps coming toward her. The final step brought his foot to within inches of her face. He stopped muttering. "It's time," he said. A heavy blanket fell over her, and he hauled her up and over his shoulder. Every bruise and broken bone jarred, and Dara screamed. Her voice was muffled by the blanket.

She had no sense of direction. Her head was swimming, but she counted the second until they stopped moving again. The killer waited for fifteen seconds, then continued walking. A traffic light? He didn't have any qualms about ripping people apart, but he drew the line at jaywalking?

Dara counted to 217 before he stopped again. This time, he dropped her on the ground and pulled the blanket off her. He checked the blindfold, added a gag. When he cut the binds on her legs, Dara recognized the opportunity to fight back, but she was too weak to do any damage. He slapped her hard across the face for her efforts.

He was retying her legs to something, like a post in the ground. When he was done, Brendon Z turned his attention to her wrists. Her arm was broken. When he cut the binds, it hurt. When he brought her hands forward, it hurt even more. When her retied wrists were pulled up so her weight hung on them, Dara began wishing for death.

She thrashed her head, trying to knock herself out again, but all she managed to do was dislodge the blindfold from one eye. They were outside, surrounded by tall buildings that looked like enormous black bricks in the night. Her vision was blurry; she didn't recognize any of them.

But she did recognize the giant metal claw that rent the air on her right.

Oh, God. He'd chosen the location for maximum effect. When he was done, it would look like the tiger had torn her apart. She didn't have to look into his mind to know that whatever message he decided to scrawl with her blood, it would include the word *beast*.

You bastard! She wanted to scream. How dare he desecrate the beautiful thing like this!

But Dara had bigger problems than a bloodied statue.

Brendon Z was spreading the blanket on the ground in front of her, laying out a collection of gleaming knives. There were all shapes and sizes, and he arranged them precisely in a row, not a fraction of an inch out of place. He looked up at the sky, searching for something.

Ritual. Tristan had been right, Brendon Z needed to see the stars above him. His eyes closed and his mouth moved in something like a prayer. To what, she didn't want to know.

Dara couldn't take a proper breath. She was in agony, lightheaded, and a moment away from either passing out or dying. She wanted to scream for help, but the only sound she made was in her mind, and even that was feeble. Why wasn't she passing out? God, she'd been beaten to within an inch of her life; why was she still alive?

The killer passed a reverent hand over his knives, then picked one out and stood. He was muttering under his breath again as he came to stand before her. His violet gaze was fixed on her chest, not even looking at her face. She tried to reach out to his mind, command him to stop, but it only made her head hurt more. Dara was helpless to do anything but hang there and watch him spread his arms wide in a sort of supplication.

Desperate for this not to be her last sight on Earth, Dara sought Tristan's face in her memories. She drew on the summer day, a meal shared with friends, and built a world around it, pretending that was the end of her story. Sharing happiness and sunshine with the man she'd fallen in love with. Dara needed that tranquility to comfort her now.

But even that little thing was to be denied her. Her mind was fractured, couldn't hold on to the image and she was expelled right back to the present and the murderous psychopath before her.

He brought the tip of the knife to her chest and cut.

He'd lost her. One moment he'd been flinching at the blows to her fragile body, and the next she was just… gone. He'd torn the training room apart in his rage, felt people outside herding others away from him. Tristan didn't care about any of them. The moment he'd deciphered the jumble of images Dara had sent him, he'd been running out the door.

Common sense told him there were others who could help. Calen and MacMurphy hadn't left his side since he'd returned here after scouring block after block without finding the smallest hint to track. They could be out there looking for her, too. But he didn't have any common sense left. He sprinted down one block, then another, looking for the landmarks Dara had shown him.

He'd failed her once already. He wouldn't—*couldn't*—do it again. Her life depended on Tristan making sense of what she'd risked her life to get for him. Helpless, hurt, and so damn brave, Dara had put her trust in him. He *had* to find her.

This city was vast, and all the buildings looked the same. When he heard sirens behind him, he ran faster, not about to be stopped. But the transport pulled up alongside him and Calen stuck his head out. "Get in," he said. "We'll find her faster if we drive."

"No," he said, his voice inhuman. Instead, he shoved what Dara had given him at the man. The transport swerved, nearly colliding with a lamppost.

Calen swore and steered back toward him. "Go straight three blocks and turn right," he said. "I'll check out the other sites." Then the transport peeled away, sirens blaring. Soon the night was echoing with a chorus of them.

Tristan ran in the direction Calen had pointed out. Three blocks. He turned right. Three more blocks. Nothing.

He stopped. Drew air deep into his lungs. Closed his eyes to focus, searching, searching. Hunting for his prey. The killer didn't have a scent. Just like in his dream, he was a void where something ought to be. He ignored him for the time being. Dara was his priority. He'd memorized her scent long ago; it was now part of him. Tristan could track her by it anywhere.

He had to do it now.

A rare breeze, kicked up by the traffic of police transports, tickled his nose with a hint.

Tristan breathed it in again, fangs aching. *—I'm coming, Dara.—*

He turned right and ran as fast as his legs would carry him. They were outside. And the farther he ran, the stronger her scent became. He was getting closer. Her fear, her blood maddened him, gave him strength to push on. The killer hurt her even more…

Around another corner, he emerged in a small square. Three hundred yards in front of him, the giant tiger's tail curled to one side. Tristan heard a faint voice, barely a whisper at this distance, but he still heard it. Male. Chanting.

He stalked out, death in his stride, in his claws, aching and curling, ready to rip and tear into flesh. Tristan sought a mind; found *his*. Looked through his eyes and saw a knife poised against Dara's chest. It cut before he could stop it. Dara sobbed.

Tristan broke into a run, taking control of the killer's mind at the same time. He made the bastard freeze, then back up, far away from his mate. And he relished the pain it caused the son of a bitch. He rounded the statue and launched himself at the killer, changing as he flew through the air. The tiger roared in triumph, landing on top of the violet-eyed monster who would not die. Tristan would show him how it worked.

Mercilessly, he drew his claws slowly down the killer's chest, cutting him open a few inches. Not enough to kill, just scoring the skin and scraping bone. Tristan didn't allow him to make a sound, all the while holding his gaze and letting him know exactly how he would die. Slowly. Painfully.

He relished the panic clouding the killer's mind, the voices that screamed at him, tearing him apart from the inside as the tiger cut into his flesh from the outside. One thing to mess with a mind already messed up. Another to mess with the body attached to it, bringing a shadowy demon to flesh-and-blood life. The tiger became the demon the killer had learned to fear.

He stepped on his prey's arm, leaned his weight on it, crushing bone. The knife fell out of its hand—*its*. The killer was no longer human, but a thing. To be played with. To be ended. He reared up and let his weight drop on it again and again. Once for every time it had hit Dara.

And he was just getting started.

"I think I see them," John said, and Jeremy turned the corner, following his directions. "Christ," the man muttered. Jeremy had to bend low over the steering wheel to identify what he was looking at.

Dara was strung up against the tiger statue. He couldn't tell if she was conscious, or even alive. She wasn't moving. "Do you see Hunt?"

John hesitated. Then he sucked in a breath. "Jesus!"

Yep, he saw him. Jeremy turned off the sirens and drove onto the square, stopping a reasonable distance from the tiger playing with his prey. The killer wasn't yelling, but as Jeremy got out of the car and pulled his gun, his mind was assaulted by mental screams so horrifying, he had to shut them out. Hunt wasn't letting him scream out loud. *Jesus…*

John motioned for him to circle around from the other side. It was a stupid idea, but they had no choice. The tiger was growling, almost a gleeful purr as he dug his claws into his prey. He knew where to cut to cause pain, but keep the killer alive as long as possible. Normally, Jeremy wasn't a big supporter of torture. Normally.

As he took in Dara's condition, he began to reconsider. "Hunt," he said in a carefully level voice. He'd given his word to stop Tristan. With a bullet, if need be. But he would do everything he possibly could to not have to honor it. As far as Jeremy was concerned, Hunt was justified in everything he did to the fucker.

The tiger growled at him, flashing enormous fangs. *—Don't interfere.—*

"Tristan," he tried again. "Dara is hurt." She wasn't moving. Her jacket and shirt were cut open, but he couldn't see if the cut had been deep enough to injure her.

Again, the tiger growled, ripping into his prey even more. Jeremy blocked out the killer's mind. He didn't want to know. He'd be having nightmares about this for the rest of his life as was.

"Tristan, she might die."

That brought his head up. He stared Jeremy down, then glared at John, who'd been trying to reach Dara. The older man stopped in his tracks and held his hands up. "Easy," he said. Tristan looked over his shoulder at Dara, making a pained noise.

The other transports were nearing. John would have told them where to go and to turn off their sirens. It was anyone's guess what the tiger that used to be Tristan Hunt would do if something spooked him. Best-case scenario, he'd run off. Worst-case, he'd go for the nearest neck and take out as many people as he could before Jeremy brought himself to pull the trigger. He didn't want to. Didn't want to have to go back and explain to Pixie what he'd done.

Hunt could hear the others approaching already. It didn't seem to bother him. At least not as much as the sight of Dara, beaten and unconscious, strung up in the statue's jaw—a statue that uncannily resembled him.

It's my fault, he'd said back at HQ. Would he see this as a sign that he'd been right?

When he turned his gaze back to the killer, Jeremy was sure the man knew his end was coming.

Tristan snarled and bit into his neck, mercilessly jerking his head to break it. The killer was left bleeding, paralyzed, but alive. For now. Tristan shook himself out, turned his back on the killer, and stalked toward Dara. He dislodged the ropes tying her legs with his claws, then, before Jeremy's eyes, the tiger transformed into a man. A very big, very naked man.

He took one of the knives laid out on the ground, put his arm around Dara to catch her, and cut the rope binding her arms. She fell limp against him, and he cradled her in his arms, sitting on the blanket with her. "Call an ambulance," he said to them, without looking away from her.

"They're on their way," John said, waving at Jeremy to holster his weapon.

As long as he lived, Jeremy would never forget the sight they presented: a man and his mate, sitting in the shelter of a giant tiger protector. Dara would live; Hunt wouldn't allow her to do otherwise. She would heal and regain her strength, and soon she would forget this had ever happened.

Jeremy heard sirens approaching and met John's gaze. The older man shook his head, his fingers pressed to the inside of the killer's wrist. Just as well. It was cheaper to bury a psychotic serial killer than have him stand trial. Jeremy holstered his gun and went to intercept the ambulance.

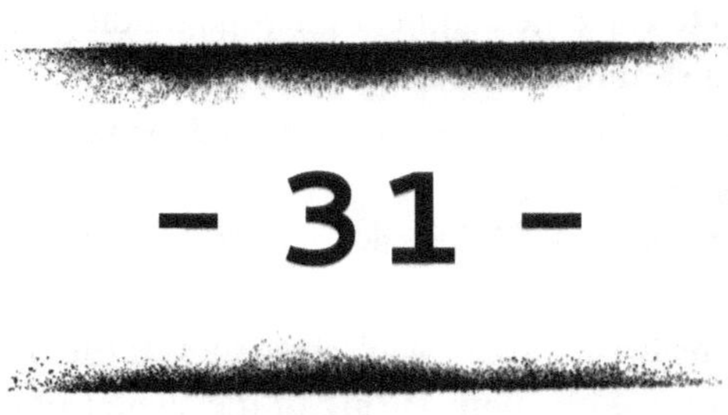

– 31 –

August 14, 3028

Two months later, the story of the Blood Moons killer was still in the headlines. With the killer dead by a confirmed case of animal attack, the police were happy to tell the public that his latest victim, Katie Grayson, had been retrieved and, after a short stay in the hospital, returned to her family, safe and sound.

The city of Gray Dublin returned to its artificial routine, none the worse for wear. It seemed that everything was happy and normal again.

But it wasn't.

Not in a claustrophobic hospital room with a small window looking out onto another building where Tristan sat by Dara's bedside, watching over her sleep. A coma, the doctors said. The blow to her head—or a number of them—had caused enough damage that, after Dara had lost consciousness out there, she hadn't woken up.

Bandages were still wrapped around her broken ribs. The cuts and bruises she'd sustained were healing rapidly. Minor surgery had fixed her broken arm. A more involved operation had done everything humanly possible to stop the intercranial bleeding and mend her skull. But the damage to her brain, they warned, could possibly be permanent.

She might not wake up—ever.

Tristan had run out the last doctor who'd said that to him. Only nurses came in now, bringing him food and checking on Dara's vitals, making sure the intravenous fluids were okay. They'd talked to him in the beginning. Now they came in, hastily did their job, and left again.

For the first couple of weeks, the little girl, Pixie, had shown up, too. She'd never come in, just peered inside around the door at him, watched him for a few minutes in silence, then disappeared again. Then her brother had come in one day to tell him that he'd done all he could to clear Tristan's name.

The Special Unit had been given custody of him, and they would be responsible if he got out of hand. Calen had told him that no one at the unit believed he would be getting out of hand anymore. He'd assured Tristan that they wouldn't be following him or checking on him anymore, but might drop in for a friendly visit, and not to take it personally. Apparently, some of the younger ones had taken a liking to him.

And they did continue to show up, at least once a day, to look at the weretiger guarding Dara. They even talked sometimes.

All of it fell on deaf ears as Tristan read Dara's favorite book to her. He ignored everyone who came in, focusing all of his attention on her. Because if he slipped, even for a second, he had no idea what might happen. He couldn't breathe. His stomach was in knots constantly. He rarely slept anymore because every time he did, he dreamed of her. But it wasn't his Dara who floated like a vision through his unconscious mind. It was just a projection of a ghost, a memory.

Dara was sleeping, far away where he couldn't reach her. He couldn't even find her in her mind. At first, he'd been frantic to find her. But as the days had gone by and still there'd been no sign of her, Tristan had realized that the brain damage might have cut her off from him telepathically. The only recourse he had, then, was to reach her with his voice.

So he read. He'd read her favorite book to her three times now. It was a story set in ancient Scotland, in a mighty castle sheltered by the sea on one side and a forest filled with mythical creatures on the other. The story had clan battles, magical faeries and demons, political struggles, and even murder mysteries. But at the core was the tale of a man and woman, a chance meeting, and a fated love that overcame all adversity.

Such a simple concept—love overcoming anything. He understood now why she would read this story over and over again. Understood every heartfelt phrase she'd highlighted and bookmarked. Even before all of this, Dara had known the world as only few people could ever know it. She hadn't had the luxury of ignorance; every dark corner of people's hearts and souls had been open to her from the first.

Faced with so much darkness, she'd turned to the only light she could find flickering softly between the pages of books where everything always ended happily. He wanted to give her that happy ending. Even if she never knew it. As soon as the doctors cleared her for transport, he wanted to take Dara someplace beautiful. To build her a fairy tale she could dream about, wherever she was.

Tristan turned off the electronic reader and set it aside. He rubbed a shaky hand over his face and unfolded from his seat. His entire body was cramped, but he didn't care. He sat on the edge of Dara's bed and watched her sleep. Bandages were wrapped around her head, but the bruises on her face had already faded to almost nothing. Soon there would be no sign left that she'd ever suffered so much pain. He took her hand in his, brought it to his cheek, wishing he could take the pain for her.

He brushed her cheek, kissed her still lips. Cursed whatever power or universal design had brought this all down on someone so wholly undeserving of it. "Dara, open your eyes," he whispered. "Please, baby. I need you. Wake up."

She didn't respond. The monitors showing her heart and brain activity never even flickered. Tristan stayed close, needing to feel her breath. He strained to hear even a whisper of her thoughts.

There was only silence.

"You've been sitting in here for hours," a nurse said from the doorway.

Tristan didn't acknowledge her. —*I love you.*— He sent the words as deep as they would go. Dara had to hear him; she had to know.

"You should go outside for a while. Take a walk. Go eat something."

"No," he said. If Dara woke up and he wasn't here… —*Dara,*— he tried again. —*Come back to me. Ah, God, love, save me.*— Or, if not him, then everyone else *from* him.

"Your friends were here again, but since you told us not to let anyone in anymore…"

Tristan touched his forehead to Dara's. Her steady breaths assured him that she was still alive, her heart still beating. He'd give his life a thousand times over to see her awake again. If he thought it would help, he'd jump out the window, smiling all the way down. If she would just wake up. —*Wake up…*—

"She's not waking up," the nurse said peevishly. "Maybe it's time you moved on."

"*Get out!*" he roared at her, turning feral, glowing eyes on her.

She screamed and fled, slamming the door behind her. He could still hear her screaming all the way down the hall.

When he heard the door open again a few moments later, his claws sharpened, ready to kill someone. *Go away,* he willed silently. *Leave us be.*

"You always did have a unique way with women."

Tristan looked up, disbelieving. "You…"

Amelia smiled a little, cautiously closing the door behind her, and came a couple of steps closer, but not too close. "I heard what happened," she said. "I'm so sorry, Tristan. For everything." She looked so young, dressed in a pair of jeans and a sweater with the sleeves rolled up. But her eyes showed the strain of her years. And a lot of it, he knew, he'd caused.

He didn't think he'd ever see her again. He swallowed past the lump in his throat to find his voice. "Can you help her?" He dreaded the answer.

"May I come closer?"

He nodded, but didn't relinquish his place at Dara's side.

Amelia approached with wary caution. "You know," she said, keeping her voice steady, "I read up on tigers a little. They're very solitary creatures. They don't mate for life, and aren't possessive of their mates. Females raise the cubs alone, and males have been known to kill another's cubs to mate with the female themselves." She took Dara's chart and read through every entry.

"So?"

She shrugged, glancing at him briefly. "Just saying that you can't blame me for your attachment to her. Your tiger instincts have nothing to do with it. If anything, they should work as an antidote for… whatever you do suffer from." Her lips twitched, Tristan noticed. He didn't see any humor in the situation.

"Maybe it's fate, then," he said, turning Dara's hand palm up to trace her fingers. Texts ancient and modern were filled with stories of destiny and fated paths, people meant to find each other, fight each other, or love each other. Was it all just human imagination, and if so, why would they place the power over their own lives so far out of their own reach? Why let someone or something else decide whether they got to be happy in their lives? Why bind themselves to someone who might or might not show up—might not even *exist*?

It almost seemed more reasonable to believe there *was* such a thing as fate. *Something* had given Dara the ability to witness a murder. Something had brought her to him light years away, on a different planet. Something had made him love her so much it killed him to look at her now and not see her looking back. That *something* needed to bring her back to him again.

"Stranger things have happened lately," Amelia said. She turned her attention back to the chart. "Says here she's on the mend. Her injuries are healing very well and her body should be back to normal very soon. They're blaming the coma on brain damage, but there doesn't seem to be anything in her scans to indicate where or what kind." She was still looking over the chart as she spoke.

"You're saying they lied?"

"No, not at all. The brain is a complicated organ. Doctors can estimate what a spleen, or a liver, or a stomach should look like, but the structure of the brain is unique for every individual, shaped by memories and experiences. By definition, a telepath would create different perceptions than other people. Hence, her brain structure is vastly different from, say, mine. It could be that they just can't see where she's hurt."

"But you scanned her in New Alaska," he said. "You could compare the scans and find the differences."

"Tristan," she said softly, "even if I could do that, it probably wouldn't help. I could fix the structure, the brain, but not what's inside."

"Her mind," he supplied. He hadn't really thought it could work.

Amelia nodded. "Can't you reach her?"

Tristan shook his head. "I can't find her. It's like walking through an empty maze. Even when I reach the center, she's not there." Could be she was just as lost and they kept missing each other. But if that was the case, it would take much more than just him to find her.

Tristan started. "Genius," he said.

"What? What did you figure out?"

For the first time in weeks, Tristan felt his mouth want to smile. He raced out the door, yelling back at Amelia, "Do *not* leave her side!"

~

It would take an army to find Dara in so much empty space. And Tristan realized he already had one. Amelia pulled some strings to have Dara moved to a bigger room, and now thirty-two telepaths crowded around her, eager to try a new experiment with their abilities. Half of them were trainees, but he couldn't afford to be picky. Their boss, MacMurphy, would keep them in line to keep them safe from Tristan.

Calen and his sister weren't there. They'd left Earth a few days ago, MacMurphy said *on vacation*, but they both knew that the siblings probably wouldn't be coming back. It bothered Tristan. The girl was strong, and she had something the rest of them lacked—an innate intuition about people and how their minds worked. If anyone would have found Dara, it would have been her.

"Listen up," Tristan said. "We'll go slow. You follow my instructions *to the letter*. This isn't playtime. If something goes wrong, Dara could die." Thirty-one people drew back a step. "We go in the order of experience. Seniors first, trainees last. One at a time. Understood?"

A fifteen-year-old boy somewhere in the middle of the throng raised his hand high to be seen. "What do we do when we find her?"

Good question. "You alert me. I'll take it from there." *Somehow...* "Are we ready?"

"Wait!" Amelia pushed through the telepaths to reach Dara. "I think I have one last miracle in me," she said, holding up a syringe.

"What is it?"

"It's a kind of adrenaline cocktail. A neural stimulant. I haven't had a chance to test it properly, but if I'm right, it should make her mind more active and easier to find."

Another experimental serum. What a surprise. But this was Dara she wanted to test it on. "How certain are you that it will work?"

"Hey, if you can put together a search party, at least I can give you a beacon to follow. I'm ninety-six percent certain it will work. There's a point two percent chance it will cause side effects."

"What kind of side effects?"

"Hyperactivity, possibly depression, maybe some minor memory loss. But they should be temporary." She was waiting for him to make the decision.

"Maybe we should go in first," MacMurphy suggested. "Get a feel for our surroundings. When something changes, it'll be easier to spot."

The man had a point. If this worked, it might be doable with fewer people. The less they interfered in her mind, the safer it would be for Dara. They were—*he* was—already taking a risk with this plan. "Okay, senior agents first. You'll follow my lead. Amelia, I'll give you a signal when it's time. Call in more help only if it's absolutely necessary."

Amelia flipped a switch and typed something on a small pad on the side of Dara's bed. When the scanned image of her body appeared above her, Amelia focused it on Dara's head and brain. "Just in case," she said.

Tristan glared.

"What?" she said. "You don't know what this might do to her. What if something goes wrong? This way we can at least see *where* it goes wrong."

"And you have a great way to observe and document physical evidence of telepathic activity."

She blushed, but didn't turn the scanner off. "It's a win-win, as far as I can see." Amelia had learned her lesson all too well in New Alaska. She wasn't about to start experimenting again, especially not on someone's mind. What drove her was sheer curiosity, the scientist in her always wanting to look for answers. Tristan supposed there was no harm to it.

"Are we ready?" he asked the team.

Senior agents—ten of them—stepped up, and everyone else backed away toward the walls to give them room.

"I'll wait for your signal," Amelia said, her syringe at the ready.

"I'll go first," Tristan said.

MacMurphy nodded, trying to reassure him. "We're right behind you."

Tristan took Dara's hand in his, needing to feel her with him in any way he could. Then he closed his eyes, steadied his breathing, and sank slowly, carefully into her mind…

There was fog all around him. So thick, he couldn't see his own feet. Nothing had changed since the last time, then. He was walking blind, feeling his way with the toe of his shoe before he put his weight on it. One careful step after another, he made his way, arms outstretched to feel what was before him.

The next step brought his foot onto something hard. Wood. Old, grooved, but sturdy enough. Planks nailed together to form a bridge of some sort. No, not a bridge—a pier. He almost stepped right off the end of it. Tristan crouched low to trace its edges, then reached over to feel for water. There wasn't any. He had to duck his head below the level of the pier to see the dry, sandy bottom of what used to be a lake.

He sat up again, commanded his physical body to move his hand. He didn't care whether the others were in by now. They'd just have to deal with it. "Hello!" he called. "Dara!"

After a moment, the fog stirred. He could feel a breeze, but couldn't tell which way it was coming from. Tristan stood up, looking around for any sign of movement. There! Somewhere in the distance beyond the pier, a pair of flickering red lights, like fireflies. Barely visible, but there. At the same time he saw them, someone else sounded the alarm, "pointing" in that direction.

Tristan took off at a run, fell off the pier into a deep ditch—the lake bed. He picked himself up, changed shape, and loped blindly toward those lights. He tripped, he fell. He got up, never once looking away from those lights, afraid they'd disappear and he'd be just as lost as before.

The other end of the lake was even deeper. He collided with an almost sheer wall of brittle dirt and sand. He shook himself off, backed up a few steps, then jumped, hoping he'd make it. His front claws just dug into the edge of the precipice, but the earth crumbled beneath him and he slid all the way back down.

Growling, he backed up farther to get a running start and tried again. He got a better grip this time, dug his hind claws into the sheer side and hauled himself up over the edge. The fog was thinner here; he could see a few steps ahead. The lights were brighter as well.

Where were the others?

Immediately, three lights winked in the distance around him: the other telepaths announcing themselves. They were coming toward Dara, too. The tiger bristled to have others so close to his mate, but the man knew he might need them.

He kept running, chasing the red fireflies, dry grass changing to mud beneath his paws, then to foliage. There were suddenly fallen trees to jump over, thick shrubs he had to claw his way through. He was in a forest, giant trees forming shadows against the fog all around him. Tristan slowed. He knew those trees.

The red lights winked out for a moment, then reappeared, but they were fading. Fear of losing them spurred him on and he ignored every-thing except his path. As the fog thinned even more, he began to hear sounds, birdsong and insects. A howler monkey somewhere high above him. It was a melody he was all too familiar with.

Again, the others announced themselves, four of them this time. They were closing in on the red lights. Tristan picked up speed, needing to get there before the others. He roared at the top of his lungs, sounding his position. The red lights swirled madly, then winked out again. Tristan ran headlong in the direction they'd been, not daring to blink.

They took longer than before to reappear. If he didn't find them soon, they'd disappear completely.

"Over here!" someone shouted. Tristan followed the sound, ran across a fallen tree, and landed in a clearing shaped like a hexagon and bordered by giant, twisting tree roots. He could just make out MacMurphy to his right, and a woman on his left. Knew there was a third on the other side of her, and someone else catching up.

Tristan didn't acknowledge any of them. He was frozen, staring at a giant pillar of what looked like crystal standing in the middle of the clearing. There was no more fog here, and that crystal shone, as if lit from underneath.

Inside it, Dara stood, her hands placed on the smooth walls, looking at him. She could move in there, he realized, but couldn't get out. He approached slowly, changing along the way, then matched his hands to hers. A brilliant tear glittered its way down her cheek. He couldn't feel her through the thick wall.

Tristan leaned his forehead against the crystal, pushing to get a sense of her. Any small hint.

Like a punch in the stomach, he got her memories…

Pain. So much of it he couldn't breathe. Darkness. Then just barely catching a glimpse of a knife poised at her chest. She ran. Retreated so quickly, she shocked herself. One second there, about to die, the next running across a grassy field, death nipping at her heels, grass wilting behind her as she ran.

Running, running, so fast… She dived into the forest, looking for him—her safety net—to catch her. She ran until she found his lair, a clearing surrounded by lush flowers. Bordered by giant roots as a defensive wall.

She tripped. Fell. Sensed the knife's cut. Ducked for cover as a massive boom shook this world. Then she sensed the threat retreat. Knew it was safe again. Got up to run back…

And collided with the crystal wall.

Tristan shouted and punched the crystal, pounded at it, trying to break through. He circled around, looking for a weakness. The crystal was smooth from all sides, rounded at the top like melting ice, but solid all the way around.

Christ, he was losing it again. He could feel his chest going so tight he couldn't take a breath. What he was seeing was affecting him physically, and the physical distracted him, pulling him back out. He fought it with everything he had. He had to get Dara out somehow.

The others were on the other side, conferring, putting ideas together. There had to be a way. Nothing was ever perfect. Everything had a flaw; Tristan just had to find it. He sank to the ground, leaning his back against the crystal and digging his hands into the soft earth to think.

Then he looked at his hands. In the dirt.

He turned around so fast he startled Dara, but she shook it off quickly and met his questioning gaze. She looked down at the ground on her side, and when her eyes met his again, they were filled with stubborn determination. She nodded.

They dug into the earth at the same time. Tristan changed again, the tiger more suited to this than the man. He braced his hind legs and dug down with his front claws, scraping them against the crystal, but he didn't care. Blocked out the cloying screech it produced.

Tristan knew it would take Dara longer to dig a hole big enough from her side by herself. He wouldn't meet her halfway, but dig himself all the way to her if he had to.

The crystal wall was two feet thick. By the time he got down to its edge and across the bottom of it, Tristan was completely underground, with the others waiting for him outside.

He was digging his way up now, dirt falling into his eyes, his nose; he ignored it. There should have been complete darkness, but he could still see where he was going. Finally, the ground above him began to give way. He widened the tiny hole, made it bigger, big enough for a person to pass through.

When he caught Dara's hand, he was human again. Fingers curling tight around her wrist, he pulled...

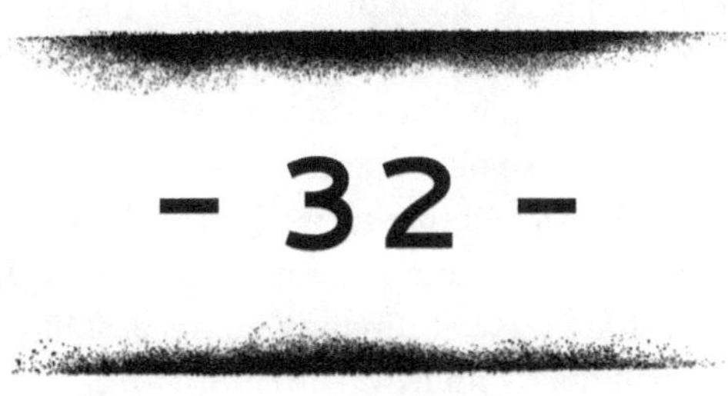

– 32 –

September 27, 3028

"You are *not* building a castle here!"

"Why not? The Jenkins, two parcels south, are building a cathedral. And it's not even an original design. They're copying Notre Dame, down to the last pew."

Dara sputtered, turning another circle on the hill where he'd taken them for a *picnic*. There were vast open spaces as far as she could see. On one side, the hill lowered gently to a bright white beach and a lake the size of Gray Dublin. On the next side, the slope was almost a sheer, jagged drop into a thick forest. She refused to go too close to that edge. And on the third side the hill was *tiered*, as if someone had cut into it halfway up and made a level platform.

Tristan put his hands on her shoulders. "Stop spinning. You'll make yourself dizzy," he said with a self-satisfied grin. "This is the perfect place for it."

"Not to mention," Calen chimed in dryly, "that Torrey doesn't have official building regulations yet. If you're going to build, now is the time. And it just so happens, you're not the only whimsical idiot on this planet, either. I heard of at least three more castles going up, and those are developers. They'll be building entire villages to go with the castle."

Whimsical was definitely the right word to describe Tristan. As if the past decade had never happened, as soon as he'd stepped foot on Torrey, he'd completely let go of it all, and it was like watching a brand-new person look out over the world. He was carefree, playful, took joy in every little thing, like a kid who still saw wonder. On this world, that didn't seem so out of place.

Dara had asked him about that a few days ago. Looking at her with his eyes glowing with emotion, he'd said that he was getting a new start and he wouldn't waste it dwelling on his past life. He'd rather live the one he had now, with her.

He was determined to make this one a fairy tale. But just how literal was it going to be?

Dara stared at Calen. "Why are you encouraging him?"

"Why shouldn't I?" he returned, grinning. "I'm not the one who'll be living in it." No. The Calens had bought themselves a nice lakeside cottage with an acre of land, where he'd already begun planting an orchard.

Pixie laughed and twirled around. "This is where the ballroom can be," she said.

Dara shook her head. "No. No, this will not be happening."

Tristan turned her toward the lower tier and pointed to it. "See that there? That's where the bailey will be," he told her proudly. What the hell a bailey was, she had no idea.

"Stop talking like it's a done deal. I will *not* be living in a giant cave on a hill. Period. And where would you even get the stone, anyway? Not to mention, *how* would you even haul it here?" She held her hand up when Tristan opened his mouth to reply. "No, don't tell me. I really don't want to know." Knowing him, he'd probably already thought of every contingency before he even told her about all this.

What was it with that man and castles? Ever since she'd woken up in the hospital, he'd talked about fairy tales and happy endings, and every time he'd mentioned their future home, he'd called it a castle. Until now, Dara had thought he was talking metaphors.

"Pixie, you want to help me out here?" Tristan said.

"Wha—don't bring her into this!" That was all she needed. One more person trying to persuade her that this was a good idea.

"Why not?"

"Because *she*'s not the one who'll have to live here!"

"I might," Pixie chimed in.

"Whatever happened to the wild tiger who couldn't be cooped up inside for more than ten minutes at a time?" Dara questioned, crossing her arms over her chest. "Whatever happened to sleeping underneath the stars?"

He made a grumbling noise. "Haven't we been doing that enough lately?"

Most definitely, she thought. Tristan had bought the land here with the money he'd gotten from the Special Unit as payment for stopping a serial killer. But it was *only* land. There was no man-made structure on it that even vaguely resembled a house. For the last two weeks, they'd been sleeping in a rough shelter made of tree branches.

And it had rained three times in those two weeks.

"Then build a house!" She was starting to feel as if she'd have to stomp her feet and hold her breath to get him to let this go. "A shack. A freaking tent would be nice at this point."

"Woman, I'm building this castle, and that's final."

Her eyebrows shot up. "*What* did you just say to me?"

"Uh-oh," Pixie said, hiding behind her brother, who was having a coughing fit.

Tristan shifted his weight, looking away uneasily. "Er…"

"Because it sounded like you said *that's final.* And I just know you'd never say *that* to me." Taking her out of Gray Dublin had been one thing. She'd been so happy to leave it behind, she hadn't even questioned where he'd be taking them, or how they would live. With her own payment for her services, which included very nice hazard pay and a hefty disability premium, they had a small fortune to live on, so she didn't mind settling on this brand-new, clean and shiny, nearly unoccupied planet.

But the days of him pushing her around were over. Apparently, she'd lost a great deal of her telepathic abilities, now reduced to *sometimes* feeling other people's emotions if they were too strong. She didn't miss it. It actually made going out among people easier, and Dara wanted to take advantage of it and socialize. Which was difficult enough now, when they weren't living in town—a glorified village, really—but in the woods, without as much as a set of plates to eat from.

So Dara had been teaching Tristan how to compromise. Because there were now new lines drawn with her, and there would be dire consequences if he crossed them.

This castle was one of those lines.

She would *not* be living in seclusion up here, away from the rest of civilization, no matter how much she loved her husband.

He backed up a step for each one she took toward him. "Well, yeah, but I didn't mean *final* final," he said.

"Really?"

"Really." Tristan smiled wide, looking around for an escape. He faked right and ducked left around her before she could back him up all the way to the beach-side edge. "I meant the drawings and plans have been finalized. As structurally safe. And they're ready for your inspection." He nodded, as if his own explanation had satisfied him. "It's all negotiable. Trust me." This was the Tristan she'd only seen glimpses of before. Now that all immediate threats were gone, he'd channeled all of that intensity to his playful side. The side that made her heart melt for him and made her forget that life *wasn't* a fairy tale.

"Uh-huh." Dara squinted into the distance. "What's that on the lake?"

"Er…"

"Maybe we should go," Calen suggested and started pulling Pixie away, but she wouldn't budge.

"Tristan?" Dara prompted.

He winced. "That's the… barge. Bringing the first batch of stones."

Dara sighed, grasping for patience. "But it's all negotiable."

Calen lifted Pixie off her feet. "Yeah, we will definitely be going now," he announced and took off down the hill. The damn castle wasn't even built yet, and already they were losing what few friends they had!

"Absolutely, it's negotiable," Tristan said firmly. "Besides"—he put on his most seductive, I-am-your-hottest-fantasy-and-you-know-it look, smiling enticingly—"I never said we'd have to live here full-time." He caught her hips and pulled her to him, linking his hands loosely at her back.

Dara refused to be charmed. She would hold steady. She *would*, damn it! "I will *not* be cleaning a hundred and sixty rooms."

"Good God, no," he said, laughing. Then he ducked his head to her ear. "I have much better uses for you than that, lass." He showed her in her mind exactly what he meant by that.

Dara shivered, and her cheeks burned. "Shameless," she accused breathlessly, tangling her hands in his hair. *—And I love you all the more for it…—*

Tristan stilled. He drew back, searching her gaze.

"What?"

A slow smile spread over his face, his eyes sparkling with gold.

It wasn't until much later, after they'd made love on the beach, and then again in the soft grass, and then once more in a secluded, shallow part of the lake as the sun set over the hill, that Dara realized she'd thought him the words.

The End

ALIANNE DONNELLY was a wordsmith long before she became a reader. Driven by an insatiable curiosity about everything from history and mythology to science and philosophy, she grew into a fiction writer who hates coloring inside the genre lines. Her books all have elements of romance, with different series sorted under paranormal, science fiction, fantasy, and erotic. And then there's *Wolfen*…

Alianne lives in California, doing hard time in a corporate 9-5, while secretly scribbling away any chance she gets. She loves pizza, hiking, and avoiding small talk, and hopes to one day win the lottery jackpot. To find out more about Alianne's books and works in progress, visit her website at AlianneDonnelly.com.

www.ingramcontent.com/pod-product-compliance
Lightning Source LLC
Chambersburg PA
CBHW030614170726
48283CB00002B/604